# SCORCH

## THE ARDELEAN BLOODLINE
### BOOK FOUR

SARAH JAEGER

BEARLY CONTAINED ROMANCE, LLC

THIS BOOK WAS WRITTEN BY A HUMAN
HUMAN
I DON'T SUPPORT AI BOOKS OR ART
GENERATED

© Bearly Contained Romance

E-Book ISBN: 979-8-9900360-0-0

Male Model Paperback ISBN: 979-8-9877001-9-8

Wolf Paperback ISBN: 979-8-9900360-1-7

*Editing - Indie Edits with Jeanine*

*Proofreading - Indie Edits with Jeanine and Nay's Notions*

*Book Cover - Sandra of Mando Designs*

*Director of Public Works - Kelsey Schneider*

# Scorch

River Mts.
South Pass
Big Sandy R.
Green R.
Snake R.
Soda Sps.
Malade Cy.
Bear R.
Logan
Corinne
Brigham Cy.
Ogden
Evanston
Bryan
Bridger
Ft. Bridger
Uintah Mts.
Echo
Coalville
Centreville
SALT LAKE CY.
Gt. Salt L.
Toano
Great Desert
Strawberry Valley
Provo
Utah L.
Spanish Fork
Uintah R.
White
Onaqui Mts.
Oquirrh Mts.
Silver Cy.
Mt. Pleasant
Little Mts.
White R.
U T A H
Sevier L. & R.
House Rge.
Deep Cr.
Egan Range
White Pine Rge.
Manti
Gunnison
San Rafael R.
Fillmore
Green R.
Grand
Dirty Devil R.
Beaver
Sevier R.
Sage Brush V.
Rail Road Val.
Highland Rge.
Parowan
Wahsatch Mts.
Pioche
Colorado R.
Virgin City
St. George
Hyko
Meadow Val.
White Mesa
Vegas Rge.
Spring Mts.
Muddy Rge.
Gr. Cañon
Little Colorado or Flax
Bill Williams Mt.
Mt. Sitgreaves
Picacho Mt.
Cerbat
Black
Hardyville
Mohave Cy.

*To anyone who ever felt like they were unlovable.*
*You weren't then and you aren't now.*

Salmon

Malade R.

Mc.Arthur R.

Camas Prai

Snake

R.

Soda Sprs.

O

Green R.

d River Mts.

South Pass

Swe

Sweet

Plain

Cr.

Malade Cy.

Bear

R.

Logan

Corinne

Brigham Cy.

Ogden

Evanston

Bryan

Bridger

Ft.Bridger

Bit

Bish

Echo

Coalville

Centreville

Uintah Mts.

To no

Great

Gr. Salt L.

SALT LAKE CY.

Strawberry Valley

White

Desert

Utah

Provo

Uintah R.

Spanish Fork

Deep Cr.

House Rge.

Stansbury Mts.

Wahsatch Mts.

Little Mts.

White R.

H

Mt.Pleasant

Silver Cy.

Sevier L. & R.

Manti

San Rafael

R.

Green R.

Gran

U

T

A

Fillmore

Gunnison

White Pine Rge.

Egan Rge.

Sage Brush V.

Dirty Devil

R.

Beaver

Sevier R.

Parowan

R.

R.

Hail Road Val.

Meadow Val. Mts.

Pah Rand Rge.

Cañon

Colorado R.

S

Virgin City

White Mesa

Caleb

St. George

Muddy Rge.

Virgin

Gr.

Colorado

Yuko

Little Colorado or

Cerbat

Black

Cañon

Bill Williams

Picacho Mt.

Mt. Sitgreaves

Mo

Mts.

Hardyville

Mohave Cy.

Agua

Plateau

Col

"Now I have to remember you longer than I've known you."

— C. C. AUREL

"We have not touched the stars, nor are we forgiven, which brings us back to the hero's shoulders and the gentleness that comes, not from the absence of violence, but despite the abundance of it."

— RICHARD SIKEN

Malade R.

McArthur R.

Camas Prairie

Snake R.

Soda Sprs.

O

Gage Cr.

Salt R.

Malade Cy.

Bear R.

Green R.

River Mts.

South Pass

Sweet

Sweet

Plain

Logan

Corinne

Brigham Cy.

Ogden

Evanston

Bryan

Bridger

Ft. Bridger

Bit

Bish

Uintah Mts.

Echo

Coalville

Centreville

SALT LAKE CY.

Strawberry Valley

Toano

Great

Gr. Salt L.

Provo

Utah L.

Spanish Fork

Uintah R.

White

Desert

Wahsatch Mts.

Oquirrh Mts.

Silver Cy.

Mt. Pleasant

White R.

Deep Cr.

House Rge.

Sevier L. & R.

Manti

Little Mts.

Green R.

Grand

D

A

U

T

A

H

Fillmore

Gunnison

San Rafael R.

Egan Range

White Pine Rge.

Rail Road Val.

Highland Rge.

Sage Brush V.

Sevier R.

Beaver

Dirty Devil R.

Parowan

Wahsatch

Pioche

Meadow Val.

Hyko

Sevier R.

Colorado R.

S

Gr.

Cañon

St. George

Virgin City

White Mesa

Calabe

Vegas Rge.

Spring Mts.

Muddy Rge.

Virgin R.

Cerbat

Black R.

Cañon

Gr.

Bill Williams

Mt. Sitgreaves

Little Colorado or Flax

Cot

Picacho Mt.

Mogollo

Plateau

Hardyville

Mohave Cy.

Agua

# A QUICK NOTE ON CONTENT

This book is a traditional shifter romance book. As such, it contains events such as physical on-page violence and discussions of death. These events may be handled or discussed in ways that may not be acceptable by all readers.

Scorch is a book based in a world very much like our own and deals with a wide variety of heavy topics. These topics may cause individuals to have negative feelings or reactions.

The list of topics includes, but is not limited to, mental health, revelations of biological parentage, drug and alcohol use, addiction, sexual intercourse, gambling, misogyny, conversations relating to firearms, use of firearms on individuals, infertility, medical trauma, health struggles, suicidal ideation, and suicide.

Ansel and Morrigan must overcome their own diversity and trauma within this book. Some of these topics include, but are not limited to, childhood sexual assault, childhood neglect and abandonment, sex trafficking, domestic violence, death of a parent, attempted sexual assault, food insecurity, poverty, and homelessness. Also included are scenes related to the judicial system, incarceration, and interactions with police.

These topics are not always handled in the most politically correct way. As often seen in real life, my characters can sometimes be insensitive to those around them and their struggles.

None of these words written were chosen without thought. All choices were debated at length. Ultimately, it is my intent to highlight the struggles of humanity as we work toward acceptance of all the differences among us. Even if that means allowing my characters to be imperfect as part of their growth, as part of our growth.

And while it is never my intention to cause any reader any distress: reader discretion is advised.

If based on this warning, related to the potential triggers listed above, you have any additional concerns or questions that you'd like addressed, you may reach out to me, the author, via email: sarah@authorsarahjaeger.com or on Instagram: @author.sarahjaeger

# ANSEL'S HOUSE
## FIRST FLOOR

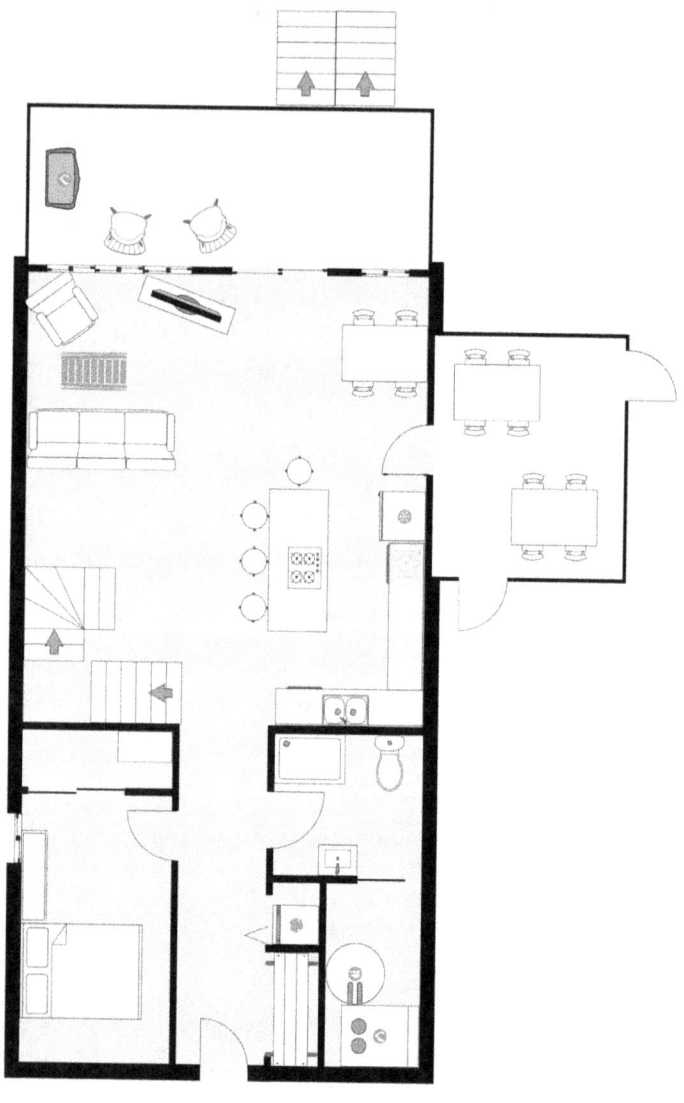

# ANSEL'S HOUSE
## SECOND FLOOR

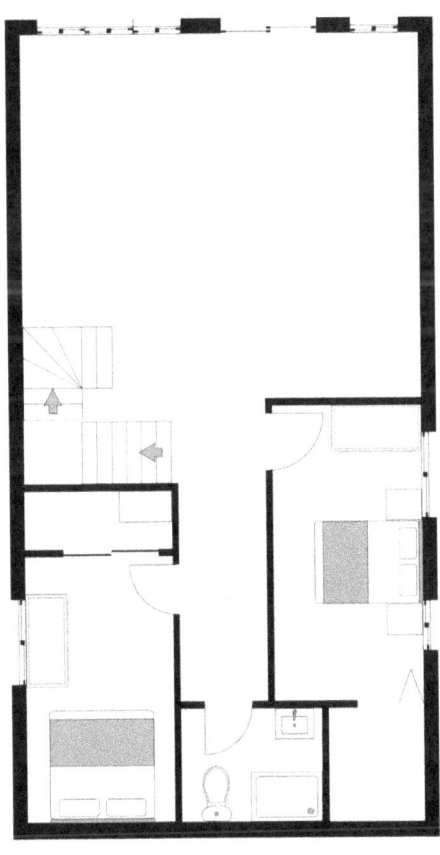

# ANSEL'S HOUSE
## THE KENNELS

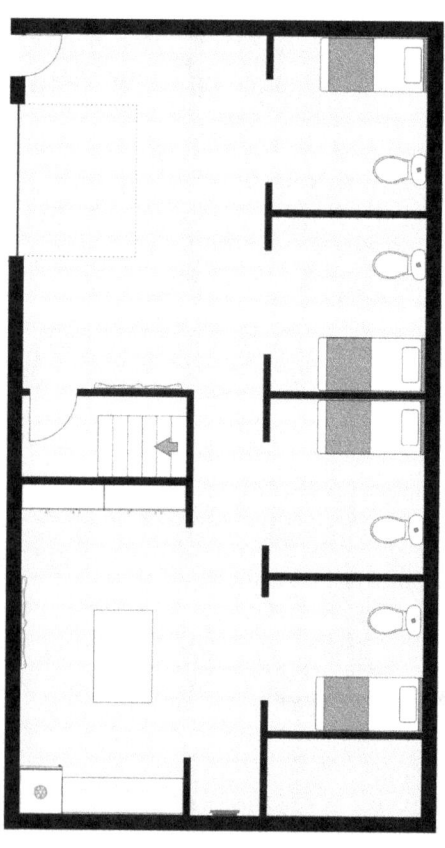

# ANSEL
## TWO YEARS EARLIER

We've had a lot of fun. Well, if killing people is fun. But does it count as a bad thing if it's almost a whole pack gone mad? I could feel how fractured and broken they were becoming from the time we rolled up on the property. When a wolf pack goes sick, from the Alpha down, there's no stopping it. Even the wolves who manage to leave the pack, and don't fracture, become haunted by that horrible reality: they were almost next.

Like now, after the bloodshed.

Dinah's safe, tucked up in the back of an SUV with Ezra and Deacon, on her way home to hopefully heal. I get to sorting the rest of the wolves — from fractured to mostly whole.

A sniveling blond kid is kneeling in the mud before me. He doesn't smell sick, just cold and dirty. He's probably seventeen. Plenty of time for him to make better choices after seeing what not to do.

"He lives to die another day." I shake my head to Judah and Cade standing at my side.

Judah's been different; he's darker and not his usual unsettled but stable self. He snarls loudly at my statement, his wolf thirsty for bloodshed. It's not normal, Judah calling for violence. Today is different. He does so without being sorry about it. It was his little sister they tortured, after all.

He growls.

Cade tries to stop Judah's slaughter. "Fate worse than death?"

"There's no such thing," the boy says boldly. But the look I give him has him backpedaling. He stutters. "What? You'll torture me?"

"Not our style, kid," Cade huffs and wiggles his fingers, probably from the feeling of skin healing. It always does tickle.

"Ansel?" Judah presses me to rule on the kid's future. "His scent is all over the house."

*He's just a kid.* It doesn't sit right killing him, but what's the harm in scaring him anyway? Who knows what he did or didn't do?

"A fate worse than death is knowing about your death. Maybe the date or the time? Maybe one day of the year, you live in complete terror of that day being your last rotation on the earth? Or the time so that every minute it ticks closer every day?" I explain further.

The kid shakes his head in disbelief.

"No, maybe not the date or time . . . maybe the how is worse? Like, say it's a car accident. Happens every day. What do you do? Give up drivin' and ridin' in cars? Maybe move to the city so you can walk to work. Only for a car to jump the curb? Or you go to live in the middle of nowhere, and a family takes a wrong turn and runs you over, ruins the family vacation." I keep asking questions, watching him squirm.

My wolf loves watching people squirm.

The boy stops looking at me. His whole body shivers. The stench of fear hangs in the air.

The darkness of it all leaves Harry pacing back and forth under my skin.

He could keep killing. That would be fine with him. Ending the rest of the pack wouldn't bother him. Harbinger is judge, jury, and executioner. The only thing that keeps Harry from killing everyone is my small ability to wrangle him and only end those who need to be ended.

"Could be worse. I can tell you the smallest bit that seems unimportant: a stick, a rock, or a bump to the head. Maybe a heart attack or a stroke. Those happen to unsuspectin' people all the time." When I lay my gift out like this, I understand why some of my cousins refuse to talk to me about it.

Judah growls, "So, which would you rather have? Death today? Or the knowledge of what's to come?"

The sick way Judah is hoping the kid is suicidal is worrisome.

The kid looks like he's about to go into shock. "I don't want to die."

I let my gift take me. The vision easily comes forward.

*An old man in his bed. Wife and children around him. Holding his hand. A tiny girl whispers, "Goodbye, Great-Grandpa, I love you."*

I let the vision cut away. I don't need anything more. No sense in going for details.

It's cruel. But I say it anyway. "The last thing you'll ever hear someone say to you is I love you."

Harry hears a sound off in the brush. The Leviathan must hear it too, because Cade and I snap our heads in that direction.

I walk away, leaving the kid in the dirt. *Now to hunt down that sound.*

An hour later, Cade and I are dressed and sitting in his SUV.

He turns to look at me. "That was uncharacteristically cruel."

I shrug. "For now anyway. He dies late in life, family all around. I don't get to write it. His path could change. But for now, it's the bed he gets to die in. Maybe this is the conversation that gets him to that end path."

# MORRIGAN

## SIX MONTHS EARLIER

The music is loud but nowhere near as overwhelming as it was the first time I snuck out a few months ago. It's freeing to be caught up in the bumping of the bass, moving back and forth with the sound. I can just dance. No thinking, no worrying, no fear that something bad will happen. It's me and the middle tones swaying together.

But soon the song changes and the rhythm slows, a little, but enough. It's time to take a step off the warehouse's makeshift dance floor.

The tables they've set up as a bar along the back wall are mostly empty except for a group of girls. Their cat and wolf eyes refract differently in the same way I'm sure mine do, glinting and gleaming in the pulsating lights. We're predators mixed in amongst the humans.

LA is a big place, but our pack is tight knit given how Gerad runs it. We're expected to know everyone. But I don't know *any* of them.

I approach, purposefully coming to the bar near where they've congregated.

"Hey." One of them, a cat of some nature, beguiles me.

She leans against the counter, rolling her head and looking at me with a slow blink, pupils turning to slits as she watches.

I nod in response, flagging the bartender. He knows me; we have a deal. With a wink, he gives me a bottle of water and palms me my drug of choice: ecstasy. In exchange, I give him a heads-up as to where the pack will be so he can flirt with shifters who may want to get off on banging a human. All he wants is a chance to go through heat with a wolf. Ridiculous since there's no way the scrawny human will ever be able to placate or keep up.

"Who are you?" A second girl wraps herself around me, her arm dragging across the back of my shoulders.

"I'm a nobody," I answer, trying to shrug her off.

Her eyes glint before she nods to the water bottle. "You party. I know the pack here doesn't tolerate that. They're too sophisticated."

"I don't exactly care." I step out from under her arm.

"We're passing through, we travel and follow the party." A blonde smirks at me. "You strike me like the kind who doesn't play by pack rules."

She's not wrong. But you don't run off with people you just met. That's how you end up dead in a ditch somewhere.

"I'm Bubbles," the first says. "Take that. Then come dance with us." She glances between the water bottle and my face a few times to imply her meaning.

It's not an invite. It's a command. Begrudgingly, I head out to the floor. It's a well-ingrained, strict reminder that outside of my stepfather, my mother, and the few 'trusted' advisors, no one is to know that Alpha Commands don't affect me correctly.

We dance for another hour or two, and exhaustion is setting in.

The Molly kicked in shortly after I took it. It's more fun to have a pack that's wild with me. From the looks in their eyes, some of them are riding the high with me. I don't feel unsettled with them. There's a belonging that I'm not sure I've ever had before.

"You should come with us." Bubbles beckons me with a siren's call for adventure as we head outside the club. "We're travelers."

Shaking my head, I sigh. I turn to walk home. "Not possible. They'll notice I'm missing soon. It's complicated, but I can't."

"Aww, come on. Join the pack." The blonde laughs as she grabs my wrist. "It'll be fun. We'll party and travel. And the best part is we'll have each other, so we won't have to worry about being packless."

"Bubbles is an Alpha Female. She can keep us together." A brunette smiles.

I don't pull too hard, but it's enough to release the blonde's grasp. Despite pulling away, my objection isn't strong enough.

Their offer is tempting. So. Tempting.

I deny them, and myself, again. "And what do you do for money? Partying and fuel aren't free."

"It's no different than the deal you have with the bartender here." Bubbles laughs, and it's almost condescending. "Humans are willing to pay extra to say they've had a shifter. You flash them the eyes, and they go nuts for it."

"My bartender is different. I don't fuck around." I hate her accusation. My deal with the bartender isn't about my body.

"Alright, well, if you're not into hooking up, then you'd have to hold. We've an arrangement with a few dealers. It's some side money." Bubbles takes a step closer to me, and her eyes light up with her wolf. They're pale yellow.

She's trying to draw out my wolf and gain her allegiance. It won't work.

Dealers that travel? Sounds like the cartel.

I shake my head and step back. "I'm sorry, it's been great, but I have to stay with the pack."

"We'll be here again tomorrow night if you change your mind. After that, we're leaving," Bubbles states.

It's phrased like an offer but said like a warning.

"I'll think about it." I walk away, diverting around the corner.

*There's no way I'm thinking about it.*

"Morrigan!"

Gerad is calling for me, and, per usual, I turn my music up louder and start the next seam through my machine. I work the cotton fabric of my jacket under the presser, focusing on each rise and fall of the needle through the dense cotton fibers.

My headphones are ripped off my head. This time, they don't survive the force of being slammed against the floor. The broken pieces skitter across the room and end with a small crash against the wall.

"Morrigan!" Gerad, my mother's mate, stands there yelling at me like we're not even a foot apart. His face is beet red and his eyes bulge. "Get dressed. You're not even ready? We have company. You need to be presentable."

He claps his hands at me, punctuating his demands.

"I'll get ready. No need to yell." I make eye contact with him.

His hand lands squarely on my face, and I turn my head aside with the blow.

He's seething. "Insolent child. Get presentable. You have

five minutes. If you're not ready, I will send someone to get you ready."

He wouldn't dare hit me with anything more than an open hand. After the last failed attempt to fix me, Gerad resolved to invite 'company' to see if I'm suitable, and now he won't do anything that'll leave a bruise.

The door to the room where I live slams shut behind his explosive exit. This place is a prison of sorts. I'm cloistered away like the disgrace I am.

*We'll be here again tomorrow night if you change your mind.* Bubble's voice plays back in my head. Six more hours until the partying starts. I can play nice for six hours, and then I'll be free. Running off with people I just met is no worse than what I'm dealing with now. *Is it?*

PRESENT DAY

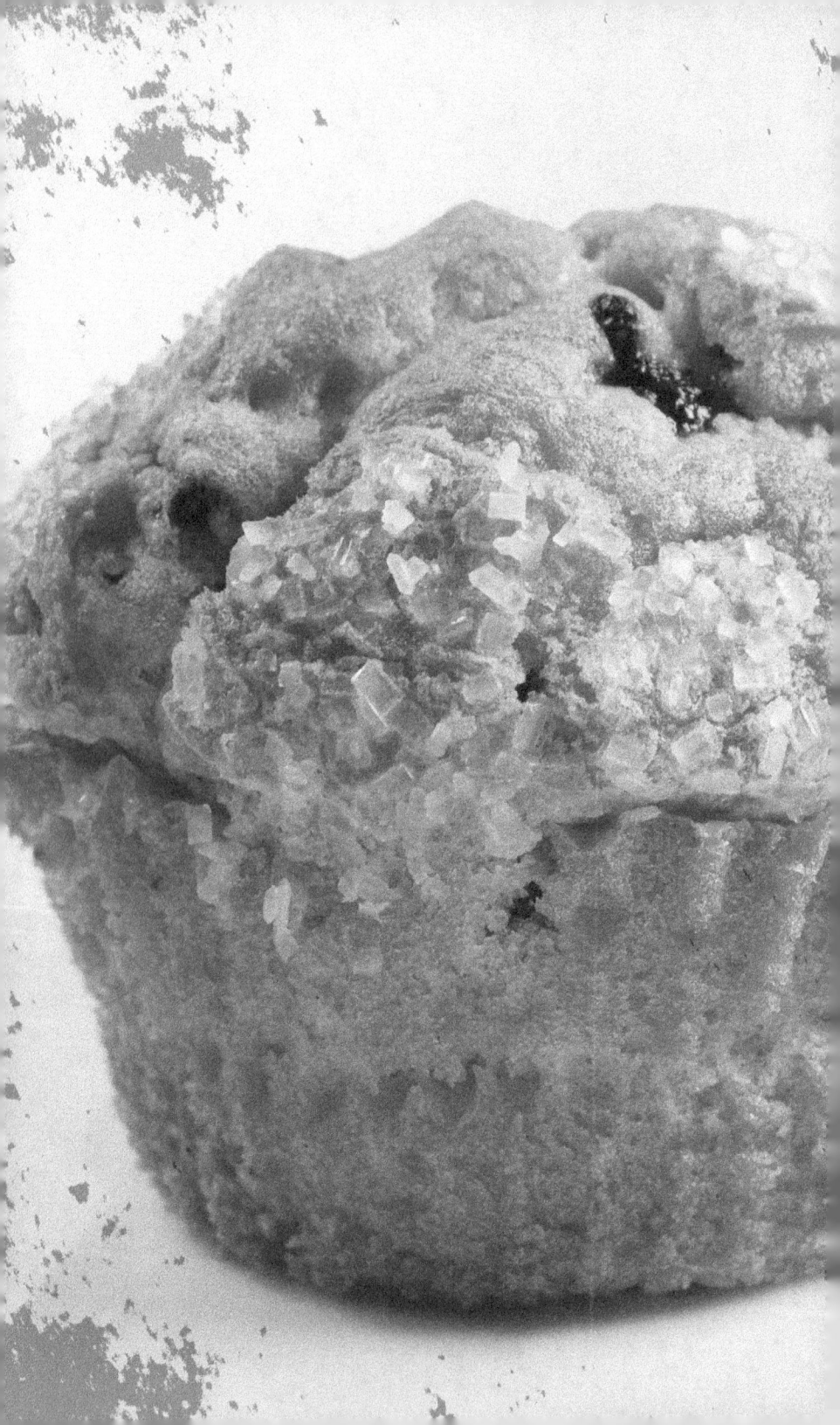

# CHAPTER I
# ANSEL

Salt Lake City is a nice enough place. The humans are a little weird, but I suppose that's true about most cities. The government center is right where the little GPS thing told me it would be. I've been here once before, but nothing worse than getting lost and being late.

Plus, I bought a blueberry muffin at this little mom-and-pop shop as they were opening for the morning. Delicious way to start the day. Maybe getting lucky enough for a muffin is a sign of other good things that will happen today.

There's hope. It's become my thing, holding on to hope. I'll hold on to hope for as long as I possibly can.

I park my truck at the far end of the lot, away from the door where humans may want to park. The pickup doesn't take up a lot of room, but sometimes it's a tight squeeze.

Cade's government liaison told me the usual: absolutely nothing helpful for what I'm getting myself into today. No name, no gender, no clue what they're being held on, and no way of knowing if I'll even be able to save 'em. It's not his or his liaison's fault, I don't think. Robert's liaisons were worse. I ended up in the wrong state more than once before.

Today, something feels right. I'm positive I'm where I need to be.

Case number, my ID, and checkbook in hand, I open my little banking app on my phone and double-triple-check. How long will it take me to get used to seeing the big numbers there again? It's a huge sigh of relief knowing that I got this kind of financial leverage back.

Cade taking back his throne as Sovereign Alpha ended my days of negotiating with the bank and the utility companies. It's been a couple months since he got me full access back to The Ardelean Fund. He'd been doing massive transfers to my account, but now to be back to the big fund . . . It's no less strange than the first time I gained access.

At exactly 7:00 a.m., I walk to the building's front door.

The woman at the desk starts, "Sir, we're only open for shifter pickups."

"Yeah, you should have at least one today. I got the case number?" I offer her the slip of paper I wrote it down on as I approach the desk.

"Oh." Her eyes go wide.

She does a cute little nod while trying to keep herself from feeling some sort of way.

Harry doesn't see her as prey. She certainly doesn't smell like it, so maybe not fear?

I suppose her not recognizing me as a shifter comes with being the runt of the family. My cousins are almost exclusively over the six-foot mark. I don't think I've ever found a full adult male shifter smaller than me. I get the job done anyway.

It takes her a minute before she takes the slip of paper, her hands careful not to touch mine. It's interesting to watch her work as I wait for her to look up the information. She doesn't have a very good poker face. With heavy clicks on the mouse, she furrows her brow, then raises them in what looks like shock.

She addresses me. "Alright, I need your ID and a few signatures. Then the judge is ready to see you right away."

It's not surprising that the judge is waiting to see me. I'm sure Cade's people told him I'd be coming. Most governing bodies want nothing to do with having shifters in their cells. For all the dumb shit Robert did, the one good thing he negotiated quickly and pretty okay was the process for getting shifters back into custody of our people. Well, mostly to me.

Though, the bit he fucked up was giving up our rights to a fair trial. If you claim shifter status or are found to be a shifter by the government during your arrest, you've seventy-two hours to have a claim put in for you by your people. That claim says that we're taking liability and we would like to deal with the consequences of their actions. Once a claim is put in, the clock starts again.

Before I even get a call, the countdown has already begun. We've seven days to pay the incarcerated person's fines and collect them. My worst nightmare is for the time to run out without having the chance to save someone.

The woman from the front desk directs me where I need to go, pointing me down a long hallway and giving me an office number.

I find the door and knock.

A long time passes before an older gentleman in his sixties opens it.

"You must be Ansel Abbot." He smiles while stepping back, giving me entry into his office.

The room is nearly the same as you'd expect to see in a Western movie: wood paneling, lawbooks, a massive desk with leather, and cowboy apparel. It's cool.

"Yes, Your Honor." I keep the formalities that are important to the humans. Just because I don't want anyone calling me Alpha doesn't mean I can diminish someone else's title.

"Please have a seat, I'm having the bailiff bring her up now." The judge offers me a seat in one of the worn leather chairs in front of his desk.

*Her*, I note. It's not unheard of for female wolves to fracture, but it's very rare that they find themselves in any sort of trouble. Usually, packs keep them well protected. Women are revered and precious — mostly.

"I've been told you do this sort of thing regularly." He sits down at his desk across from me.

I nod. "Yes, sir. It's my job among the wolf packs to manage wolves who find themselves in difficult situations."

Is it weird that he's found people to talk about me with? Maybe he asked Cade's people?

"That is the politically correct answer?" The judge raises an eyebrow at me.

Without an answer, I sit silently, resting my hands on the chair's arms.

The judge narrows his eyes at me. "If I send her with you, is she at risk of being killed?"

"A significantly less risk of being killed with me than if she stayed here with you," I answer with a short nod, driving home my harsh words.

It's the facts of the matter. But I shouldn't have been rude.

Bowing my head a bit and changing my tone to be humbler, I answer again. "My job is to do anything in my power to keep wolves alive. But I have the primary responsibility of keeping humans safe from wolves. No one's told me who I'm here to pick up or what they've done. Their fate depends on them."

"Accused of." The judge corrects me with a firm shake of his finger. "No one's on trial here. No one's being convicted. I still believe in justice for all." He taps his fingers on the cream-colored folder in front of him. The scolding becomes softer. "As far as I'm concerned, when she walks out the door with you today, this meeting never happened. She's a young lady who is in some need of guidance. I'll meet with you once, around the six-month mark, to confirm things are on the right track, and in a year, we'll reconvene and check that everything is as it should be, then this folder disappears."

A smile crosses my lips. Holding on to hope sometimes pays off. A year is a pretty okay timeline to make sure a wolf is solid. Six months is a little iffy, but we'll see.

"While we wait, let's get started on some of this paper-work." The judge opens the file. "We have Miss Morrigan Camilla Hart, nineteen of Los Angeles County, California."

My whole body drops — my jaw, my shoulders, and my stomach. *Walt's Morrigan?*

I don't want to believe it. But there's no way it isn't her. What is she doing in Utah?

"She's racked up quite a commission. Underage drinking, possession of alcohol, three counts of possession of illicit substances with intent to sell, property damage in two instances, past curfew, bribing a police officer, fleeing from the police, and assault on an officer." The judge looks at me.

I run my hand down my face, pulling at my beard. *Are they really letting me take her? That's a lot of really big charges.* The blood drains from my face.

The judge questions me. "Are you okay, Mr. Abbot?"

*What caused all this? Where is her pack in all this? Her fucking mother?*

Harry feels my fear. He stirs, looking for the threat.

"Yeah. Sorry, I just . . . I'm so sorry for the officer. Was he hurt?" I shake my head.

5

"He has a few scratches and bruises on his arms. The department wished to press charges." The judge narrows his eyes like he disagrees with their decision.

I don't know for sure, but I don't think it's his decision if they do or don't.

It's their right. She hurt someone.

I promised her father I'd keep her safe. I would say I'm waiting for the other shoe to drop, but maybe that only applies if there are only two things of bad news. I'm now waiting for the third bit of bad news: the price tag for her life.

"So, that being said," the judge starts.

There's a knock on the door behind us.

The judge stands from his desk, and I remain seated, not remembering the protocol.

"Ah, yes, thank you. Ms. Hart, would you please come in?"

My heart hammers in my chest as I turn my head. Looking over my shoulder, I get a look at Morrigan for the first time in five years. I'd like to say I'd recognize her anywhere, but had I been walking down the street and seen her in this condition . . . it would've taken me more than a single glance.

She's too skinny. I can see the muscles in her neck. Her eyes lack all fire, and she looks like she hasn't slept in weeks. With how big the jail's clothing is on her, it's impossible to say what the rest of her looks like.

Morrigan is still in handcuffs. I'm pretty sure they're as tight as they can possibly go. Her wrists are so small. But the way she's being monitored makes it clear they're distrustful of her. Rightfully so, even a small wolf can take down a human by themselves.

The man who escorted her to the judge's chambers stands off to the side, slightly behind her, as Morrigan sits in the chair to my left. Her hair falls in her face, shielding her eyes from me.

I pull my gaze from her to look at the judge, watching him return to his desk.

Harry, who usually paces constant circles in my mind, stills inside me, observing her.

"Ms. Hart, you've caused quite a bit of legal trouble for yourself." The judge waits, but Morrigan doesn't respond. After a few moments of silence, he continues. "Do you know everything you've been charged with?"

Morrigan nods but says nothing. Gently, I nudge her shoulder with the back of my knuckles, prompting her. Humans are verbal creatures.

Obediently, she speaks. "Yes, sir."

"Now, I've convinced the department that if you pay the fees and show a good effort of staying out of trouble, they'll forgo any further legal action." The judge nods to her and then looks to me before looking down at the paperwork in front of him.

That information should settle me, but it doesn't. I brace for bad news.

"According to the fee schedule set by the federal government and the state of Utah, restitution is three hundred and ten thousand five hundred dollars." The judge reads the number slowly.

Morrigan's head whips toward me, and just as quickly, she diverts her eyes back down to look at her lap.

Her shoulders shudder slowly as she whispers, "Ansel?"

Reaching over, I give her shoulder a quick squeeze.

"That won't be a problem, Your Honor," I answer firmly.

I need to call Cade. I owe him significantly more than just the money in the bank. If it weren't for him, I wouldn't be able to take her home. Not today. And without it, I would have had to scramble everything, the house, the property, everything to save her.

And I would have.

I'd give every last single thing I have to save her.

The judge looks at me. He purses his lips before turning back to her. "Ms. Hart, based on these charges, if you have another altercation with the law, you will not be released back to your people."

He swings his gaze back to me. "Mr. Abbot, you're willing to sign the agreement that you are responsible for her actions for the next year? Be mindful, given the gravity of her crimes, she will need to be available for further evaluation on a random interview at least once. She will have to appear here in Salt Lake City." The tone of his voice is as if he's doubtful.

Anything he asks for, I'll do it.

Speaking clearly, I try to convince him I'm here to go the distance for her. "I have no issues signing any paperwork to take Morrigan home with me, and she'll be easily available as I'm a resident of Utah."

Harry's focus stays firmly on Morrigan and the way she's barely breathing.

"Those I've spoken to have told me that you do this regularly, Mr. Abbot," the judge states. "And, our records confirm it, if it's not a family member who bails a wolf out, it's you."

He's not wrong. There have only been two wolf executions by the government.

It makes me sick knowing I couldn't have helped them or at least given them an honorable end. But killing humans is taboo in our culture and illegal in theirs. I would have never been allowed to give them the proper rites to their deaths as wolves.

"Yes, our people are very connected. We make it a priority to take care of each other. If someone is lost, we help them find a way. We want everyone to have a place where they belong," I assure him, motioning to Morrigan with an open hand. I need him to believe I can easily care for her.

"Ms. Hart, if it weren't for Mr. Abbot's ever-growing positive record with wolves' rehabilitations and the complete lack of repeat offenses, there is a distinct possibility you would not be released." The judge's voice carries a dangerously serious note. He drives in those last few words hard, pointing his finger at the papers on his desk.

We're all silent for a moment.

The judge starts again. "That being said, I believe you're young and made a mistake. That's not worth the death penalty."

Morrigan makes herself smaller, sinking into her seat. Her entire body is curling in on itself, trying to hide away from the fear. She's scared.

Shit, *I'm* scared. Even with the judge pretty much saying he's letting her go, I'll be scared until she's out of those handcuffs and in my truck.

And then I'll be angry.

"Alright, let's get this paperwork signed." The judge looks at the bailiff. "Ms. Hart understands the gravity of the situation. We can release her."

The bailiff is hesitant but unlocks the handcuffs. She instantly wraps her arms tight around her middle like she's guarding herself from coming attacks.

No one will be attacking her. But there will be some serious conversations about her actions. And at least one angry phone call to her mother.

Satisfied with her behavior, the judge starts going through the paperwork. Morrigan only speaks when spoken to; she keeps her head down and answers questions concisely.

I'm fighting a battle between keeping my attention on the legal papers and Morrigan, making sure she's staying where she's supposed to be. It's nearly impossible. I'm not comprehending everything entirely, but when I asked for copies, the judge didn't hesitate to have them made.

He doesn't have to know it's because I'm afraid of what humans can do if I don't play by their rules. I'll try rereading them at home, and when I get stuck, I'll run to town, see if old Judge Whittaker is home, and I can buy him a cup of coffee to talk me through 'em, again.

Stopping her from doing something stupid before we get home is the first step.

TWO ADDITIONAL HOURS AND WHAT FEELS LIKE A HUNDRED signatures later, I finally get to walk Morrigan out of the judge's chambers. She stays glued to my left side as we follow the bailiff to the clerk's desk. I cut the biggest check I've ever written and hand it over to the older woman at the desk. She looks at me wide eyed before stamping it and running it through her machine. Evidently, she's shocked when it spits out a little receipt. I can't blame her. If it weren't for Cade, I'd be surprised too.

Shortly before noon, we step through the final glass door outside the government center. Morrigan stretches and yawns, raising her hands high to the sky like she could grab the clouds.

Harry, still laser focused on Morrigan, shakes himself out from the heavy feeling of being in that sort of building.

I give Morrigan a minute to feel some freedom before we get cooped up in the truck for the three-hour ride home.

After fishing my phone out of my pocket, I check the messages. There's exactly one. It's from Ben, my pack Second. Even if he doesn't want to be, he is.

Texting him back, I'm a bit distracted.

"Okay, well. I'd say it's been good to see you but . . ." Morrigan's voice is smaller and farther away than it should be. "Well, thanks for bailing me out. I'll get out of your hair."

She's ten feet down the sidewalk. *Stupid cell phones.*

The growl starts before I can stop it. Harry's ready for the chase, anticipating her next move. Begging for her to run.

I, on the other hand, would do anything to avoid making a scene.

With her head held high, she's wearing a shit-eating grin like she outsmarted everyone. Which isn't entirely true, but she's been released from human jail, so she's bound to wolf laws. And they're a lot less strict on women folk.

Unfortunately for her, Harry doesn't care that she's young and female. Prey is prey.

Death and discipline are my job. She'll have to remember that.

"The only place you're going is home with me. You're officially my problem for the next year." I shake my head, crossing the pavement toward her.

Placing my palm between her shoulder blades, I move her across the parking lot to my truck.

We've walked halfway before she shrugs my hand off. Glaring at her and flaring my nostrils is enough of a threat for her to keep walking. Morrigan keeps her head high, trying to maintain that she is not under my control.

That attitude will change, or it'll be a long year.

Morrigan looks at my truck like she hasn't seen one before. Her thoughts of making a break for it are obvious with her sideways glances in various directions.

Harry dares her to. Hunting prey is his favorite activity. Damn wolf forgets we aren't supposed to kill for fun.

"Really, Ansel, I'm good. It won't come back to bite you. I'll be on my way." Morrigan shrugs, taking a step back from the truck.

I step around behind her and open the passenger door.

As we stand at a stalemate, her pig-headed, challenging nature fuels a fire I'm unfamiliar with. I don't usually let myself get angry.

But even Harry's growing more and more impatient.

I tap into Harry's dominance and command her, "Get in the fucking truck, Morrigan."

With a huff, she stomps over to me and rounds the door. It would be more impressive if she wasn't emaciated and her footsteps didn't sound like fat raindrops hitting the pavement.

Once she's tucked inside the truck, I flip the little child-lock latch down before closing the door so she won't be able to open the door from the inside.

*What happened to her? Where the fuck is Ersilia?* My jaw is clenched tight, and I try to relax it, pushing down my shoulders while I walk around behind the truck.

It's useless. Fear has faded, and I'm already angry.

Long strides get me to the driver's side before she has the smart idea to try and escape that way. I'd rather not make chaos for the good people of Salt Lake City, but I'm not afraid to if that's what it takes.

I'm starting the truck when she speaks.

"You could drive me to the bus station, and I'll disappear. You tell everyone I died." Her voice is sharp, the jolt of anger likely caused by what she believes about me.

"No." I pull away from the parking space. I snarl at her, "End of discussion."

"Fine," she snaps. Her teeth click as she closes her mouth.

I can't offer her more words, not without better control first. Snarling at wolves you've bailed out of jail isn't a good way to start. Even if she was raised better than this. I know for certain she wasn't this fucked up. Well, up until her mom took her to California, anyway.

Sure, she's always been a spirited child, but never like this. What sort of shit has she gotten into?

With how tiny she is, I can barely see her out the corner of my eye. She's smart enough to stop arguing with me about the stupid bus station.

Back on the highway, the tension from her side of the truck slowly starts to fade, and I risk a glance over. Her head is slumped to the side, the heaviness of sleep taking over her body.

My anger remains.

Harry has been glued to listening to her and constantly insisting I take more glances and check in on her. The way he's focused makes me nervous. He only pays attention to those he's seen marked for death.

Morrigan's sleep sounds haven't changed since she was little. They're little almost snores.

As a child, Walt would drive her around to get her to fall asleep when nothing else would work. So the almost four-hour drive home will keep her sleeping.

*How long has she been alone?* Wolves aren't meant to be alone. A few manage without a pack, but for the most part, the community we build makes our own stability. We naturally gravitate toward a group. It keeps us safe and fed and gives pups a safe place to learn how to love and take care of themselves and others.

*Why is no one loving her?*

ALMOST HALFWAY HOME, HARRY INSISTS WE STEAL EVEN MORE glances at her. The longer we're together, the more obsessed he gets.

*Please don't make me end her.* I plead with Harry.

I gotta find out why she's alone and in a heap of trouble and fix it. Fix her.

Unsurprisingly, Harry doesn't answer. He never has. Everyone says their wolf talks with them somehow. The Leviathan gave Cade the cold shoulder for years, but the two of them talk now. I don't remember ever having that experience with Harry. Before I really met my cousins, no one ever told me wolves were supposed to talk.

But that's the toll of being different. When the people who found me figured out I was an Ardelean and what my gift was, Ebenezer assigned me to the station of Reaper. Hadn't even met the guy, and he had more say over my life than I did. It came with a lot of perks, like a house, even if it still doesn't feel like mine. It probably never will. Guess it's better than being homeless.

I learned a lot of things from the last Reaper 'bout how things are supposed to be between people and their wolves. I mostly see three things: feral, fractured, and odd. Determining the differences between them isn't always as easy as it should be. Feral wolves look very similar to fractured wolves. But sometimes, if you look closely at some, you see they're not damaged, just odd. When he told me what it was like and that if someone couldn't hear their wolf, they needed to be ended, I kept my mouth shut. Self-preservation and all that.

My eyes drift over to Morrigan. I've always wanted to do my job differently because I'm different. And, maybe, that different can save more people. At the very least, it keeps me alive.

# CHAPTER 2
# MORRIGAN

"Morrigan." My name is called softly.

My eyes fly open, readying for whatever is coming next. The surroundings aren't expected. I forget where I am. Then, through the fog, the last two days come back to me. The party, the cops, jail, and landing in my own personal nightmare: Ansel's house.

It's not unexpected. I purposefully had them call the Sovereign Alpha's people over my parents. I'm not surprised Ansel is handling the wolves coming out of the government's jails. We're supposed to do everything we can to not get involved with humans, especially not their police. We have our own jailer, and I'm all too familiar with him and his house.

The truck's driver's side door slams shut. I try the lever on my door, but it doesn't budge.

In no particular hurry, Ansel Abbot walks across the front of the truck to free me.

Ansel's house hasn't changed. Brown wood siding with a rusty-red shingled roof, and a two-car garage with a faded green lift door next to it. I bet the inside will be exactly the same as my memories too.

Ansel opens my door and steps aside. With a sweep of his arm, he gestures for me to get out.

My shoes have barely touched the dirt when his lecture begins. "We're over an hour run in wolf form to the nearest town as the crow flies. That's, of course, assuming you remember which way. Followin' the main road, the run takes about two hours. And I do mean running — at top speed — the entire way. People in town call if they see someone or something suspicious or new. There are no buses, car rentals, or other mass transportation in town. You could try hitchhiking. No one's been successful yet. My truck never has a full tank of gas, and if you were dumb enough to try and steal any of the others' vehicles, they've got tracking on them and won't have full tanks either."

Ansel pauses and waits for me to look at him. Our eyes meet, and he nods, then draws a deep breath before continuing. "You've the privilege to sleep in a bed upstairs. I don't have any habitable cabins right now, it's on the top of the work list. If you prove untrustworthy, then when I'm not home and at night, I'll put you in a kennel downstairs."

Without any further commentary, Ansel takes a step back from me and the truck. Tossing his head, he beckons me to follow him to the main house.

The fact is, it's virtually the middle of nowhere in Utah. There's no easy escape from here. I remember driving here from the Denver airport with Dad, but there was so much road, and I was so excited to see him, that I don't remember much of it. If I'm running away, I'll probably have to follow the road. Growing up here, Mom and Dad kept me corralled close to the main house. But what I remember of the time before Gerad is fuzzy.

There aren't a lot of happy memories left to hold on to.

Left alone in the driveway reminds me that Ansel truly doesn't believe I'll flee. If I can keep the trust between us, I'll be able to leave soon. Earn trust, then use it in my favor to escape.

I won't forgive Ansel for what he did. I can't. My only chance of surviving the same fate as Dad is for me to escape. There's no way in hell I'll be a victim of Harbinger.

At the back door to the house, Ansel calls out, "I've got chicken quarters thawed out. Brussel sprouts and carrots for sides, and there's some cookies left for dessert."

The door closes with a thud against the house.

While the promise of food triggers a growl from my stomach, my feet stay glued to the ground. I turn my head to the sky, closing my eyes. The afternoon sun overhead feels so warm despite it being mid-winter.

I'm alone. Regardless of the perfect opportunity to run away, I'm drawn to stand here with the wind brushing against my skin.

I can't remember the last time I was in natural, peaceful surroundings. Nature can be cruel and deadly, but city parks and 'green spaces' are a disappointing experience. When I pull my face from the sky, my gaze drifts out to the distant landscape. The vastness of the land before me is another reminder that a dandelion, growing through a crack in the pavement, has nothing on seeing the horizon line from Ansel's driveway.

It's been seven years and a lifetime ago since I lived here and over five since my last visit. No place this dark and full of death has any business feeling this much like home.

Closing my eyes again, I bask in the glory of what I don't hear. A lack of distant sirens and people shouting. No bustling sounds of children and traffic. Instead, it's replaced with the sounds of birds, small game, and . . . footsteps on hardened earth.

I turn around, and a man is walking up the driveway. Instinctively, I start backing away from him. There's only one place to go: toward the house. And I swear laughter comes from his direction.

In favor of speed over keeping an eye on him, I turn and jog to the door. It's only a few yards and I'm tired. My foot catches on the bottom step, and I fall forward, landing hard against the stairs. My ribs scream as I scramble to my feet, using the railing to help me the rest of the way to the door.

Keeping him in my peripheral, I struggle with the knob, my fingers trembling. The man keeps stalking toward me. Finally, I push on the knob, letting myself in.

With the door out of my way, I step into the house, but I'm stopped by another mass with a thud. Ansel's strong hands hold my shoulders, steadying me.

Stepping backward, he examines me, his head cocked to the side, brow furrowed, and lips pursed. "Why is your heart beatin' so fast?"

Footsteps sound on the small deck behind me, and I jump. A huff of air escapes Ansel's lungs as I collide into him again.

A man's voice I don't recognize drawls out, "You rang?"

Ansel laughs and steps back from me. "You're formally invited to dinner, and could you?"

He looks at me and back to the man behind me.

*What is he asking for?*

When I look at the man from the driveway, muddy-hazel eyes look at me. He reaches his hand out and quickly brushes the back of his knuckles on my forearm, where I've rolled up the sleeves of my hoodie.

I pull away. *Fucking weirdo.*

He looks me up and down once before looking at Ansel. "She's good. I don't think you need to sleep with the lights on or anything." The man shrugs and walks out the door again.

"Take your shoes off, stay awhile." Ansel invites me.

Standing so close to him gives me the opportunity to further examine my father's murderer. He's older now. But so am I.

His hair is significantly longer and hangs loose around his face, and he now sports a short beard. He goes about his day like it's nothing, like he's not the entire reason my life's a mess. Blissfully, Ansel is unaware that he's the reason I almost died at the hands of humans today.

"I keep a bunch of extra clothes in various sizes in the closet and dressers in the upstairs bedroom. The one straight across from the stairs. Bathroom up there has a shower if you want to get cleaned up," Ansel instructs over his shoulder, walking back to the main part of the living space.

As I follow him, the door on the left of the hallway smells intensely of Ansel — his bedroom. The main floor bathroom and laundry machines are on the right. Then the hallway opens to the living space. To the left are the stairs leading down to his basement.

I freeze, and my eyes fix on them.

I was never permitted down there, and I never had the desire to see the basement. A distant memory of snarls and howls when Ansel would open the door at the bottom of the stairs flashes through my mind.

"They're unlocked right now. No one's down there if you wanna go have a look for yourself."

When I look over at the kitchen, his back is to me as he pulls items out of his refrigerator. Sometime while I was distracted, he tucked his hair up into a messy bun.

I turn back to the stairwell, and morbid curiosity takes over. Nearly involuntarily, I take a deep breath and head down the stairs.

The door handle isn't your usual knob shape; instead, it's

one of the spinning locks like a bank vault set into the middle of the door. I grip the metal and pull it open. The door is thicker than the width of my hand, and it's heavy as it turns slowly on its hinges. I push it all the way open, making sure it won't close me in before I walk into the space.

A dull glow of light comes from around the corner, but it's still not as bright as upstairs. My eyes begin to adjust to the darkness. A chill ripples down my spine, and I shiver.

The Salt Lake County jail cells were more welcoming. Harbinger would have the best prison.

The basement is mostly empty. A large lifting door, similar to the garage door, plated in steel with massive hinges, is to the left. It matches my memory of seeing the doors from the outside while running around the house as a child.

On the long wall opposite the door and stairs are two cell doors facing the center of the room. My brain whirls, taking it all in and propelling my feet across the sloped basement floor toward the cells.

Four cells in total are built from heavy concrete blocks, the walls nearly two feet thick, complete with steel bars on heavy tracks that lock into place.

I step closer to them, reaching out but not touching. I wouldn't be able to wrap my hand entirely around the bar; it's too big. It's built to keep wolves in — at all costs.

I attempt to swallow, but my throat is tight.

Knowing they're animal cages, it's not surprising that the insides house the bare minimum. A small concrete portion raised off the floor by maybe six inches, with no mattress, seems 'bed-like' but only in the sense that if someone's wolf is smart enough not to piss on it, they'll be out of a mess that doesn't run down the sloped floor to the drain. It's inhumane to think this is all some people live in at the end.

If you're lucky enough to end up down here as a human,

Harbinger at least gives you the dignity of a toilet. A steel toilet, no sink, just a toilet, but with how the cells are laid out, you get the appearance of having privacy.

Four cells seem excessive. Why would Harbinger even keep that many people around? Even murderers get lonely, maybe?

Rounding the stairs, I look past the horrors of the cells. My hand finds a light switch on the wall, and when the fluorescents flash on, my eye is drawn to the large stainless-steel table. Sterile but not clinical looking. It looks like a butchering table.

My blood runs cold before I can pull my eyes from it. Unfortunately, where they go next isn't any less harrowing.

Restraints and chains of various sizes hang along a wall.

My heart hammers in my chest, and I move my gaze around, trying to determine someplace safe to look. A bank of countertops, a sink with upper cupboards like a kitchen would have, another cabinet with vials and white packages. And then a hose wrapped neatly by a spigot.

I've seen enough of Harbinger's torture chamber.

When I turn to leave, my eyes pick up something I missed on the wall with the kennels.

A lump forms in my throat.

I've seen this terrible thing on television. I'd never imagined I'd see it in person.

At the very end are the drawers they put bodies in at the morgues.

I ball my hands into fists.

My stomach clenches in a knot.

Is there someone in there? When did Harbinger claim his last victim?

Which cell was my father in before Ansel pulled him outside to murder him? I squeeze my eyes so tight that tears prick at the inside corners while I try not to think of Dad down here. I don't want that image to be how I think of him.

Ansel's a monster. What kind of psychopath can keep a smile on their face day in and day out yet have a torture chamber in his basement?

Staying here isn't an option.

# CHAPTER 3
## ANSEL

MOST PEOPLE KNOW THE RUMORS OF WHAT I KEEP IN THE BASEMENT and stay as far away as they can. Yet, today, little Morrigan walked right down and opened the door. *Brave girl.*

I catch her out of the corner of my eye when she comes back up the stairs and then rounds to the second set, heading straight to the loft without saying anything.

Plate of food for the grill ready to go, I partially slide open the glass door to the deck when the faint sound of sobbing stops me dead in my tracks.

Harry tunes in. I'm forced, by my wolf, to redirect away from the deck and turn to watch the loft's closed bathroom door.

Fighting against his control, I move us away from watching for her and instead force my way outside. Going upstairs probably won't help her.

She needs time. Morrigan fucked up, and now she'll have to learn to deal with that.

When I round the corner toward the grill, Ezra scares the shit out of me.

Sitting in one of the Adirondack chairs with his eyes closed, he starts talking. "She's overwhelmed by the luxury of your bathroom. Which, low standards, but living on the streets will do that."

Ezra, with the gift of listening in on other people's thoughts, has no issues helping me when he's here. One little touch, and if you're thinking, he can listen.

*Can you ever not be thinking?*

Opening the lid on the grill, I explain my confusion. "She went to the kennels. No one goes down there without being asked, an emergency, or by force."

I'm busy tossing chicken quarters onto the grill when Ezra's shoes thump on the boards of the deck as he walks across to sit on the railing next to me.

He doesn't wait for me to look at him before telling me what he can hear. "She wants to know which one her father was in."

That feels like a punch to the gut. Images of Walt flood back. All the time we spent together. The almost trouble we always seemed to be so great at finding, and how he'd beam when he'd see Morrigan.

Closing my eyes, I struggle against the feelings of losing my best friend. It's been too many years to keep feeling like this.

*It's not my fault she's here. It's not my fault he's dead.*

I may have killed him, but I was doing what I had to do. What I still have to do. Even if that means I . . . have to end her too.

"*Don't keep blaming yourself for this.*" Ezra's voice inside my brain draws me out of my thoughts.

I open my eyes and see his hand touching my forearm, which explains why his voice was so loud in my head. It's weird how useful his gift is.

Having my attention, he lets go of my arm and speaks.

"You've been given the most difficult gift. Yet, you wake up every day and do your best to prolong life. Your predecessors didn't give them the time of day. They didn't bring them here or even try. Every day you give someone a gift, don't cheapen it."

Done with the grill, I pat his shoulder in thanks before heading back into the house. Maybe there's hope for him yet.

The fact that Ezra releases a hard, quick laugh lets me know he's continuing to use his gift. I try to mentally flip him the bird, but all I can picture is that cute parrot spinning around on someone's finger like a gymnast. Mrs. Hoppe's daughter showed it to me on her phone when I picked up groceries last week. Kinda cute, but not effective at telling Ezra to stuff it.

The thought of the cell phone sends me fishing mine out of my pocket. I should call Ersilia and let her know Morrigan is safe. She'd be worried, right?

But it wasn't Ersilia who called me to save her. It was Cade's people. Maybe not involving Ersilia is best, for now.

I slide my phone back in my pocket. I'll give Morrigan some time before I make any phone calls. Something tells me involving her pack won't be helpful in getting more information. Morrigan being alone didn't happen by accident. Figuring out why is important.

I promised Walt I'd take care of his girls if something happened to him. Yet somehow, Morrigan ended up locked in a human jail. It was way too close of a call for comfort. A chill runs down my back at the thought of a police officer having been hurt.

I draw a deep breath, fighting off the thought that this mistake could have cost her the life I swore to protect. I trusted Ersilia to keep her daughter out of danger, and in doing so, I failed Walt.

I won't fail twice. Anything and everything I can do to keep her free and alive, I will.

*I know you fixate on those you want to kill,* I beg Harry, *but please, don't make that our only option. Help me find another way.*

If there was ever a time to keep him under control, it's now.

# CHAPTER 4
# MORRIGAN

I start washing from the top down. It's the most logical way to remove the grit and grime. As I wash my hair, strands upon strands pull out, slowly unwrapping from the mess. It's been over a week since we found someplace to stay that we could afford, even for the night. Beyond that, it's been a month since I've had a hot shower and enough shampoo to actually care for my hair. I take full advantage of the opportunity.

After massaging conditioner into my dark strands, I start scrubbing everything else. The shower from the jail was cold, and I did the bare minimum to be clean enough to be presentable. It was uncomfortable. In the privacy of Ansel's guest bathroom, I scrub, hard. The washcloth is turning brown, as are the water and the suds as they come off my body.

Only when I'm clean and the water turns clear do I take a minute to pause, the cleansing water trying to do more than wash my body. I'm exhausted, both mentally and physically. Something inside me wants to be lighter. It's searching for hope in a hopeless place.

Leaning my forehead against the tile wall, I release a heavy breath before turning off the water.

I step out of the shower and tightly wrap a big, fluffy towel around my body, then scrunch my hair dry with another one.

My reflection catches my eye. I thought I knew what I looked like. But the person staring back at me isn't right. I lower the towel and look at the woman in the mirror. She's skinnier than I've ever remembered seeing myself, my ribs protruding over my stomach. Clean, I can see how bad it really is, from discolorations of my skin to my brittle hair.

"Morrigan, dinner." Ansel's words are echoed by the clanging of dishes against the countertops.

For now, I'm safe.

Ansel is a monster, a murderer, and my new jailer, but I know that in his care, I'm safe. Unless he kills me, but I won't stay around long enough for that to happen.

In a few months, I'll be in better shape. I can formulate a plan and run. I won't be kept in a cage, not by Ansel and not by anyone else. I redirect the hope that tried to find me in the shower, pushing it toward a better life.

As I make my way down from the open loft, I look over the banister and see a massive amount of food on the counter. It's unexpected. There are several plates of chicken and, as promised, a variety of grilled veggies. Ansel's making a plate when I round the landing to the final four steps down to the first floor.

I freeze.

The weirdo who touched my forearm stands waiting. His eyes find mine.

"Nice to meet you. I'm Ezra Alloway of the Ardelean Bloodline. I prefer freak over weirdo, but points for trying. And for the love of anything or anyone holy, don't call me gifted." He pops a smirk and gives me a wink.

*How did* . . . It's like he plucked the words right from my mind.

I'm unsure if I should finish my descent. I know Ansel's gift and that it's rumored all the Ardeleans have one. I just haven't been in the same room as another wolf from the bloodline. What is the entirety of Ezra's gift?

*Mind reading, but to what extent?*

"It's pretty much I can hear you. If we touch, I get pictures and memories and a direct connection to talk through your mind, all stealthy like jinns. But let's be real, it's obnoxious." Ezra laughs, dishing up food for himself. "Besides, most people aren't interesting enough to listen to long term."

"Ezra, quit scaring her. Morrigan, come eat," Ansel instructs us both.

Nervously, I descend the final four stairs and cross the house to the kitchen. Next to Ezra, I pick up a plate. It looks delicious, but I can't bring myself to put anything on it.

Gerad's voice echoes. *Morrigan. That's enough. You don't want to see your lunch sticking out of your stomach later. What is wrong with you? Why are you eating so much? I've never seen a woman or wolf eat that much before.*

The plate is pulled out of my hand. Startled, I jump, and Ezra rests his hand behind my shoulders. "Go sit down. I've got this."

I do as he says, following Ansel to the small table by the windows. I sit in the spot farthest from Ansel.

Ezra follows a few moments later with two plates piled high with food and sets them on the table before retreating to the kitchen. He comes back with two glasses of water. Then, on a final trip, he returns with silverware and glasses of orange juice.

Quickly, I divert my eyes when his meet mine. He motions with his fingers, the movement in my peripheral catching my attention.

When I look back at him, he gestures to my plate. "Eat. No matter whose voice that is — if you're hungry, eat. If you're not hungry, don't eat. There are seconds in the kitchen if you want more. If you don't like something, don't eat it."

Growling comes from down the table. Ansel's voice is barely distinguishable from the growl. "What?!"

"Ansel," Ezra barks. He looks away from me and narrows his eyes at Ansel. "Not now."

Ezra sits next to Ansel and starts eating.

Ansel stews in a rageful silence for a few minutes before he takes another bite. I finally feel comfortable enough to do the same. I've never had someone stand up for me like Ezra. Even if it was a little creepy how he heard my inner voice. Having someone on my side feels good.

They say if you're starving, anything will taste good. It's not true. If you're starving, you'll *eat* anything. Your body will make you want to eat more of it, but you know it doesn't taste good.

This is delicious.

I'm picking meat off a chicken thigh bone when a man knocks on the sliding glass door from the deck. Before Ansel can say anything, the door opens, and he walks in. He looks vaguely familiar.

"Boss, Ezra." The man tips his head to them. His head snaps back, and he looks between the three of us before pointing at me. "Not what I was expecting."

"Ben, you remember Morrigan." Ansel introduces us,

pointing his fork between the two of us, the brussels sprout speared on the end threatening to fling off.

Ben nods. He's tall, at least six and a half feet. He didn't have to duck coming through the door, but it was definitely close.

He steps toward the table. "I do, it's nice to see you again."

I shrug.

He returns my shrug but keeps speaking. "We only met a few times when you were here to visit your dad. I'm sorry for your loss."

His words sting. I don't respond. No one's truly sorry. No one here means anything when it comes to Dad. If he's been here the entire time, he could have saved him and didn't. He could have let me say goodbye.

Ben heads into the kitchen, and I focus on the rest of my chicken, begrudgingly knowing I'll have to start the vegetables sooner rather than later. Ezra and Ansel are quiet, both pushing their food around on their plates for a moment. Then Ezra finishes his food and heads to the kitchen.

No sooner is Ezra out of the chair than Ben sits down in it.

"Night, Ezra," Ansel says before the back door closes.

Ben and Ansel don't speak, but they seem comfortable in their silence. I try to observe them, but their silence doesn't leave a lot for understanding.

*How close are Ben and Ansel?*

Much like Ezra, Ben eats and heads out before I even manage to choke down all my vegetables. Ansel stands as soon as he feels I'm probably done eating. Which he's right because I refuse to eat any more of these putrid things.

He nods toward the kitchen, then beckons, curling his fingers as though I'm to follow him.

Without being told, I help him clean up after dinner, moving slowly as dread builds, waiting for a lecture. I know it's coming. Growing up, Ansel would talk things out with the wolves he's tried to save.

I wring the bottom of my T-shirt.

From what I remember, those conversations were always difficult. I've seen grown men cry after talking to Ansel.

I won't. I refuse to. He doesn't deserve my tears.

# CHAPTER 5
# ANSEL

She hasn't spoken a single word since I made her get in the truck. Quiet, withdrawn, reserved, and well behaved were not words I would have ever used to describe Morrigan. Walt didn't want his daughter to be afraid to find her place in the world. So, she always had free rein to be herself. Even if that meant the child outsmarted both of us on a number of occasions. We even told Ersilia that her first word was 'dada' instead of the honest 'fuck.' Spent the entire morning while Ersilia was at work teaching her any other sounds than eff.

This girl doesn't seem like the same person. Compared to the last time I saw Morrigan, she's a hollow shell. Sure, she put up a tiny fight in Salt Lake City, but how can I believe this is the child Walt had to drag kicking and screaming from the rodeo? All because he wouldn't let her bring home a pet bull. I'm clearly missing something in this puzzle.

This silent treatment from her is getting to be more frustrating by the minute. More than pulling cactus spines out of the guys when they played a dumb game and I was out of duct tape.

*Why isn't she behaving like a normal wolf?*

"Why were you in Salt Lake City?" I draw a deep breath and look across the kitchen island at her.

Standing there, with her fingers resting gently against it, Morrigan doesn't appear to be ready to speak. Maybe there's a logical answer that explains at least some of the charges.

Wrong place, wrong time? A misunderstanding.

Morrigan doesn't say anything.

I'm hot around the collar. The lack of any sort of attempt to defend herself, to explain something. Fuck, I'd take anything at all.

I slam my fist on the counter. There has to be something she'll react to. I'd rather not resort to shouting and making noise, but something to get her out of this zombie state.

With a delayed jolt, like she's been hit by lightning, Morrigan backs from the countertop and wraps her arms around herself.

Finally, she groans and, without hurry, gives a half-assed answer. "We were on our way to a show in Denver. My friends and I got separated when the cops showed up at the party."

"Who are these alleged friends?" Harry and I watch her closely.

Morrigan squirms, holding my gaze. Her body twitches as muscles spasm from the battle of dominance between us. It's no battle. I'll always win; Harry always makes sure of it. Especially since her eyes have yet to flash the gold of her wolf.

"I've only known them a little while. They're not all wolves. It's a group of girls who all share similar experiences." Morrigan pulls her eyes from mine and twists away from me.

It doesn't go unnoticed, but the vague nature of the 'experiences' goes unasked. Anger, sadness, and confusion flood my body. Anger settles in my fists but tingles out into all my limbs. Sadness sinks into my stomach.

"What did you do for money? You were all sleeping in a van? Where are their parents?" I punctuate.

*Where the fuck is Ersilia?* No. I can't get tied up in her.

Morrigan shrugs.

I'm starting to hate the shrugging and lack of commitment to anything more than the radio silence.

She hangs her head. "They don't have any. We traveled around, following the party. Score some, then flirt with guys, and trade for food."

They don't have any parents. Suspicious. I guess, logically, I'm not the only foundling orphan in the shifter world. But a whole group? Unlikely. Trade what for food?

I run my hand down my face. How did this fucked up situation happen? Could I have done something to fix it? Is this my fault for not staying in contact with Ersilia?

All these questions make my head spin.

Harry snarls and snaps his jaws. My anger is becoming his uncontrollable aggression.

Her voice gets small. "We always had a plan for if the cops came, and when they did, one grabbed my wrist. I was trying to escape but couldn't get free. They drove off. I couldn't get to the van."

"Some friends," I mutter without thinking about the consequences of my words.

Morrigan shields her face with her hands for a moment before pulling them down.

*Fuck. She's going to shut down.*

When she speaks, her voice shakes. "It doesn't matter. It was my night to hold the stash. I'm normally the quickest one, but I got stuck. You know the rest."

"Where are they going?" I growl at her, letting Harry rise to the surface.

"Denver," Morrigan snaps.

I want to be excited to see her fire, but the timing of her defiant nature isn't good.

"For what, where? When?" Her repeating answers to things I already know isn't helping anyone. *I want to help them. Let me help.*

"What does it matter?" She fights. Her arms go wide, making herself bigger like she can scare me off like another predator, but her wolf doesn't back her actions or words. "You take them back to their packs, and they'll disappear again. Besides, how is their pack any less valid than any other?"

She's been without guidance too long. There's no stability in her life. It's the only reason I can see that would leave her so back and forth with her responses. She's a small female wolf. Even with her father's coaching to be strong, Morrigan should have a lot more fear than she does right now. Face to face with Harbinger, her wolf should be guiding her to submit.

I snap back against her, trying to see how much harder I have to push for her to submit. "It matters because you got caught with drugs. Packs don't deal in drugs. You didn't have food or a home or shelter. Packs need stability, none of which you had. Morrigan, surely, you're not stupid enough to believe that was okay."

"Nice, Ansel." She rolls her eyes, pulling her arms back in and tossing her head. "Pretty sure you didn't even graduate from high school, and you're calling me stupid."

"Let me put it this way for you, Morrigan." I bite my tongue for a moment. *Walt, what I wouldn't give to have you back right now to deal with her.*

Harry pushes forward. I'm holding him back from exploding through me. Something about Morrigan and her defiance pushes his buttons more than ever.

I spell out the severity of what's happening and what our future looks like. "You're *mine*. My responsibility, my pack member, my obligation to fulfill to the federal government and to the state of Utah. *Mine.* I am offering to do what I can to help your alleged friends, who, I'll remind you, can't be that great of friends because they left you behind, to save themselves. I'm not the one who ended up in a cell with a death sentence."

Harry is right behind my words. He snarls, and I do in kind.

My teeth snap shut and my lip twitches. My fingers gripping the countertop stop me from closing the gap between us.

This could've been a mostly pleasant conversation. This could have gone so much better, but we're already here.

I keep going. If she wants difficult, then I'll be difficult. "So, if you want to play the victim in all this, you'll have to come up with a hell of a better explanation for what took you down this path. 'Cause as of right now, all I'm seeing is that Ersilia took you to Los Angeles, put you in prep school, and let you lose sight of who you are. You're using drugs."

"Fuck you, Ansel," she spits. "I wasn't even partying. You think living with Gerad as a fucking possession I just found a way to sneak out all the time? Then, what? I decided a drug addiction would be a good idea?"

"I didn't say that. I need you to tell me, should I be worried about withdrawal?" I feel warm, but our tension is raising the temperature of the room.

"I was drinking only what the guys at the party were buying me. I don't— I haven't used drugs since I left California. If you dip into the party stash you have to work it off. It's double for us what we charge the buyers. I was trying to save money to leave." Fat tears well in her eyes.

Morrigan retreats, backing away before heading up the stairs to the loft. She slams one of the bedroom doors, and it echoes through the house and rattles my bones.

I don't know whose head I want to rip off first. Ersilia for letting her get so lost. Gerad for being such a shitty Alpha that he didn't hunt her down. Morrigan for her complete lack of common fucking sense. Or . . . my own, for letting this ever happen to her in the first place.

Something is wrong if I can't keep my cool around her. This didn't have to be hard.

Harry is still too far forward. He's pushing my control.

I walk out the glass door and down to the firepit. The sun sinks lower with each passing moment. I light a small fire and drop myself into my seat on the wooden swing. At least, out here, if I can't hold him back anymore, he won't be able to shred the couch and mark the bedroom door.

Watching the flame dance in the firepit, I let Harry's thoughts flood my brain.

He brings forward screams, snarls, pain, and suffering. Bloodlust and the primal memories of the violence we've lived. Everything we've survived is fair for him to torment me with.

*My wrists ache. The metal cutting into the skin. They've locked both of them this time. I know it means it'll hurt more. I don't understand why they're doing this. What did I do wrong? I've done everything right. I scrubbed the floor until they couldn't see the stains. I cleared the plate of mush they fed me.*

*Boots scrape across the floor, and my whole body curls into itself. If they can't see me, they can't hurt me. If they can't hurt me, maybe the angry voice inside my head will stop talking.*

*He tells me to kill them all. He tells me how, but I don't understand. I don't understand how I could be a wolf. I'm not an animal. I'm a boy.*

*Boots with the metal tips poking out, the ones that wore through the leather, are standing next to me. It's David. He's the worst. He always hurts me the most. His boot nudges my side, and I try not to move with his push. It won't make a difference. Maybe he'll only beat me.*

A DARKNESS, A BLACKOUT, HAS PLAYED CONSTANTLY IN MY BRAIN FOR nearly the last three decades.

*WE KILLED HIM? HANDCUFFS CAN'T HOLD WOLF PAWS.*
*The voice told me we are wolf.*
*And it must be true. We ripped David limb from limb. His blood covered every surface of that terrible, awful room. The first to die.*

THE MEMORY FADES AWAY AND IS QUICKLY REPLACED.

*RIPLEY'S SNAPPING. THE BROWN AND GRAY WOLF SNARLS, EYES LOCKED on whatever I can't see. I try to push the vision, trying to see. Snapping jaws, the clacking teeth.*
*"Ripley. Don't do it." Ben's voice.*
*The sound of gunfire and an echo with voices shouting.*
*The sweet taste of blood in my mouth.*
*Roughly three months from now.*

"ANSEL," BEN'S VOICE CALLS.

I shake my head, scrunching my eyes closed. They're dry from the smoke of the fire.

He stands on the other side of the fire pit with his hand held out like he had been snapping for my attention. Ben's been around long enough to know that if I'm lost to Harry, he shouldn't approach. Touching Harry results in violence.

The chaos Harry rattled through my brain sated him for now. He sulks back, leaving my brain a hopeless and cold place.

"You with me?" Ben shifts his shoulders to see me around the billowing smoke.

Drawing a deep breath, I exhale, "Yeah. Sorry."

"How'd it go with Morrigan?"

Ben breaches the sitting area and slowly lowers himself into one of the plastic chairs across from my spot on the wooden swing.

"You couldn't hear it?" My voice is flat while I run my hand back through my hair.

Ben shakes his head. "That good, huh?"

I grumble, "Worse."

"She's getting her first taste of the kennels?" Ben tries to assess.

"Went up to the loft." I indicate with a lazy wave of my hand toward the second story of the house. "I'm not messin' with the system. It's worked this long. She's like any other lost wolf."

Ben laughs. "If you say so, boss."

He's the best Second I could have hoped for. Stable and completely, almost completely, normal. He understands my process and has never caused an issue. Out of all the wolves forced to visit, he's my only permanent nonrisk, reformed resident. Mostly because no matter how many times I try to kick him out, he won't leave. Part of me, the tiny selfish bit, doesn't want him to.

When my silence doesn't give way, Ben starts again, "You gonna be okay with her here?"

I rub the palm of my hand against my nose. "I don't have a choice. Humans only signed her to me if I agreed to bring her in for proof of life, I guess? Sometime in the next year."

"Shit." Ben snorts. "Well, could be worse. What do her parents think?"

"Haven't called Ersilia." I grit my teeth. I refuse to acknowledge Gerad as her parent. Even if he's the fated mate of Morrigan's mother. "One question has been buggin' me for a bit though. Why did she have the humans call the council and not call Ersilia?"

"What did Morrigan say?" Ben offers his hand out like he's handing me an answer with his question.

"She said that this group of girls she was running with all share the same experiences." I shake my head. "It didn't make sense. Then she said they didn't have parents. I'm fairly certain, at least, pretty sure, that if Ersilia had died, someone would have told me."

"Ansel," Ben says slowly, like I should understand what he's hinting at.

"Ben," I say slowly, like he should know I don't understand what he's hinting at.

Ben shakes his head. "No. I won't sit here and fill your head with ideas of what that could mean. You need to ask. To quote you, there's no sense in gettin' upset until we know what we're upset about."

Harry groans and eases slightly, but it's a relief I take with a sigh. One that Ben seems to think is my acceptance of the situation.

"Give her a few days. Maybe Morrigan comes around and opens up a bit." Ben doesn't sound optimistic as he shuffles chairs to escape the smoke trail again.

As I hem and haw over it, I don't think it'll work, but I acknowledge it.

Throwing my hands up in defeat, I change subjects. "Everything go okay today?"

Ben fights a smile. "The worst of it is that Princeton, the

new kid you picked up after Ireland, is complaining about living conditions. Apparently chopping wood isn't good for him."

We both snort at that. The new guy has been here two months and complains about everything. I understand why his pack shipped him out more and more by the day. Between his attitude problem and anger issues, he's borderline toxic. All that to say, he's perfectly unpleasant to be around, and that's without mentioning the early indicators of a fracture with his wolf.

Ben scratches his head. "Sherman wants me to look at one of his chickens, he says he thinks it's becoming a duck. So, there's that. Oh, and Ezra's struggling with the neighborhood."

"Good. Won't be long now before he decides he needs to find his place. I knew he wouldn't want to live here forever." I smile at my stroke of genius.

Purposefully putting my cousin Ezra, the mind reader, in the unit directly between my most recent shit starters was probably one of my brighter moments. He needs to see that living in the middle of nowhere isn't all it's cracked up to be. Ezra's a little lost. I have no doubt he'll find his way eventually.

Knowing what I've done, Ben laughs with me. "I can't blame Ezra though. Even down on my end of the road, I get sick of their bickering."

"Everyone is. But it's building character. Hopefully working out conflict in a controlled-ish environment will be good for gettin' them on their way home." I hang my head and finish the thought aloud. "We've had too many people comin', stayin', and dyin' here. It's about time we lose friends to healthy packs and relationships."

"If only," Ben agrees.

Then it dawns on me. "Wait, a duck?"

Ben cocks his head at me and raises an eyebrow.

"No, of course. That would be dumb." I shake my head. *Would be cool though . . .*

WINTER STILL HAS ITS CLUTCHES ON THE EARTH, SO EVEN THOUGH IT'S barely six in the evening, the world is plunged into darkness. The last log on the fire dies out, and Ben and I are saying goodbye while I soak the firepit to be safe.

I'm exhausted. The cool night air makes me crave sleep, but also, today was more than I bargained for.

Back in the house, I head to my bedroom. Normally, I'm all for the notion that if you're sleepy, you should sleep. Your body knows what you need. But if I go to bed now, I'll be up at two a.m. and baking, which my newest house guest won't appreciate.

At the bottom of my closet is a medium-sized safe, locked per usual. I adjust the dials and swing the little door open, then pull out my wallet and slide out Morrigan's driver's license.

Normally when I get new arrivals, I've got to take their personal effects: ID, bank cards, cash, and personal cell phones. I keep them secure in my safe in separate baggies. Cutting off those required to be here from the outside world isn't my favorite part of the job. It is, however, the best way to keep someone here with no opportunity to find a way out.

I don't want them completely helpless, so after some finagling with Cade, we've come up with a system of 'dumb phones' that only call a select group of people.

But it's weird. Other than her driver's license, Morrigan didn't have anything to put in the safe. It was the only thing the courts gave us back of her belongings.

Before I close the safe door, I pull out five hundred in cash and put it in my wallet. Morrigan came with nothing, and I'll need to get her things: clothes, toiletries, and who the fuck knows what women need that I don't know about.

My stomach growls, and when I look at the clock, it shows it's six thirty. I'm tired, but a couple of cookies and a movie wouldn't be awful. After reheating leftovers and grabbing some of the oatmeal scotchie cookies out of the bag, I get ready to unwind for the night.

Before I turn on the television, I walk over to the floor beneath the loft and listen to the sounds from upstairs. Morrigan is muttering in her sleep. It's not peaceful sounding.

Do I wake her up? But if dreams are the way we work out our worries, maybe it's best she works it out on her own.

Feet up on the coffee table, I turn on the dinosaur flick I've seen at least a couple hundred times. It's still cool to me. Humans in the movie running back and forth from the wicked smart dinos they've brought back from extinction. *Why did anyone think that was a good idea?* Unless you really understand what the responsibility of taking control of a monster means, don't do it.

By the time the final credits are rolling, my eyelids are heavy. Passing from the living room to my bedroom, I listen again to the sounds from the loft. Morrigan is still sleeping, but she's significantly more settled in her sleep.

Harry lingers, listening to her, his attention more intent, but I drag us away from the loft.

I want a shower and to pass out until my morning alarm rings.

The door to my bedroom clicks closed, and immediately, the sound of a wood step creaking follows.

Closing my eyes, I focus on the telltale sounds of weight shifting from one stair to the next, coming down to the main floor. *Come on, Morrigan, go to the kitchen. Get a snack, go back to bed.* I urge her, hoping to hear the sound of the fridge and not something worse.

The loose board in the living room floor creaks. She's careful but not good at sneaking out. The last sound in the house is the sliding glass door opening and closing. I give her enough rope to hang herself, and she does.

Blowing a raspberry, I trade my pajama bottoms for jeans, tie my sneakers, and grab the flashlight from the cubby above my shoe bench before following her scent out the back end of the house. Without wind, her trail stays fresh. There's no rush in chasing her. She's fueled with the nervous energy of escape, and despite eating with us this afternoon, her body doesn't have a lot more fuel to burn. She'll be forced to walk or stop soon enough.

Images roll back as Harry shows us the clear outlines of her bones against her skin, as if I needed further reminders.

Morrigan's path makes it clear she's got no idea what she's doing. We're twisting and turning across the desert. She's turned down a path in the exact opposite direction of town, headed toward the gorges that go on for a few miles, separating us from the national park. It's dangerous terrain, even if you know what you're running in.

This has officially gotten too dangerous. *Time to stop.*

Standing still, I listen for her footfalls up ahead. She's still moving, and each step she takes is a weird stride mixed with heavy panting.

"Morrigan," I call, "I get your desire to escape. However, you're headed into really dangerous terrain. If you got to get fleeing out of your system, I don't mind chasing you all night, but I would really rather not risk you gettin' hurt."

I pause. Her footsteps keep moving, getting farther away.

"And now that you know the footsteps behind you are real, not in your head, it kind of takes away the hope you'll escape." I try to reason with her. But her feet keep moving. *The hard way it is.* "So, options: you make a sharp left, and we keep going across more flat ground while in an equally wrong direction, or you stop running, we talk, and head back to the house. And since I know you're wonderin' if you should go right, if that might be the way back to town, you've kinda run in a circle because that's the direction back to the house."

Footfalls stop. Her heavy panting does not. It's a wheezing sound, air being pulled into lungs that aren't used to the elevation and a body not used to running. The wheezing isn't getting better. She starts coughing.

Even borrowing Harry's sight, the starlight isn't enough to see more than the shape of her ahead.

I turn on the flashlight.

Twenty yards ahead, she's bent over with her hands pressed on her knees. Her whole body shudders when drawing in the night air. She staggers, nearly falling over.

I close the distance between us and try to steady her by keeping her hands on her knees. She pulls away into a coughing fit. Her independence is fierce, and I know better than to push. Instead, I sit crisscross applesauce on the dirt, resting my elbows on my knees and watching her try to recover on her own. The flashlight illuminates the ground beyond us toward the drop-offs. It's eerie seeing the light fade off into the abyss.

Minutes pass, and my gaze goes skyward. Satellites are dancing across the sky.

When the coughing and wheezing stop, I lower my gaze and let my eyes adjust, seeing that Morrigan mostly put herself together.

Brown eyes hold tight to defiance. She debates bolting, as made evident by the way her eyes do a quick scan of the horizon.

Unfortunately for her, while her brain may have a lot of fight, her body doesn't.

I stand up and dust off my ass. "Ready to go back to the house?" I yawn and stretch my hands above my head, then drop them, thumb pointing toward the house.

It's late. She won't like how the rest of the night goes. I'm not too thrilled either. Best get it over with.

Morrigan limps along, barely in my peripheral line of sight. She huffs in either anger or pain with each step. But her following along is all that matters. Little bit of pain won't hurt her. Maybe it'll help with the attitude.

Insects make noises, and a hare darts out of our way as we head back. It's a nice night to have to hunt her down.

She really did run in a circle, so it was only a fifteen-minute walk back to the house. Despite having gone out the glass door, we're now on the front end of the house by the driveway. I go up the small stairs and open the door, letting her in behind me.

After I toe off my shoes, she walks past the stairs to the basement like she's going to go upstairs. This is the shitty part.

I let the words come out slowly. "Where ya goin'?"

"To bed." Her voice is hoarse from forcing the thin, dry desert air down into her lungs. The flat tone comes across easily though. Her disgust with my question.

I don't want to do this. There's no pleasure in it, but I can't bend the rules. She needs structure. She needs an Alpha who is willing to steady her.

Consequences suck.

"I warned you about being untrustworthy." I tilt my head toward the basement stairs.

"You're joking." She coughs, hand covering her mouth.

I shake my head, knowing even in the darkness of the hall-way, she can see me. "Downstairs, Morrigan."

"I'm not spending the night in one of your creepy kennels."

55

Her tone doesn't carry fear. It's aggravation. Impressive, all things considered.

"Not a suggestion. You're spending tonight, and tomorrow while the guys and I go to work, in the kennels. Go on your own, or I'll force you. I can't trust you not to run, and actions have consequences." I try offering her kindness while being firm.

I don't have to let her go down on her own. *Does she see that? Does she really not understand how badly she's fucked up?*

Harry is locked on to her, daring her to defy me.

The clock on the wall ticks.

I've been awake nearly twenty hours, and I've used up all my patience. The command comes out, and it's harsh. I don't hold back my anger. "Move. Downstairs. Now."

Morrigan has almost no choice in the matter. She tries to fight it, but her body is tired. One foot in front of the other, she makes her way down the stairs.

I follow with similar reluctance.

She pauses at the bottom of the stairs. When I flick on the light, she walks through the door. It's exactly five full paces from the door to the most central kennel. I slide the door along the track, leaving it open for her.

Her command ended at coming down here. I try to leave her choice in the matter by motioning to the kennel one more time.

No movement from Morrigan, and I command again, "Go in the kennel, Morrigan."

Lip curled in a snarl is all she can really do to fight.

I let Harry flash her his eyes. We mean business.

When it comes to fractured wolves and my position, gender doesn't matter. If she wants a fight for dominance, I'll give it to her.

She's in the kennel, and I slide the door along the track. It latches into place automatically with a click. I flick the lever for the primary lock on the kennel door.

"There's no mattress or blankets or anything," Morrigan complains.

I walk over to the cupboard and fetch her a roll of toilet paper and a blanket. From the mini fridge tucked under the counter in the medical bay, I grab two bottles of water. As I pass them through the bars, I'm not surprised when she tries to hold eye contact. Defiant to the bitter end.

"You saw the kennels when you were down here earlier. You knew what you were getting into. Next time, you'll think twice before running. The kennels aren't built for luxury. Deal with it."

It's chilly in the basement, so I adjust the heat against the cold, and the furnace kicks on. It'll take the chill off the lower level.

On my way out, I hit the main latch for the kennel doors. Once I've closed the security door and spun the latch, she's secured. No one escapes the kennels.

The farther up the stairs I go, the harder it is to leave her down there. I don't take joy in being an asshole, but leaving her in a kennel feels different. Not good or bad, but not the same as anyone else I've locked downstairs. A day away from her to think this through might help.

No one died today. It was a good day. It could have been so much worse.

# CHAPTER 6
# MORRIGAN

THAT ASSHOLE FORCED ME DOWN HERE, GAVE ME PRACTICALLY nothing for a blanket, and then left me in the dark. Dark-ish.

My whole body hurts. My feet, my legs, my . . . everything. I wrap the blanket around myself, and it nearly wraps all the way around me twice. It's cozy, compared to the cinderblocks, but it doesn't relieve the pain in every part of my body when lying on the raised portion of the floor.

The furnace kicks on again, and the white noise helps stave off the feeling of being alone. Tears are welling in my eyes, but I blink them back.

*He's not worth the tears.*

Ansel is exactly like the rumors say he is. The speculation that Harbinger is all fake happiness is true. As long as someone's watching him, Ansel is kind and laughs. But I saw the truth. The minute we were alone, the anger came out. Only he'd find a reason to put me down here alone in the dark.

Why does he keep dragging it out? Why am I the one he lets his guard down around? I get to see Harbinger's darkness.

*Lucky me.*

I don't cry. It's not who I am. But tonight, despite Ansel not being worth the tears, I let them flow. And I'm positive it's from how much I hate him.

I don't hear Ansel come back down here, but when I wake up, the lights have changed. He left the overhead light on above his torture table. The fluorescent bulbs give off more light than the dinky one from last night. In the corner, by where my cell door opens, is a cooler and thermos.

My stomach gurgles. Stiff from sleeping on the concrete slab and feet sore from trying to run barefoot through the desert, I make my way agonizingly slowly over to the food. The world spins and my body protests, but I finally make it across the cell.

There's coffee in the thermos. The smell alone wakes me up and pushes the tiniest smile on my face. Coffee used to be my lifeblood. I've missed it. When I draw a slow sip, the liquid is still piping hot. Ansel brews his coffee strong, but he added creamer, cutting the acidic taste down.

The cooler has a scrap of lined paper taped to the lid. I ignore it in favor of looking at its contents. There are three additional bottles of water, some disinfecting wipes, two different kinds of sandwiches, some beef jerky, a baggie of homemade cookies, and a bag of chips.

I pull open the baggie with the cookies, and it's another smell that pulls on fragments left of happy memories. Ansel used to let me help him bake. He never objected to adding peanut butter, the best ingredient in the world, to almost every single batch.

I open the note. What are the chances it's how to get out?

*Morrigan,*
*You didn't get up when I asked if you wanted food. Here's lunch.*
*Be back after work. What kinda life do you want?*

*-AA*

He spelled my name right. His handwriting is messy and all over the place, but he remembered how to spell my name. No one gets my name right on the first try. Did he look it up on my ID he's kept away from me, or . . . does he remember from my childhood? The longer I think about how he cared or that he spelled it right, the softer I feel about it. I don't want to be soft about Ansel.

I read the note again, focusing on that question 'What kinda life do you want?' It's such a bullshit question. I have no life. This is where it'll come to an end. He'll murder me like he did Dad, and that'll be the last of it. I crumple the paper and toss it out of the cell so it lands on the floor of the main area.

Asshole. What does he expect me to do all day? Sit here and contemplate his pathetic attempt at a deep thought question? *Yeah. Right.*

BEGRUDGINGLY, I EAT THE FIRST SANDWICH HE LEFT FOR ME. IT'S peanut butter and strawberry jam. This stupid lunchbox is a punch in the nostalgia. The food relieves the ache of hunger in my belly and a little of the dizziness, but it doesn't matter because my eyes well up with tears again. Stupid traitorous emotions. Why now?

The sandwich disappears before I've even really tasted it. Food holds no more interest for me, so instead of picking through the rest of it, I drape my paper-thin blanket over myself before curling up into a ball huddled against the wall.

I've made so many decisions that led me here, curled up on the floor in Harbinger's kennels. So many decisions that maybe I didn't think all the way through. Does anyone other than the government know I'm here? I refused to give the cops Mom and Gerad's numbers when they told me I had to call someone.

Calling Mom and being forced to go back to California would have been back to square one. It would be me letting Gerad mate me off to whomever he saw fit. I ran for a reason, and that led me to pick the only option that wasn't California: claiming shifter status.

I'm not big on staying up with the news, but I knew that claiming I was a shifter would put me on a short timetable for the Sovereign's people to rescue me. If they didn't make it in time, the human government would execute me. And maybe that should have been a deterrent against calling them. Maybe I wouldn't have, except I heard the pack whisperings that the Sovereign made a vow not to let any of our people die behind bars if he could help it.

Despite knowing that being in trouble as a shifter could lead to death, I chose to admit what I am. Well, what I was born. My mistake didn't register until I saw the green-eyed devil. I didn't think about what would happen to me in the hands of our own people.

I traded the government's guaranteed death sentence for the hope that Harbinger won't kill me because I was too afraid of the devil I knew. Why didn't I think about just running away from Gerad's again? A little part of me knows better than to think that was an option. That little part of me knows that if

Gerad had collected me, it would have also been a death sentence.

Six months ago, I ran with hope for a better life. I'm alone in the world, locked in a cage, and waiting for death to find me, and I can't bring myself to really be afraid. Everything feels pointless, but I try not to dwell on it.

Clutching the blanket, wrapped in my little burrito, I roll over to my other side.

*How did I get so turned around last night?*

I can't believe I ran in a circle. How did he find me so fast? It must have been the stairs waking him up. I have to be quieter with my next escape, if he ever lets me out of here. Asshole is probably all set to leave me locked down here for the rest of my life, which may end up getting cut short.

A tiny sliver of fear creeps in the back of my mind, permeating my pity party. When we moved to California, there was a girl a little older than me. She didn't believe me that we came from Ansel's pack. It's where I first heard the threats to behave. *If you're bad, Harbinger will come and lock you in his cages. When he gets tired of feeding you or bored, he'll torture you. Best behave, or he'll come and take you away.*

It's fiction, right? But if I walked back over to the cell door, I'd see what I found last night. Ansel has all sorts of things that could be used to torture someone; why else would he have them?

I'VE NAPPED THE BEST I COULD GIVEN THE COOL CONCRETE FLOORS, paced this cell for what feels like hours, and eaten more than half the food in the cooler. There's nothing to do and no indicator of the time of day. One thing's for sure though: the pity party is over and I'm fighting fear with rage. I pull on the bars, as hard as my frail arms allow, trying to slide them. They're locked and barely wiggle.

I can't reach the top to see if I can do something to open the lock. The lunchbox, maybe? The little day cooler has a handle, but it seems pretty sturdy. Lining it up with the bars, I place one foot on it and test it with some weight. It wobbles, unstable.

Five or six tries later, I give up. The box is too tippy, and I can't even see if it's possible to unlock the latch. My frustration grows thick.

"Hello?" I yell to the void.

I haven't tried asking to be let out. Maybe it's a possibility? Ansel probably won't let me out, but if there was someone else here? Ezra seemed like he could be on my side of things.

There's no response.

I try again. "Can anyone hear me?"

I shout louder. "Help! Someone! Anyone! Let me out!"

I keep screaming until I cough and my throat is scratchy from yelling. *It's no use.* With deep breaths, I try to recover from the exertion of screaming. The cool air burns in my lungs. Exhausted, I sink back to the raised bit of floor with my blanket.

*Why wouldn't he have soundproofed kennels?* Makes it easier to sleep at night if you can't hear the cries from your victims.

One thing is for certain, when I get out of here, he'll never be able to catch me.

# CHAPTER 7

# ANSEL

I'T'S BEEN A LONG DAY, BUT BEFORE MY BOOTS COME OFF, I HEAD straight down the stairs to the steel door leading to the kennels.

All my spare thoughts have been on Morrigan. Even the guys noticed I was distracted, making comments that the newcomer must be dangerous if I was this distracted about them. Integration with the rest of the pack normally happens within the first few days. But I'm worried it'll be too much for her. How do I make this work for her?

Practiced and honed over the years, I spin the kennel door lock open and pull the door back before stepping in to find Morrigan slumped in the corner of her cell. Her head snaps in my direction, and she shoots daggers at me with her eyes, but she doesn't stand up.

I hit the release button for the locks. A crumpled-up piece of paper is on the floor. My guess is the note I left. Picking it up on my path to unlock the secondary lock and latch, I don't bother uncrumpling it. It gets shoved into my jeans pocket.

The bars slide back with ease without the latches.

Even with the door open, Morrigan doesn't move to get up. Usually, I struggle to get out of the way of people wanting out of the kennels after a stay down here.

*Maybe she's intimidated?* I take a step back and see if that helps.

She doesn't move.

Leaning against the block wall by the opening, I try to coax her out. "You wanna come out for a few hours, or should I plan to bring your dinner down?"

She makes a noise of disapproval. What do they call that? A scoff? I wait, and she rolls her head back and forth against the wall.

"Listen, Morrigan," I start, trying to pitch her the ideas I've come up with to help her get back on the right road.

"No!" Her voice is hoarse. Probably, from screaming her fool head off trying to get someone to let her out. "You listen."

As instructed, I stand and wait for her to talk. Giving her some control over her life is part of the plan, so now's as good a time to start as any.

"I'm not interested in your voodoo hippy bullshit. I want to live my life. I don't need or want you to interfere. Let me go. I'll be out of your hair, and we never have to see each other ever again."

She started that rant spittin' mad, but it quickly turned into emotional pleas that tug on my heartstrings.

Harry isn't impressed. He retreats from the front of my thoughts.

It's hard watching her when she's resigned to feel this way. I press my lips together but don't respond. She dug this hole. I've offered to help her climb out, but if she wants to stay in it, then that's on her.

"Why don't you talk like a normal person? Say anything!"

Her strained voice pushes out words. She's panting now just from trying to yell. "Why do you have to be such a freak?"

"You're not leaving. I've got about five hours before I hit the hay. Would you like to spend them out here, on this side of the bars, hangin' out with me and Ezra or not?" I yawn. I've more control today and don't engage with her rage.

Morrigan still doesn't move from her spot on the floor. It's odd, and I don't like that she hasn't stood up. Bending over and picking up the lunch box and thermos, I give her one last look. *Maybe she just doesn't have any fight left in her, and the quiet will do her good.* "Suit yourself. I'll bring your supper down. Anything you don't like?"

She doesn't answer. Apparently, silence is her way of dealing with people problems.

Per protocol, I pull the cell door shut and engage the secondary latch and lock before hitting the main lock on my way out the door. The steel door slides closed and locks.

I'd like to leave it open so I could hear if she'd like to come out, but something tells me that the time in the kennels will do her good. Give her a chance to get herself sorted.

*Why does she have to be so difficult?* I understood the fight from her as a child, testing limits and figuring out pecking order within wolves, but now she's rude.

Finally, I get to untie my work boots and toss them over the vent to dry out. After pulling off my socks, I toss those directly in the wash. I'm not hungry, but dinner isn't about me; there's a half-starved little wolf in the basement.

I open her lunch box to find only half the food eaten. I rifle through, trying to remember in my half-sleep state what I packed her. She ate the PB&J but left the ham and cheese. The sweets are gone, but the salty snacks are still here. *Woman after my own heart.*

I shake my head, trying to clear those thoughts. *No, don't think thoughts like that. What's wrong with me?*

Opening the fridge, I take a quick look at what's left from my trip to the grocery store two weeks ago. Two frozen pizzas are the only thing that sounds even slightly appetizing.

Ezra comes in the back door. He hasn't been saying a lot lately, and I'm not sure if that's good or bad. I've always been closer to Judah, but this is more than uncharacteristic of him.

"I'm fine. My neighbors suck." Ezra plops down on the stool with a sigh. "I think it might be time for me to get out of here for a while."

"You don't say." I smile, shaking my head. "There's nothin' wrong with you, Ezra. You're imagining it. Your wolf is fine. I bet there wasn't a single incident where you felt strange when you were helping Cade keep Thalia safe."

"He's so loud and so present." Ezra defends himself. Though, he doesn't deny my observation of his time away from my little piece of the world.

On and off, over the last year, Ezra's been here. Not that he needs to be, but Ezra does everything in his own time. He's working through some demons. That doesn't make him fractured.

I put the pizzas in the oven, stacking them on different racks. Someone once said they don't cook right that way. But if you rotate them halfway through, nothing comes out funky. I twist my chicken-shaped egg timer to the appropriate amount of time and look at Ezra.

He's drumming his fingers on the countertop.

I give him another minute before sitting on the counter-top, facing where he sits at the island. "When you came here, Judah and I, well . . . we never did the paperwork. Neither of us was sure about what you wanted, and we didn't think you were ready for us to ask. You're free to leave. But Judah and I agree, there's no reason you'd have to go back to Maine. He wants you happy. If Maine isn't where you're happy, then . . ."

Ezra's sudden change in facial expression makes me smile. He's furrowing his brows with puffed-out lips.

"Surprised?" I ask, tipping my head.

"Yeah." He nods before running his hand behind the back of his neck. "I mean, not that I'd think Judah would ever want me to be unhappy."

"But you're not used to Judah tellin' you to do what's good for you. It's never been to take care of you first." I offer him bits of the conversation I had with Judah about his treatment of Ezra. Sometimes, the problem isn't with the wolf who ends up here.

Ezra points at me. "That."

"You're a lot like Cade," I say slowly, hoping he gives me a chance to finish. "You get a bad rap for not wanting to help. Yet, you've been given an awfully big burden to start with. I think the time apart has helped Judah see your struggles. He knows he's been a bad brother, a bad Alpha for you. When you went to different schools, it was easier for him to get on without you. Judah could stand on his own two feet 'cause he didn't have the pack to worry about. When the two of you went home, and he took the Alpha position, it was natural of him to drag you along too. Not drag, include?"

Nodding, Ezra drums his fingers a bit more. Something is still eating at him.

I try one last thing. "I'll talk to Sherman about keepin' it down and fightin' with Ripley. But I think it's time you take a road trip. Swing into the pack in Colorado, maybe head down to New Orleans, and if it still doesn't seem right, work your way north to see Cade. Hang out there for a bit, and if you're not happy, move on again. Your wolf is stable, you're strong enough to keep the both of you outta trouble until you find the right home."

Ezra doesn't say anything. His face twitches as he runs through things in his head. I hop off the counter before my chicken timer starts squawking. I'm already moving the pizzas around when it does.

"You'll be okay without me?" Ezra asks as I close the oven door.

*That's a weird question.* I look over my shoulder at him before setting the timer again. I rest my hands on the counter behind me. "Why wouldn't I be?"

Ezra tosses his head over his shoulder to the basement stairs.

Ah. I swallow hard, looking down at the floor. *I need to sweep.* "Yeah. As nice as it was to have a mind reader around here, I think we'll have to figure this out the hard way."

"Want my two cents or want me to stuff it?" Ezra offers.

*Do I want his opinion?* I've been doing this for so long that I should have it figured out. Take the help when you can get it, right?

I nod, looking back at him, and wait for him to go on.

Ezra gives me a soft smile. "There's no one, anywhere, fighting for her. She knows it. Morrigan wants to belong somewhere. I know she's focused on being on her own, but she doesn't know how to fit in somewhere to even give it a chance. I'd be willing to bet she believes she has no one in this world. Morrigan would rather fight to prove that she doesn't need anyone than learn to accept there is someone who wants her to succeed."

Ezra, per usual, makes a shit ton of sense.

I'm struck with the 'I don't know what to says'.

Ezra keeps talking. "Yeah, she blames you for making her alone in this world. But you didn't do that, Ansel. It wasn't your responsibility to care for her then. She had a mother and stepfather who were supposed to give her love but failed. Everyone's always tied up in who wronged them. Very rarely does the blame fall in the right place. We all point fingers, in different directions, and hope someone's more at fault than we are. Morrigan's not right with her pointing. What she needs is someone to show up, to be consistent, and fucking care."

I open my mouth to say something, but there are still no words. Is he wrong? I can't let a difficult first day set the tone for Morrigan's stay here. If I take food to the basement and not make her come upstairs, that's the rhythm she'll expect. I don't know if I can get through to her that I care, but I can be consistent.

# CHAPTER 8
# MORRIGAN

THE DOOR TO THE BASEMENT OPENS, AND THE DELICIOUS SMELL OF pizza wafts in. My stomach growls in response. Ansel doesn't have a plate with him. Figures, the monster will starve me for this incident, just like Gerad would. He goes through the clearly well practiced motions before pushing my cell the door open along its track.

Ansel steps back, inviting me out of the cell.

I don't move.

"Get up," Ansel commands.

I stand and hold my head high. He doesn't know I don't have a wolf, and I'm not sure what would happen if he found out. So, I follow the commands that have no effect on me. But only to their very basic extent.

I smirk, and Ansel gives me a look. He didn't say to do anything other than get up. Militant compliance is my favorite way to get around rules, and I'll do so absolutely.

"Get out here," Ansel commands again.

Moving forward and out of the cell, I stand on his side of the bars.

Ansel steps away from me, and this time, he doesn't command but rather beckons in a more polite tone. "Come on."

My stomach knots. There's food, and I want it. I push forward, following him up the stairs.

I'm panting by the time we make it upstairs, and my head swims with the exertion.

Sitting on the table are two plates, silverware, and two glasses of water. Ansel invites me to sit down without words, and then he serves himself a slice of pizza.

I don't want to sit at the table and pretend I'm not eating with the enemy. But escaping can't happen if I don't fuel my body. From what I remember of Ansel, he isn't the type to drug someone's food.

Watching him make no move to plate food for me is a better reassurance. Cautiously, I move and put a piece of pizza on my plate. Ansel says nothing. He eats the front half of each slice with a fork and knife while I pick mine up. Shuffling his cut pieces around on his plate, he waits for them to cool before putting them into his mouth.

*What a wuss. Man up and eat the pizza.*

Ansel doesn't pressure me for anything more. Asshole made me leave the cell, but he hasn't initiated any additional conversation. *Not that I'd want to talk to him anyway.* It's spooky quiet in his house. I eat all my pizza down to the crust, and Ansel raises an eyebrow. *Hypocritical asshole. You use a fork, but I should eat my crust?*

"It's about two hours before bed," Ansel announces. He sits back in his chair, his green eyes trained on me. "Would you like to stay up here and watch a movie, or would you like me to let you back into your kennel?"

"Wait, I thought you let me out?" I bat my eyelashes, hoping he'll take pity on me.

Pulling his hair up into a messy bun, he laughs. "Yeah,

battin' those eyelashes at me won't work. Harry doesn't do puppy privilege. I've no reason to believe I won't be chasin' you all over the backcountry tonight if I leave you out. Last night, you almost ran off a cliff. You'll be in the kennel until you prove trustworthy. Then we'll try the loft again. If that goes well, we'll see about getting you down the hill and in your own cabin."

Without waiting for permission, I shove my chair back and abandon my plate on the table. I move with a specific hurry to the stairs leading up to the loft away from him. If I can't sleep in a real bed like a person, I might as well fucking not smell like an animal locked in a cage. After slamming the bathroom door shut, I turn on the shower.

I let the bathroom fill with steam before undressing and letting the hot water nearly scald my back. Standing there, staring off into space, I try to find a happy memory in the few my brain has retained, and all my muddled and garbled thoughts run back to Dad.

I was younger, couldn't see over the kitchen counter, but he let me climb up on it and help pour seasonings into a bowl he was mixing for dinner. I can hear his voice. *That's it, pup, look at that. You're gonna be a pro in no time. Do you 'spose they have competitions for shakin' seasonings? I bet you'd win.*

My tears mix in with the hot water. *There has to be a way to not end up like Dad.*

The facts don't change though . . . There's nowhere to go. Nowhere to run to. Even if Ansel lets me stay on this side of the kennel bars and I escape, where am I going? I won't have anything. Denver was the pack's next stop, but if you're caught, they'll never trust you're not working with the cops or with a Pack Alpha. They're too paranoid. I'd be on my own.

I'm too tired to wash my hair, so I settle with getting the grime of the basement off my body while reflecting on the only thing I've learned today. I traded one prison for another and then another. Gerad's, Utah's, and now Ansel's. I fled Gerad's with the hope that someday I'd be able to live a simple life. The woman in the mirror hasn't changed in appearance since yesterday, right down to the red and puffy eyes from crying.

*Who is this crybaby I've become? Furthermore, why? Is my dream really so unobtainable that the only thing left to do is cry about what I'll never have?*

I refuse to be another victim of Harbinger. I've given nearly everything for my freedom, and I'm not going to stop fighting for it now.

# CHAPTER 9
# ANSEL

"ASSHOLE," MORRIGAN SAYS AS I TURN OFF THE LIGHT TO THE kennels.

I leave a night-light on in the medical bay for her. I imagine the basement is creepy to someone who hasn't lived here.

Using the Alpha command is not my favorite thing to do. It's draining, and Harry gets squirmy inside, wanting more space, and that's uncomfortable.

Morrigan is so much like her father: stubborn. Climbing the stairs, I reflect on what Ezra said: consistency. I hope he doesn't mean making this a nightly thing. What am I supposed to do with her? Command her into behaving for the rest of her life? That doesn't sound fun for either of us.

I've had harder wolves to work with. Ones I've tossed scraps of food through the bars to, running a clock down to when I have to give up on them. They're the ones who either pull it together or they die.

Morrigan's different. She's not fractured, but she's physically unhealthy. The panting, leaning, and last night's tiny escape attempt, all clear indicators. Getting her physically well is the priority. Then we'll talk about what's next.

If I can survive the attitude problem.

Pajamas on, I lie in bed and stare at the ceiling. Harry begins hunkering down inside me, circling and nesting, ready to sleep.

No one died today. Today was pretty alright. Take the win when I can.

# CHAPTER 10
# MORRIGAN

Morrigan,

What do you want to do when you leave here?
How can I help you reach that goal? I'll be back after work.

-AA

I COULD DO WITHOUT THE PATRONIZING NOTES AND THE RIDICULOUS self-help. What's wrong with him? I hate this. Does he do this to everyone, or am I getting special treatment because, at one point, Ansel and Dad were friends?

I drag the lunchbox back over to my bed slab and wrap my blanket around my shoulders while I eat. The note is still there, mocking me.

I know what I want. It's what I've always wanted. I want to go as far away from Gerad and his 'advisors' as possible. I want to go someplace where people leave me the fuck alone. Where I can sew to make money, get a pet, maybe a cat or dog, and be happy. There's got to be a place in the world where I fit, somewhere. Anywhere.

But I'll never tell Ansel that. If you tell someone your dreams, they have the power to crush them. I'll guard my tiny little hope for a future and a better life away from everyone.

Today there are two PB&J sandwiches and no lunch meat and cheese. I eat the first one slowly. I'll leave the second one for later in the day and graze on my snacks.

Not knowing what time it is makes the day that much longer, maybe? This is so fucking ridiculous. Lying on the cold floor of the utilitarian basement, I'm uncomfortable. While the blanket helps, it's nothing compared to the feeling of the bed after that first meal here. I toss and turn a few times until I'm not completely uncomfortable and just a little irritated.

I was too rushed in my last escape attempt. That spat with Ansel wasn't worth running from. I was angry and let it get the best of me. My feet are still sore, and it furthers my need to plan better for next time.

A place to call my own is at the top of my priority list, and if I get to leave here, I've got to find a way to make it happen. But I need to be more calculated about it. It doesn't matter where I move. New York City, maybe? Dallas? Georgia? Anywhere that's not fucking Utah or California. I need a plan.

# CHAPTER 11
# ANSEL

"Fucking freak," Morrigan whispers when I close the door.

For the briefest moment, I thought she said my name again softly, but it wasn't worth reopening the door to find out.

She's mad. I'm exhausted. I don't have the energy to fight with her. I wish I did. I want to dedicate more time to getting her out of the kennels and on with a better quality of life. The kennels aren't meant for long-term occupancy.

Morrigan is getting stronger. It's only been a couple of days, but in the four and a half hours out of the cell today, I could see she wasn't quite as exhausted as she had been. She's eating a little bit more and getting her appetite back. She needs to get outside more.

The problem is the pack is falling apart. I take a deep breath and remember it's about balance. I collapse into bed, not even making it under the covers.

Sherman's lucky to be alive today.

Morrigan is lucky not to have Princeton as a neighbor in the kennels.

No one died today. Could have been a hell of a lot worse.

# CHAPTER 12
## MORRIGAN

Morrigan,

Do you have your diploma? Do you want help enrolling in college classes? It would be nice if you'd like to try socializing

I'll be back after work      -AA

What a joke. Asking me all these questions. I haven't answered one yet. Why does he keep trying? Why does he even care?

Full of frustration, I let out the scream I've been keeping inside. No one's going to hear me having a breakdown anyway. It feels good to just let it out.

When I'm done, I'm panting. I look at the note and roll my eyes at the irony. I'm locked in his fucking basement. Hardly seems like he'd let me out to go to school. Though, if he did, I'd absolutely be able to get someone to help me. I've had plenty of practice in California. With a little flirting, human boys will do anything you ask them to. I'd be on my way to freedom in no time.

Being alone down here does give me lots of time to plot an escape and rest in hopes of healing. When I run, I'll have to stick with my plan of following the driveway. It'll take longer, but I won't get lost. I'm sure I won't get another chance. And there's got to be plenty of businesses with shitty security in Nameless. It'll be easy to get a couple bucks and steal a car like Bubbles taught me.

Ansel brings me upstairs, and once again, we're alone.

I'm tired, but being upstairs out of the cold kennel is nice. I feel like I can breathe, and I draw deep, calming breaths while looking out at the landscape through the windows. The sun still sets early in February, but it's been good to see it.

Dinner isn't done cooking, and Ansel doesn't argue when I head to the shower while it finishes. But when I come back down, it's like two and a half rounds of twenty questions all evening.

Except I don't get a turn to ask.

Ansel constantly asks questions about the girls I was with, where I want to go in life, and how he can help me. I'm so sick of his condescending tone and assumptions. This idea that he'll be the one to 'help me' is ridiculous.

The darker the world grows outside and the more questions he asks, the more angry I am. It feels like a growing inferno in my heart. The fiery flames of upset stave off the remaining coolness within me from the basement. He holds himself so high and mighty, but it's all his fault. It's all his fucking fault. Maybe I should let him try and 'help' so he can fail at that too. Maybe after a failure, he'll give in and let me go.

# CHAPTER 13
# ANSEL

"MURDERER! YOU KILLED HIM, AND YOU DON'T EVEN CARE!" Morrigan shouts as I ease the door to the kennels closed.

I spin the dial and rest my head against the door. *Walt. Please, what am I supposed to do with your fucking kid?*

She's constantly back and forth between anger and sadness. On the occasion that there's something remotely stable about her, it's gone in the blink of an eye. I can't figure out the source. She won't trust me and it's frustrating both of us.

We were doing so good tonight. It started out fine, as a regular conversation, and then she started shutting down until we ended up where we have every night.

I pull myself up the stairs and can hardly believe it's only been four days. *I need a break.* I'd hoped she'd be ready to talk and be civil by now. I tried asking her about every subject I could think of. *What can I do differently? I'm not failing her.*

Today was a good day. We had close calls, but no one died. Another wolf is on my radar, and it could be soon when I get the call, but maybe tomorrow is a better day.

# CHAPTER 14
# MORRIGAN

Morrigan,

What do you do for hobbies? Is it something
you'd like to turn into a career or a lifestyle?
I'll be back after work

-AA

HOBBIES? REALLY? I'VE BEEN LOCKED IN A BASEMENT WITH NOTHING
to do all day for five days. Fucking asshole. Even if I told him
my hobby, it's not like he'd actually let me do it.

But I'd love a sewing machine. Fuck, I'd be happy hand
stitching if it was something to kill the time. What if I told him?
What if I gave in and answered his note? The thoughts of
running fabric through the machine, the soothing hum and
clicks, would be a nice change to the monotony.

If I'm spending a year down here . . . Or maybe not the
year . . .

A shiver reminds me where I am and yanks me back from the happy place that sewing has been. Asking about my hobbies is probably just Harbinger's plan to be rid of me. He'll make me think of all the things I'm missing. It'll make killing me easier and more justified for him if I fracture out of boredom. He can treat me like every other reject he's murdered. That's all I matter to him; why am I surprised?

Ansel killed his best friend. No one is safe if Harbinger gets his eyes locked on them. Especially not me.

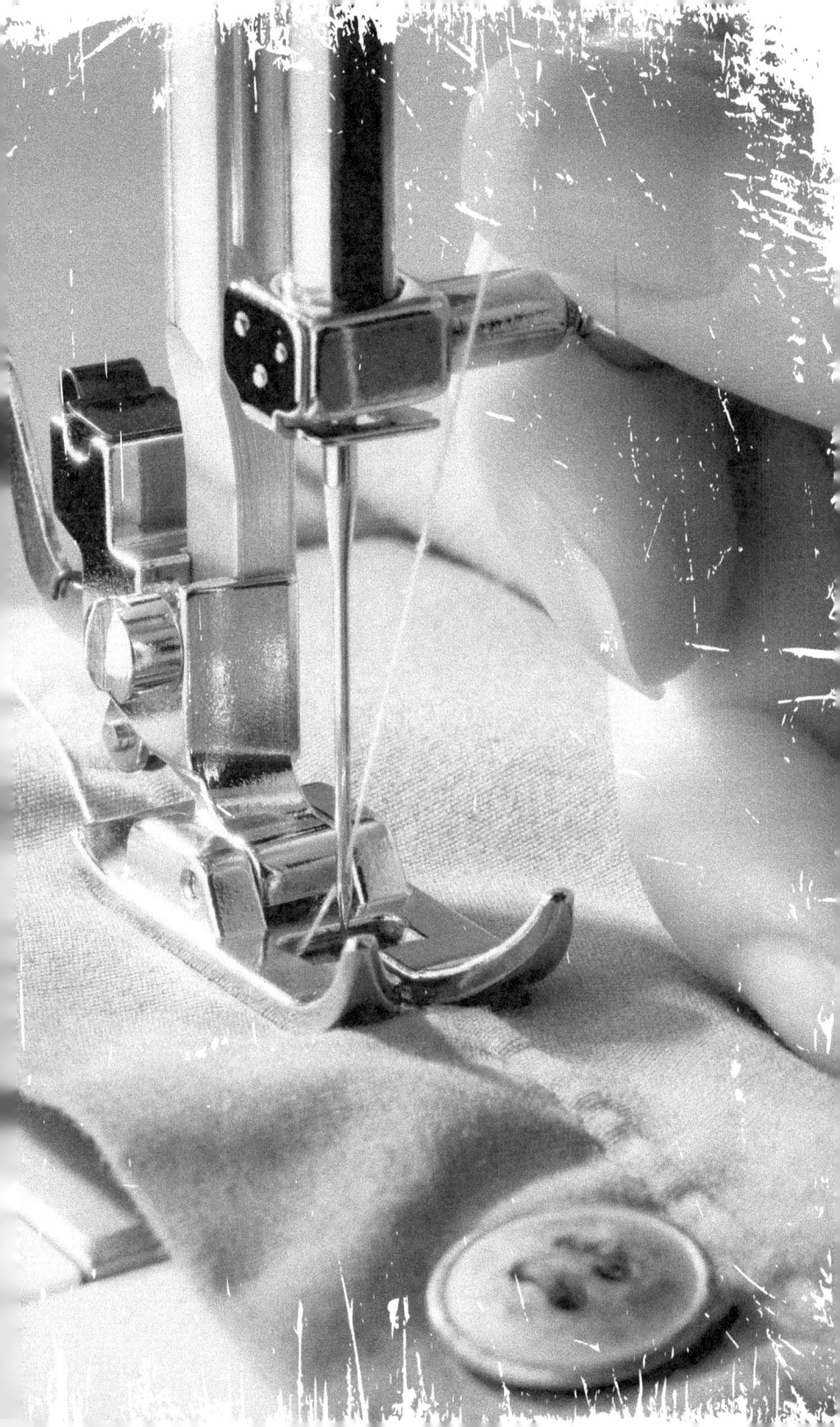

# CHAPTER 15
# ANSEL

"You know, my mom says that even if you didn't kill him, you're the entire reason Dad is dead." Morrigan goes with a new angle tonight, trying to poke me for a reaction by bringing her mother into this.

She's only hostile down here in the kennels. I get her upstairs, and she's completely stoic and nearly shuts down. Trying to talk to her where it's more comfortable isn't working. Maybe tomorrow morning I'll try talking to her down here?

My heart hurts, an ache in my chest that gets stronger when I'm around her. Years of sadness build up to all this pain.

I hand her a water bottle through the bars, keeping my voice as controlled as possible, letting her have her grief. "I'm sorry your father is dead. I'm sorry you're hurting."

"Liar," Morrigan spits and throws the water bottle back through the bars into the open area by the external doors. The plastic doesn't stand a chance, and water goes everywhere. "You think you're so special keeping a woman locked in your basement. There are hundreds of other serial killers who do it. Did you just want to be part of the club?"

*She's much stronger today.* I've thrown one of these water bottles before, and it takes a bit of force to get them to break like this. I pick up the plastic as the water runs into the central floor drain and take it upstairs for recycling. She's snarling even as I lock the door behind me.

Tomorrow, I'll try again. No matter how long it takes, I'm not going to give up on Walt's daughter. Not even if this pain in my chest kills me. I'm not giving up.

Ben is in the kitchen when I get back to the top of the stairs. I shake my head. He growls but doesn't say anything before heading back out the door he came in.

I muster the energy to get undressed and flop down on my bed to avoid further bending my back, which would only risk tearing the healing wounds of breaking up a wolf fight.

No one died today. Today was shit, but at least no one died.

# CHAPTER 16
# MORRIGAN

Morrigan,

What makes you happy?

I'll see you tonight

-AA

It's getting really fucking old, him talking about being happy and hopeful for the future. I'm not here for therapy. These questions make it seem like he thinks my life is so full of possibilities. I start shredding the little slip of paper, tearing pieces smaller and smaller until I can't pick them up anymore. The actions don't calm me like I'd hoped.

Does he really have no idea what kind of hell my life is because of him? Is Ansel blissfully unaware of everything? By now, he should have talked to Mom and Gerad. There's no way he wouldn't know that an arranged intention is waiting for me on the off chance he doesn't kill me.

Running my fingers through my hair, I work out tangles from sleep, but that doesn't soothe me either. I'm frustrated with no way to get it out.

Ultimately, my life will be tragically short. I won't live that way. Either Ansel kills me or what Gerad has planned as his last attempt to fix me will.

# CHAPTER 17
# ANSEL

EVERY INTENTION I HAD OF TALKING TO MORRIGAN THIS MORNING WAS shot to hell before the day even began. Howls from out at the cabins had me out of bed before dawn, and I had to rush through making her lunch before I went back to mediating Sully and Princeton. Even the question I wrote today was short, and really, I haven't expected her to answer any of them, but certainly not 'What makes you happy?'

The pack is falling apart, and I'm splitting too much time in too many places. Tomorrow, I've got to try harder to get through to her. I've got to find a way to get her integrated into the pack so I can focus on them all.

I almost thought I was getting away without a new Morrigan insult, but as I flick the light off in the med bay while leaving on the night-light, Morrigan starts cussing me out.

Harry pays closer attention to her today. Closer attention than he even paid Sully and Princeton during the physical altercation.

I shake my head and urge him to ignore her. *Don't, Harry.*

*Let it go.* I keep walking. After double-checking the locks on the kennels, I walk out of the basement and seal the fire door.

Someone's going to die this week, but no one died today. I don't know if today was a good day or not. Things are getting muddy, and I'm so fucking tired.

# CHAPTER 18

# ANSEL

IT'S BEEN SIX DAYS OF THE SAME ROUTINE. I GET UP, PACK HER lunches, leave her in the kennels, come home, let her out, feed her dinner, and lock her back downstairs. She spews profanities and curses my name until I can't hear her anymore through the fire door. I will say her profanities are quite colorful. Walt would be proud.

But frankly, I'm tired of the routine, and the pack is suffering for it. Today, come hell or high water, I've got to figure out how to get Morrigan on board. The best way through it might be a mistake, but I'll try.

I need to be checking in with the pack more, especially in a one-on-one setting. Being off balance, flirting with the teeter-totter of having Morrigan so hot and cold and Princeton being twenty-two going on sixteen, I don't know which way is right. They're both all bark and unstable emotions.

With Princeton, it's like he and his wolf haven't settled together properly, and I don't think they ever will. But I promised his Alpha I would try. I don't give up easy. But I don't know that I can fix him.

They're not my only problems though. The nightmares and visions from the last few days, of another wolf running the clock, were answered with a phone call from a Pack Alpha wanting help. I need to go and figure out how to handle it. What do I do if the wolf is stable enough to be put back together?

The house is almost out of room because I have to assume Morrigan will eventually get back upstairs to the loft. It doesn't sit well with me to have both her and another male on that floor together. More so if he's fracturing.

Harry growls inside, thinking of another male. He's never liked them in his space before.

Overall, my system is falling apart. I can't figure out how to get Morrigan to start trusting me, and I'm running out of hours in the day to get that other cabin back to habitable. I don't like the idea of her being neighbors with Princeton, though, either.

I'm still untying my boots when there's a knock at the door immediately on my left. Two quick knocks and then a slow one after. Ben.

Normally, I'd just tell him it's open, but with how close I am to the door, if he opens it a little too fast, it might be cause for a collision. Momentarily abandoning my boot, I open the door and let him in. He steps past me before toeing off his sneakers.

"Ezra packed up and headed out today. Did he call you?" Ben asks.

"He stopped by the jobsite on his way out of town. He's swinging into a few different packs. Ezra needs to find his place in the world."

Ben chooses not to engage in the discussion of my family. He motions to the stairwell. "Want me to let your delinquent out of the basement?"

I slide off my socks and wiggle my toes. The workday is

over, and I'm so glad to be able to relax. I slip on my plastic yard shoes. "If you don't mind."

"Take a load off. You're working too hard."

Ben goes downstairs while I slip out to grab the bags of groceries I picked up.

Across the driveway and back to the house doesn't even take me two minutes. But when I open the house door, arms full, it's to screaming.

*Shit. What the fuck!?*

I drop the bags of groceries and dart forward. After jumping down the flight of stairs, I find Ben backed into the open space by the exterior fire doors, away from the kennels. His hands are up along the side of his head in surrender. Morrigan's standing and screeching at the top of her lungs, inside her kennel toward the back but not against the wall.

"What are you two doing?!" I shout over Morrigan's shrill screech.

I raise and lower my hand, attempting to get her to bring the volume down, at the very least. The basement echoes, making it feel so much louder. None of us are hard of hearing—yet.

The scent of fear fills the basement, and Ben backs even farther away from her.

Harry is watching Morrigan and only cares about her. Prey in his little cage.

Morrigan's eyes move back and forth between the two of us, and she eyes the stairs behind me.

"Why are we all so afraid?" I pull my hair out of the binder I had it in and run my hand through the strands, shaking it free from the restraint.

She's still panting from the explosive scream. "Why is he fucking down here?"

"To let you out?" I answer slowly, dropping my hand from

my hair and gesturing to the kennels where she's standing. *What else would he be doing?*

Morrigan shakes her head and comes forward out of the kennel, then takes large sidesteps, putting me between her and Ben.

I look over at Ben. "What am I missing?"

"I think she's implying that I'm here because she's vulnerable and alone," Ben says quietly.

*Vulnerable and alone? Vulnerable and . . .* Oh, what sort of shit goes on in Gerad's pack if that's a thought that crosses her mind? I motion with my head for Ben to leave.

I wait for the rustling of plastic bags from Ben picking up the groceries I dropped before I speak. "Ben's safe. He's stable. If you don't want to believe anything else I say, then so be it, but the only way someone here will ever take somethin' like that from you is over my dead body." I pause and shake my head, my fist clenching. The idea of someone hurting her and not being there to stop them has bile rising in my throat. "And if someone's doin' that to you back home, give me names, and I'll remove them from this earth for touching you or anyone else like that."

Harry pushes the idea of murdering an entire pack across my brain. He likes how we helped Dinah. Apparently liked it enough to want to do it again for Morrigan. I should pretend to be surprised.

*Not unless we have to,* I remind him.

Morrigan's no longer panting, but the acidic scent of fear still hangs in the air.

With a hard swallow, she nods in understanding.

"You good?" I offer my hand out to her in case, despite being out of the usual, she'd like to behave like a wolf and want some grounding.

She nods but doesn't take my hand. "I'm good."

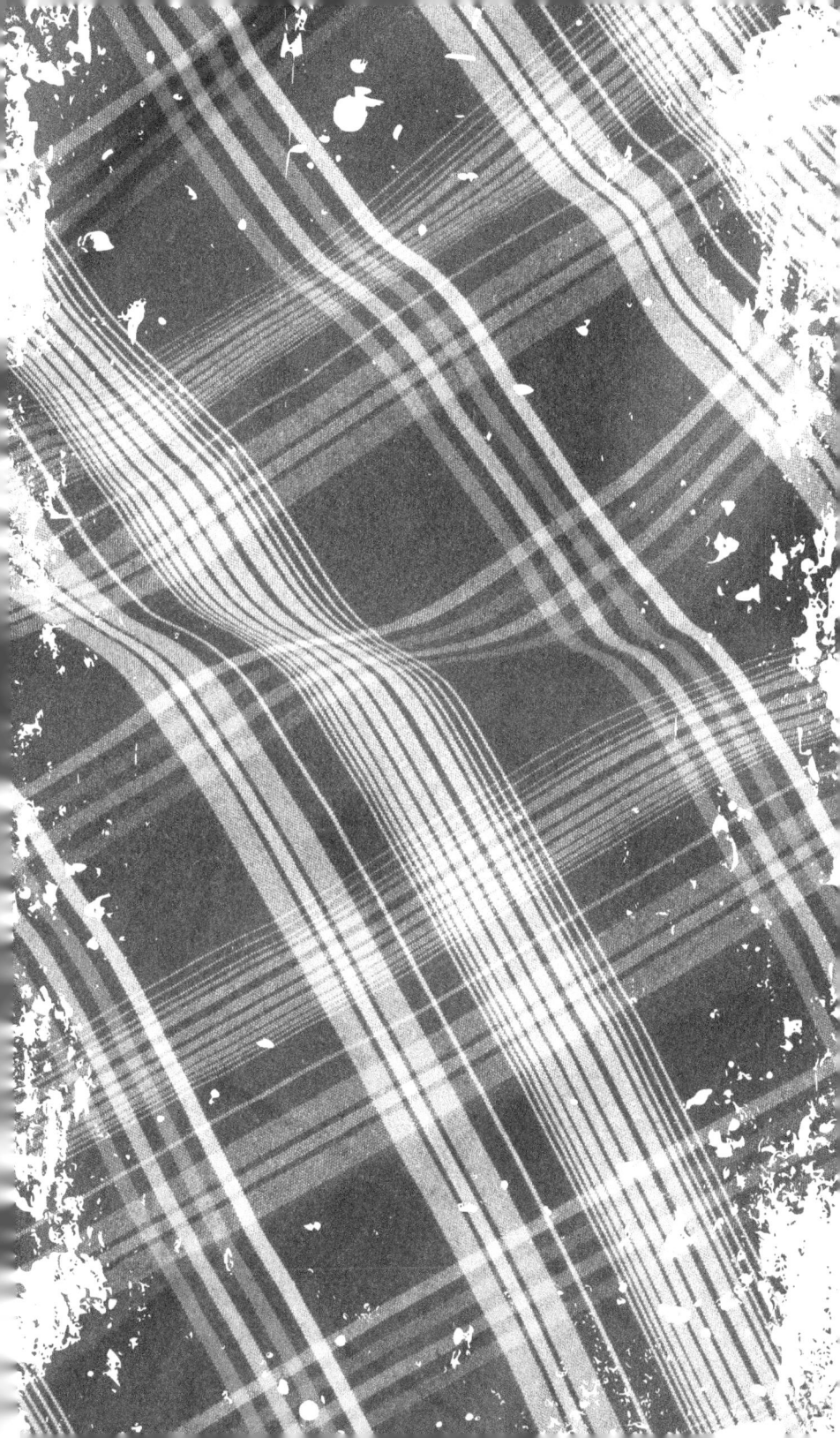

# CHAPTER 19
## MORRIGAN

*Harbinger would kill for me.* He would, without any questions, kill someone if I said they hurt me. Nothing makes sense because he's hell-bent on destroying me . . . right?

My heart hammers in my chest, rattling my lungs and making it hard to breathe. Fear burns off quickly, but it's racking my mind with new questions that are making cracks in all the thoughts I've had for the last week.

Ansel walks back up the stairs, but I take a minute to stand there in the silence. *Did that really just happen?*

He killed my father. And I'm standing here trusting he'll keep me safe? Granted, I don't have a ton of options, but this is fucked up. I do believe Ansel would protect me. He means it. Ansel would kill for me, and I . . . Maybe I'm wrong about him?

When I finally head up the stairs, my heart has stopped running a marathon. I can tell I'm stronger than I was a week ago because I'm not out of breath, even after the screaming in the basement, and climbing the stairs is much easier.

Ansel is nowhere to be seen, but the main floor bathroom door is closed.

Ben is putting groceries into the fridge. I pause and take a good look at him. In terms of physical size, there's no comparison. He's tall with blond hair and bigger than Ansel. I'm right. If Ben wanted to hurt me, he could, but Ansel trusts him. I'm conflicted as I stand in place, my thoughts running rampant as I try to make heads and tails of what just happened.

*Harbinger would kill for me.*

"I didn't think of the impact unexpectedly coming downstairs may have had on you, I'm sorry." Ben turns to look at me. His eyes hold sincerity, and his eyebrows are drawn together.

The apology is genuine. I can hear just how much he means what he said, and it has me lowering my shoulders, but I'm caught off guard and speechless. No one apologizes to me about anything. Well, condolences about Dad being the exception.

Ansel comes out of the bathroom, eyeing the two of us. "We good?"

I nod because I know he's not actually asking Ben. He's asking the problem child.

Ansel descends the stairs to the basement and returns with the lunch box and thermos. It seems weird to stand in the middle of the walkway, watching them in the kitchen without anything to do. I walk past the living room seating area, over to the large sliding glass doors, and look out at the scrub brush landscape.

"Did you want to call your mom?" Ansel offers.

"Ha. No." I push my hair out of my face.

The generic shampoo and conditioner are doing the best they can to restore it. But it's a lost cause. I should chop it off to my shoulders and start over.

What way was I running when I wasn't heading toward town? I went straight out the door. But when we came back, we were on the other side of the house to the left. No, scratch that.

It's safer to follow the road. Even if it's the long way, I won't be able to get lost. My feet are almost completely better. I could run again as soon as he lets me out of the kennels to sleep in a real bed at night.

Ansel snorts. "Yeah, kinda how I feel about her too. You don't have to, but thought I'd offer."

Ben snorts but doesn't say anything.

*Wait, what?* I turn and watch the two of them. Apparently, that being the end of the conversation, they keep doing kitchen stuff.

I turn my eyes back to the landscape, trying to figure out where my mistake was.

"So, wanted to ask," Ansel starts but waits. I turn my eyes from outside to look at him, which prompts him to continue. "Would you like to come to work with us this week?"

"Work?" I raise my eyebrow and roll my head toward him. The ungraceful, staggered movement would have driven Gerad mad.

Ansel doesn't play into my defiance. "Fine, suit yourself. If you'd rather spend another week downstairs, it won't hurt my feelings."

"No, I'm listening." My words come out desperate, more interested than how I wanted to sound.

The undeniable fact is the basement is boring. I'm doing nothing but sleeping, and I've forgotten what it's like to sleep on a mattress. *I need to keep control. He can't see me crack.*

"We're working for Ben this week." Ansel nods toward Ben.

Ben's working with ground beef, and he starts forming them into patties. Burgers sound amazing right now. My stomach growls. I don't even know the last time I had the juicy goodness.

*Why would Harbinger work for someone else?*

I make my face stay neutral. It's the exact expression I

know Gerad hates. My 'indifferent to the world around me' face. But I don't know what's going on. Neutral is better than offensive. I need to stay neutral. The sooner I convince him I'm fine, the sooner he'll let me go. If . . . he'll let me go. There's a chance he won't, and he'll kill me instead.

Ben speaks next. "I'm a vet. Ansel and the guys are helping with getting calves and cows rounded up. One of my clients is bringing in their herd, most of them have calved, but some of them haven't yet. So, we're running them in, inoculating, tagging, and branding as appropriate. Separating out those who aren't calved yet and then turning the others out into the smaller nearby pasture. The whole operation will probably take two days. It's a large farm."

"Right, but —" I stop myself. *Don't be stupid.*

"Why does the Alpha work for the Second?" Ansel finishes. He draws his lips into a flat line.

I don't answer. That wasn't what I was about to say.

Ansel answers the question he posed himself. "Keepin' this place running takes quite a bit of money, and I've found that stabilizing pack members is easier if we have tasks to do. It helps them find a way to come together."

"Wait, there's more than the three of you here?" I raise an eyebrow in disbelief.

I force them back to neutral. I need to not give away that I'm looking for more information. Surely someone here wants to escape as badly as I do. Were there more people here when I was younger? I remember a lot of coming and going. But I thought he brought them here to kill them.

Ansel tips his head, his hands still from where he had been unpacking the lunch box. His words come out slowly. "Well, Ezra left, but yeah, it's more than the two of us here. The pack register is a total of eight. Ezra comes and goes as he pleases.

Some stays are longer than others. But usually, it's me, Ben, Sherman, Zero, Ripley, Vito, Sully, and then Princeton for now."

"I didn't know you were allowed to have a pack. I thought you were required to live alone because your wolf is sick." That tone of voice, sardonic with a pinch of defiance, would have gotten me smacked back home.

Let's see him confirm the speculations and prove he's the monster everyone says he is.

Ben lets out a low whistle. "Is that the kind of rumor they're starting about you now? Harry's sick?"

"I don't even know." Ansel shakes his head and frowns. "I don't know if I wanna know."

He doesn't even flinch at my tone of voice. He's indifferent to it? How can he be so relaxed? Gerad would have been livid that someone was speaking negatively about him. He would have grilled me before sending someone off to squash the rumors. Ansel though . . . lets my words slick off him with not another thought. It's almost like he's a pacifist.

"Anyway." Ben moves on, drawing out the syllables. "The ranch had a bunch of quads, but the widow is struggling to get someone out there to fix them in time to bring the cattle in. She asked if I knew of some cowboys or riders who could bring them in. And most of the guys can ride, but we'll try and see how the cattle handle our wolf form. If it stresses them out too much, we'll go back to horses, but it would be much faster if we could do some of it as wolves."

"I don't think it's a good idea for me to do that. I've never even seen a cow up close and personal. The only time I see them is from the safety of a car window and the freeway when we'd go out to the parks to run, and other than pony rides, I've never ridden a horse." I distract from my dark secret.

He doesn't know I don't have a wolf, and I won't tell him.

Though without a wolf and on a horse, which is huge, it seems highly probable I'd get bucked off.

*This is so not helping my case of don't lock me in the kennels.*

Ben shakes his head. "It's actually why I'm hoping you can help me. Ansel needs to be out with the guys to keep them stable. Historically, introducing someone into this pack without a while to warm up isn't good, but I need another set of hands. I can hire a tech for the day, but it's expensive and I'd like to keep the cost down for the client."

I shrug and try to be noncommittal. The idea of getting out of the kennel loses some of its appeal — but not all of it — when I still feel like a prisoner.

I'm locked in for days on end and now put to work like some sort of prison work camp. For an idiot, the exploitation of those he allegedly cares about is well thought out.

Ben washes his hands before moving to a sack of potatoes. He starts peeling the potatoes onto a brown paper bag before setting them down on the cutting board. Something about how he looks at me gives me a bristly feeling like he doesn't like me.

He doesn't have to like me. I don't like him.

With a firm point to the cutting board, he presses, "You could help."

Begrudgingly, I move away from the door. It's not like I was finding a way out of here today anyway.

Approaching the workspace, I eye the cutting board.

Ben sets a knife down on it. "Don't make me regret giving you a pointy object."

I curl my lips into a devious smile. To be fair, I can see where that statement comes from, considering how we started the day.

Ansel snorts, holding back a laugh.

It takes real force to keep my smile down. Even in jest, it shows too much joy. I can't enjoy it here. I won't.

*Don't start getting comfortable.*

ANSEL DOESN'T FORCE ME DOWN TO THE KENNELS TONIGHT. HE DOES give me a scolding look. "Make me chase you down, and you won't be goin' with tomorrow. There's some jeans and different shirts upstairs. I think I got your size right."

I try the clothes on before getting into bed. The jeans fit. But the shirt is still too big. It'll be fine once I knot it. If I had my sewing machine, I'd put a dart in the sides. It would be easy enough.

That thought makes my face hot. I blink hard. Someday, I'll get another machine. Someday, I'll have a place. This is a stepping stone to escape. I'll figure out how to get out of here, and it'll be okay. No escaping tonight. Tomorrow, I'll map where we are and take notes. We've got to head toward some civilization.

# CHAPTER 20
## ANSEL

I KNEW I WASN'T GETTING A FULL NIGHT'S SLEEP. I WAS READY TO RELY heavily on my pot of coffee to get through today. But the three times I woke up to check on Morrigan, she was right where she was supposed to be. It ended up being a lot more sleep than anticipated.

I'm not dumb enough to think she's accepted that it's not worth the effort to escape, but I'm feeling pretty confident she doesn't want to sleep in the kennels anymore. It's best not to assume because if you assume something, one of you ends up with a free donkey. That's the absolute last thing I need, another being to keep alive.

Standing at the end of the balcony to the loft, I call, "Morrigan. Time to get up. We're leaving in thirty minutes."

There's a groan, and it's louder than every morning I've tried to wake her up downstairs. I wait to make sure she's actually up. When her bed creaks and the sound of her feet on the floor follows, I get a move on.

Morrigan hasn't really turned her nose up at anything I've put in her lunchbox consistently. So, I whip us up some breakfast burritos we can eat in the car on the way to the ranch. I fry eggs and sausages quickly, then toss them with cheese into tortillas.

Hearing her feet on the stairs, Harry hums. His focus is tight on her again, watching how her body moves as she steps lazily down the stairs, each foot falling hard onto the stair below. Standing at the ready, Harry feels the drive of the hunt.

She's braiding her hair as she walks down the stairs. Rounding the banister, she stops, looking at me. Eyes going wide, she quickly diverts her gaze.

I blink. *Damn it, Harry.* He retreats but is still focused on her.

"Sorry," I say. "He isn't normally so active. We're stressed about today."

Morrigan approaches slowly, flicking her loose braid over her shoulder. "It's okay."

She lies, nowhere near as badly as Cade's mate, Thalia, but it's still blatant. But I ignore it for now and move forward with our morning. "Do you want a hair tie?"

"Yeah, that would be great."

I finish wrapping the last of the burritos in tin foil before pulling a fresh hair tie out of the cupboard. I set it down next to her on the counter with one of the burritos.

She snatches it up and starts wrapping her braided hair into a bun at the nape of her slender neck. In a flash, she's focused on the burrito, pulling back the foil and taking a bite right away. Her eyes are distant, like she's zoned out as she eats. It's an auto-pilot-type movement that's simply functioning.

"Coffee?" I offer, gently shaking the pot in her direction to catch her eye.

Morrigan nods, and I pour her a travel cup.

Trucks rumble up the driveway, signaling we're out of time.

"Ready?" I turn away from her and grab my food before heading out the door.

I don't wait for her because I want to give the guys a quick assessment before we take off.

TODAY WAS A GOOD DAY. NO ONE DIED, INCLUDING THE COWS. No one got hurt, including the cows.

Morrigan and Ben seemed to tolerate each other, more than anticipated. Overall, I'm really proud of my entire pack. I was worried that with their prey drive, the need to hunt and kill, they'd be unable to bring it together. Despite not being cattle dogs, my pack of partially fractured wolf shifters seemed to do fine.

Unfortunately for me, Harry was hard to control. He constantly watched Ripley with more focus. He's slowly running out of time. His metaphorical clock keeps winding down. Something used to interfere and give him more time. Now, it's moving steadily. Every time we see his death, it's sooner and sooner.

Harry still sees him as sick. I don't know that I'll be able to save him at this point.

MORRIGAN PASSES OUT ON THE DRIVE HOME. HER HEAD RATTLES against the side window, and I drive slower, swerving to avoid jostling from the potholes in the dirt road.

When we pull up to the house, I pull into the garage, alongside Walt's truck, and leave her to sleep for a bit. After quietly closing the door on my side of the truck, I walk over to the house and sit on the back steps.

I've put it off for a week now, but I have to make a call. *The call.*

Morrigan has to stay here. By pack law, I need to update the register. Morrigan's an adult. So, technically, I don't have to call anyone other than her home pack's record keeper to get her transferred here. Which I would do, but there's no way their record keeper will transfer the daughter of the Luna without telling her. I'll avoid a headache later by cutting the confrontation off with Ersilia now.

Ersilia Gardner's contact lights up on the screen. The last time I called was so long ago my phone doesn't remember. Hopefully, she hasn't changed her number in the past five years.

Hitting the little green button, I draw a deep breath. While the phone rings and rings and rings, I close my eyes. I'm fairly certain it'll go to voicemail or be a wrong number, but it picks up.

"Ansel?" Her soft voice hasn't changed.

"Hey, Ersilia," I answer slowly.

"Do you have her? Is my baby alive?" She's almost whispering.

"I do. She is. Did I catch you at a bad time?" Seems weird Ersilia's whispering, but she took my call.

"No, I stepped out of a meeting. Gerad is very upset that she's been missing for so long." Ersilia's voice gets a bit louder between the sounds of high-heeled shoes clicking on a hard floor.

"I wanted to make sure she needed to be here before I called. Figured that a week wasn't too long, seeing as how she's an adult." I don't offer more information, hoping to learn more than I give.

"A week?" Ersilia asks shortly. "Ansel, she's been missing for six months."

Alright, so I made a mistake in not calling her mom sooner. Probably rude, making a mother worry about her kid. *Probably.*

Six months. That explains a lot about her physical state. Her wolf's been starving physically and emotionally. I assumed she'd been running with those girls for a month, at the most, maybe.

Trying to find words, I pull my hair out of the tie at the nape of my neck and stretch the rubber with my fingers, fiddling with it. "I don't know what to tell you, Ersilia. She's not okay. But she's here. She's safe. I'll do what I can."

The voice on the phone line changes. It's a sharp bark. "Ansel! It's Gerad Gardner. What's the status of Morrigan?"

*I fucking hate this guy.* My shoulders are tight, and I sit up straighter. It's dumb to square off to no one, but my body is on edge. "Morrigan isn't stable. I'm still tryin' to figure out what's going on with her." I answer with the least amount of detail I can.

"There is something very wrong with her. She is not fractured and not your concern. Morrigan needs to be brought home and seen by a medical professional, evaluated, and treated." Gerad lists off demands and how he thinks this process should go. *Thinks.*

Harry bristles, looking for the source of my anger. Wolf doesn't understand the phone but stays on edge.

Mostly in agitation but partly in disagreement, I shake my head. He's so used to calling the shots that he thinks he can talk to everyone like this. Pulling out my best impersonation of my cousin Judah and his flowery language, I explain how this'll go. "As an Ardelean Alpha, I have the exemption of returning her to her home pack. I will take it under advisement that you're asking for her to be returned as soon as possible. Ultimately, the decision is mine and mine alone. I will do so when it is in Morrigan's best interest." *Which is definitely not going back to California.* I leave that part out.

"You can't do that, Ansel. She's intended to another pack. They're expecting her. I need her ready to go to them on Vernal Equinox." His voice raises.

*About a month. He thinks I'll . . . That's ridiculous.* It's always the same talking to him. He's talking at you and ordering you around, but that's not how this is gonna work with me.

"I was unaware that she's been intended. However, that does not change the facts of the situation. Please have the Pack Alpha she's been intended to reach out to me. I'll gladly explain the same situation." My voice trails off at the sound of footsteps on the gravel parking pad, drawing my attention away from him.

Morrigan walks toward me, arms crossed and with the meanest glare I've ever seen.

I keep talking to Gerad, trying to finish this quickly. "The government says she has to stay here for quite some time, and in addition to that, I have my own concerns. I'll send the documents over so you can reimburse the pack fund and start paying for her room and board. Once the documents are handled and some time passes, we can talk about circumstances for her return."

Gerad goes to argue with me again, and I hang up. *Damn cell service in the country. So unreliable.* I laugh at my thoughts, sighing as the laughter fades.

"Should have known you're working with him," Morrigan accuses.

There's no hiding the irritation in my voice when thinking about him. "I'm not working with Gerad. I'm actively trying to do whatever I can to not. I'm guessing you missed the part where I said 'for quite some time.'"

"That's not what it sounds like." Rolling her eyes, Morrigan untucks her arms from around her, and they plop down by her sides. Her lower lip quivers, but she forces it still, pulling it between her teeth.

I shake my head. Her mood swings are like watching a damn tennis match, but one thing is for sure, Gerad's a major pain point for them.

"Did you know you're intended with someone?"

"See, that's all he cares about too." Morrigan starts walking away from the house.

On her way back down the driveway, she mutters under her breath. I recognize all the colorful names and insults; they're the exact same ones Walt used to use when I'd piss him off. He'd go on a ten-minute walk to clear his head before coming back more under control and ready to hash it out.

I let her keep walking and text Ben. She's been angry with me this entire time. Maybe it's time to switch tactics. I'll let the two grumpies hang for a bit.

ME:

Morrigan's headed down the driveway. You seemed to hit it off with her today. Can you try to tell her that I'm trying to help?

BEN:

Sure.

Let me know if you can't catch her. I'll hop in the truck.

Sure.

# CHAPTER 21
# MORRIGAN

*Should have fucking known he'd be working for Gerad. Of course.* Ansel's trying to figure out the best way to get rid of me. Why wouldn't he pass me back to Gerad?

I'm not surprised that Gerad claims I'm intended to someone. It's his final game plan to 'fix me.' I'm not the perfect daughter of the Pack Alpha. And since Mom couldn't give him more pups, it's always been 'Morrigan, you have to be perfect. The pack needs to see how good we are. How strong we are.' Knowing Gerad, whoever this jerk is, willing to take me as an arranged mate, they're probably someone from his inner circle. Whoever would put an intention in on me is probably way older and wants more of the same: an obedient, tiny mate. Then I'll be his problem to try and get a wolf back into, one way or another.

Maybe that's Gerad's game: see if Harbinger can fix me before shipping me off. Or worse, Harbinger will murder me in cold blood like he did my father. Gerad wins either way. I'll no longer be his responsibility.

Bile rises in my throat. I may not love my life, but I don't want to die.

I thought maybe Ansel wasn't as he seemed. For a moment, a tiny hope that he was different lit up my chest. It's been extinguished. *How could I have been so stupid?*

Ben is standing up ahead on the road by a turnoff I hadn't noticed this morning. He's rolling a rock around with his boot in front of him.

"Want to give me a lift?" I ask suggestively.

He might not know what happened between Ansel and me. Maybe he'll get me out of here. Surely, he isn't okay with Ansel keeping me locked in a basement. His coming down to the kennels wasn't a coincidence. Right?

"Sure, hop in." Ben motions down the path behind him.

Ben's white vet truck sits in front of a little cabin. It's weird in an 'I'm a murderer. Welcome to my mostly intact shack in the woods' kind of place.

"Is this where you drive me back up to Ansel's house and drop me back off at the door, or are you driving me out to the desert to kill me?" I raise an eyebrow, crossing the driveway away from Ben.

He might have been a bad choice. This seems far too easy.

Ben glares and then scrubs his hand down his face. "Morrigan. I'm sure someone thinks your repugnant personality, wild accusations, and inappropriate advances are cute, but it's not me. Ansel might let you get away with whatever insults and slander you spew at him. He might even smile and nod while you do so, but I'm not about to let you get away with this bullshit." His strong voice is laced with a growl.

Ben's phone rings. He fishes it out of his pocket, keeping his eyes locked on me.

"Yeah, boss." Ben goes quiet as he listens.

Try as I might, his phone is turned down too low for me to hear the other end of the conversation.

"Yeah. I'll make it work." Ben hangs up and walks away from me. "Come on, let's go for a drive."

I follow as instructed. He's an Alpha wolf, and if I'm keeping up the ploy of faking having a wolf, I have to keep up pretenses.

Ben unlocks his work truck and opens the passenger door for me. After moving a stack of papers, he dusts off the seat. We're both filthy from wrangling baby cows, but it's a nice gesture.

As Ben drives down the driveway away from the house, we're silent. I'm not hopeful, but our course takes us closer to town. It gives me a second look at the road for when I run again. Not tonight, but soon.

Taking a hard right, Ben practically drives us into the brush. I barely noticed what used to be a road between the overgrowth before he turned. The truck bounces lightly as it rolls up a hill and past some gnarly scrubby trees. We come to a stop at a clearing with the remains of a burned-out house — charred framing mixed with a collapsed roof, and a dilapidated shed in a similar state but no scorch marks. It's leaning so far over it might as well be lying down.

The air feels heavy, and I shiver with the change of atmosphere around me. I raise my eyebrows at Ben as he unbuckles his seat belt and climbs out of the truck without a word.

I don't want to go. A hollow knot grows in my stomach, and my whole body fights as I force myself out of the truck. Leaving the door open, I walk slowly over to where Ben's standing.

"This is where you, your dad, your mom, and Ansel first moved to when they came to Utah. They found out who he was and what was going on with his visions. The last pack Reaper gave him this stretch of land and the cabin. Ansel was hesitant to actually own something. He'd never had anything before, especially something so valuable. Your dad did everything he could to help Ansel adjust. When I arrived a few months later, Ansel was still calling it 'The Reaper's House.'" Ben pauses and looks at me.

"What happened?" I don't remember this place at all. I lived here? And I don't remember this place? The disconnected memories feel strange. Why can't I remember?

"It was a fucking death trap, but once Ansel started to feel comfortable with the pack fund and having money from the Ardelean Bloodline, he broke down and built the house he's in now and set up the cabins." Ben motions at the burned-out house. "When your dad died, Ansel came out here and torched the place. He sat right there and watched it burn down." Ben points to a space by a mangled tree of some sort. "Honestly, I thought I would be ending Ansel after that day. I'd never seen him so broken."

"Good." The word is sharp as it comes out of my mouth.

Ben shakes his head and holds his hand out at the house. "Fucking hell. You're so wrapped up in yourself and your own head that you have no empathy for anyone else, do you?"

"For the man who murdered my father?" I ask flatly, holding back a dam, ready to burst, full of anger. Not anger, rage.

With a nod, he confirms. It's the drop of water the dam can't endure.

"You want me to have empathy for him? I suppose you can't empathize with me. Hmm? It seems like you care more about how I feel about Ansel than I feel as a person. Which, great, good job, you're his friend, but . . . like . . . I'm just supposed to be fine? Your Alpha ruined my life." Fire burns in my chest, and my words come out sharp and angry.

If I could growl and snarl and make him see how fucked up this is, maybe then someone would see me. See my hurt. *No one cares about little girls with daddy issues.* I clench my fists against the reality. I'm nothing, to anyone.

Ben's eyes turn dark. "You don't know what happened. You weren't here."

"That's not my fault." I cross my arms in front of my chest. I huff and push out more words, letting them drip with the acid I feel in my heart. "Are you gonna tell me, or is this some big mystery boys' club bullshit?"

"No." Ben shoos me back toward the truck. "Let's go. You clearly weren't ready for this yet."

I stand my ground. *Fuck, I wish I had a wolf.* I could growl at him. What I wouldn't give to be more intimidating. *What I wouldn't give for one tiny snarl.* "I'm not some child you can dismiss, Ben."

It's like Ben chooses not to hear me. He flicks his hand toward the truck again. After a minute of a staring contest, I remember this should intimidate my wolf and I should feel the push to look away.

Begrudgingly, I get back in the truck and let Ben drive me back up to Ansel's house without further insistence on going to town.

When we get back, Ansel's truck is gone. *Where would he go?* I look to Ben for answers. "So, I'm free?"

"Ansel had to go do his job. You're stuck with me for the next couple of days." He leaves me behind in his work truck as he goes toward the house.

I follow, frustrated that Ben is so quick to dismiss me.

*What does Ansel being gone mean for me?* I have exactly one guess, and it involves sleeping on concrete. It was stupid of me to try and run on the first day. Had I waited, this would have been a better opportunity.

Ben's untying his work boots when I come through the door. I stand there dumbly, wanting more answers but not ready to ask the questions.

"Take your shoes off. Go grab a shower. I'll make dinner in a minute. We can work out how this situation will go while we eat."

Ben is so pragmatic, and it grates my nerves further. I thought I had the ice princess gig down, but with how flat his words are, clearly I could use a lesson from the indifferent master. I know Ben hates me, but not showing any emotions at all? It's impressive.

# CHAPTER 22
## ANSEL

HARBINGER IS SATED. HIS BLOODLUST WAS SATISFIED THROUGH THE sacrifice of a fractured wolf. He rests easily under my skin as I get dressed.

Toweling off, I run back everything I saw. How the man's wolf wouldn't settle. The gold of his wolf's eyes flickered unsteadily. The snarling and snapping at nothing, completely unprovoked, almost like he could see threats not there. His fate was sealed before I even forced the vision of his death. It was sealed before he shifted at the dinner table yesterday.

Putting my wet hair back up, I leave the guest bathroom and find the Alpha's house abuzz with quiet conversations. There's always a lot of mixed emotions once I've done my job.

However, the Alpha here is nice. The pack will be fine.

I'll probably be here again sometime in the next five years to do this again. Older Pack Alphas like him — being that he's in his sixties — are too old to put down fractured wolves. It's not a reflection on him; it's just how things are. While we age a bit more gracefully than humans, it happens all the same.

Walking the layout of the house, I find my way back to the

Alpha's office. He sits behind his desk, head resting on his hand, reading a document. I knock on the doorframe.

Startled, he stands up. "Ansel. Thank you."

I nod as he gestures me into the room with an open hand, indicating toward a chair. I carefully sit on the edge of the offered seat. Tender new skin on my back from my fight threatens to rip open.

"Thank you for coming." He struggles to find words. Sitting back down, he tries again. "Is there something I could . . ."

"Do differently?" I offer, waiting for him.

Nodding sadly, he picks up his pen and flicks it nervously. "I've never had a wolf fracture. Ever."

"Is the pack stable overall?" I ask, trying to diagnose the problem behind it all.

He nods quickly and convincingly. "There was a small hiccup. When Cade took the throne last year, there was some fear. The young kids were mostly unruly and challenging our laws. Parents and I got involved, and they mostly piped down. We . . . couldn't . . ."

I press my lips together into a thin line. I can't give him answers. There's no rhyme or reason, as far as I can tell, to why a wolf will or won't fracture. Maybe it's stress, and it affects some harder than others.

I nod, trying to be the vague wizard person they all make me out to be. "Change is hard. I think we're all seeing the after-effects of it, but not all change is bad."

Looking away, he goes back to business. "Is there anything else you need from me?"

"No." I shake my head and stand to leave. "Everything's in order. I'm sorry for your loss."

"Ansel?" the Alpha says as I reach the doorframe.

I turn back to face him.

He gives me a soft smile, the kind that he doesn't mean, but it's the effort that counts. "Thank you."

"You're welcome," I answer.

Soft conversations follow me out toward the front of the house to the door. I'm finishing the knot in my shoelaces when the door opens and someone barrels over me.

The growl erupts from Harbinger, waiting and ready for whatever's happened.

A pup yelps, and I go completely still. A tiny blond child with bright blue eyes has fallen on top of me. His lips curl up into the start of a wail. He's barely two and a half feet tall.

I laugh, righting myself from where I ended up on my side. I stand up, picking him up with me. "Hey, little guy. You scared me. You're awfully strong for such a little dude."

The wail that was starting stops as we look at each other. His feet settle on either side of my hip as he looks at me. I hold him, looking at the future that doesn't seem so dark.

He smiles wide. "Are you . . ." He stops, drawing his eyebrows together and wrinkling his nose back and forth. "Who are you?"

"My name is Ansel." I smile at him. "Who are you?"

"I'm Eu—"

"Oh, Harbinger. I'm sorry. I'll take him." A woman briskly comes into my peripheral view and gently plucks him out of my arms. "Eugene, what did I say about running through doors? So sorry."

She quickly turns and walks away.

The little boy waves at me, clenching his fist as he says goodbye. When I smile and wave back, he smiles with a crooked grin that feels weirdly familiar. Cute kid, for sure. Kinda reminds me of Ben with those darker blue eyes and floppy blond hair.

*What would it be like to have a pup running around out at the house?*

*Where did that come from?* I suppose, though, seeing puppies always makes you think about how much fun they can be. *I don't know, they're probably more trouble than it's worth in my life.*

Harbinger and I watch as they disappear through a small crowd. He feels a little lighter and less wild.

I give a quick wave to the people who have congregated to see me off. Generally, their wolves like witnessing when death leaves. They watch as I head out the door and across the yard to where I parked my truck late last night after our almost two-day road trip.

It's earlier in the evening than I arrived yesterday, so it's not even worth a second thought. They'd have hosted me for a night; apparently, customarily, they're supposed to ask, but my presence isn't helpful. Packs take time to adjust after death. My being there only delays the adjustment period. I've not once stayed longer than I have to.

I want to get back home and see how she's doing. Morrigan's so back and forth. It's evident she and Ben aren't friends. I don't normally care this much. It's probably because she's Walt's kid. It's gotta be that.

Harry's focused on her again. It's like he's rushing me, trying to get me to go faster. But we've a long road trip home. He'll have to settle down.

# CHAPTER 23
# MORRIGAN

ANSEL'S BEEN GONE FOR FOUR DAYS. I THOUGHT HE WAS ANNOYING. But in the ways that Ansel was cautious and by the book, Ben is worse. His rules make no sense. He takes everything too seriously. He even asks if I brushed my teeth before bed. Weirdo.

I'm free to sleep upstairs since Ben sleeps on Ansel's couch each night, but I'm locked in a kennel during the day while all the guys I met a few days ago do whatever the fuck they want because Ben goes to work.

I'm loathing the time down there. It's punishment, and I haven't even done anything wrong. The isolation is making me feel more hollow. I'm starting to miss the littlest things I took for granted. A hug from Mom or sleeping in the tight vehicles with the girls. The physical touch and comfort of another person, even if they didn't love me, was better than nothing. I'm never taking another hug for granted.

Begrudgingly, I draw myself out of bed and debate making a bedsheet ladder to climb down the side of the house to avoid going back to the kennels.

"Ansel should be home today." Ben smiles.

It's crooked and weird, and he shouldn't do that again. Ever.

He pushes a plate of breakfast toward me when I round the bottom stairs.

I sit down at the plate and begin picking apart my breakfast. The slower I eat, the less time I spend down in the kennels alone. Even if it's five minutes less, it's something.

Minutes pass as if they're seconds, and Ben starts whistling while cleaning up.

There's a break in his tune. "What do you say we bend the rules today? Think you can handle the responsibility of trying not to run off?"

"You bend rules?" I huff.

Ben is the epitome of not fun. I don't expect him to mean it. Probably a sick joke.

"You were really good with the cows. Today, I've only got one stop." Ben turns to face me, crossing his arms in front of his chest. "Normally, I wouldn't take someone so new out with me without Ansel being able to come back me up if I needed it, but I'm fairly certain I could take you in a fight, and I know with those scrawny chicken legs you won't be able to outrun me."

"Wow." *Does he even hear himself?*

Though it might kill him to be nice, the whole 'growing a heart' thing might warm the frigid asshole up too much.

Ben raises an eyebrow at me, and I lower my head, submitting to him.

"Do you want to come with, or do you want to go downstairs?" Ben asks flatly, cocking his head toward the kennel stairs.

"I wanna go." I force myself to let go of my frustrations and answer him, keeping my head bowed.

Ben huffs. "That's what I thought. Go put on some jeans. We'll leave in ten."

"You know he isn't all bad, right?" Ben asks before we make it down to the end of the driveway.

"Is this where you try to tell me to forgive the man who killed my dad because he's your best friend, and he's helped you and now you're indebted to him, but even if you weren't, you'd tell me this anyway?" I sigh, rolling my head over to look at him.

"Nope." Ben pops the *p* on his word. "Was saying you don't have to forgive him for killing your dad. But you do have to accept you're stuck here, and you can either count down the days until you leave from downstairs in the kennels —"

"Three hundred fifty-four," I interrupt him.

"Or" — Ben gives me a scolding look out of the corner of his eye — "you can learn to live with your anger and behave. Ansel will move you out of the main house into a cabin, and you can work with the guys or me for the next year."

"Three hundred fifty-four days," I repeat. *Quit trying to make this prison sentence longer.*

His proposition is tempting. Cabins down the hill and far away from Ansel are probably a lot easier to sneak out of. *On to a better life? As soon as I figure out how that works.*

"Right," Ben mutters. He continues. "Make your life hell or make your life easy. You don't have to forgive him, but you're the one in charge of how you have to interact with him."

I don't answer him. But I understand what he's saying. The cabins down the hill are farther from the driveway, and they're closer together. Sneaking out of the cabin means I would have to pass more wolves to get where I'm going. They're definitely pack mentality. From driving the cows, I know they have a strong hierarchy, and the chances of me breaking into that is slim. Unless I'm able to get one to take interest.

I don't want to be put in the kennels, but down in a cabin isn't good either, not unless I can figure out how to traverse the desert.

I DON'T REMEMBER HAVING MUSCLES IN ALL THESE PLACES. BEN'S IDEA of 'one stop' is about the same as 'just up the road' . . . on the 91 . . . during rush hour . . . on a holiday weekend. He has the decency to pull his truck all the way up to the main house rather than park down by his cabin, but I stumble out of his truck and curse with every step.

A large stack of boxes sits next to the steps going up to the house.

"Odd." Ben scratches his head as we get closer. "Your people sending you some stuff?"

The snort comes out before I can stop it. "They don't love me that much."

Ben picks up the first box. It's smaller, and he shrugs. "Guess Lena went shopping."

"The Ardelean submissive is sending packages to Ansel?" I look at the boxes, and sure enough, 'Lena Alden' to 'Ansel Abbot' graces the box in a scroll of messy handwriting. "Can none of the Ardeleans write?"

Ben doesn't answer and picks up the stack of boxes. He orders, "Open the door." And I swear there's the slightest hint of an Alpha command.

Despite how bad my feet hurt and how hard it is to move, I push as quickly as I can; if it was a command, it has to be followed. There's no risking it.

As I hold the door open for him, Ben carries the boxes low in his arms. They must be heavy because Ben picked up a miniature horse like it was weightless today.

Ansel peeks his head out of the kitchen.

I jump, startled.

He looks at Ben and the boxes. Then his eyes fall on me. "I see we're breaking rules now."

"Bending," Ben corrects, setting the boxes down on the floor by the island.

"I didn't even hear the mail truck," Ansel says. "Sorry, Doc."

"Not a bother. But it's not her fault. I offered to take her. She behaved. Animals seem to like her." Ben points to me.

I watch the floor as I toe off my shoes. Blisters on my heels and the sides of my feet soaked my socks. I can't pull them off, or he'll notice something is wrong. Ansel's attention is focused on me.

Avoiding his gaze, I walk down the hall, past Ben and the mountain of boxes, toward the stairs. The weight of his eyes grows heavier.

"Are you okay?" Ansel probably wants that to sound concerned, but the way he looked at me when said 'breaking the rules' makes me uneasy.

"I got spit on by a llama, and I want a shower and to change." I walk up the stairs. *Ben said I could go with him. What the fuck is Ansel's problem?*

He didn't command me to stop or come. There's no reason to listen. So, I do what I want.

"Dammit. Ben, what am I gonna do with her?" Ansel hisses under his breath.

*Do with me? You're the one mad that I got one fun day. Okay, maybe fun is overselling getting out of the house.*

I get to the top of the stairs and walk straight into the bathroom. If he's going to talk about me, the least he could do is wait until I'm in the shower.

# CHAPTER 24
## ANSEL

MORRIGAN CLOSES THE DOOR TO THE BATHROOM, AND HARRY'S FOCUS falls off her.

"I'm trying with her. I am really trying. I don't know what to do. She doesn't want to hear an apology. She doesn't want to talk about it." I scrub my hands down my face.

"Okay, but did you try to apologize or just assume?" Ben leans against the countertop and crosses his arms over his chest.

"I tried to apologize." I pull my hair away from my face and secure it with a tie. "I've tried to make amends. But it's not going so well. Did she give you any trouble?" I ask, gesturing to the kitchen tool drawer.

"Surprisingly, no." Ben shrugs, handing me a knife. "She was a bit mouthy but fairly respectful otherwise. I didn't have to use force to get her downstairs during the day."

"I don't understand her." I sigh.

Empty kennels, a missing Morrigan, and Ben not here put me more on edge than I should have expressed. Having her back in the house calms both me and Harry.

Taking the knife, I slice open the first box. There's a bunch of new DVDs.

Seeing them lightens the mood a little bit more. Something new to watch is really exciting. I open two more boxes, and there are more movies, a few new books, and a few physical catalogs for home delivery services with notes telling me to use them with account numbers and app-y stuff for my phone.

Ben pulls boxes across the counter and looks inside as I open them.

After a few minutes of going through the small boxes, he speaks. "I may have explained the cabin policy for you. Tried to sell it that if she behaves, she can at least be away from you."

The middle-sized box contains stacks of new T-shirts, flannels, a knit sweater, pajamas, and socks. They're packed in there so tightly I struggle to get them out. After moving one of the flannels aside, I find another DVD case with a note.

Little Orphan Annie,

I love you VERY much. I know you don't take care of
yourself beyond the essentials, so I tried to find some fun
stuff for you. If it doesn't fit you but fits the guys, share
or donate. Let me know what size you do need.

All these movies are safe. I've put notes in the cases of the
ones that are a little sad. Please don't be mad, but later,
people will be coming by to get you some security
equipment, etc. Cade's worried that your current system
(literally having no road signs) isn't enough preventative
measures for stupid people looking to see the wolves.
We just want you safe.

Thank you again for stopping Finn from getting into
trouble in Ireland. You always know what I need, and for
that, I can't repay you enough.

Love always, Lena

PS. If you pick his side over mine ever again,
I'll cut your balls off.

I look at the DVD case with the note and pass it to Ben.
"Did you know they made another dino flick?"

Ben laughs. "I really need to get you out more."

While I'm opening the final two boxes, Ben takes the other
DVDs to the entertainment center and shuffles things around
to make them fit.

The largest box is a bunch of new jeans, a pair of dress
slacks, two pairs of boots, two pairs of tennis shoes, and dress
shoes. It's two years' worth of new clothes. Well, if the guys
don't get stupid and I'm not forced to shift through them.

"What do you think the new security system is?" Ben asks, looking over the note one more time.

"I'm not sure I want to know." I sigh and shake my head. *Fuckin' hope it's not something ridiculous.*

I start pulling tags off clothes to toss them in the machine, but Ben is lingering.

I look at him, tipping my head. "Say it."

"I'm wondering if you need me to referee. The last time you two were here together, it got a little heated." Ben raises his chin and crosses his arms over his chest.

I listen over the top of my shoulder. The bathroom door from the loft opens.

I call out, "Morrigan, do you want dinner?"

"Whatever," she grumbles.

"Yeah, we'll be fine." I nod my head, assuring him. "Go get some rest. Thanks for helping."

MORRIGAN COMES DOWNSTAIRS THIRTY MINUTES AFTER THE BACK door closes. From where I'm starting spaghetti sauce, I watch her limp across the house toward me. It's not in her hips or back. She's not carrying her shoulders odd. It's her feet?

"What's wrong? Ben didn't tell me you got hurt today."

"I'm fine." With a nonchalant shrug, she lies to me. "Sore feet. Not used to walking so much, is all."

I debate letting it go, but there's only so much I can ignore. Her physical safety is where I draw the line, so I push a little harder. "Morrigan, walking all day shouldn't cause an issue. I know you were a little malnourished when you got here, but you should be getting stronger."

Morrigan rolls her eyes and brushes me off. "I am."

"What's going on with you? You're quiet. You're limping.

It's like you're not healing." I try giving her examples, hoping she sees it.

"Nothing." Morrigan shakes her head. "Working with Ben is hard. I didn't anticipate needing to be a bodybuilder for 'one stop.'" She uses her fingers to make air quotes around those last two words.

It doesn't sit well with me. I know she's lying, but about what? *Everything, most likely.*

I try moving the conversation away from that, picking something I'm hoping we can get out of the way.

"The guys are anxious to get to know you." I laugh.

They practically swarmed the house when I got home, ready to ask questions. Getting them to give me space was a little harder than normal. They're too damn excited to have someone who isn't a potential loss. Explaining to them that she's safe helped with the morale.

Morrigan bristles, watching me. She sits straighter and eyes the back door.

Harry watches her. The idea of a chase through the brush crosses our joint mind.

I keep browning the hamburger in the pan before me. "I think Sully is the most excited. He has four sisters, so the lack of estrogen around here is driving him nuts."

Less shifty eyed, Morrigan settles in.

"Can we clear the air a bit?" I try inviting her into this conversation again.

This'll probably come back to bite me in the ass but no time like the present. I'd like to know what I'm dealing with.

She shrugs without commitment.

I keep my eyes glued on her while carrying on the one-sided conversation toward something that she might want to discuss. "So . . . you're intended to another pack."

Where Morrigan has been quiet verbally, her body

language here does the work. She grits her jaw and her nostrils flare. She's not looking at me directly, but I'm sure I'm in her side vision.

"You're not going anywhere you don't want to go." I try to get her to listen to me, hoping she'll read between the lines.

A laugh comes out of her mouth. "Yeah. Sure, whatever you say."

I try something a bit different. "Do you want me to arrange a visit here with the man you've been intended to? I've got pull to make it that he's gotta spend time with you before your year is up."

"I'd rather you find a reason to kill me," she murmurs, which almost feels like a growl.

"I'm not killin' you," Drawing a deep breath, I battle against myself. Anger hasn't gotten me anywhere with her. I try again. "You will not be mated off against your will. Especially not to a stranger. If you want to get to know the guy, then I'll make it happen. If you don't, Gerad will stuff it. This is why you left home?"

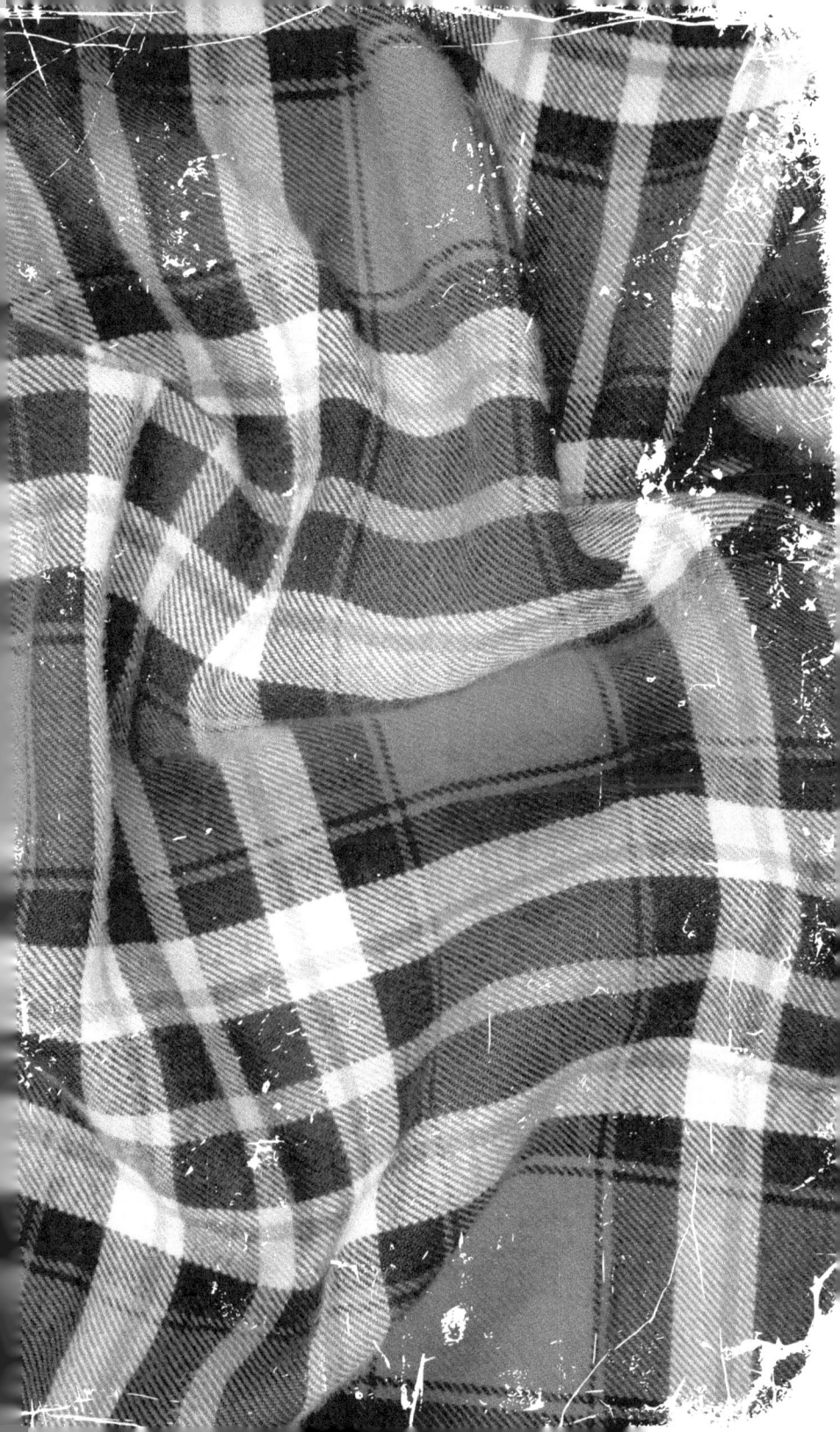

# CHAPTER 25
# MORRIGAN

A NAIVE PART OF ME WANTS TO CLING TO HOPE THAT ANSEL TRULY cares about what happens to me. But I'm not dumb enough to believe that he and Gerad haven't been talking. Why else would he have offered me to get to know the man that Gerad's intended me to? It's probably safe to assume that Ansel knows my shame too. Gerad probably told him. But if that's the case, why was Ansel surprised I was limping?

I don't know if I should ask. I don't know if this makes sense. Do I wait for Ansel to spill what he knows?

Watching Ansel cook is such a unique experience. Gerad doesn't even touch the plate to serve himself food. Ansel, however, has made multiple meals, all demonstrating that he's more than a little dedicated to eating. He's browning beef for spaghetti and Bolognese, and I'm impressed.

He's a handsome monster. His hair is shoulder length, and it's clear he's a guy about it. It's fuzzy, and there are split ends everywhere. But somehow, the messy, unkempt look is appealing the way he wears it.

SARAH JAEGER

"I want to help you, Morrigan. More than anything, I want to know how to help you." Ansel's green eyes lock on mine.

I hold his gaze, then I choose to divert, hoping to demonstrate respect. *Why does it sound like he means that?*

"Please, Morrigan." He sighs. His voice nears a begging tone. "Give me something. Tell me what the fuck caused you to leave your mom. Ersilia said you were missing for six months."

"You really are playing this whole innocent card? Saying that you have no idea what's wrong with me?" I shake my head, watching him pour tomato sauce from a glass canning jar into the pan with the meat.

*Why am I being so difficult? I can hear he's trying to be genuine.* There's a part of me that can't help but be contrary.

He stirs all the ingredients in the pan. "Morrigan. I hear you. I know you think I'm workin' with Gerad. I'm not. Cade's people called me to get you. Then, after a week-ish, I called your mom to tell her you were here and safe. It didn't sit with me that the Sovereign's people knew where you were but she might not. At one point, I did call your mother a friend." A growl takes his voice as he continues to explain what happened. "And then Gerad jumped on the line."

Ansel's words ring true. Somewhere between the beginning of this conversation and now, I let my guard down. No, somewhere over the last week, despite how angry I've been, Ansel's stayed steady.

Anyone with half a brain cell could see how honest Ansel is in the way he lives his life. His being honest and open about this should feel reassuring. And it does, kinda. Maybe I need to trust, if not him, my feelings.

"I don't agree with Gerad's kind of pack dynamic. There should be no need to tell you how much I dislike the guy." Ansel is growling. It's soft but constant in the undertone of each word. He drops his shoulders, rolling his head back and

164

forth. He forces the tension from his body and changes the subject again. "Morrigan, in the courthouse, I was fucking terrified I wouldn't be able to save you. When they said assault on an officer, I was wondering why they even bothered telling me to come. Then, for it to be you I could have lost —" He scrubs his hands down his face, and a whole swamp's worth of emotions bubble through his green eyes. "I couldn't let that happen." He draws a breath and tilts his head, watching me. "I don't know what caused you to run from your mom. An uneducated guess says it was Gerad." Ansel pauses again, this time for longer. He gently taps the spoon off on the side of the pan before setting it down in a spoon rest.

*What is happening?* This is starting to feel surreal. The air in the room is shifting from the hostility between us, and I don't know where it's going.

Ansel drops his shoulders, and we lock eyes. The look on his face is soft and vulnerable. I've never seen a man so deadly look so approachable.

"I know I'm public enemy number one and that you don't understand what happened with Walt. You don't understand because if you did, you'd let me hurt with you rather than push me away."

The way he says those words. There are so many feelings it gives me chills. I shake my head. *No. No, we don't have empathy for Ansel. No.*

But empathy is what's growing. The feeling of connection has been rooting for a while, but I've been squashing it down every chance I get. I pushed him away, shouting insults when it felt too real.

*What if what Mom said about Dad fracturing was true?* He's the only other person who really knew Dad.

"Morrigan. Please." Ansel's words hold a depth of unexpected emotions. "I know something's not right. I can't help you unless you tell me. Please just let me help you."

"I —" My mouth starts speaking before my brain is ready. *No one says please to me.* His green eyes are soft and caring, and his patience has the words I've held back flowing out. "I've been starving myself and doing everything I could to be perfect. If I could be what Gerad wanted me to be — quiet, small, and seen but not heard — then maybe he'd leave me alone until I was old enough that he'd give up on me."

Ansel stays quiet. He lets me find my way through the words.

I look away from the intensity of his focus. It's so freeing to tell someone.

But at this next bit, my voice falls to a whisper. "Gerad figured it out."

"I need you to be specific; what did he figure out?" Ansel's tone is sharp. The growl is back.

Like the first day I was here, the words cut, but this time, it doesn't feel like that frustration is meant for me.

I close my eyes. "Ansel, I don't have a wolf."

"You've a beautiful gray wolf," Ansel says, the end of his sentence raising but not quite to the level of a question. His eyebrows draw together like he's thinking.

Shaking my head, I move past his objection. Even if he doesn't believe it, I know the truth. There isn't a wolf to be found inside me. If I tell him the worst of it now, I won't have to tell him later. I won't have to say this more than once. "He started . . . doing different things to get me to shift. When the traditional methods didn't work, he moved onto advice from older packs and apparently what he could get access to out of the archives."

The gas range clicks off, and Ansel's voice comes out as a growl. "What did he do to you?"

Bubbles told me, 'If you don't tell someone what happened, then it's not real.' If you don't talk about it, then it never really happened.

Ansel's hands find my shoulders. He spins my stool to the side to face him.

*How did he get here?*

He runs his fingers across my face and brushes warm water droplets away.

"I'll kill him, Morrigan. All you have to do is tell me what he's done." His voice is soft, and his hand moves to petting my hair. "He won't hurt you again."

I don't answer. Sitting here feeling his touch is cathartic. It's comfortable. The most comfortable I can remember being since my life changed. *How can the simplest touches become so affirming?*

"I don't need details. Name the act, and it will seal his fate." Ansel vows the kind of salvation I'd held hope for deep inside.

His words are the ones I wouldn't even let myself dream about. I could never picture someone walking in and saving me from the pain, least of all him.

*Why is the man I blamed for causing all this the one promising to fix it?*

"I don't want you to kill him." I can't believe the words that come from my mouth, yet they breach my lips with a heavy sob. "You can't kill him. Mom doesn't deserve to die."

"Shhhh. Morrigan, it's okay." Ansel draws in closer, and I let my head fall against his chest. His heartbeat thrums in my ear between calming words. "I won't kill him. Not right now, at least. But I need to know if he's hurting people."

"It's me. He's only hurting me. Not . . . any sort of way the humans would find him guilty for." I pause, trying to draw a breath. *Maybe Bubbles was wrong. I need to tell someone. Let it be real.* And then move past it. "Because I don't have a wolf, Gerad

167

reverted to every historical solution that he could get to try and fix me."

Ansel is quiet. He doesn't move.

I'm safe in his arms to tell him. So, I do. "They say that a hungry wolf is a dangerous one. So, they withheld meat. I lived like a stupid rabbit, but no matter how hungry I was, there was never enough hunger for a wolf to come out." My stomach rolls with the memory of what starving was like.

Ansel runs his hand into my hair, stroking my scalp gently.

"Next, it was that I was too distracted for my wolf to connect. So, they left me in the dark for her to find me." A sardonic laugh comes with that one, only to pass quickly. "Then there's that saying that if you're afraid enough, your wolf will save you. So, they put me in danger."

The feeling of a gun to my head comes and passes. The sound of it ringing in my ears. This and other horrors that hurt too much to think about.

The memories that do surface trigger word vomit. I can't stop them, and they keep coming out faster. "They ran out of ways to scare me. Apparently, there are records of lost wolves being able to be gifted back. So, they tried. I was hunted in the mountains. For two days, they stalked me until . . ."

I shake my head against Ansel's chest. The memory of the pain of being torn apart and bitten bone deep is still fresh. I want to climb into the safety he's providing. If it were possible, I would disappear into this feeling.

There's nothing more I want to talk about. But I fill in the answers for why Gerad might want me to go back to California. "I left shortly after I recovered from the hunt. Gerad arranged me a mate, and I'm guessing it's because they want to breed one into me."

Ansel is growling. He holds me firmly to his chest, the soft petting of my hair having turned into a fierce protective hug.

Tears roll down my cheeks and soak the fabric of his shirt. The last five years of my life and the reality of the situation hurt more now. I've blamed him all this time, yet Ansel is the one holding me as I relive it. The man who isn't really responsible let me blame him and hate him, and now, in the end, holds me together like it's his one purpose on this earth.

Harbinger, the wolf of death, is holding me together when the reality of what I've survived sets in. He squeezes me to him. Little movements soothing me with firm pressure as if he's afraid to let go. A long few minutes of silence and safety pass before he relaxes his hold.

"That won't happen," Ansel growls. He clarifies, "I won't let anyone take you from me. I won't let anyone hurt you. Ever. You'll be safe here."

Snot is clogging my nose, and I can't breathe. I push myself away from him, and he grabs a box of tissues off the side table in the living room. He runs his hand back through my hair and kisses my forehead, then returns to the stove.

As I straighten myself back out, I'm reminded how weak I am. I hate crying. I don't get emotional. My eyes are still watering, but I look at Ansel through the moisture.

He's stewing. His jaw clicks back and forth as he grinds his teeth. Guilt washes over me. I shouldn't have told him. Ansel will have to deal with the mess Gerad's made. The unhealthy pack dynamic and weeding out unfit wolves . . . it's his job.

"You won't kill him, right?" My voice doesn't come out anywhere near strong enough.

Ansel nods, still stirring the frying pan. "I promised I wouldn't kill him right now. I can't promise that time won't come. But for the near future, I won't."

"I'm sorry." The words come out stronger this time.

Ansel turns the burner down low. "This has to simmer for a bit. Want to go for a walk?"

I do. I want to spend time with someone who understands my pain, who makes me feel protected and like I'm not alone in this world.

I never thought I'd feel this way again. And if someone had told me I would volunteer to spend time with Harbinger, I would have never believed them, but right now, I want to go outside. If my feet didn't hurt so bad, I would willingly spend time walking with Ansel. But I shake my head. I can't walk like this.

"Fuck, your feet. I'm sorry." Ansel pulls his hair into a hair tie he fishes from his pocket.

After putting a lid on the pan, he offers me his hand. "Let's go sit outside. It always makes me feel better when the world isn't quite right. Life can't be too bad if you can still go outside."

I try not to let my discomfort show as I step down off the stool, but the sharp breath I draw gives away my pain. With the hand that had been extended toward me, Ansel pushes my hair out of my face. When our eyes meet, he's the first one to look away. His head bows, and he picks me up, knocking my legs out from under me.

He walks slowly with me in his arms to the back door. With only the slightest jostle, he opens it.

"How were you not this sore after doing the cows? Or running off in the dead of night?"

"There wasn't a lot for me to do with the cows. It was standing still and handing Ben things," I grumble. I hate being reminded of my fuckups. But I answer him anyway. "And my failed escape attempt? I still had blisters and calluses from life before. It didn't hurt this bad."

Ansel lowers me into one of the low-seated deck chairs. Instead of sitting in the other one, Ansel goes back inside the house. He returns with a few ice packs. After pulling over the detached footstool, he lifts my legs, his strong hands raising my calves with no issue, and rests the ice pack below my knees.

"Cold!" I object loudly, trying to pull my legs from the ice.

Ansel laughs while effortlessly holding down my legs. "Probably, but it'll help."

When I sit still, Ansel lets go. I squeeze my fists, trying to ignore the cold on my legs. Ansel closes his eyes as he rests in the chair beside me. Tilting his chin toward the sky, he seems so content and at peace.

"You're not asking me any questions?" I try closing my eyes like he's doing.

"Nope." Ansel pops the *p*.

Must be contagious since Ben does it too.

"So, why not?" I let the end of the sentence hang but dig my fingers into the wooden armrests, waiting.

If it were me, I'd have a hundred questions.

Ansel takes a moment before he answers. "You have a wolf. I've seen her. She's dormant. That's concerning but not dangerous. You're not fractured. When you're good and ready, we'll talk. I've gotta find a way to make it safe for you to integrate into the pack in a more controlled environment."

The sting of the cold is still strong, but my feet ache less. We sit in silence, and unlike where we were a week ago, it isn't torture. I don't hate sitting here with him. He's the man who killed my father, but I'm starting to think there's more to know.

Somehow, Ansel's no longer the monster in my story. I'm starting to doubt he ever really was.

# CHAPTER 26
## ANSEL

HARRY PACES INSIDE ME. FEEDING ON MY ANGER AND HATRED, HE demands bloodshed, but I'm not sure he understands where the anger is coming from. He doesn't pull any particular image of an instance of bloodshed for me to view. So maybe it is understanding after all. I'm angry, but it's with myself.

I have to believe that whoever left me, mother or father or guardian, had no idea what would happen to me once they were gone. It's easier to think that they didn't know. Because they left me with monsters, and those monsters made Harry and me who we are. No one should want that for their child.

And somehow, knowing me and knowing all this, Ersilia let this happen to her daughter. No, not this; it's not the same. Morrigan is strong. She escaped before it got too far.

*Who willingly lets someone hurt their child like this?* She lives with Gerad day in and day out. What monster lets wolves maul her daughter? I can only imagine what kind of danger they put her in. *If I knew the truth, I'd be breaking promises.*

Morrigan squirms next to me, pulling me from my

thoughts. I move quickly and help her take the ice packs out from behind her legs. She's shivering from the cold.

"Come on. Let's get you inside. I'll start the pasta."

Tenderly, Morrigan makes her way to her feet. I probably shouldn't have carried her out here, but I couldn't let her walk like that. I follow her into the house and close the door behind us. She's hobbling a bit less, and it's only slightly painful to watch.

Sitting back down at the bar, she watches me start the pasta and stir the sauce.

"Ansel?" Morrigan's voice is so quiet I almost miss it.

I look at her, waiting for a question.

"Why did you kill Dad?" She chews on her bottom lip.

That's not what I was expecting. Someone once told me grief isn't an emotion, but if it isn't, I don't know what I've been feeling all these years.

I start trying to have the conversation I've anticipated over the past five years. "It was past his time. He, uhm." *Fuck.* It's so much harder than I expected. I assumed I'd have to answer to her for this one day. But I didn't expect it to feel this heavy after all this time. I pull in a large breath before trying again from the beginning. "After your mom took you away, he started going downhill. Walt handled losing Ersilia to her fated mate pretty well."

Tasting the sauce gives me some time. *How do I say this? I don't want to blame Ersilia. It's no one's fault, is it?* In my mind, it is though. I've always blamed Ersilia. But she's Morrigan's mother, and this isn't about me.

The words I pick are as neutral as they can be. "As long as he got to see you, Walt was perfectly content with the arrangement. Then, when she said they were taking you to LA with them, Walt fractured."

I can't look at her. I know I should. She needs comfort in

this. But I can't. The day he broke haunts my nightmares. Harry makes sure of it.

"He held it together for the most part. Summers were obviously easiest for him since he got to see you. But your mom started getting difficult about visits for holidays. She started making excuses, and every time Walt called to talk to you, she'd brush him off. I got involved, and Ersilia and Gerad behaved for a bit. But not seeing you was killing him."

I finally force myself to look at Morrigan.

Her eyes are wet with tears, but she's not shutting down. She's listening.

"I did everything I could. I waited too long. Your dad made me promise I wouldn't make him live out his days in a kennel. Everything I did was for him in those final months. Then, your mom canceled your flight for spring break, claiming it was too expensive. I paid for a new ticket. It was a no-brainer, and fuck, I had the money. I thought maybe you could see him just one last time. But Morrigan — I left him in the truck for ten minutes to get a fucking haircut, and when I got back, he wasn't there." I look to the ceiling, hoping for some strength to get through this. All the things I never say. He's the person whose end I refuse to talk about. "I found them in an alley. A woman taking out the trash. He didn't kill her. Only because Harry is faster."

*Do I keep going?* Tears are welling in her eyes. I don't think I should. But maybe she needs to hear it?

I bite my bottom lip but get the words out. "I managed to get him calmed down to bring him home. In the end, he knew he had to go. Walt was ready. He didn't want you to see him that way. He didn't die alone."

Morrigan nods, but it's almost empty. Like her head is moving because she knows it should, but she's not there. I've scooped her insides out with my words and left a shell.

I don't know that a hug solves this one. I stand watching the pot boil. I know it's not going any faster doing so, but at least it's something to do.

WE NEVER RECOVER FROM THAT CONVERSATION. IT WAS HEAVY. I honestly didn't expect us to, but we do watch one of the new movies from Lena. Begrudgingly, Morrigan lets me put ice packs behind her knees again to help her feet. And now, after the film, her steps are a little less tender as she walks up the stairs.

When she hits the top of the landing, I turn to clean up the kitchen and go to bed.

"Ansel." I look to see Morrigan standing at the balcony. She gives me a nod. "Thanks."

"You're welcome?"

Morrigan doesn't say anything but turns to go to bed.

I watch her go.

LYING IN BED, I STARE UP AT THE CEILING. I'VE SEEN HER WOLF. I know I have. I dig back in my mind, looking for exactly what her wolf looked like. I know it's gray, but markings?

Harbinger is restless thinking back that far. He struggles. Fighting against me, he tries to protect me from looking too far into our past. Anytime I try to remember back more than a few years at a time, it becomes a horrible fight between us.

Finally, I can recall a memory of a pack run. Morrigan's gangly wolf still growing. She's all legs. Gray and white wolf with black flecking. There was never anything wrong with her.

I went digging too far into my past. Memories of violence flood, ticking into my head.

*"BOY. CLEAN THIS FLOOR. YOU FILTHY FUCKING PIG," A MAN I DON'T recognize yells at me.*

*The bucket he drops on the floor is full of water and almost as big as I am. It sloshes as he sets it down, getting my feet wet. He throws a rag at my face and laughs when I don't catch it. My shoulder hurts, and I still can't move my arm right.*

*"I said clean the floor, pig." He grabs the back of my head and pushes it down into the bucket.*

*I can't push myself out of it.*

*He holds me down.*

*I can't breathe.*

*THE MEMORY GOES BLACK.*

*MY ARMS ARE TIED IN FRONT OF ME. DAVID AND JAKE, WHO DROWNED me before, drag me along in the mud behind them. I try to walk, and every time I step too quickly, I fall over. Everything's dirty and I'm hungry. I try so hard not to cry, to not make a sound. They don't like it when I make a sound. They punish me. I don't want to be punished.*

*David drags me up next to a guy's car. He smells like the rest, dirty, like cigarettes and sickness.*

*The man grabs my chin. "This it?"*

*"He's one of them. Creepy little fucker," they say.*

*"Show him what you can do." Jake smacks me upside the back of the head.*

*I can't do what he wants me to on command. I don't even know*

*I'm doing it most of the time. David puts his hand around my throat and squeezes.*

THE MEMORY FADES, AND I'M LEFT PANTING, SOAKED IN MY SWEAT ON the bed. I roll my head to the clock and see it's only two in the morning.

I need to get out of these clothes.

I put on some dry pajamas and take the wet ones to the laundry machine.

Listening up to the loft above, I can hear Morrigan sleeping peacefully. Light murmurs and soft breathing are calming. It's nice having someone else in the house.

*Please let this be the turning point for us. I can't help her if she doesn't trust me. I'd like her to forgive me, but I've no right to ask for forgiveness.*

But tomorrow is a new day. Today was good though.

# CHAPTER 27
# MORRIGAN

Is this what it's like to have someone care about you? I was too tired to think about it last night. But I've been up for a few hours now. Lying here and not moving shouldn't be this exciting given all the time I spent in the kennels.

Ansel told me his side of the story. And the longer I think about what he said, the better his version fits what I remember. Her hushed phone calls filled with angry voices before she would tell me I wasn't visiting Dad. Those calls never made sense. If she was fighting for me to go there, why wouldn't she have let me hear the fight?

Dad fractured. But I don't remember him seeming any different when I did get to visit him here. He was just . . . Dad. Maybe that's what's happening to me? I don't feel any different except there's no wolf inside me. Gerad's said before that those who fracture, left unchecked, ruin packs. It's why he's never let someone stay who has had one in their bloodline. Is that why he arranged an intention for me? He knew . . . Did Mom?

"Good morning, Morrigan." Ansel's voice reaches the loft from the ground floor.

"Morning," I answer, pulling myself out of the cozy sheets.

I can't hide away up here forever. Something changed last night, and I've got to face it.

Downstairs, Ansel is starting breakfast. He's shirtless, but plaid pants hang low around his waist. Ansel's back, shoulders, and arms are covered in tattoos. Skulls, snakes, flowers, feathers, and leaves decorate his skin. There are more than I remembered. A lot more.

"Are you ready to formally meet the pack today? I figured we'd do some small one-on-one meetings before we go to a full group hangout tomorrow, depending on how it all goes?" Ansel turns to face me.

The muscles of his stomach form a thick V, drawing my eyes low. Forcing myself away from following the muscles, I bring my eyes back to his. No need to fake having a wolf anymore. And eye contact is probably better than staring too closely at his body.

"Yeah. It would be nice to put names to faces again."

It's been twelve days since I was brought here. There are three hundred and fifty-three days left in my mandatory year with Ansel. I should get to know his other prisoners.

"I'm happy to hear that." Ansel smiles, directing my attention to the table with a toss of his head. He's set out plates ready to eat.

No one should be this smiley and happy in the morning. But it suits him. The way the corners of his eyes wrinkle gives me butterflies. Butterflies that aren't afraid of fluttering lower. *What on earth* . . . I try to squash the uninvited guests in my abdomen. This is *not at all* on the menu.

Instead of being woken up and locked in a kennel, I slept late today, and we're having a late brunch. I was starting to think these guys work seven days a week. Anything that's not sitting in a kennel in the basement sounds like a good time.

Once Ansel serves the food, my mouth waters at the sight of eggs Benedict. Poised with my knife and fork, I'm ready to dive in.

Ansel takes his time and pulls on a T-shirt that was draped over his chair before sitting down. It covers most of his tattoos, and it's almost a shame that he hides all the work he's had done. But it's not exactly polite to eat shirtless, I guess.

He clears his throat. "I would like it if you could start working with us. We haven't had any more late-night jogs, and maybe getting out more might help you."

*Oh fuck yes. No more kennel.*

I try to play it cool by nodding. "Yeah. I'd like to see the sun a little more."

He chews his bottom lip for a moment but shakes his head like he's decided not to ask a question. *Was he referring to my lack of wolf?*

His words echo in my mind. The things he said we could talk about when I was ready. I don't think I'll ever be ready. But I'm curious enough to pretend. "Do you think you can fix my wolf?"

Ansel blows out a raspberry. "I don't know."

His admission hurts. The little hope I had is crushed. It's been ground to dust in three little words. With nothing to say, I nod.

"Don't lose hope. I'm positive you had a wolf." Ansel gives me a soft smile. "If you work with me, we'll see what we can do. Never have I ever heard of a wolf up and not being a wolf anymore. So, that means there has got to be a way." He looks over my shoulder at the clock. "Also, really glad you said yes because we've about thirty minutes before the guys have mandatory scheduled appointments, taking turns to say hello. Some of them are more thrilled than others."

I'M HALFWAY THROUGH MY PLATE WHEN A MASSIVE BANG COMES TO the back door. I jump in my chair.

"It's open, and I'm not getting up, so let yourself in," Ansel yells, leaning around the side of the table past me.

I turn to look over the chair at who is coming in.

"Hey, boss!" One of the guys from the crew comes in the back door. He's wearing a massive smile and sporting a fresh black eye.

"Ripley? You and Vito again?" Ansel groans from behind me.

Ripley is stocky. I've never seen a wolf so compact but built.

He smirks while he retorts, "It's not my fault he can't park."

"You're early, but there's extra if you wanna sit and eat." Ansel sighs and his fork clinks on his plate.

I turn back to my plate and start poking around, trying to eat. Nervousness washes over me. I shouldn't be nervous like this.

The sound of a glass being pulled from the cupboard is followed by the refrigerator being opened, then something is poured, and Ripley comes and sits at the table with a glass of water and a smile.

"Nice to meet you. I'm Ripley, as in, believe it or not."

"Believe it or not?" I ask, looking him over.

His eye is super swollen and looks angry, but Ripley doesn't favor it, and it doesn't seem to hamper him from smiling and going on with the questions. "Yeah. You know, like the record books? And the oddities?"

Shaking my head, I indicate I have no idea. There's something in the air that's unsettling with him here. It's intimidating, but maybe it's because of the healing black eye?

"What do they teach kids these days?" Ripley looks to Ansel with an exasperated sigh. "Not the important stuff. Clearly."

Ripley hangs out and tells stories about being 'my age,' and I'm fairly certain he thinks I'm sixteen and learning to drive. Despite not knowing what he's talking about half the time, I can tell he's funny and kind, not that I let anything show beyond a flat face.

Twenty minutes later, he's finished his glass of water. Ansel clears his and my plate, and Ripley says his goodbyes.

"I think Zero is next." Ansel furrows his brow, thinking. "Or Sully?"

A soft, solitary knock comes to the back door.

Ansel nods. "Zero, it's open."

The door opens, and I lean over to see the man entering. He's tall and lanky. Catching my eye, he looks away quickly. *A submissive? Or polite?*

Despite his monstrous height at almost seven feet tall, he bends down and unties his shoes.

"I think I'm early. Sorry." A genuine apology rings in the air. His voice is deep and carries well throughout the house.

Zero is absolutely a submissive. It's evident in everything he does. Only two have cycled through Gerad's pack, that I know of. They never wanted to stay long. Even if Gerad offered them the best accommodations. They're big on vibes. Gerad didn't pass the vibe check. This surprises no one. And thus, it was unsurprising to me they didn't want to stay.

He sits on a stool, and I'm pretty sure he's not any shorter sitting down. But both Ansel and I are children in size compared to him.

"California, huh?" Zero asks, opening the conversation.

I nod. "Yeah, it smells like pee, and California is a culture itself. You're not missing anything."

"Oh, so it's like here, but it smells bad." Zero winks.

Ansel rolls his eyes but then focuses on me. "Mind if I hop in the shower?"

*Trusting me with Zero?*

I shrug. "Yeah, that's fine."

With a clap of his hand on Zero's back, Ansel passes by, and I hear him go back and forth from his bedroom and then the bathroom.

"So, they send you here because you're too tall? Stand out in the pack photos?" I try to crack the joke, hoping he thinks it's funny.

"I mean, at least for me, no one had to sit on the floor to be in the same frame." He jokes right back.

"I'll have you know I'm not that short." I stand up off the stool, which does nothing for my point. I'm still lying to people when I say I'm more than the inch and a quarter over five feet tall that I am.

I get a laugh out of Zero.

He's easy to talk to, and I've said the most words I've said in a long time to anyone. I even teared up about my sewing machine and how I've always wanted to have a pet dog or cat.

The bathroom door opens and closes, then Ansel's door does the same. I hadn't realized all that much time had passed.

"I'll let you go so you can have a few minutes before the next guy gets here. Sherman's always early." Zero nods and smiles. "It was nice to meet you."

"It was nice to meet you." I could see myself being friends with Zero.

Ansel comes out of his bedroom with enough time to give a quick goodbye.

When I'm sure Zero's away from the door, I turn to Ansel. "This isn't bad, but how many more of these are there?"

"Four." Ansel furrows his eyebrows, then holds up his hand

and counts, confirming with himself. "Sherman, Vito, Sully, and the new kid, Princeton."

A thud that rattles the house comes to the door.

The person on the other side doesn't wait for Ansel to call and let him know it's open.

"Helloooo!" a voice booms.

Zero is tall and lanky, but the man walking through the door feels larger. Everything about him is imposing. He walks fast, not taking his shoes off.

He doesn't stop.

He nearly bowls me over as he picks me up into a bear hug, pulling me off the floor. My feet dangle.

"Sherman!" Ansel scolds. "Did you ask first? Why are your shoes on?"

"Oh, sorry." Sherman sets me down much more gently than when he picked me up. He straightens the sleeves of his shirt with his head bowed and then mutters, "Sorry, Ms. Morrigan."

With that, he retreats to the back door and takes his shoes off.

He comes back, starting over again, "Hello. I'm Sherman."

He offers his hand out and shakes mine much more daintily than when he lifted me. It feels very practiced. Sherman is so intimidating, but there's this part of me that wants to protect him from everything scary in the world.

"It's nice to meet you, Sherman." I smile at him, assuring him it's okay. "How's your day going?"

"It's so good. My chicken isn't a duck." Sherman nods. His voice has a very thick Southern accent. "Ben said she's just tall. I call her Sally Lou."

"Oh! Well, I'm very glad that Sally Lou is still a chicken. How many do you have?" I ask and step back from him, inviting him to sit at the counter with me.

187

"Four hens." Sherman nods. "Ben said I can't have a rooster 'cause the girls are enough."

"Well, I trust Ben, he seems like a very knowledgeable vet." I sit farther away from him than I did Zero.

I didn't realize Ansel had stopped moving when Sherman entered until his movements draw my attention from the corner of my eye.

He pulls out glasses from the cupboard and slides them over to us before pouring water. His silence and still movements are uncharacteristic. I take a cue from him and move more cautiously as well.

# CHAPTER 28

# ANSEL

I'M AMAZED BY HOW EASILY MORRIGAN TALKS WITH SHERMAN.

He scares almost everyone.

Sherman is a lifetime resident. I'll never release him to go to another pack. I would love to be able to, but he's nicknamed after the tank because he's a fucking beast. He's a little slow on the uptake, but he gets by. He needs everything to be steady and cohesive. If his schedule changes too much, it takes him a bit to process, and if he gets upset, he's very violent and quick to shift. But he's not fractured, and his wolf isn't feral. He just needs more time than others. So, I'll keep him until I can't anymore.

Consciously or not, Morrigan handles him well. She didn't freak out when he picked her up in a hug, and she sat there talking and taking an interest in what he was saying. It was the easiest full introduction with Sherman to anyone else I've ever had.

"Thank you for chatting with me, Ms. Morrigan." Sherman plays with the hem of his shirt. "Sorry for picking you up. I'll remember to be gentle."

"I appreciate you remembering, Sherman." Morrigan smiles at him. "I'll see you later."

INTO THE EARLY AFTERNOON, WE CONTINUE THE CYCLE OF PACK members through formal introductions.

Vito, per usual, is late in coming up to the house. Where Morrigan was relaxed in talking to Sherman, she's terse and tense with Vito.

"Oh, uhm. I'm getting hungry. Maybe a good time to catch lunch?" Morrigan runs her hand over her stomach.

"That's a good idea." I agree quickly. Tossing my head toward the door, I motion for Vito to leave. "We'll catch up with you later."

After Vito leaves, I text Ben, asking him to tell Princeton and Sully to cool it and give us an hour.

"You okay?"

Morrigan sighs but nods.

Turning from Morrigan, I start setting up to make some BLTs for lunch.

I let her sit in silence while I fry the thick-cut bacon.

"Sorry," Morrigan mutters. "I'm tired. They're a lot."

*Did I go too far? Should I have split this up, maybe over the weekend?* My brain runs that back and forth, and I try to keep my eyes on her. I could tell Sully and Princeton to come tomorrow morning before yard games and activities.

"Sherman is a sweetheart. But I'm guessing he's not all there?" Morrigan says quietly.

Not wanting to look a gift horse in the mouth with her wanting to talk to me, I'm quick to answer. "No, I don't think he's all there. He's a big dude and really particular about how things are in life."

The bacon grease pops and bites at my skin, and I shake my hand to cool off the sting.

"I don't like Vito or Ripley. Nothing against you, I know you don't pick who comes here," Morrigan grumbles. "They're off. It's like they're aliens trying to pretend they're wolves."

"It's the fracture. That's a good analogy for it." *A really good analogy for it.*

Silence suits us for a bit, but after I fry three pounds of bacon, I have to figure out what we're doing today. "There's two guys left. Sully and Princeton are both closer in age to you. But they're both kinda big personalities. We could hold off on them until tomorrow mornin' before pack lunch if it would help you."

"No, with a break and some food, it'll be good." Morrigan nods.

Her words are hesitant. I'm not sure I should trust what she's saying. The problem is she needs to be allowed to make her own decisions. Independence within the confines of the pack is important for getting better. Not that there's anything wrong with Morrigan, mostly. What I've been doing has been working for a long time, and there's no sense in changing it. There's a lot of reasons for a wolf to go dormant, but probably the best thing for a dormant wolf is time and improved health.

"Can I help?" Morrigan points to the bacon. "Or is bacon lunch."

"Uh, sure. There are tomatoes in the fridge. You could slice those. BLT's for lunch."

Morrigan is quick to move around the counter to the fridge. She looks through the condiments and pulls out a jar of mayonnaise. The sigh that comes from her starts at the top of her head and slumps her whole body.

"Write what condiments you want on the notepad on the fridge. Or, if you want, you can do the grocery run with me on

Wednesday, and we can look at what the store has." I hold back a laugh but try to solve her need for more complexity than a traditional BLT has to offer. "I've got some chipotle seasonings in the cupboard if you want to mix that with mayonnaise and sour cream for a sauce?"

"Ooo!" Morrigan squeaks, rushing to the spice cupboard next to the stove.

SULLY AND MORRIGAN WEREN'T FAST FRIENDS. HE'S A BIT OF A ladies' man and laid it on a bit thick, but by the time I have an apple pie going into the oven, they're talking more naturally.

Harry huffs inside me, pushing around and wanting space. Having Sully close to the house and in our space regularly unsettles him to start with. But this is a bit more than the usual.

"It's a knickknack, Patty Wack, give the frog a loan. His old man is a Rolling Stone." Sully finishes the end of his joke.

It's one I've heard him tell a hundred times, and as much as it pains me to admit, it's still kind of funny.

Morrigan laughs until tears are in her eyes, and she draws a deep breath. "That was a good one."

"Alright. Well, I'll catch you around." Sully bites his lip at Morrigan.

I turn away and roll my eyes.

PRINCETON SCOOTS HIS STOOL CLOSER TO MORRIGAN'S AGAIN, AND this time, the cutting glare I give him isn't enough of a deterrent to keep him from getting into her space. He doesn't move, so I push out a growl.

"Jeez, Ansel." Princeton rolls his eyes but moves back a small slide away from Morrigan.

He doesn't let that break his conversation with her.

I have to focus on keeping Harry locked inside. Harry doesn't like Sully in his space, but it's a mild irritation when compared to his reaction to Princeton.

Nothing I can think of stops him from smashing against the walls I have holding him inside.

Since Princeton's only been here for a couple of months, we have yet to come to a healthy balance. Accepting his place as a pack member doesn't seem to suit him, but even in the instances where we're toe to toe, Harry doesn't normally have this severe of a reaction.

Princeton has a temper. Only last week, he snapped a shovel handle and put a dent in the back end of the work truck with his fists.

That has to be the start of where Harry's rage against Princeton began. Deep in my gut, though, I know I'm being protective over Walt's daughter.

I don't have any issue with the guys hooking up. It's unreasonable to expect them to be celibate. From time to time, most of them have flings with humans in town. And the one time a year we open the place up for a holiday, the same bunch hook up.

*But Princeton and Morrigan? I don't like it.*

Harry growls. It echoes my sentiment, and I let it escape as Princeton's hand again advances toward her.

Walt would be pissed the fuck off if I let someone so violent move in on his daughter. They may be closer in age, and Princeton may have a sister, but he sure doesn't treat women like he does.

I've only taken him to town twice because of our issues. The women around town are more cautious around him.

That's enough for me to be more than a little wary of him in close proximity to her. He's not stable, and I don't want to pretend he is. While I haven't looked for his timeline, my assumption is that it's short. *Shorter if he keeps it up with Morrigan.*

"Well, Princeton." I cut his time two minutes short. "I think it's best you be going down the hill."

"Oh, well, I thought maybe . . ." Princeton looks to Morrigan like she'd be able to overrule me.

"Yeah. I need to start answering some of the questions Ansel's written out for me." She lies flawlessly to him.

*Impressive.*

I take the time to personally walk Princeton out the door and then lock it behind him. I hurry back to the oven and get the pie out, then set it on the cooling rack.

Morrigan slumps against the counter the minute the oven door is closed. "How could I forget how awful that feels?"

"Hmm?" I turn the oven off and start pulling out chips and salsa for a snack before dinner.

"Faking being nice to guys." She waves at the door where Princeton left. After a yawn, she continues. "Especially slimy sleazeballs who are way too focused on me."

The admission that she hated his attention as much as I did soothes Harry nearly instantly. I draw a deep breath and finally get to relax.

I pour out chips and salsa for both of us without saying anything.

Relaxing back into the stool, more at ease, Morrigan flips her hair from one shoulder to the other. That shouldn't be attractive, but the simple act sends a jolt through my heart and then down much lower.

Closing my eyes, I shake my head and dismiss it.

Morrigan sighs with what seems like an unawareness of

my inappropriate thoughts. "It's hard having to watch first for wolves and then for human scumbags. I hate feeling so powerless all the time."

That stops me dead. It's been a long time since those feelings, powerless and unable to control something, have hit me.

Harry moves back to being bloodthirsty.

I understand his rage. Humans let other humans hurt each other with such ease. But at the very least, wolves try our best to keep the women folk safe at all costs. It's why I very rarely have a female tenant.

They mostly never — Lena and Dinah probably don't count — go anywhere far from home alone.

But then again, pack law and how we govern our people failed Dinah. A whole pack failed her until . . . I blow out a breath, needing to stop thinking about it.

But pack law failed Morrigan too.

Her voice falls. "I didn't mean to get you upset."

"I'm not upset with you. It's okay. I needed to know." I assure her, meeting her gaze. "I don't want you to feel powerless here."

# CHAPTER 29
# MORRIGAN

THIS MORNING, ANSEL TELLS ME HE HAS A BUNCH OF PAPERWORK TO do, but he offers me free rein of all the DVDs he's amassed or the few books he keeps on the coffee table.

Opting for a rom-com I've seen a couple of times over the books that were required reading for me in high school, I snuggle in with the quilt Ansel left draped over the back of the couch.

It smells like him, and for whatever reason, that makes it cozier.

Ansel mutters to himself as he does math of some sort. The murmurs are barely audible over the sounds of the TV. I try to keep it down so he can focus, and I'm tempted to ask if I can help. Not that I probably know what he's doing, but two heads are better than one.

Ansel has his hair pulled over to one side with his fingers fisted into it as he supports his head. The light from the big picture windows illuminates his face, and he nearly glows in a god-like fashion.

*Don't be weird. He's the Alpha. No matter how attractive he is.*

*Very,* comes a faint echo.

I look over the back of the couch for where that whisper could have come from.

*Wolf?*

It sounds silly to talk to her . . . if it is her. Do I believe Ansel is right? I don't remember shifting, but he wouldn't lie, would he?

The voice doesn't happen again.

A LOUD THUMP COMES TO THE BACK DOOR BEFORE IT OPENS. THERE'S a hustle and bustle as the sounds of people taking the house by storm rattle through the hallway.

"Let's play some bags." Vito claps his hands together and rushes through the house and out the back sliding door.

The rest of the guys follow barefoot into the dirt yard.

Ansel shakes his head and gathers his papers. He goes the opposite way toward his bedroom, where he puts them away.

Credits roll on my movie, and I turn it off.

Back in the living room, Ansel shoos me with a short flick of his wrist toward the sliding glass door. "Pack bonding. It's mandatory."

Pulling off my socks, I follow him outside. Not grabbing shoes will probably bite me in the ass, but I don't want to be weird and stand out since the rest of them went barefoot.

THE GUYS, AS A GROUP, ARE HILARIOUS. THEY RIB EACH OTHER BASED on nicknames. Bad puns, limericks, and sexual innuendos fly around. The most creative being Sully, who somehow rhymed come and ransom. He lets me be his partner for beanbags in the tournament. Despite being completely unathletic, I'm surprisingly good at throwing the beanbags.

Ansel doesn't hover, but he's always watching, and he steps in when anyone has to take a break of some nature.

I'm constantly aware of him. We've locked eyes, several times, and it feels like we're catching each other looking. The protective nature and constant watching are easily explained, but it feels like more. The looks sometimes feel heated but not in anger, like it's something . . . hotter.

BEN SHOWS UP AROUND THE TIME WE SHOULD START COOKING DINNER. He brings hamburgers, hot dogs, and all the fixings. The idea is salivating.

"Morrigan helping in the kitchen?" Vito asks with a huff.

I raise my eyebrows and blink at him dumbly. "Vito, I know you didn't imply that a woman's place is in the kitchen."

"Uh." Vito stumbles. "I just meant."

"Ooooo." Sully laughs. "He stepped in that, didn't he?"

"I . . . just meant . . . that maybe she'd be more comfortable." Vito stops talking.

Ansel, who had been sitting on the swing reading a book, shouts, "Vito, you're on kitchen duty with Ben. Ripley, you get to help too."

"What did I do?" Ripley shouts at him.

With a laugh, Ansel taps his eye, indicating Ripley's mostly healed black one. "Teamwork. You two need to work out whatever the fuck is causing your constant bickering, and maybe cooking together will solve it."

Tossing my beanbag, I end our game, winning by six points. Sully high-fives me.

The guys start congregating around the fire pit, and Ripley and Vito begrudgingly head into the house with Ben.

The number of chairs is enough for us for when the kitchen crew returns. But the remaining guys all sit in every other chair. Sully sits closest to Ansel.

I'm most comfortable with Zero, who sits on the opposite side, but I'm drawn to the side of the fire between Ansel and Sully. Princeton and Zero don't seem as friendly when sitting next to each other. Princeton strikes me as an instigator, and while yesterday he was creepy, today, he seems more dangerous than before.

Ansel gives me a soft smile when I opt to sit next to him on the swing. It feels genuine, like he wants me there. He puts his book down and rests his hand on it. He's so close to touching me.

Watching him too intensely, I pull my eyes away, only to be startled when he blows a raspberry.

His voice is authoritative but respectful. Ansel talks like they're all equals. "It's been a great day. But I'm not ready to let Morrigan run with us. She'll come to work with us, but until she's better integrated, it's safer. We haven't had a woman out here in a while."

They all hang their heads and mumble in agreement with Ansel.

After the great day we've had, it seems unfair that he lets them think it's about them and not really about me. But it's better than the alternative: them knowing how vulnerable I am.

I want to fit in. What does that say about me? Would staying here with them — with Ansel — be the worst thing? Who even knows?

Ansel's hand is still on the book, and I can't read the title.

"What's the work this week?" Zero asks, breaking me away from my thoughts.

His deep voice is so interesting. When we joked earlier, I was tempted to keep him talking so I could hear it for longer. That phrase about I'd listen to him read the phone book? One hundred percent applicable.

"Mr. Hoppe needs help with a pole shed. The corners of the tin weren't nailed down right, and now everything's warping. He wants us to see if we can straighten it out and, if not, replace it. Probably a one-day job." Ansel shakes his head. "Then after that, we've fence lines to mend going into the weekend."

Zero nods along.

Sully groans. "I might go crazy if you keep us doing these fence projects."

His words feel unfair. It's not like Utah is bustling for work. It doesn't exactly scream City of Industry.

Before I think better of it, I let out a huff. "Right, because you weren't crazy to end up here in the first place?"

"I mean . . ." Sully goes quiet.

I've evidently said something he disagrees with, but I'm not wrong.

He chews on the side of his cheek, grumbling.

Ansel ignores what I've said and addresses his complaint. "Apparently everyone else finds it mind-numbing too. But it gets us out of the house."

"Are we not getting fun projects because we fucked up out at that lady doctor's house a month ago?" Vito asks as he and Ripley approach the ring.

They sit as far away from me as they can, and Vito gives me a stink eye.

I look to Ansel for guidance, and his entire body seems to have straightened as he looks at Vito. The hand that was resting on the book moves into his lap. *To Kill a Mockingbird.* Another required read. Interesting.

Ansel's voice holds the rough quality of a suppressed growl. "Her name is Doctor Cross, and she's a female and apparently a very skilled heart doctor. But we're not doing any more large projects because there aren't any more large projects. We might help with moving shelves at the library, but that's still up for debate."

"Kinda nice to not have a buncha jobs," Sully offers.

"I mean. I like being busy, but there's plenty of stuff we could get done around here," Vito agrees.

Ansel nods, only relaxing slightly. "Eventually, I've got to get that last cabin back in order. I'll order in supplies for it when I know we've got downtime."

"Bet you're looking forward to getting your house back," Princeton, the predator, draws out. A glint crosses his eye. "Sharing with Morrigan can't be all that great."

"You sayin' I'm bad company?" I snap at Princeton.

The way he looks at me puts me on edge, but furthermore, why does everyone talk around me like I'm not sitting right here? First at home and now here? I'm a person!

Princeton growls, clenching the armrests of his chair. His lip curls in a snarl.

It's hardly a logical response to my question.

I snarl back and snap my teeth at him before smiling, trying to end the fight. I'm all bark and no bite, and this was a bad idea.

Time moves slowly when you're in danger.

And before I know what's happening, a wild dark gray wolf springs toward me, but Harbinger is in front of me.

I don't even have time to react.

The wooden swing Ansel was occupying lurches back and forth wildly. *How does he shift so fast?*

The pale wolf of death is as I remember, light white fur flecked with gray around his neck. He tangles with Princeton's deep gray tones.

I can't move. I don't know where to move.

I seem to be the only one frozen in fear as Zero and Ripley start backing away toward the house. Dangerously, Sherman steps closer to the fray. Sully weaves by my side, shifting his weight back and forth from foot to foot and back again.

Growls and angry snarls escape from Harbinger and Princeton as their wolves battle. It's a blur of fur and movement.

A crunch is followed by a loud yelp. Within the space of a heartbeat, Harbinger ends up on top. He stands above Princeton, and it's clear who the winner is.

As their fight ends, Sherman pitches forward. I put my hands over my mouth to try and not scream.

*Sherman, no!*

His wolf, a striking gray with russet red accents, throws itself toward Harbinger. Dust flies as Harbinger's body hits the ground with a thud.

I haven't seen fights like this since I don't know when. My heartbeat is so loud in my ears I can't hear the snarling of wolves over it.

Princeton lies broken on the ground, breathing shallowly, but Harbinger isn't fazed.

*If Ansel dies, what happens to me?*

Moments of fangs and teeth and blood splattering against the sand pass before Sherman stills.

I guess I don't have to worry about asking my question.

I watch with bated breath, focusing on Sherman's chest. It rises and falls with proof of life, and I exhale in relief.

Harbinger turns slowly and looks at Sully. Sully looks away, offering Harbinger his neck in submission.

In the briefest second, I diverted my eyes and Harbinger moved. Now he stands maybe a yard away from me, bearing his fangs.

I meet his glare and squirm under the scrutiny of his demonic eyes.

In submission to the force of his power, my head bows and my eyes drop to my lap. I'm sure I reek of fear.

# CHAPTER 30

# ANSEL

BEN IS RESETTING PRINCETON'S SHOULDER THAT I DISLOCATED AND broke. In his wolf form, Sherman skirted along the yard's edge and down toward his cabin, no worse for wear.

Harbinger refused to tuck away for nearly twenty minutes. Even now, Harry is uncharacteristically pressing forward. He got to spill blood, yet I can feel him on the edge of my skin.

Nothing in my arsenal of happy thoughts calms me down. *Sunset, stargazing, running through the woods with Judah's pack, watching movies.* Nothing. Even without a solid grip on Harry, I've got to keep working.

When I turn back toward Morrigan, she bows her head again quickly.

"Morrigan. House. Now." The growl and Alpha command roll out of me like a bulldozer.

I know she isn't connecting with her wolf, but I let the Alpha command out anyway. It won't work, but it gets the point across.

Smart enough to mind, she scrambles out of the swing and

up toward the house. I stalk after her as Princeton yelps when Ben pulls his shoulder back into the socket.

Harbinger wags his tale to the sound. Would they let me be the keeper of the fractured if they knew how messed up he was? Or would I be put in the ground myself?

We're barely in the house, and Morrigan starts. "I'm sorry. I didn't think."

I'm seeing red. My tongue runs across my teeth, and I contain as much rage as I can.

"That's the problem right there, Morrigan. You didn't fucking think!" My voice comes out at a yell.

The growl coming from my chest rattles me hard.

I stalk over to my bedroom and push in the door. After throwing on a shirt and jeans off the pile of clean clothes from Lena, I come back out to the living room. I'm covered in drying blood, but I don't care.

Morrigan's arms are at her sides, and her head is bowed.

I take a few deep breaths, trying to further cage Harbinger back.

*She's a kid. She's made a mistake. She doesn't know the rules.*

Harbinger pulls back a bit.

The problem is, even with reminding myself and him, I'm still angry. They didn't need to get hurt today. She caused this.

"Do you know what you did wrong? Or is this something I've got to explain to you?" I manage to hammer the growl out of my voice by the end of my questions.

"I said I was sorry." Morrigan articulates in her own tone of anger.

Standing before her, I grip her bottom jaw and tilt it so she looks at me. Her black hair falls out of her eyes. They're drawn together, full of anger.

"If he had hurt you, I would have had to end him. The only

reason Princeton is still alive is because I was next to you and fast enough to get there." I shake my head at her.

Morrigan pulls her head out of my hand. "Let me go, drive me to town, give me a couple grand, and I'll be gone. Problem solved."

My whole hand wraps around her upper arm, and I pull her back toward me. She struggles, but I'm so much stronger than her it's useless.

"You're not going anywhere but downstairs." I lead her over to the top of the stairs.

She laughs. "You know I don't have a wolf. You can't make me go down there."

"Morrigan. You're what, a hundred pounds soaking wet?" The laugh that comes out with those words is much louder and far darker than I want it to be.

The fact she thinks she can escape me to avoid the kennel is laughable. I toss her over my shoulder before she has time to object.

Her ass is so close to my face. The idea flicks across my brain to take a bite out of the soft denim-clad thigh pressed against the side of my head.

*What the fuck?* I shake my head, ignoring it. What did Ezra call that? Invasive thoughts? *Nothing to worry about. Probably.* Ridiculous time to think of anything other than the task at hand.

It's a little harder to spin the dial on the vaulted basement door with my left hand, but I manage. After flicking the locks open on the kennel, I walk her to the one she's practically lived in and set her down at the opening. I shove her a little to get her out of the way of the door and slide it closed, then lock the secondary mechanism.

"I didn't do anything wrong!" Morrigan argues as I hit the main lock button.

"I'll bring your dinner down later. The fact that you don't understand that you're the one who fucked up in this situation is really telling," I snarl.

I close the vault door behind me, leaving her in the darkness of the kennels.

SULLY AND ZERO TAKE PRINCETON DOWN TO HIS CABIN FOR THE NIGHT and come back up for pack dinner. As we sit out on the porch and eat our burgers, the meal is significantly quieter than the earlier day's festivities had been.

"So, no pack run?" Zero says, pushing broccoli around the grilled vegetables on his plate.

Ben shakes his head and assures him with a smile. "We'll still go. It'll be good."

Zero nods.

Sully leans over and rubs shoulders with him, assuring him. "Besides, it's been too long since you outran me."

That makes Zero smile. Everything about Zero is long. Wolf form and human, he's all limbs. I swear he can run at least fifty miles an hour, but it's not like we've ever tried clocking it. Maybe that's something we could do for fun this week: see the top speed of the guys.

"Why is she so bitchy?" Ripley, of course, decides to ask. "Is she going into heat? Or is that what younger females are like these days?"

"Ha." Sully laughs. "No, I've got four younger sisters, and if any of them were as disrespectful as that, my mom and dad would skin them alive."

Ripley nods, biting the side of his cheek. Ripley's in his late forties, and it shows sometimes with his expectations of people. He shakes his head. "Maybe this is why I was never blessed with a mate. Women folk are —"

I cut him off with a quick thud of my fist against the table. I'm not having sexist bullshit here.

"Sorry, boss." Ripley stops without me having to say anything.

"She will be dealt with. She's got issues. Might I remind everyone that none of you were as stable as her when you arrived here." I look between them and point at Ripley first. "You were hanging on by a thread and wouldn't shift into your human form for a week and a half. I threw scraps of food to you through the bars of a kennel." I point at Sully next. "You were catatonic and didn't speak for four weeks." I point across to Vito. "You literally told me to kill you for a whole month." I turn my finger to Zero.

"I couldn't eat." He shrugs, admitting his own shortcomings. "I was starving."

I number off the rest. "Sherman couldn't string a sentence together, Princeton literally couldn't stop growling. In the spirit of honesty, I'm not sure where he's headed. And Ben?" I laugh when I get to the end of the roll call. "Well, Ben hasn't changed at all."

"I resent that." Ben snorts. "I'm not sorry for what I've done."

Shaking my head, I sigh. "Okay, no, you've got a point. You're still not sorry 'bout what you've done, but instead, you've come to be the only one holding it together around here. I'm not sure what I'd do if you weren't here. Fuck, if you find a mate and I've got to try to replace you . . ."

"Oh, that's never happening." Ben laughs, his eyes wide with terror.

Zero laughs really hard — it rumbles like thunder — and

he gasps for air. "Better . . . knock . . . on wood. You . . . jinxed yourself."

We're all laughing within a few seconds. Ben leans over and taps his knuckles against the side railing of the enclosed porch.

I wipe tears from my eyes. It's a relief to remember that today could have been worse.

It was almost catastrophic, but it wasn't. Today was a success, even if it was rough.

THE PACK GOES OUT TO THEIR CABINS TO SHIFT. BEN STAYS BEHIND FOR a few moments, helping me clean up from dinner while I make a plate for Morrigan.

Ben nods toward the basement stairs. "You put her in the kennels as punishment, but she's young, and let's be real, no one is ever really prepared for a situation with them all at once until it happens. You can't take your frustration out on her forever, Ansel."

"I'm not." My answer is quick and snappy. It surprises me.

Ben raises his eyebrow at me.

*Am I?* It's uncomfortable to think about this. Something's not right.

Harry pushes against my skin. My confusion about Morrigan flusters us both.

I look away from Ben. "Shit. I am. What's it about her that gets under my skin? I'm better than this."

I walk toward the basement stairs, leaving her plate on the counter.

"She's Walt's kid, and you haven't forgiven yourself for him yet," Ben says softly.

Frozen, before I take that first step down the stairs, I listen to him.

He sighs. "Ansel, I know you've heard it before, and it irritates you to hear it, but I'll say it again: you did everything you could have for Walt. He didn't want to live in a kennel. Her not seeing him that way . . . was better for her." Ben adds that last bit in there, and my heart throbs.

My hand rests on the railing, and I hang my head. *When did I get so emotional? I don't get invested, and I don't lose my head.*

Drawing a deep breath, I start down the stairs and let the air escape my lungs with each step. I spin the lock open and enter.

So we're not blinded, I flick the switch for the lights on the far side of the basement before walking in. Morrigan sits up from her slab but doesn't say anything.

"You ready to be civil?" I ask quietly, tucking my hands in my pockets, watching her watch me.

Morrigan rolls her eyes before running her hand back through her hair. It tangles, and she pulls forward the shed hairs, flicking them off her fingers.

Harry huffs with an agitated pressure against my skin. Her lack of sense and respect for us grates him.

When I don't prompt her for an answer again, she finally gives in. "I'll behave."

"Sorry doesn't cut it round here." I unlock the main latch and then, once at her cell, hit the secondary and slide back the bars. "You've lived with a pack, but from what I know about Los Angeles, it's a lot more civilized than here. You don't fight for pack placement. The old laws rule here. When someone new comes or goes, it disrupts the pecking order. Things get bloody. So the problem of what to do with you is causin' enough of an issue. That's without your smart mouth and bad attitude egging everyone on."

She walks out of the kennel through the gap and tries to stay as far away from me as possible. But it's not far enough.

I grab her upper arm. She tries to jerk it away, and a flash of fear rips through her. It passes across her eyes as she goes rigid.

I let go.

What I was saying doesn't matter anymore. That reaction I missed earlier is so telling.

*I'm an idiot.*

Harbinger protected me when I needed him. Her wolf abandoned her. I have to do better. *I will do better. How many people have given up on her? I won't.*

Morrigan stands controlled behind me while I slide the kennel door closed.

Ushering her out of the basement, I work to make things better. "If you're not too mad, I'd like you to sleep upstairs tonight. Tomorrow, you'll come to work with the guys. More exposure for them will help you settle."

Morrigan's silence says a lot, mostly about how she's not forgiving. But when we get to the top of the stairs, she quickly goes to the plate I set out for her and starts eating. The food goes down quickly.

"Hey." I stop her, putting my hand on her back and sliding the plate a space away from her chest. "Easy. There's more. It's not going anywhere."

She swallows, the panic leaving her eyes, and takes the next bite slower. I pull out the leftovers and set them in front of her, showing her there's more.

A chorus of howls outside calls to Harbinger. We both want to be running with them. My skin itches, and I scratch the back of my neck, shuddering.

"You can put me in a kennel if you want to run with them," Morrigan volunteers. "But I won't make a break for it if you leave me out either. I don't have a death wish."

*Tempting.*

I look over at her, but the answer is in the way that she isn't looking at me. Morrigan needs me here. "No, putting you in a kennel isn't getting me anywhere. I've forgotten what's been done to you. I can only imagine what I've done to try to help you has set you back in healing. I'll do better."

I haven't been perfect. Shit, I haven't even been good. I lean forward and rest my elbows on my knees. Part of my heart wants to go to her. It needs to comfort her. I'm being strangled by feelings I don't know. I rub at my sternum over the soft texture of my T-shirt. While it's a bit soothing, it's not right. It's not enough to stop whatever it is I'm feeling.

"Whatever you see fit," Morrigan grumbles lowly.

There's no way I can let this go. I can't go into the darkness of night with her feeling like no one really cares about her. She doesn't see what she's done wrong, but that's not her fault.

Ben's right. I'm not putting the blame where it belongs. She's reaching for the storage container across to the other side of the counter without getting out of her stool. It wobbles, threatening to topple.

Pointing to it, I ask, "Do you want one more or two?"

Her eyebrows raise in shock, and she bites her bottom lip. "Two patties, one bun?"

Harry hums inside me, settling.

Trying so hard to assure her, I force a smile. It's weird I don't feel smiley, but I know she needs it. Caring for her, meeting her physical needs, has to be the start of both of our healing.

## CHAPTER 31
# MORRIGAN

EMOTIONAL WHIPLASH IS WHAT THIS DAY COMES DOWN TO. I AM mentally exhausted from yesterday, and then today was a roller coaster soaring to new heights.

Ansel slides my plate with the delicious double-stacked, California-style burger over to me, and I could melt. Cravings are cravings, and this is one I was afraid I'd miss out on.

"I need you to work with me," Ansel says as he leans back, stretching his arms high overhead.

His shirt is a hair too short for his long torso, giving me another view of that salacious V shape I got a glimpse of yesterday. My eyes go wide, and I train them back on my plate again. *It's been way too long since I've handled myself if I think this is a good idea for my first time.*

"Morrigan?" Ansel presses.

This seems to be our new normal position. Him on one side of the island and me on the other. It's oppositional and totally uncomfortable. *But with the rogue dirty thought, maybe the space between us is a good thing.*

SARAH JAEGER

"Work with you how?" The words come with a small growl — a small growl such as a wolf would make.

It surprises me, but I don't want him to know that.

"Work with me. Talk to me. Tell me what it is you're thinking." Ansel rattles off words. He continues in another breath. "Tell me when you're uncomfortable, if something's buggin' you, if there's a way I can make it better for you."

The food in my mouth turns tasteless and gross. I swallow it before putting the burger back on the plate.

"You could let me go." It's the first thing that comes to my mind.

"No." Ansel shakes his head.

I shake mine right back at him and mimic his body language, sitting tall and leaning back. "Listen, I'm obviously not a fit here. I don't have a wolf. I'm not meshing with the pack. Clearly, I'm more trouble than I'm worth. A little cash, and I'm on my way out the door. No one would have to know."

Ansel runs his hand down his face and pulls on his beard before motioning to me from top to bottom. "Will you stop trying to run from me? I'm trying to help you."

As much as I'd like to believe that Ansel can help me, that's fucking laughable. There's nothing that hasn't been tried before. Really, what do I expect Ansel to do? I snort.

"What are you going to do about it, Ansel? Spank me?" I snark at him. *Punish me for not obeying Alpha's orders? I'm not a child.*

Ansel turns to look at me, and his gaze darkens.

Harbinger is there.

What I don't expect is the seductive laugh. The laugh he used before he tossed me over his shoulder and carried me down the stairs. When my body was pressed against him and the promise in that laugh sent goose bumps over my skin, distracting me from the gravity of the situation.

220

With a downward tilt of his chin, he smirks. "Why? Does it work?"

My pussy clenches. *Traitor.*

He steps closer. Harry is still there looking at me. Something in the last second changed between us. "No, seems you like that. Punishment isn't effective if you like it. How much pain can you take, Morrigan?"

I swallow hard. My mouth dries out. He wouldn't really do this. *Would he?*

"Or is that the problem?" Ansel pauses. When he moves closer again, the overhead track lighting flickers in his eyes. "You're acting out because I'm not taking care of you enough? The right kind of care."

Ansel rounds the island, closing the distance between us. He stops short, just out of reach.

My pulse quickens. There's always been tension between us, but it's shifted. Why does it feel sexual and devious now?

His voice hits that low tone when he pushes the Alpha command at me. "Morrigan, I need you to tell me. How do I help you?"

A tiny tingle runs slowly down my spine, causing me to shudder.

"I don't know what I need." I whisper the truth.

Not knowing is not allowed in Gerad's pack. You're expected to know or find the answer. Not knowing and telling Ansel that I don't know feels defiant. *But does he see it that way?*

Ansel takes one more step forward. He wraps his hand firmly around the back of my neck and pulls me toward him.

I resist, slightly pushing back against him.

He growls.

Instantly I still.

Sliding off the stool, I get myself closer to him. When I step into him, he drapes his arms around me. My head rests against his chest, and I listen to his heartbeat. It's steady. Not racing like mine.

After a long, ragged breath, Ansel steps away from me. My body steps forward, instinctively following him. I tilt my head up to look him in the eye, and my gaze stops on his lips. They look soft and kissable.

*What would happen if I . . . went for it?*

Ansel steps away from me again, and this time, I don't follow.

"Finish your burger." His voice has a different kind of growl to it.

It's not Harbinger in his throat. Instead, it's that gravelly tone guys get when you cut them off. The gravel of arousal.

*This isn't right. Why am I feeling these things toward him?*

# CHAPTER 32
# ANSEL

Mr. Hoppe's pigs are a pain in my ass. And I wish that was one of those fancy metaphor things. Big boar came right up and took a bite at the back end of my jeans.

The whole caravan of work trucks comes into the city limits, and we pull over at the fuel station. I start our ritual of giving the guys enough money for fuel to get the trucks home and back to town again tomorrow morning for the next day's work. They go in and pay while I let my pump run, the numbers slowly going up.

I walk over to Morrigan's window, and she looks at me expectantly.

"Peanut butter malts?" I offer with a smile.

They were her favorite. Walt and I used to joke she was no less than half peanut butter.

Liveliness flickers in her eyes, but it's not her wolf.

She squashes her excitement down, and with a shrug, she answers, "That wouldn't be so bad."

Well, at least we're back to half-hearted answers instead of flirting with danger.

I open her door, and she hops out. After stopping the pump and putting the hose away, we walk together into the convenience store. I can feel eyes on my back as we walk past the guys, but I pay them no mind. They've all had special treatment of their own nature when they've come to live with me.

If it takes a softer hand and gallons of peanut butter to get Morrigan's wolf to come out . . . I'll buy a peanut farm.

"How's your day, Ansel?" Mr. Feldman asks when I open the door.

Zero, the straggler in the store, touches my shoulder on his way outside.

I'll have to check on him later. It's odd for him to search for physical touch.

"It's going well, Mr. Feldman. Tourists been treatin' ya good?" I ask as I open my wallet.

He wobbles his head a little. "Not as many of them as I'd like, but season is early. At least I've always got you boys to keep the pumps running."

I nod and give him a smile. "I don't know what I'd do if I didn't have to stop here twice every day."

Morrigan snorts and rolls her eyes.

Mr. Feldman looks at me before saying quietly, "First time I've ever seen you with a woman in your truck. Gah, she looks like Walt."

*Please don't let her explode over that statement.*

Puffing out my cheeks, I take a beat before answering. "Yeah. She's Walt's kid."

"Morrigan, right?" Mr. Feldman smiles at her.

She gives him a polite wave and a tight smile back.

He continues. "Gah, I miss him. You two were thick as thieves." Mr. Feldman nods, patting my hand as he hands the change back to me. "It's a shame. But you did the best you could."

I nod, tossing the change in the charity jar, and turn toward Morrigan.

She's actively avoiding me and the conversation about her father. Much like Zero did to me, I reach out and gently brush my hand against her shoulder. Morrigan leans into my touch and follows me out of the convenience store.

Trying not to read into her accepting my touch as comfort, I lead her back outside. The next door over, on the same block in town, is the ice cream shop.

Holding the door open for her gives me the view of Morrigan biting her bottom lip. Her eyes are lit up with excitement. Without any prompting or encouragement, she walks up to the glass case and looks at all the different flavors.

"Oh my lord. Ansel, is that who I think it is?" Mrs. Hoppe, with wide eyes, looks between me and Morrigan.

"Morrigan, do you remember Mrs. Hoppe?" I ask, prompting them both.

"Oh gosh, the last time she was in here . . ." Mrs. Hoppe turns to Morrigan. "You were at least a foot shorter, but by the looks of you, probably weighed about the same," she croons before tapping her finger on her cheek. "Let me guess, peanut butter malt with sprinkles and whipped cream. No cherry."

*How the hell does the woman remember that after all these years?*

Morrigan nods.

*When did she get to be so shy?*

Mrs. Hoppe moves about behind the counter, making a peanut butter malt for Morrigan, and then she starts a chocolate one for me.

After Mrs. Hoppe finishes, she hands us our shakes. We both look at Morrigan, who has stars in her eyes as she stares at the frozen sweet goodness in her hands.

"What brings you back to Utah, dear?" Mrs. Hoppe asks, pulling Morrigan out of her trance.

Morrigan licks her straw and looks at me to cover her ass. When I don't, she swallows and shrugs. "I suppose the same thing that brings everyone back to where they grew up."

With a nod, Mrs. Hoppe accepts the answer.

After a small fight about wanting the ice cream to be on the house, Mrs. Hoppe lets me pay and tip her for the malts.

Morrigan heads outside and back to the truck. And my view falls south as she walks. It's been two weeks that she's been here. And it's put a healthy bit of weight on her. Her ass is starting to fill out her jeans. *Fuckin' hell. Walt's daughter. Get that out of your head.*

To distract myself, I look around the town as we walk. A few other people on the sidewalk wave as we pass.

"Why is everyone so nosey?" Morrigan grumbles when we get back in the truck.

Sipping on my malt, I drive one handed. I pull the truck away from the fuel pump and merge back onto Main Street, heading down the block toward the hardware store.

It takes a minute, but I come up with an answer. "'Cause they want us to belong. Humans are kinda like packs in a way. They want to invite you in and know your life and struggles. It's important to them that the people around 'em feel safe. It's why, even before we were outed to the public, many of the people in Nameless knew, in not so many words, that me and the people round me were shifters."

"Wait, what?" Morrigan turns in her seat, apparently not buckled in, to look at me.

"Put your seat belt on," I scold.

With a grumble and a lip curl, she complies and goes back to sipping more of her malt.

"It was impossible for me to keep it quiet. If I was maybe

228

having wolves potentially running wild through people's property or needin' them to be able to get out and socialize, someone had to know. So, I slowly let a few people in on the secret." Chocolatey goodness soaks my tongue as I wait for Morrigan's shock to wear off.

"And other wolves knew you did this?" Morrigan shakes her head, playing with the straw in her cup.

"The important ones did." I nod. *Cade knew. Close enough?*

I pull up in front of the hardware store and park in a spot a little way down the block. Armed with a small list of supplies it'll probably take to keep the pigs out of everyone's butts, I'm ready to go when my phone rings.

It's been about a week since I talked with Ersilia and Gerad. So it's not surprising they're calling, but it's not welcome.

I unbuckle my seat belt and fish the list from my pocket. The feeling of Morrigan's eyes staring at me across the narrow cab doesn't make staring at Gerad's name and number on my phone more pleasant.

"It's Gerad. If you want to sit here and listen, you're more than welcome to, or if you trust that I'm not scheming with him, you can take the list into the hardware store and start picking things out." I offer the note out to her.

Morrigan looks between me and the paper.

The phone rolls the call to voicemail, but it immediately starts to ring again. *Needy bastard.*

Morrigan nods at me. "Answer it."

I push the button and raise the phone to my ear. "Hel —"

"Where are you?" Gerad's question is more of an angry statement the way he says it.

"Oh, doing great, thanks for asking." I shrug at Morrigan and roll my eyes.

When Gerad growls, I answer his initial question. "Same place I always am, I suppose."

She's stock-still. Morrigan is barely breathing. The malt is held loosely in her lap as she waits with bated breath for Gerad's response over the phone.

"I'm at your house. You're not here. Where the fuck is she?" Gerad seethes.

His heavy breathing wheezes through the phone. It's gross sounding, and my lip twitches involuntarily.

I blow my lips out with a raspberry and laugh at him. "That sucks for you. My house is pretty boring. TV only gets two channels. I'll be home after I finish this run into town. Morrigan is with me, so it'll be a bit. If you see Ben, want to tell him that his truck is getting an oil change, and I'll have Morrigan —"

The disconnect jingle happens, and my phone lights up, showing that he hung up. I shake my head. "Rude."

Morrigan turns from me and looks back at her malt. She uses the straw to stir the mostly empty cup. The way her shoulders slump hurts my heart. But I don't know what I would do if the men from Harry's memories were to show up. Can't hardly blame Morrigan for this response.

"He'll wait. Don't worry about him being here." Realistically, I know those words won't comfort her, but it's something.

TWENTY MINUTES LATER, I'VE GOT ALL THE SUPPLIES FOR BUILDING A hog-proof fence loaded in the back of my pickup truck and we're ready to go home. Well, we're ready to deal with the other pain in my ass today.

"Goodbye. You be a good boy." Morrigan pets the hardware store's resident dog. He followed her everywhere around the store, always wagging his long tail at her praises.

It brings a smile to my face to see her behaving sweetly toward another being. She's starting to warm up out of her shell, and who knows how Gerad being here will change that.

"Ready to go?" I ask, tipping my head toward the truck.

Morrigan shakes her head. "I won't ever be."

"I get that."

A DINKY LITTLE RENTAL CAR IS PARKED IN THE MIDDLE OF MY PARKING pad, blocking both main spots in front of the house and my garage. Pulling the truck more into the 'yard,' I sigh, trying to displace the frustration before I start dealing with public enemy number one.

After putting it in park, I climb out of the truck and look across the cab at Morrigan.

The whole flight or fight response has picked one, and she's sitting there, looking out the window, like a deer hoping a car doesn't see them in the middle of the road. The car, of course, being Gerad.

Through the windshield, I can see him with his arms crossed in front of his dress-shirt-clad chest. He's trying to look intimidating and self-important. Trying.

"Stay here," I offer Morrigan. The course of action is set in my mind. "He won't stay long after he hears what I have to say."

I close my truck door and stride across the driveway, tucking my hands in my pockets. I'll at least try to have a civil conversation with him.

"Where the fuck have you been? I've been waiting for three hours." Gerad scolds me as if I'm a petulant child.

There was a two-week period when I thought he was kinda okay as a person. It was short lived, started seeing right through him. It's really rude that whatever powers that be in the universe, who control fated mates, would give Ersilia someone so cruel. But I don't make the fated mates.

Walking toward him, I answer, "Well, first we went to work, then to the fuel station, oh then got some malts, then the hardware store —"

"You knew I was waiting," Gerad growls.

"You called me two hours ago. How was I supposed to know you were here longer than that?" I fight with logic.

Harry snarls inside, and I hold him back. *Keep it together.*

With a shrug, I motion to the house door he's blocking. "Doors unlocked. I told you the TV worked. It's not my fault you showed up unannounced."

"I came to get my daughter," Gerad snarls at me, and his lip curls with the threat.

Grinding my teeth together, I take a second. *Is it worth it? Shit, fuck it, of course it is.* The imaginary gloves come off. "Morrigan isn't your daughter. Let's stop pretendin' you're worth even half the weight Walt was. You could only wish to sire someone as sweet as her."

Gerad laughs. "Clearly you haven't met the child if you think she's sweet."

"What do you want, Gerad?" I bypass his statement.

He extends one long finger toward the truck, pointing at Morrigan. "She's coming home with me."

Harry and I watch him intensely. The way he stands before me, his arrogance in the matter, is so silly.

Gerad keeps talking. "Get her ready to go. If you can't put her wolf back with whatever yogi bullshit you do out here, that's fine. I have a mate lined up more than willing to breed one back into her. Just own up that your methods aren't perfect. I'll take care of my daughter."

*What the fuck is yogi?* Anger roots in my stomach, but I keep

SCORCH

it there. I won't let him see he's getting to me. Not any more than I already have.

I wobble my head back and forth as if I can't make up my mind. "No can do, Gerad. State of Utah and federal government signed her over to me. Nontransferable. She's got eleven and a half months left here. You'll have to tell her intended that their mating is delayed. If you're scared to talk to them about it, fine — you've got my number and evidently directions to get here."

Gerad steps forward, so there's maybe three feet between us, getting in my face. He's growling.

Mrs. Hoppe would tell me that he's adorable in her condescending tone. The one she reserves for the teenagers of town doing stupid shit. That sarcastic tone echoes in my head with the thought of ending him.

Harry pushes forward with excitement toward bloodlust. The anger I've kept under wraps blooms.

I yawn lazily. "Listen, Gerad, I 'preciate you comin' out here for a discussion, but I'm not able to give you what you want."

"She's still a child, Ansel. The laws don't apply. I'll petition the Sovereign to bring her home," Gerad growls.

"What the fuck do you mean? She's nearly twenty," I snarl.

"It's ridiculous you've made it to be the Reaper but you're clueless about laws and old ways."

Gerad talking down to me doesn't bode well for the thorns in my anger. "I'll spell it out for you. Female wolves who haven't gone into heat are considered juveniles. They're property of their parents. Not their Alpha. And I am her father, and Ersilia wants her home." Gerad smirks, using those claiming words over her.

His words hit my brain like a sledgehammer, opening up a wall I'm not prepared to demolish, but I can't focus on the meaning behind them. All I can do is focus on the fucker

233

swinging the hammer. *Think fast, Ansel. You need an answer. Give him a reason he can't take her.*

Lightbulb moment. "For all purposes and intention things, she's human until she's not. But pup or not, Morrigan can't leave. Human laws keep her here, and as an Ardelean Alpha, I've the right to overrule any of the laws, new and old. It's my blood right."

*I think. Cade will back me up, and that's good enough.*

"Is that it, Ansel?" Gerad asks. "You think you can keep her to yourself?"

"Don't be gross, Gerad. She's a pup and the daughter of my best friend. The only thing I'm doin' is protecting her from your dumb ideas on how to fix a wolf. Go back to California. Give Ersilia my regards. I'm not entertainin' this conversation further." Growling seems to get Gerad's attention.

Harry comes forward to the point I'm not sure I can hold him back. The deep brown-black color of his eyes scares most wolves. Gerad falls in the category of most. The breeze blows around the house and pushes his scent right up my nose. Acidic, thick, and, in some sort of way, enjoyable.

"Go home, Gerad," I order, pressing a command to him, hopeful it might work.

Only Cade should be able to command another Alpha, but sometimes, if someone's afraid of you enough, it works.

Gerad shakes his head, and his snarls and growls turn into a half-assed grumble. "You'll regret this, Ansel."

"Mm-hmm. Have a nice day. Appreciate you stopping by. Don't come back." I dismiss him.

I stand in the driveway, and he squeezes into his stupid little rental car. He mutters as he backs around into my makeshift yard before speeding toward the main road. If I cared, I'd call him and tell him to go slow, or that dinky tin can will end up in the brush. But I don't. Would serve him right to crash it.

"Thank you." Morrigan's voice behind me startles me.

"It's nothing I wouldn't do for anyone else." I lie to her.

If she was anyone else, I might have folded, called the government, and seen about options for transferring her care to someone else. But she's not anyone else, so it doesn't matter.

Unfortunately, what Gerad told me about Morrigan makes complete sense. It also happens to change everything. It colors the way I've been feeling about her. My mouth goes dry as my stomach sinks.

*Can't be. Don't even think it.*

# CHAPTER 33
# ANSEL

THE JOB AT HOPPE'S FARM, WHICH WAS SUPPOSED TO TAKE ONLY ONE day, has taken the whole crew two more days, as suspected. Two more days of testing my patience. I'm over this week, and it's only Wednesday.

Princeton's shoulder healed up most of the way, and he's been more help than anticipated, but Morrigan's presence is still causing issues. She's snapped more than a few times at the guys, and while I've been mediating, her headstrong nature is doing nothing to protect her from what's going on.

Top it off, Mr. Hoppe's pigs broke through their regular fence as we were trying to leave today. The prey drive of my fractured pack and the chase were almost too much to resist. But I can pleasantly say that no pigs were hurt in the process of wrangling them back home. Sully and Zero ended up scuffled and trampled, but the pigs all survived.

Morrigan and I are covered in sloppy, dirty poo mud from trying to grab the little piglets and carry them back. The stench alone has us driving home with the windows down. I'll have to let the truck air out overnight. Maybe wipe the seats off in the morning.

Morrigan pulls her shirt off over the top of her head as we walk in the back door.

My breath hitches in my throat, and I cough. "Really?"

She stops and holds it before her, looking over her shoulder at me. "What, why take it upstairs? It's disgusting. I'll toss my clothes in the machine here."

The coy glint in her eyes gives away that she knows what I mean. Not persuaded by my statement, she finishes sliding the dirty piece of clothing off her arms and steps over to the laundry closet.

My tongue feels thick in my mouth as she bends to open the washer and casually flicks the shirt into the bottom of the stacked machines.

I messed up on Sunday. Somewhere between the anger and the fear, my head got turned around. The last two nights have been filled with dreams I don't know how to comprehend. Unlike visions of people's deaths or the musings of Harry running back through the violence of our life, these dreams are pleasant. I'd go so far as to say happy. That is, until I remember who she is.

My heart beats hard against my chest as I look at her. *Why am I feeling this?* No, she's Walt's daughter. This isn't happening.

I shake my head, trying to clear it like one of those little doodle pads.

"You okay, or are you having a heart attack over there, old man?" Her shoulders rise and fall while she toes out of her shoes.

Temptation in a five-foot package wiggles her way out of her jeans that a few weeks ago were too large. Now, they cling to her thighs, which have come back to a healthy weight and tone.

*To sink my teeth into those thighs.* My cock throbs.

Even her smallest movements talk to my body on a level that can't happen.

"You need more clothes," I observe, trying to move past the inappropriate things I want to do to her body.

*I mean, at least it's not thinking about killing her?* I try and fail to cut myself a break.

Turning away from her, I sit on the bench. The wall of the closet that I converted into a shoe bench gives me only a bit of safety from the perfect view of her body. I focus on my boot laces and their frayed ends, untying them carefully and, most importantly, slowly. Buying myself some time for her to disappear up the stairs.

Harry, however, focuses on listening to her. It's not enough, and he pushes more intensely to lay eyes on her again.

"I really could use a bra. I've never had boobs this big," Morrigan grumbles.

I pull hard on my lace, and the leather of my boots creaks under the tension. *No. What is wrong with me? No, I'm not looking. No.*

Harry pushes, focusing harder on Morrigan. I struggle to hold him back. Why is he so interested in her? *We've seen a naked woman before. There's no reason to look at her.*

"We can take a special trip into town this week. If the store there doesn't have what you need, then on Saturday, we'll head down to Moab. They've got more options." I let out a slow breath.

There's nothing left to do. I've untied both boots. I pull them off slowly and slide out of my socks. Opening the tongue, I give them room to air out.

The problem is I haven't heard her move. I can sense her, and she's no farther away than when I sat down.

Morrigan speaks. "That would be nice." Her voice takes a funny tone. "You could also give me a grand and leave me in Moab. Then you'd never have to see me again."

That doesn't sound like the same tone she used that told me she really wanted to go. It's like she's poking me for a reaction.

"I told you. You're my responsibility. You're goin' nowhere." I keep looking straight ahead. *Mine.*

I can see her in my peripheral vision. If she doesn't move, I'll have to. Probably. *What are the odds I could stay here all night? Bench isn't that uncomfortable.*

Morrigan huffs. "Right. You keep saying that, but it's been two weeks. Have the humans even asked about me? No. Let's face it, you're constantly watching me. It's like you're on the verge of killing me. You don't need me here."

Harry huffs somehow as if he disagrees with her statement. He's focused on her still.

I can't exactly explain to her that it's not my fault the wolf is obsessed. I'm doing what I can to protect her. It doesn't feel murderous. But I don't recognize these feelings. Harry must be confused.

We're both confused. That's all. Maybe I should call Dinah? Mercury or some other planet might be doing some sort of dance. It's got everyone crazy and it'll pass?

"You're safe." I stand up and face her.

Morrigan's leaning one shoulder against my bedroom door. Her arms are wrapped around her, pushing up her small breasts.

They're probably the perfect size for my palms. The composure I had is retreating again.

*Fuck, I can't be doing this. I really can't be thinking like this.*

"Neither of us believe that, Ansel." She bites and releases her bottom lip before looking down my body, like she's thinking about me or somethin', but instead turns to walk away.

Something in me snaps.

# CHAPTER 34
# MORRIGAN

His hand wraps around my forearm as I turn away from him. The roughness of his fingers is different from how I anticipated his touch would feel. It's the first time he's touched me since Sunday, when we had . . . whatever that was in the kitchen. I can still feel that hug when I think about it. But more than that, the unusual desire is still burning.

He spins me back to face him, and my eyes meet his. I'm locked in place, watching the bright green fade to the rich, deep brown, nearly black, of Harbinger.

"Trust me, Morrigan. You're not near death." His words are a heavy vow I didn't expect to feel in my soul.

It feels heavy but it fits.

I'm not sure how long we stand like this, eyes meeting and holding steady.

Something stirs deep inside me. Pushing around, it squirms and causes me to shiver.

The corner of Ansel's mouth turns up into a small smile, and he steps into my space.

I divert my gaze by dropping my head away from him, submitting.

Harbinger deserves that respect. I've been grossly out of line. It was on purpose, but since Sunday, I've been wondering if Ansel would come up with a new way to punish me. Is that what the distance between us has been about all along?

It's not what I want. I don't want to be pushed away or dismissed. I want to be closer.

In contrast to the roughness of his fingers on my arms, the softness of his lips on my forehead is wildly unexpected. When they leave my head, it's like we're both frozen, waiting, unsure where to go.

If I want to see what this is between us, this might be my only chance. *There's no rule saying you can't be the one to initiate your first kiss.*

Ansel shifts his weight, preparing to take a step back.

*And, even if there is . . . fuck the rules.*

Following his step back, I rise on my tiptoes, step up to him, and press my lips to his.

Kissing is different from what I expected. Not because I initiated it, but it's more. Movies depict sparks, fireworks, and silly leg lifts. Those aren't accurate representations. Maybe that's the problem with movies; they can only show you a stand-in concept for an abstract idea.

This is the fire of desire. It's a burning pulse. It's a part of you that comes alive.

I press my tongue forward, and he lets me kiss him deeper, taste him fully. His tongue gently plays with mine. His hand leaving my forearm and running up my shoulder into my hair fuels the flame. I step closer to him. Everything in my entire body wants more of Ansel.

No, it's not a want. It's a need. If this is what kissing is like, it's a wonder that anything else in the world gets done. I'm consumed and overwhelmed by the way Ansel kisses me back.

My hand finds his T-shirt, and I curl the soft fabric in my fingers. He feels my intention and pushes himself against me. The denim of his jeans brushes my naked thighs. I draw a deep breath and pull in the thick, heady smell of wolf, fur, and earth, but there's also something more, a woodsy, sweet scent. Cinnamon?

Ansel presses against me. Stepping along the outside of my legs, he guides me until my back meets his bedroom door. It's off limits through that door. I've seen glimpses inside but haven't entered. If we opened it, I could be completely surrounded by his delicious scent. We could lie among his sheets, wrapped up in his bed.

*I want that.*

Harbinger's low growl grounds me.

I'm no longer concerned about being wrapped up in his scent. *No, fuck. More.*

I want to be wrapped around the bulge pushing against my stomach.

I pant quickly against our kiss. Pushing up on my toes, I try to get closer to where he would fit inside me. Does he know what I need? *I need.*

Stop.

Vacant.

Empty.

Cold.

Ansel has stepped away.

He shakes his head and covers his mouth with his hand. Ansel turns away from me and picks up his tennis shoes before going out the back door.

I'm alone, naked, and rejected.

One moment, we're locked in an embrace, pulled together by our own gravity, and in the next heartbeat, I'm lost in space. Floating and alone in a desolate place, I'm left to crash-land on my own.

# CHAPTER 35
# ANSEL

I saw them. The eyes of her wolf are hauntingly beautiful. Pale yellow that almost look green. They drew forward in a slow wave.

Then I lost control. *Why would Morrigan's wolf, finding its way back to her . . . affect me?*

But seeing her, seeing those eyes, I lost control.

Shame pours through me like water from a leaky bucket. A small part of me understands why this is happening to me.

Walt would gut me from chin to stomach and lay me out for the vultures to find.

I gag. I take a few steps out of my yard over to the scrub brush and lose my stomach's contents.

*What the fuck is wrong with me? How the fuck did I lose control?*

I kissed her back. I don't have words.

What my first heave missed comes up in a second wave.

Harry pushes the memory of the needy sound she made and how her naked body felt against ours. Even through my clothes, it was tempting.

*Why? Why now?* It's only been blood and death. Blood and

death I know. It's natural. It's my life. Why is he now pushing something new forward?

I don't want this, especially not with her. Relationships don't go well, not for someone like me. The few times I've ever engaged in anything more than hookups at the holidays only ended in painful acceptance of my station and role in life. It's better not to hurt her and push her onto a better life.

Pulling on the collar of my shirt, I try to cool myself off. My cock is hard, uncomfortably so. I adjust my jeans.

This, kissing, inappropriate thoughts, anything other than my job to protect her and get her whole, can't happen again. I'm here to keep her safe, evidently mostly from herself. This isn't a relationship. Morrigan is here as ordered by the government. I'm keeping her here until the terms are over. Then I'll settle her into another pack. Somewhere far away from Gerad, her mother, and me because that's what's best for Morrigan.

Seeing her wolf proves she's not fractured, just dormant. It proves that Morrigan is here for now, not forever. There's nothing wrong with her.

I run my hands back through my hair. Pulling at the binder, I release it and then put it back up again. I tighten the pull, getting the strands off the back of my neck.

There's got to be an answer to why this is happening. I've got to talk it out.

I walk down the slope of the driveway, knowing right where I need to go. Past the scrub brush tree, which somehow has decided to thrive right here, I walk directly to Ben's deck.

It's not surprising when Ben opens the side door to the house and steps out with a bottle of scotch and two glasses. He walks out to meet me.

I only come down to his house when something's wrong.

"Ben, I don't know how to ask this." I settle my butt into the chair by the door.

Slumping, I rest my elbows on my legs.

"Oh, this'll be good." He groans as he relaxes gracefully into a hammock chair adjacent to me with a drink in hand. With a second thought, he asks, "Have anything to do with the rental car that was here Monday?"

My shoes have become fascinating, apparently, because I can't bring myself to look away from them. "Wolves sexually mature before nineteen, right? Usually like sixteen or seventeen?"

"Boss, you're pushing it, calling yourself probably mid-thirties. You're just now asking about the birds and the bees?" Ben isn't talking down to me as much as I was expecting, but there's a punchy undertone, letting me know the goat still has horns.

I drag my eyes off my shoes long enough to look up at him, hoping he somehow understands what I'm thinking. Ezra might be the mind reader, but Ben's pretty sharp.

A long moment passes before he lets out a low whistle. "The hellcat hasn't gone into heat. Ever?"

I raise and push my hand out to him, handing him the answer.

"Shit." Ben leans back, sipping from his glass. "What are your thoughts?"

"Well, you know about the wolf issue. I know she has one. I saw her shift when she was younger, and tonight we were — Doesn't matter." I stumble on my words, not ready to say that I pushed her up against my bedroom door. I draw a breath and try again. "Well, I saw her animal in her eyes. But, obviously, my first thought is for her health and if there's something wrong." I pause and puff out air before speaking. "My second thought is wondering, because of the last few years, if she's, I don't know, stunted?"

"Both are possible," Ben confirms with a nod and another

sip before continuing. "I'm absolutely positive she won't want to talk to me about it. Even if she did, I'm not equipped to handle feminine issues."

I look at Ben. "You're a vet."

"I'm not an ob-gyn." Ben shakes his head, raising his glass to punctuate the statement.

"Right." I nod, trying to make my point. "A vet and we're wolves."

"That's not how this works." Ben rolls his eyes.

I lean back in the chair. A cold sweat breaks out over my skin. *Time to come clean.* "There's another piece to the issue."

"Oh?" Ben snorts, leaning forward and setting his cup on the side table. "Do tell."

I don't like these thoughts Harry feeds me. His darkest desire of her fuels my fear of what might be coming.

Saying this out loud to Ben feels dirty. "If it is that she was stunted, now that she's in a stable place, having consistent meals, and taking fucking care of herself." My voice trails off. I can't even bring myself to say it. "She's never . . . She's never gone into heat ever, which means that . . ."

"You could be her mate, and that's why you're having all these interpersonal issues." Ben finishes the thought in a more pretty way.

I look up at the sky. Maybe a rogue lightning bolt will hit me? Slim chance, seeing as how it's a beautiful day. No clouds in the sky. But still, chances are never zero.

I'm in over my head. I can't believe I'm even considering telling him the incident between us. Not because he'll judge me, but because he'll have no choice but to try to fix it. The only other option for her is an Ardelean Alpha or her pack of origin. I'm not ready for those options.

"It gets worse." I keep watching for some deity to throw a lightning bolt my way.

Ben lets out a whistle. "How much worse could it be?"

"Way worse — I kissed her." I admit it, and it feels as dirty as I thought it would.

I drop my head from the sky to look at him. Waiting for him to tell me I've got to send her away. That I need to brace myself for disciplinary actions. *Death.*

"Welp, you're screwed." Ben shrugs. Then he laughs. "Can't fight fate. What do you do?"

I throw my hands up. "I have no idea. Frankly, I don't exactly feel great thinking any sort of thoughts about Walt's kid. She's a minor by our laws, Ben. I've fucked up."

"First, our laws are a dumb technicality. She hasn't gone into heat because of what's happened to her, not because she isn't old enough to consent or know what she's doing. It's to protect real children, not grown-ass women with attitude problems. Second, Walt wouldn't want you upset over this." Ben picks up his cup again and pauses before taking a sip. "He was a good guy. He wanted his kid and friend to be happy."

"Fairly certain he wanted those things separately." I sigh, scratching the top of my nose with my palm. My stomach is unsettled again. "Damn it, Ben."

"Call Dinah. Have her fly out, or you and the little hellcat could go to Maine. Maybe some time with an actual functional pack will help ground her." Ben now goes into fix-it mode. Fixing the problem I initially brought up. He swirls the ice in his cup. "Though, with how agitated you've become lately, and the working theory . . . you might not have that kind of time."

The sound of my truck driving down the gravel road cuts our conversation short. I crack a smile. "Well, she was due to try and steal that or burn the house down."

"Or both." Ben stands up out of the hammock. "Here, take my keys, I'll go and make sure your house is still standing."

# CHAPTER 36
# MORRIGAN

WE KISSED.

Ansel and I kissed.

My first kiss.

We kissed.

I loved it.

If he gave me the opportunity, I'd be under him in an instant. Or if he wants me on top. Would he be more force-ful — *No, don't think about this.*

Then again, it's not like I haven't imagined what my first time would be like. It's never been with someone so . . . rough around the edges? Off limits? I don't know because my brain is one of those stalled-out planes, screaming 'mayday' and circling toward the ground. I'm panicking but, at the same time, lost in a blissful free fall.

We haven't even talked about what Gerad said to him about me being a 'pup.' I'm coming up on twenty. It's a techni-cality that I haven't had my heat. There's nothing juvenile about me. But the way Ansel responded — evacuating the premises — tells me he doesn't feel the same way I do.

I've showered and gotten dressed. The odds and end clothes from the dresser all fit differently. I don't recognize my figure, and the tag size on the clothes has to keep getting bigger. It's bad enough that they're mostly all hand-me-downs. Now I'm changing sizes. I've never been this strong, and it's an adjustment.

Ansel isn't in the house, and it feels empty. I don't have to listen downstairs to know he's not here. I feel it. He didn't take his keys with him when he went outside.

Whatever happened between us, those dreams meld with when we were so close in the kitchen. I don't get it, not entirely. Something has changed between me and Ansel over the last few days. The tension between us has shifted. It's no longer fueled by anger and irritation. Something about him draws me in, and I don't fully understand it. I've never been one of those girls who fawn after guys. But there's something . . . growing. It's led to my behavior today, provoking him, and then that kiss.

I've been dreaming about the possibilities since he threw me over his shoulder to take me downstairs.

For every ounce of confusion I've had with Ansel, there's another sickening feeling in my stomach. It's one I haven't had time to think about because I've worked with Ansel's crew every day since it happened.

But the fact is Gerad knows I'm here. By showing up on Monday, he's proven he is not afraid to come here, to face Ansel, and stake whatever claim he thinks he has over me. There's no way I'll give him a chance to take me. I'll only go if I'm kicking and screaming. He'll have to make me.

Gerad is resourceful. If there's a pack law or a loophole, he'll find it and exploit it. He'd petition the human government and get me transferred back to his care if it came down to it.

When it comes to getting me back, there is no level Gerad won't stoop to.

And I've already given him a two-day head start on finding a loophole.

*I can run.* If his keys are where I remember seeing them and I go right now, I can make it. Leaving Ansel isn't what I want, but hiding from Gerad is more important. *Unless Ansel pulled the truck in the garage.* I don't know if I could get it unlocked.

I dart down the stairs, and Ansel's keys are right next to where he was sitting on the bench. After slipping on my tennis shoes, I open the front door slowly. The truck is right where we got out of it with the windows rolled down. He's airing it out from the stench of the pig farm.

Ansel isn't in the side yard, and I don't hear his footsteps anywhere nearby. The coast is clear.

*Freedom.*

I dart around the vehicle and clamber into the cab. As I sit forward on the seat to reach the pedals, something causes me to pause, my fingers hovering over the key in the ignition.

I need to go, and I need to do it now.

The engine roars to life. There's no turning back. It won't be long before he figures it out.

I put my foot on the gas. I want to go as fast as I can, but the dusty road doesn't allow for speed. Spinning out across the landscape isn't conducive to escape.

*No risking it. This might be my only chance.*

My fingers brush my lips. It may have been nice to say goodbye, but Ansel made it clear he'll never let me leave on my own accord.

# CHAPTER 37
# ANSEL

DRIVING A LITTLE FASTER THAN I'D LIKE, I CATCH UP WITH MY TRUCK, and Morrigan, about five minutes down the road. I beep the horn on Ben's truck, and Morrigan checks the rearview mirrors. She steps on the gas, trying to pull away from me. I back off and slow down. She's going too fast. It'll kill me if she gets hurt. There's no choice but to settle in for the drive.

We pull into town, and Morrigan watches me follow her in the mirrors. I know my truck is almost empty. *Please don't run it out of gas. That's a new fuel pump.* It's a hopeless request; no one trying to escape cares about a fuel pump.

Much to my surprise, Morrigan eases my truck next to the pump at the fuel station. I pull up behind her and hop out, waiting for her to take off at a sprint.

The town has seen it all before. So, it's not surprising when faces peek out of buildings along Main Street to watch. Morrigan doesn't hop out though.

I walk up to the door, and she doesn't even turn toward me when I stand there, looking at her through the rolled-up window. I open the door and step back, holding it for her.

I smile with pretend joy. "Fancy seeing you here."

"Whatever. Had to try." She moves to slide out of the vehicle, but I put a hand on her arm to stop her.

Her eyes are glassy, and my heart aches in my chest again. I know I did this. I caused this pain. It's eating me up inside. Something I did — no, I know what I did — caused her to do this. Now it's up to me to make it right.

"Pull it over to the parking space." I indicate where I want her to put it.

While she parks, I gas up Ben's truck. His veterinarian tool truck is the only exception to my 'half tank or less' rule. Not that I'd ever advertise it. The whirring sound of the fuel running from the pump is soothing. I absentmindedly watch the numbers roll.

Morrigan leans against the side fender, looking down at the ground where she's moving her foot back and forth.

It's not her fault. This escape attempt is on me. She did the running, but I pushed her to do it.

The click of the pump indicates that Ben's truck has drunk its fill.

I motion Morrigan forward, and she follows me inside the fuel station.

"Hey, Ansel." Mr. Feldman greets me. "Just the fuel for you?"

"Yeah, mind if I pay for the other truck too? I'll send the guys down to pick it up tomorrow." I motion over my shoulder at my truck.

"You got it." He pulls out an envelope from the till.

We've done this dance for years. I pull out a few twenties and hand them to Mr. Feldman. He tosses them in the envelope before ringing up what I actually ran through the pump. I put it on the Ardelean account and sign the slip.

Morrigan stays by my side, silently brooding. I usher her

out of the fuel station and into Ben's truck. Once in the driver's seat, I take a few minutes, debating what to do.

The sun has gone down, and sitting here in the cab isn't getting us anywhere.

"Can I have dinner before I get put down in a kennel?" Morrigan sighs softly.

I shift the truck into gear and pull away from the pump, heading toward the diner. It did occur to me to go home and cook dinner, but an hour from now, I'll be that much more exhausted.

"You're not going into a kennel," I answer.

The acidic scent of fear overpowers the smell of pig shit in an instant.

"Shit, Morrigan, you're not going in a kennel because it doesn't work on you. You're safe. I messed up. You don't pay for my mistakes. If you want me to call Cade on your behalf, I will." My stomach rolls. *I should probably do it myself.*

"I'll behave. There's no reason to get someone else involved. This isn't your fault." Morrigan's voice rattles.

While sitting down in the diner and not having to cook sounds appealing, I smell like pig shit and who knows what else. I don't want to stink the place up, so I place a quick order with the teenager working the counter and head out to the truck to sit and wait.

Silence in the cab gets more and more uncomfortable by the minute. I've never been happier to see a bag of takeout in my life. When the teen brings it out to the truck, I place it on the seat behind us.

Backing out of the space, I look over my shoulder. Morrigan looks away from me when my eyes pass her.

Once on the road, I offer, "I'm not the biggest fan of reheated food. Let's go to the edge of the property and park? Saves us about thirty minutes of more mushy food?"

Morrigan shrugs, not committing one way or another.

Through town, I don't take the turn that would normally lead up to the house. Morrigan turns her head to look at me but doesn't say anything. On the trail I've cut through, the scrub brush leads back up and around to a lower valley-like area with small hills wrapping all the way around.

When we're parked, I give her the answer. "If someday I come to a place in my life where I don't have to bring people home to rehab, I figured it'd be nice to have a spot closer to town. I didn't want to be in town. But I bought this parcel because it's closer. It's a stupid dream, but when it went up for sale, I figured land's an investment."

"It's not stupid," Morrigan answers.

She climbs out on her side and takes the bag with her. I follow out my door and along the box of the truck. Ben's truck bed is full of all the boxes and various storage thingamajigs of who knows what, but the tailgate at least opens freely for a place to sit.

Morrigan sets the bag on the tailgate and turns around, pushing herself up to sit on it.

I hop up and let her open the bag.

She opens the boxes on top first. There's a slice of pecan pie and a slice of caramel apple. She hands me the pecan one and a fork.

"Dessert first?" I question her, raising an eyebrow.

"We could be hit with an asteroid at any moment," Morrigan says flatly. Her face is completely serious when she continues. "What if we don't ever get to eat the pie?"

Finishing the sentence, she can't hold her seriousness together, and a smile breaks through.

"I can't fault that logic." *Pie first, great idea.*

Morrigan and I finish our pie about the same time, and she pulls the bag of food into her lap.

Holding it hostage, Morrigan tries to hint at something, lowering the inflection of her voice. "I have feelings."

"Feelings?" That doesn't tell me a whole lot, so I hope repeating it will get me more answers.

Through the low light and the perks of being a wolf, I watch her nod.

"Yeah. And I don't know what to do with them." Morrigan looks at me.

When I don't say anything right away, Morrigan turns back to the bag and hands me the top container without opening it, taking the second one for herself. Since I didn't exactly consult her before ordering, I guess it doesn't matter to her what she gets.

That ache in my chest is back, but I ignore it and open my take-out container.

She and I try to speak at the same time.

"No, go ahead," I offer.

Morrigan eats a french fry, indicating I should go first.

Giving it another moment before trying to speak, I draw a deep breath. "I want you to get looked at by a doctor."

"You don't have to." Morrigan shakes her head. Her voice comes fast with sharp syllables full of fear. "There's nothing medically wrong."

Obviously, I didn't lead with the right statement. But I try to meet her at her level. If no one else has listened to her before, someone has to start now. "Why do you say that?"

"You don't think Gerad has had me see dozens of doctors?" Morrigan deadpans. "I've been poked and probed, stuck with needles, and examined." She runs her hand over the top of her head like brushing off a bad memory. "No one's found anything physically wrong with me. No one's found anything in my blood work or anything else to indicate what's wrong with me. I highly doubt any doctor you can get out here in Utah can do better."

Utah doesn't have the best options. Mostly because the only wolf I know of with a medical license said no because he's not an ob-gyn. I also have to respect her decision. The knowledge that Gerad took away the right to her body makes me warm with the want for violence.

The task at hand is that Morrigan doesn't want to see a doctor. I won't make her. But if I don't offer my edge over any of Gerad's attempts, I can't know for sure.

"I was thinking more along the lines of Dinah Alloway. She tells me she's not exactly a doctor. I don't quite understand, but from my understanding, it's a bit more specialized?" I offer, cautiously watching her out the corner of my eyes and waiting for a response. Morrigan doesn't move, so I add, "And if Dinah thinks we should run some tests, then we could send them straight to Lena Alden for her lab?"

Morrigan pushes her french fry around the ketchup in the plastic container. "You would do that?"

I pull my phone out of my pocket and set it on the tailgate between us. "Say the word. I'll make the call. We'll fly out to see her in Maine, or she can come here."

"You'll use the information against me." Morrigan's voice changes from hopeful to quick with anger. "Get proof there's nothing wrong and hand me back to Gerad."

The longer she talks, the clearer and clearer it becomes. Her voice holds anger on the surface, but fear prickles underneath. There's a sting in my heart.

I try logic. "If I were gonna send you back with Gerad, wouldn't I have done it when he was here?"

Her fear fuels anger inside me. Morrigan doesn't deserve this, and I'll be damned if I ever let her truly fear someone hurting her. Gerad will never get close to her again.

Morrigan huffs, "Decoy?"

"Morrigan, nothing you and Dinah talk about has to come back to me. She won't tell me anything you don't want her to. She's my cousin, but she takes what she does seriously. This isn't some sort of conspiracy or whatever." I try to reassure the fear she voiced, but I also address my guess at the one she won't. "If, and I don't think there is, but if there is something wrong, it would be better to know than to keep guessing."

Morrigan doesn't say anything for a long time. We eat in silence, both of us taking time to look up at the night sky.

"Are those rumors true? Did you really kill Dinah's mate?" Morrigan whispers the question like it's some big secret.

"I didn't kill him myself, but yes, I let Harbinger loose on the pack when we went for her." I answer honestly and at full volume.

"You really think she'll see me?" Morrigan's voice holds this tiny sliver of hope as it grows louder.

"I know she will," I answer. Lighting up the screen on my phone, I offer, "Want me to?"

The second her head moves in the tiniest nod, I move, not wanting to give her a second to go back on it.

Dinah answers after two rings. "Yes. I'll see her. Took you fucking long enough. I'll come to you. I need a break from Judah being stupid. I'll text you my flight details once I book it."

"Bugsy, that's just rude," Judah yells in the background.

"Thanks, Dinah. Keep me posted." I smile at Morrigan. "I love you. See you soon."

"Love you too." Dinah starts talking to Judah. "I'm leaving."

Morrigan's mouth hangs open.

A few seconds after I've disconnected, she finally speaks. "Clearly you . . ."

My phone starts ringing. I debate sending it to voicemail, but I answer it the same way I talked to Dinah. "Hello?"

"Status update," Gerad snaps, cutting me off.

Harry snarls.

I agree with the anger Harry has chosen. *Why the fuck does he think he gets a status update?*

"Hello, Gerad, nice to hear from you. Weather is fine —" I start, correcting him.

"I don't have time for your childish games. What's my update?" Gerad cuts me off.

"Gerad? Can you hear me?" I crinkle my napkin over the top of the phone.

"Ansel. Where's my update?" Gerad repeats like it'll get him one.

He threatened me last time we talked, and that's not something I should brush off entirely, but I can avoid it, for now.

"I." I fight back a snicker. "Hear. Give. Call. Morrow."

Morrigan covers her mouth with both hands, but her shoulders bounce as she laughs. It's audible even through her hands.

# CHAPTER 38
# MORRIGAN

A<small>NSEL HOLDS THE TRUCK DOOR OPEN FOR ME TO CLIMB IN AFTER WE</small> finish eating. He tucks the bag of garbage farther ahead in the footwell and closes the door.

When he finally climbs in and turns on the engine, I've got to say something, anything, about what happened.

"I'm sorry I kissed you. I crossed a line. I'm sorry." The words aren't as assured as I wanted them to be. It's a genuine apology, but it doesn't hold the level of control I wanted to display.

I don't know what I can do to make it better. He seemed like he wanted it too. The way he kissed me back made me think it wasn't wrong. And then he left. But when you piss off the Alpha, you apologize. Even if it's stupid.

There's no reason I need to see what his face does when formulating a response, so I turn to look out the window. Silence stiffens the air around us, and my face heats as breathing becomes harder. I fucked up. Really, really bad.

*It felt right. He felt right but is acting so wrong.*

After a massive exhale, Ansel draws a breath. "It's not your fault. I need to get you moved out of the house. You need more independence."

*What does that have to do with anything?* I'm so frustrated I ball my fists, clenching them in my lap. *Why is this his response?*

With a deep breath, I force my fingers to straighten out against my thighs, and I circle back to where I tried to start the conversation again. "I have these feelings, and I don't know what to do with them. They aren't something I'm used to feeling."

"Let's wait until Dinah gets here to assume anything," Ansel says cryptically despite the fact that he was all talking and bonding a few minutes ago.

*Assuming? Why won't he talk about this?* My fingers lock together tightly, and my knuckles turn white as I squeeze harder. The growing attraction I have for him is new. Unexpected. But his treatment of me in this, the dismissiveness, is spiking a new level of rage toward him.

One more try, and maybe he'll hear what I'm saying. "The feelings started before I kissed you. It's different."

He doesn't say anything. Not for lack of trying. He opens his mouth to try to speak but closes it again. After a few moments, he scratches a spot in his beard. "Let's not jump into anything. There's no reason to think your feelings are anything. Let's give ourselves some more time. It'll be good for me to get you into a cabin. Space and all that."

There's no way I'm alone in this. I felt him, hard, against me. Is that why he won't talk about it?

I don't want to make any assumptions. "You have feelings too?"

Ansel's grip tightens on the steering wheel. "Let's not —"

"Jump to any conclusions. I got it." Shut down again.

I give up and look out the window.

His adamant denial of admitting to anything, everything,

screams inside my head. Ansel also has feelings and attraction. It's the only logical conclusion because if he didn't, he'd say so. I'm positive if Ansel didn't have feelings, then he wouldn't be so against talking about it. He'd want to clear the air.

I force my fingers apart and wiggle them to get blood flowing again. With nothing else to do, I cross my arms in front of my chest, trying to contain the rage in my ribcage from exploding out into the world.

If he would talk to me, maybe we could . . . could what?

*Hmmm.* The buzz of that is an echo in my brain.

It's nothing though. I'm tired, and the crunch of the tires on the road underneath us is relaxing.

"MORRIGAN?" ANSEL'S VOICE CALLS.

I open my eyes wide.

The truck has stopped moving, and I'm quick to unbuckle. "Yeah. Sorry. Tired. Stupid pigs."

"Right? Stupid fuckin' pigs." Ansel rolls his shoulders and, after gathering the garbage from the truck, leads the way to the back door.

Stalling at the top of the stairs, I wait for Ansel to order me down to the basement. He said he wouldn't, but I don't know that I trust it. Everything is overwhelming and confusing.

*Safe.* This word comes into my brain from nowhere.

Uncharacteristically, Ansel kicks off his shoes rather than untying them. He leans against the wall near his bathroom door and hangs his head.

When he lifts it and meets my gaze, the darkened eyes of Harbinger look back at me. *Harbinger isn't a threat this time.* I swallow, waiting while he examines me. *Ansel knows that too.*

When the darkness fades, Ansel sighs. "I've already decided

to break every rule for you tonight. We've got to find a better way to help you. But can we not do this again today? Dinah is coming, and by the sounds of it, soon. Let's say we did and just not? If you're hell-bent on running again, can it be tomorrow and not again tonight?"

If I didn't know any better, that tone sounds like he's begging.

He takes big breaths when I don't answer and pushes off the doorframe, extending his arm out toward the basement stairs to usher me down in front of him.

"I won't run. I didn't run from you. I ran because Gerad knows I'm here. If he knows I'm here, he'll find a way to get me back." I walk away from him and plop my butt down on the couch. "Go shower, though, you smell disgusting."

Ansel lets out a low growl. "I fucking hate that asshole."

"It's mutual, he hates you too," I retort without a second thought.

It gets a sharp laugh from him before the only noise is the sound of him getting his stuff together to shower.

The actions show trust and an expectation for me to be here when he gets done. But I couldn't leave if I wanted to. Dinah Alloway is coming here to meet with me, and more than anything, I want answers.

# CHAPTER 39
# MORRIGAN

THE MORNING LIGHT SEEMS BRIGHTER TODAY. AS I STRETCH, THE BED seems smaller. *Couch*, my brain informs me as I try to stretch out. I fell asleep? I don't even remember. The quilt tucked in around me is softer than the quilt I've used before. And it smells so much more strongly of Ansel; it's almost like cuddling him directly. It must have come from his bedroom.

"Good morning." Ansel's voice is behind me.

Sitting up, I look over the back of the couch. He's sitting at the kitchen counter with his book in front of him.

It feels too early. Rubbing my eyes, I slide out from under the blanket. "Morning."

"No work today." Ansel doesn't look at me.

Walking past him to his bathroom, I stretch out. "What time is it?"

"Close to noon," he answers without looking up. "I tried to wake you up for breakfast, but aside from what I think was you telling me to fuck off, you weren't up for it."

"Sorry." Some of my hair has fallen in my eyes, so I brush it back away from my face.

"Go get dressed. I'll make you breakfast? Lunch? Which-ever." Ansel closes his book and turns in the stool to look at me. "According to Cade, there'll be a work crew of like fifteen people here today installing the first half of the security systems. I've got to figure out how to deal with the guys," Ansel grumbles, and it's evident he's not thrilled with whatever this new security system entails.

He's not alone in his distaste for it. A new security system means more things to try and escape around. If Dinah Alloway can't fix me, then I'll need to flee and not get caught. Ansel is underestimating Gerad, and I don't think I'll convince him otherwise.

I'm halfway dressed when there's a knock at the back door.

"It's open!" Ansel shouts.

"Okay, well, that's the first security issue," a woman answers.

"Millie, good to see you again." Ansel greets the woman.

Throwing on clean clothes as fast as I can, I advance, light on my feet, to the loft edge and look over.

Ansel's pulled the woman into a hug. Green jealousy creeps inside. *Why is she touching him?*

"What? No hug for me?" A man huffs.

I look more directly down, and a man is carrying a large black tub of who knows what.

"Well, put that down, and you can have one too." Ansel laughs, and it's full bodied. He lifts his eyes to where I'm at. "You'll come down, or you gonna hang out up there all day? Either option is okay."

I'm surprised his offer is so genuine. There's no tone that would imply I'm being rude for not wanting to interact with his guests. If I wanted to, I could stay up here all day. But I want to know the security system. Know thy enemy and all that.

"Adam and Millie, meet my . . ." Ansel's voice trails off for a second.

*What was he about to say?* I school my features to keep the surprise off my face as I wait for him to finish that sentence.

"My newest resident, Morrigan," he finishes, nodding ever so slightly as I round the corner of the stairs.

Millie, the woman, smiles at me, and it seems so genuine. "Thank God. I thought this was another weekend dick fest."

That brings a smile to my face, but I don't indulge in the desire to laugh.

"I heard that." Another man carrying an additional black tub comes in through the back door.

He's unfamiliar to me as well.

He sets his tub down on the island and offers his hand to Ansel. "Michael Tate, Corinth Security."

He has a mop of dark hair and is broader, with a more dense type of muscle than the lean cut of Ansel. Michael Tate is what I pictured myself with as a mate in the past. Tall, dark, handsome, and overtly dominant, but now he holds zero interest.

"So, is this really necessary?" Ansel gestures to the two tubs. "This seems like a lot. We could tell Cade that you decided it wasn't necessary?"

Millie snorts. "Oh, Ansel."

"This is what I need to set everything up and get your house ready for internet. None of this is security equipment." Adam scratches his head.

He's shorter than Ansel, with cropped dark hair and glasses. Nervously, he keeps talking. "Cade said that if you have any questions, you could give him a call. I know it'll be an adjustment, but we brought some different sized monitors so you can pick what size you'd want. We can walk you through everything. He mentioned you might be a Luddite."

"Adam," Millie hisses at him.

He runs his fingers across his lips, zipping them shut.

Ansel pulls his hair off his neck and wraps it up into a messy bun. "The internet piece is mandatory?"

"Afraid so." Millie pats his arm. "But we can make it so only you get it here at the house and put a password on it. No one will have outside access if you don't want them to."

Ansel's body is rigid, and he doesn't seem to be breathing.

"Did you guys bring a streaming stick?" I ask Millie and then look at Adam.

"No . . . but we could get one?" Millie questions, looking at me and raising her eyebrow.

"Ansel." I draw his attention to me. "The internet can get you access to tons of movies. No more DVDs?"

That gets the smallest head cock.

He turns his attention to Adam. "No one can get on it but me?"

Adam confirms, "I can get a notice anytime a device connects too. Then I can run it past you to make sure it's supposed to be happening."

"I can deal with that." Ansel begrudgingly nods.

"I'll figure out where I can get a streaming stick from." Millie gives me a small thumbs-up from where she's crossed her arms over her chest.

An hour in, and it's clear Ansel is completely out of his element. He's trying to ask questions, and Adam tries to answer, but the two of them are struggling to come to language they can agree with.

Millie and Michael, using the dining room table, are

looking at topographical maps and talking about terrain and sensors.

"So, where does the power come into the house?" Adam asks.

"Uhm." Ansel swallows. "There's two separate power panels. One is in the basement, and one is in the utility closet through my bathroom. The basement is solar with a backup generator and can switch into the county's utilities. The house runs strictly on solar."

"You've two grids?" Adam's eyebrows are pulled together as he questions it. The 'Why?' is practically spelled out in the lines of his forehead.

Ansel nods but doesn't provide more of an answer.

"Adam, we talked about this." Michael groans, drawing Adam's and my attention. "Ansel is essentially wolf jail. The basement needs to be wired up that way."

"Oh, right. Sorry." Adam looks down, his face turning red.

# CHAPTER 40
## ANSEL

BY THE TIME I LIE DOWN IN MY BED, I'M EXHAUSTED. MY BRAIN hurts. It physically hurts. I didn't know it was possible for your brain to hurt.

Harry whines, unsettled by how frustrating today has been. All day long, it was a struggle with his territorial nature. I'm positive the next time we shift, it'll be a marking fest. Should start drinking more water now.

I didn't understand even half of anything Adam was saying. Morrigan stepped in a few times and made some things make sense. But one minute, she's helping, and the next minute, she physically withdraws and goes back to letting me try and figure it out on my own. Is this some sort of boundary I've made for us that she's afraid of crossing?

I want her to help because at least she seems to understand and somehow knows how to explain it to me. *Shit. At this point, I should ask.*

After calling Cade, I understand more about what he sees as a risk. His heart is in the right place, and this won't be the end of the world. It's just . . . hard.

Tomorrow's another long day of install. Apparently more solar panels and some satellite thing are coming. I guess the panels installed six years ago aren't supposed to be enough power for what we draw despite never having any issues.

Whatever this streaming stick thing is sounds kinda cool. But Lena normally screens my movies for me. There was an incident with one I got from a store. Apparently, it's called 'triggered,' and it was terrible. Wouldn't wish that feeling on anyone.

I've got to start telling the guys what's going on. We're putting solar panels on each of the cargo cabins and then security cameras outside. It's gonna raise some questions, but Cade's not wrong. Knowing if extra people are coming or going when I leave isn't the end of the world. Ben can't be here full time.

Overall, today was a good day. Hard, but good.

# CHAPTER 41

# ANSEL

"Alright." Starting this meeting with the guys isn't easy. I called for a pack meeting and chose to meet in the large open space of their shared driveways between all their cabins rather than bring them up to the house with the humans, but none of them missed the comings and goings of work crews. "Listen, some of you won't like this. I don't like this. But we're getting a security system this weekend. It might go into next week. There are cameras going up. You're each getting solar panels. Ben's house is getting the same treatment. My house is already getting rigged up."

"Invasion of privacy much? Is this even legal?" Princeton huffs, and it turns into a growl. "I'm not consenting to being recorded."

But, surprisingly, no one else is voicing or displaying any concerns or discomfort with the announcement.

"I'm not putting them inside. It's just the outside. There've been issues with the rest of the Ardelean packs. Rather than hoping that the fact that there aren't any directions for how to get here is enough to make people second-guess coming out, it's been demanded that we do this." I keep my voice level.

Putting him in his place would feel so good right now, but there are humans here and Morrigan is vulnerable.

Harry is back to pacing today. When Zero steps back, I know he's in my eyes and I need better control.

"Can I get a camera for the chickens?" Sherman asks sheepishly. "What if someone wants to take my girls?"

He picked up really quickly on my roundabout way of saying the fear is of intruders. It's a simple request, and if it makes Sherman happy, I owe that to him. If he can't leave, he deserves to feel included in decisions.

"I can ask them if we can do that. I don't see why not."

He gives me a smile in excitement at the possibility.

"Then I'm leaving," Princeton declares.

There's not enough energy in the world to deal with his bullshit today. "Well, that's too bad because I have your paperwork, driver's license, and cell phone. It's not coming out of the safe until a Pack Alpha is ready to take you back. So, start impressing me or start making phone calls on your dumb phone."

Sully and Vito snicker. Even though both know they aren't in any better positions to bargain their leverage out of here.

"Fine," Princeton snaps, his teeth clicking on the closure of his jaw. As quick as his rage came, it dissipates. "At least that fine piece you're keeping up at the main house is hanging round for a while. I'll occupy myself with her."

Zero steps behind Ripley and closer to Sherman.

Thunder has nothing on the growl Harry pushes out of me.

The sheer idea of this twat spending time with her is enraging. Inappropriate, but enraging.

Hiding the truth of the growl, I cover with an equally

important reminder. "There's no disrespectful talk around here. I catch another word of some sexist and derogatory shit about Morrigan, or anyone else for that matter, there are plenty of kennels downstairs we could fill. And I'll remind you that every single one of those container cabins lock from the outside."

A chorus of 'Yes, boss' flies around the circle, all except for one. Princeton is too good to acknowledge it.

"Do we understand?" I growl, locking eyes with Princeton and stepping toward him.

He draws a deep breath, trying to resist submitting to me.

It won't work. Harry is designed, destined, made, whatever the fuck it's called, to end The Leviathan. This kid is a blip of irritation when it comes to a fight to the end.

"I need an answer." I push the Alpha command at him.

As if I threw a right hook, Princeton's head snaps aside, looking away from me. "Yes, Alpha."

Normally, I'd feel bad for using the command, but well, I don't.

"So, what? No one gets to hang out with her but you?" Princeton goes right back to pushing his luck.

*Yes. Exactly.* A little jealous gremlin creeps into my brain. *No,* I correct myself.

"There's no reason you all can't come hang out at the house. I've always kept it a policy that the pack is welcome. I don't have the big fancy pack house like most alphas, but we make due." It's the right answer.

Judah would say the same thing. He'd tell me to extend an invitation. Having a controlled environment is better than letting things go unsupervised.

"You ready for us?" Michael shouts from the top of the small hill by the driveway.

The caution he exhibits is well placed. No wonder Cade

likes him so much. The watching, waiting, and deciding is the hallmark of The Leviathan.

"Yeah. Let's start at the far one and work our way back up?" I call back to him.

There's no logic in starting on the far end of the rows, but if Princeton is so concerned about security, it makes me think there's a reason to be cautious.

# CHAPTER 42
# MORRIGAN

When Ansel shouted at me that first night, I didn't think he could get any angrier. The phone call with Cade Alden, The Leviathan, is proving that assumption wholly incorrect.

"Are you fucking serious, Cade?" He shouts at the phone, holding it away from his face like he's trying to look at him through it.

*Should I show him it makes video calls?* Mmmm. No, that's probably too much technology today, even if it is really an entertaining idea.

"My fucking windows?" Ansel repeats. It's been ten minutes of yelling about it. "Cade, I don't need bulletproof glass. Who the fuck is gonna take shots at me? I live in goddam nowhere!" He paces back and forth across the short length of the house. He snarls, "I don't care that it's already here. Take it back. Surely, they can —" Ansel gets cut off by whatever Cade says.

"Yeah, Lena. I hear you." His shoulders deflate. He pulls out a chair at the dining room table and slumps into it, immediately completely disarmed. It's like a light switch, flicked off with a few words from the Ardelean submissive.

Ansel draws a deep breath, speaking on the exhale. "I don't understand why they want to change out my front door."

A tap comes to my shoulder. Turning, I look to see Millie. With a curl of her fingers, she beckons me to follow her.

Hesitantly, I leave Ansel in the house to finish his call.

After the door closes behind us, she starts. "Any chance you could get him out of here for a few hours?"

Eyebrows raised, I cock my head at her. "I don't have that kind of power."

"The crew is afraid of him. They don't want to work in the house if he's here," Millie explains and puffs out her cheeks.

"And if they don't want to work, it'll take longer." The understanding comes with a nod. "I'll figure something out."

*What will get Ansel out of the house? How long do windows take to install?* There's the obvious: making a break for it. That'll push him over the edge. No, gotta be something easier.

Just then, my answer walks up the driveway. The stupid designer clothes he changes into after work every day look so out of place in the red earth around us. Princeton wants us all to believe he's something he's not.

Millie follows my gaze over her shoulder.

She faces me again and rolls her eyes. The sentiment is shared, but there's absolutely no reason for him to know.

"Hey, Morrigan, I was wondering if you wanted to hang out for a bit?" Princeton sidesteps around Millie and practically cuts between us.

Impressive since Millie was already standing close to me.

The flirting makes me want to hurl. But it'll have to do. It doesn't take eyes to see that Ansel hates Princeton.

Playing with my hair a little bit, I push it behind my ear.

"Shall we?" He attempts to lead me down the hill toward the cabins by wrapping an arm around me.

*Oh, not so fast, creepy fucker.* "No, let's go throw some bean-bags." I dodge his advance with a sidestep.

Princeton looks at me with what I expected: the guilt-trip look. The one you get just before a guy tells you he has blue balls.

Millie looks over her shoulder at him with what I only assume is a death glare. She'd make a terrifying wolf.

"I guess," he finally manages.

Pulling the boards out of the garage, Princeton insists that only he should carry them. That they're not that awkward and heavy. The macho, tough guy act doesn't impress me, but I need him to assume things are going well.

There's a great view from the sliding glass door where Ansel is sitting, talking on the phone and staring out at the landscape, to where we are.

Standing on the same side of the board as Princeton, I purposefully throw the beanbag badly.

Evidently Princeton has the shortest memory ever.

"What, is that how you think tossing is done?" He laughs at me before launching straight into mansplainer mode. "Watch, it's all in the wrist."

Four more bad tosses later, and the classic predatory flirtation move comes into play. Princeton steps behind me, and the hair on the back of my neck raises. You never give your back to a predator, yet here I am, voluntarily letting him behind me.

The sliding glass door opens, and Ansel steps out on the deck.

*Come on, Ansel.* Can I will him into —

"Hey!" Ansel calls to get Princeton's attention.

Harbinger's dark eyes come forward.

Princeton hesitates but steps away from me.

"Morrigan, we're out of some food, want to go on a grocery run? I know we're lacking condiments." Ansel is stock-still watching us.

Now's the tightrope act. I keep a hint of reluctance. "I mean, we're kinda playing, but I guess."

"Suit yourself, but I don't know what you like, and there's nothing on the list." Ansel's fighting back a growl, his voice deeper and his lip curling up in a near snarl.

"No. I'll come." I sigh and turn to Princeton. "Sorry about our game. You can clean up, right?"

"I've got some barbeque sauce in the fridge if it helps," he offers.

How is that any better than the sole bottle of ketchup in Ansel's fridge? What is this, some sort of joke?

"No, I better go. He sounds mad." I step away from him.

Princeton reaches his hand toward me. "He doesn't own you. I saw the other dude come for you. If you need to get out of here, I'll help you."

*Is it possible to forget you're surrounded by wolves?* I shake my head. "You don't quite understand the situation. But thanks for the game."

Ansel has already turned around to head back into the house, which gives me the perfect excuse to jog across the lawn and up the stairs. Anything and everything to get away from the only person I'm afraid of here.

I barely have time to catch up with him through the house.

He snaps at Millie and tells her if anyone gets aggressive with them, to shoot to kill, but we'll be back in an hour or more.

The truck is started before I even get in, and Ansel backs out of the garage before my seat belt is buckled.

Ansel is a man on a mission, or a war path, and it doesn't seem like the fire burning in him is getting put out anytime soon. Certainly not on this trip down the driveway or on the road to town. Anytime we pass one of the Corinth Security or the solar company work vans, his body tightens.

If there was a way to make him feel better about what's going on at the house, I would do it. If I thought he'd tolerate me holding his hand or leaning against him, I'd push my luck.

There's something big between us. Anytime we're alone together like this . . . it's all I think about. Like right now, no matter how angry he is, and knowing how deadly he can be, the confined space with him should be unbearable. But instead of fear . . . I'm at peace.

*Ours*, that silly little part of my brain that doesn't fit anywhere inside me whispers.

It's a ridiculous thought.

"You gonna be okay?" I'm cautious in asking, slowly pushing the syllables out.

Ansel takes his eyes off the road to look over at me.

"I don't like you fl — spending time with Princeton," Ansel growls. He pulls his eyes back to the road but quickly looks back at me. "He's dangerous."

I bite my lips together. Now isn't the time to push his buttons, but I really want to. Instead, I change subjects. "I was talking about with the house."

"Fuckin' new windows and doors. Are you kidding me? What of my house is gonna be left by the time Cade gets done with it?" Ansel growls.

After a few minutes, he scrubs his hand down his face, stops growling, and goes quiet.

He draws a deep breath. "It's not my house. I'm lucky to live there. It's a small change. Today's an inconvenience. This weekend is a blip in the grand scheme of things."

"You don't own your house?" I question.

He's lived there as long as I can remember.

"Technically it's in my name. But I've never paid for it. The Ardelean Fund purchased it and the property around it. Cade assures me that nothing on this earth will make me leave if I don't want to, but it still doesn't feel . . ." Ansel's voice trails off. "It's too good to be true."

I'm not wise. I don't have words to tell him that if it's in his name, then no one can take it. Is that even a thing? I can't even trust that Cade Alden, the Sovereign Alpha of The Ardelean Bloodline, which really, who has a title these days, would come through on a promise like that. I don't know him from Adam. Well, okay . . . not *Adam*. The nerdy tech guy flitters across my brain.

ANSEL PULLS THE TRUCK INTO AN ANGLED PARKING SPACE ALONGSIDE the grocery store. He's a lot more calm than when we left the house.

"Ready?" Ansel asks, opening the door to his truck.

Surprisingly, when we enter the store, Ansel hands me a basket and turns me loose. I don't remember the last time I walked around a store and got to put things in the basket. Maybe never?

Less than five minutes later, Ansel finds me with a cartful of food.

"How do you . . . ?" I shake my head, looking at him and indicating to the full cart.

"List," he answers with a little wave of the piece of paper in his hand.

*Well, he does shop here all the time.* Putting one bottle of sauce in my basket, I shrug.

Ansel furrows his brow, and he looks like he's examining my entire being from the inside out. "I'll leave money up front.

You get whatever you need. Take some time. It's cold enough out that none of this'll spoil before we get home. I need some time anyway."

With a nod, Ansel rolls the cart right past me toward the front.

SURE ENOUGH, ABOUT FIFTEEN MINUTES LATER, I GET UP TO THE FRONT of the little grocery store, and a woman smiles at me. "You must be Morrigan."

"Yeah?" I load my basket onto the short conveyor belt.

"Ansel said you were pretty." Her voice is cheerful but resentful, maybe, when she says that.

"Thanks, I guess." *What do you even say to that anyway?*

The woman quickly checks my items across her scanner and then announces, "That'll be sixty-four dollars."

"Uh. Ansel . . ." My voice trails off. *Condiments are expensive.*

"Oh right, right!" The woman reaches alongside her till, pulls cash out of an envelope, and starts counting.

A few moments later, she hands me a hundred forty dollars in change and a receipt.

"Thank you." I pick up my bags from the end of her counter. *Ansel must also think condiments are expensive.*

"Have a good day! Can't wait to see you around!" She waves at me.

*This has got to be the strangest place on Earth.* I can't imagine a shop in LA keeping money up front for someone.

Once I walk out of the grocery store's entrance, I don't have to look far to find Ansel. He's sitting on the sidewalk with a bunch of kids.

One of them holds a book out in front of him.

Ansel's mood has significantly improved from earlier. His

eyes are bright, and the smile on his face is giving him little crow's-feet at the corner of his eyes.

"Oh, it's for sure the stegosaurus," Ansel explains. "With those spiny plates down its back, it's totally the most rock and roll lookin' dinosaur there is. It's my favorite."

"I don't know. The T-Rex is the king of the dinosaurs. It was this big," another child exclaims, his arms outstretched.

"They were really big, weren't they?" Ansel agrees, nodding. He looks at a little girl in the group who is being quiet and invites her to the conversation. "What about you? What's your favorite dinosaur?"

She's blonde and bashful, and she smiles and scuffs her toe in the dirt for a minute. Putting her arms behind her back, she twirls back and forth. Her little skirt pokes out from under her coat, waving with the movement.

A boy with similar hair says, "She doesn't have one. Girls don't like dinosaurs."

"They don't?" Ansel tilts his head with a look of genuine confusion.

"Dinos are for boys," the boy with the book pipes in.

Ansel looks mortally wounded and places a hand on his heart. With a gasp, he asks, "Did you tell the dinosaurs that?"

"No." The boys sound guilty, the round sound of the *o* dipping down.

"Well, I think it would be insulting to the dinosaurs if you told them not everyone could like them because they're only for boys," Ansel says, cocking his head in the other direction with an eyebrow raised. "Especially since most of the dinosaurs they find are girls."

"Even the T-Rex?" the girl pipes in.

"Especially the T-Rex," Ansel confirms, and the way he encourages her gives me the feeling women describe when they say their ovaries explode seeing a man playing with children. He's so good with them. "The biggest T-Rex they ever found is on display in Chicago. Her name is Sue. She was named after the woman who found her."

"That's cool!" the bashful blonde girl exclaims, her voice so much louder. "I like the T-Rex!"

A trio of women comes around the corner of the building from where we parked the truck to where the kids have Ansel as a captive audience.

"William and Thomas!" one woman barks out angrily at the boys.

She shakes the pharmacy bag in her hand at them. Her stern glare at Ansel has me standing up taller.

"Joey and Nadine, are you bugging Mr. Abbot again?" Another woman laughs.

"We weren't bugging him. He was telling us that Sue is a T-Rex, and she's a girl, and a girl found her," Nadine, still excited, yells at her mom.

The kids have wandered back to their mothers, and Ansel jumps up from the ground. He dusts off his ass and smiles.

"Sorry, Ansel," the woman with the blonde children says with a smile.

"Quite alright, Mrs. Dermont. It's refreshin' to have someone ask you what your favorite dinosaur is." Ansel smiles and tosses a nod my way. "Besides, all I was doing was being busy waitin'."

The mother of the two boys scowls at me. Then she runs her eyes up and down Ansel. "As long as you and your people aren't in town causing trouble."

I take it she is not a fan of the wolves.

Ansel doesn't engage in her negativity but cracks a joke. "Well, thought about goin' over to the hardware store next and rearranging all the seed packets based on color rather than alphabetical order. But if you insist on no trouble, I'll save it for another day."

With that, the third, very pregnant woman snorts. Her hand goes to her mouth to prevent the subsequent laugh from coming out.

"No baby yet, Mrs. Mullholland?" Ansel asks with his light-hearted, happy voice, and his cheeks pull up with a smile.

"My due date isn't for another six weeks, but babies choose their timeline." Mrs. Mullholland sighs. "I am getting miserable though."

"I can only imagine." Ansel nods. "If I don't see you before then, congratulations."

Ansel turns to me, and his smile falters when he sees me glaring at the woman behind him.

He points to the bags, redirecting my attention. "Find everything you need?"

"Mostly." I shrug.

He offers to take the bag, and despite wanting to prove that I'm capable, I let him.

Ansel adds my bags to the others in his truck bed, and as though he's divining the time like someone from a century gone by, he looks at the sky.

With a sigh, he asks, "Suppose the work crew will trust I've calmed down yet?"

"I mean, if you're sure the groceries won't spoil . . ." I look past him down the block, indicating toward the ice cream shop.

"I do believe I could go for a cake shake." He nods in agreement and tosses his head for me to get in the truck.

# CHAPTER 43
## ANSEL

MORRIGAN AND I PLACE OUR ORDERS, AND WHILE WE'RE WAITING, MY phone rings.

Cade's name shows up on the screen.

"Go." Morrigan nods toward the door. "I can bring them out."

*Is this the same woman I picked up a few weeks ago?* I leave her waiting by the counter and head out the door.

"Cade?" I answer the phone.

"Hey, Ansel, you holding up?" His voice is softer than the last time we spoke.

Seeing as how I nearly ripped his head off through the phone, it's surprising he even tried to call again. I lean my ass against the grill of my truck and cross my arm in front of my chest, supporting the one holding my phone to my ear. February's still winter, and I should have brought a jacket, but I was in too big of a hurry to escape the house.

Blowing a raspberry, I answer, "I'm making do."

"I know you don't get it. I'm sorry I couldn't make it out

there to be there when it all happened." Cade apologizes and continues. "I heard Dinah's coming soon though."

"Yup," I answer.

His heart is in the right place. I know it is.

"You planning on forgiving me before Equinox?" Cade asks. "Or should we reschedule your flight here for Solstice?"

Morrigan comes out of the ice cream shop and looks at me with a smile. Her lips are wrapped around the straw on her peanut butter malt, and my mind goes blank.

"Ansel?" Cade asks.

"Yeah. Uhh." I rack my brain trying to remember what he asked. "Equinox is fine."

"I love you," Cade tells me. "I wouldn't do this if I didn't."

"I know. I love you too. But I gotta go drive these groceries home." I hang up on him.

Morrigan walks over with my cup held up close to her chest. I offer my hand out to take it from her, and she steps closer to where I'm leaning against the truck.

Tucking my phone in my pocket, I ask, "So, you're drinking them both?"

"No, it's an exchange." Morrigan bites her bottom lip.

"An exchange?" I repeat.

A shake is hardly leverage for any sort of something.

"Mm-hmm." Morrigan nods. "I'll give you your malt if you give me a kiss."

*Fuck.* I eye her and then the malt. *On the forehead. Sure.* I step forward, giving up my position against the truck.

Morrigan's eyes brighten from the irises outward. They go from their natural deep brown to the vibrant green-yellow color of her wolf. It's stunning. I doubt it'll be long before she shifts.

Harry wags his tail, excited about it.

Drawing a tentative breath, Morrigan waits, looking up at me.

Wrapping one hand behind her head, I gently bring my other hand around the cup above where hers is on it. Cautiously, I lean forward and lift the cup from her grasp before pushing my lips below her hairline.

Morrigan tries to reach to take the cup back, but it's too late. Her little five-foot reach and short arm can't make it.

"In the truck." I shake my head before walking around to the driver's side.

*What the fuck will I do with her for the next eleven months? She'll give up eventually, right?*

## CHAPTER 44
# MORRIGAN

I DON'T KNOW WHY I THOUGHT THAT WAS A GOOD IDEA. OR THAT IT would work. But I do know that when I think about kissing Ansel, part of me feels more alive now than it ever has.

Our malt and shake are gone, and the cups are resting in the cupholder attached to the dash. The silence had been filled by the radio, but about two minutes ago, we crossed the point where even that cuts off.

The kiss from the other day is playing loudly in my brain again. I need more. Whatever is happening between us makes me feel, and I need to feel more.

Fortune favors the bold.

I unbuckle my seat belt and slide across the cab.

Ansel is quick to snap, "No, buckle your seat belt. What if we're in an accident?"

"With who?" I indicate to the driveway in front of us.

"The work crew?" Ansel points toward the direction of the house.

I stay next to him on the bench, my shoulder resting against his. Ansel doesn't push me away.

*It's obvious he likes this too.*

Waiting for only a few more minutes, I run my hand across the denim of his jeans.

Ansel's fast. He picks up my hand and returns it to my lap.

"Go back to your side of the truck." Ansel's words are spoken carefully.

They feel full of contradictory regret. And it's not a command, so I don't listen.

After a few more minutes, I don't move.

Ansel growls ever so softly, "Morrigan."

My hand finds its way across the fabric of his jeans. I move it to the inner thigh, where the worn fabric is thinner. His body feels so warm.

The truck jolts and swerves off the drive.

I'm tossed away from Ansel, and my fingers dig into the dash, trying to hold me steady in the cab. We come to a halt after sliding in the dirt.

Ansel's door on the cab opens. He's gone before I can even process what's going on.

I'm tracking, looking around and trying to find him, when the door on my side of the truck opens and I'm pulled out backward.

I'm spun around, and my back is slammed up against the back quarter panel of the truck. Looking up, I see the difference. The change in it all.

The green eyes of Ansel are gone. Harbinger is staring down at me.

And I'm fucking soaked in a second.

I'm in the middle of drawing an unsteady breath when his lips press against mine and cut it off. Ansel's tongue is in my mouth a second later, and we're kissing like there's no time left.

His fingers find their way into my hair, and he squeezes, pulling, keeping my head right where he wants me.

Ansel isn't gentle. He isn't pretending or playing nice. This is raw and full of need.

I take it.

I want it.

The kiss breaks, and he pulls me away from the truck, moving his hand from my hair to twist in the back of my shirt. Silently, he puts me in the cab so I'm sitting on the seat facing toward him. For a second, I think he'll scold me. That he'll turn me, buckle my seat belt, and lock me in place on my side of the truck.

But that second passes when Ansel wraps his hand around my thigh and tips me backward onto the seat. My breath catches in my throat when his fingers work the fly of my jeans.

The denim is gone, and the cold desert air prickles against my skin. Involuntarily, my legs come together to keep me warm.

Ansel snarls. It's so completely wolf that it pulls a yelp from deep in my core. Raising my head to check that I'm not face to face with the white wolf of death elicits even more sweet anticipation.

Desire looks good on Ansel. It looks really good.

He runs his hand up the inside of my leg, and I whine, collapsing back onto the seat. Graceful fingers slide beneath my panties and begin to pull them over my hips. I raise my ass ever so slightly so he can remove the one thing keeping him away from where I want him to be.

For the first time, one of us dares to speak, and it isn't me.

"Fuck, Morrigan," Ansel grumbles, but it's not with his usual displeasure. This is something much more primal and enthralling. "You smell so sweet." Ansel's voice melts me. "Is this all for me?"

It's true. I'm wet for him. He's all I can think about.

I nod and lick my bottom lip.

He runs his large, warm hands from my knee up my thighs to my core.

"Answer me, Morrigan," Ansel commands.

His thumb sinks between my lips and pauses the smallest distance known to anyone away from my clit. The sadist waits for my answer.

"Yes." The word makes it out of my throat but only at a whisper.

The reward for my answer comes from his thumb as it brushes my clit.

My body jolts involuntarily.

A finger probes lower and slowly presses past my lips inside me. Then all the tension flows out of my body, released with a moan.

I've never felt something so relaxing. Is it possible to carry all your tension in your pussy? I've heard neck and shoulders, but as his fingers intimately explore my inner walls, I feel more relaxed with each stroke.

Warmth builds, and he circles my clit with his thumb. We're panting together. I hear his heavy breaths, and he hits that sweet spot. The movements are perfect.

I'm on the verge of an orgasm.

"Ansel." His name leaves my lips on the tail end of a breath.

With it, his hands leave too. The warmth is gone.

I sit up, and Ansel is pulling my jeans and underwear off the truck's sidewall.

"Put your pants on. Let's go." His voice is quiet and somber. "Absolutely no more touching each other. At all."

We lock eyes for a moment. My body objects to the loss of the building orgasm, the painful edge of denial stinging from the core. I've never done something like this with anyone else, and now it's been cut short. *Why?*

He leaves my side of the truck and walks around the tailgate.

We were on fire a moment ago, and instead of kerosene, he doused us in water. My body shivers, and I do as he demanded, pulling my clothes back on and straightening myself.

On my side of the truck, as far away from Ansel as I can get, I wrap my arms around myself, trying to fight off the physical symptoms of rejection. *What did I do wrong?*

# CHAPTER 45
## ANSEL

THERE'S SOMETHING SERIOUSLY WRONG WITH ME. I CAN'T CONTROL myself around her. *She's a fucking child, and you're . . .*

I shake my head and squeeze the steering wheel as I drive back home. As expected, there's still a work crew bustling around, and when I put the truck in the garage, people hesitantly walk about, continuing their tasks.

"Don't stop on my behalf." I look at the crew while carrying bags of groceries inside.

Morrigan trails behind. The rustling of plastic tells me she's grabbed at least two of the remaining bags.

My bedroom door is open, and my feet come to a dead stop.

Harry bristles at the intrusion.

From this angle in the hall, I can see the window is missing, and there's a man on a ladder outside, doing who only knows what to get the new one installed in its place.

Harry is on edge. He's pressing and pacing, trying to get out. First obsessed over Morrigan, and now he's pushing violent retaliation against people in our inner space.

Millie is at the counter standing next to Adam, who is doing something with his little computer.

"Ansel, what's your birthday?" Adam doesn't look up from where he's working.

"Pick one," I answer.

"No. Ansel," Adam repeats like I didn't hear him. "Your birthday."

"I didn't stutter," I repeat back with a snap. "I don't have one. Just pick one."

"Everyone has a birthday." Adam squints at me.

"Adam." Morrigan's voice is soft as she draws his attention from me. "Ansel was found. He doesn't know when it is."

The nerd goes white as a sheet and turns to Millie for answers.

I ignore them and put the groceries away. With that load in the house, I head to the door, and my eye wanders into my room to find the window being hoisted into place.

Harry snarls, but I shove him down. It's not worth getting upset over. They're doing my house first to get it over with. It's fine. It'll be fine.

It'll be fine.

It'll be fine.

Once I'm out at the truck grabbing the last couple bags, it's not fine.

PRINCETON IS SHOUTING LOUDLY, YELLING AT ZERO, WHO IS BACKING *away with his hands up. Snow on the ground brushes out of the way at Zero's feet as he retreats.*

*"Is that it? You like her? She could be my mate!" Princeton's words become clearer.*

*Zero shakes his head. "That's not what I said."*

*The snarling is so loud it sounds like thunder.*

*Princeton's wolf shreds through him and lunges at Zero. Zero's tall wolf shifts slower and ends up pinned beneath Princeton. Long legs push the more compact wolf off him, but it's not enough. Princeton's quick to get hold of his neck.*

*But it's not Zero's clock that is running down. Harry arrives, and Princeton doesn't make it.*

I QUICKLY PULL OUT MY PHONE AND LOOK AT THE RADAR. SNOW ON Tuesday and Wednesday. *Fuck.* That's too soon. Having a wolf needing to go down with a house full of humans is not ideal.

I need to get the humans out of here by then. If something changes, if he snaps early, it would be very bad.

It's me versus the clock. *Unless I break my rules.*

That thought hurts as it echoes in my brain. As much as I dislike Princeton, it doesn't sit right with me ending him early on a maybe. Maybe he snaps? Maybe he doesn't?

It's unprecedented, but so are the circumstances. I've never had this many humans here. *Stupid fucking Cade and his damn home improvements.* My toes squirm in my boots.

What choice do I have? They finished the basement first, so the humans shouldn't need to go back down there again. That's safest.

I'll take him downstairs and give him his options. He either goes in the kennel and runs the clock or I kill him now. My blood runs cold. *I vowed to do this right. To give everyone a chance.*

The third option is that we see if he can get himself better under control . . . Which is an option, but I have very little faith in him.

*Fucking alarm system.*

I've broken enough rules recently. The work crew supposed to be gone before Tuesday. That's before the snow is on the radar.

I run my hand through my beard. There are too many things to balance.

Ultimately, Princeton is dangerous. I don't see him getting less dangerous.

Harry seems to agree as he snarls while thinking of Princeton. There's never been a moment when Harry has rested in the same space as Princeton. It's been months. Things aren't any better.

He walked in with an attitude, and I doubt he walks out.

Ignorance is bliss, right? Who knows, it's not locked in. Life is ever changing.

When I turn around, the little shit is making a beeline toward the house.

I close the tailgate on the truck and meet him before he gets to my door. "Can I help you?"

"I came to hang out with Morrigan. I saw you came back." His shit-eating grin tells me there's something I don't know that I should.

"No wolves at the house. Not until the humans are gone." Look at me making new rules left and right.

"Oh, so Morrigan will be coming down to stay in that other cabin? She can bunk with me, instead. If she'd like." Princeton offers, extending his arm and then motioning back the way he came.

"Nope. She stays where she's at. The other one isn't habitable yet, and I don't have to worry with her. Go on, get out of here. I'll come down and hang with the pack later tonight." I push my chin up, indicating toward the cabins behind him.

When he doesn't move, I step into him, putting myself more between him and the house.

His wolf floods forward, and Princeton's eyes go yellow. His nostrils flare, and his lip twitches.

*Maybe the kennel is the best option.*

Harry rises to the challenge. His haunches are raised, and he's agitated as he snaps against the surface.

"Princeton, I want you to listen very carefully." I speak slowly, hoping the dumbass listens. "If you don't get yourself under control, you'll find yourself in a kennel. You might think you're tough shit, but I promise you, that pup you call a wolf doesn't have anything on Harbinger. If you like fresh air and eatin' whenever you feel like it, I'd take the offer to turn around and go back home."

The dumbass doesn't move.

I wait before letting Harry come a bit farther forward. I can feel my eyes go dark as he pushes forward, dying for control.

*Come on, idiot. Go home.* I push him a bit, raising my shoulders and drawing in a deep breath, making myself a bit taller and giving more of a presence.

"Hey, Ansel?" Morrigan calls from the door.

Princeton's eyes snap past me, looking at her. He tries to step around me, but I drop the grocery bags and grab hold of his wrist. Pulling it behind his back, I grab the collar of his shirt and twist it around in my hands until it's secure.

"Morrigan, go open the side door in the basement," I instruct as I push him.

A few of the human workers turn to look at us, but they must have worked for Cade long enough to know not to say anything.

"Let me go!" Princeton snarls as he fights, swinging his other arm back to try and hit me.

But I tighten my grip on the neck of his shirt, choking him. If he tries to shift, it'll dislocate his shoulder. Which, from experience, hurts like a motherfucker.

Pushing hard on his back and arm, I force him around the side of the house where the side door is open.

317

Morrigan steps back and presses against the wall. She also knew to unlock and open the kennels.

I shove Princeton into the first one and quickly slam the door shut, then engage the cell's lock.

Princeton is a massive gray wolf before I can even step back. He snaps his jaws, trying to grab hold of me through the bars.

"I told you it didn't have to go this way." I shake my head while scolding him.

The wolf keeps growling and snarling.

"What happened?" Morrigan asks as her footsteps trail toward me.

"Morrigan," I caution her, my arm out to keep her away from the bars.

Wisely, Morrigan stops walking and even goes so far as to take a small step back.

"I gave him an answer to his question. He didn't like it. There's too much at stake here for him to fly off the handle like this. So, once the humans leave, I'll let him out. We can try again."

There's no point in telling her the truth. Princeton won't survive another week. It'll upset her, and who knows what that'll do to the progress she's making.

I grab a clean blanket from the cupboard and a few bottles of water from the little fridge around the corner of the kennel. I place them outside his kennel. It'll be hard for his wolf to get them, but his human body should be able to do so just fine.

Morrigan presses the main latch on the wall, and I lock the side door. Princeton starts howling, and it echoes in the basement.

"Enough!" I shout, commanding his silence.

Princeton whines and stress yawns in his kennel but still hasn't shifted back.

I put a roll of toilet paper with the other pile of supplies and leave the light on in the medical bay. I don't bother telling him I'll come down with dinner.

When we get to the steel door to close it, Morrigan puts her hand on my chest, stopping me. I wrap my hand around hers, holding it to my chest.

Her voice is above a whisper. "I explained a bit more about you to them. They won't ask anything else. I gave them Dad's info for passwords and stuff. If you don't know it, I can —"

Kissing her softly, I end her explanation of the events.

One way or another, she'll be the death of me. I've already committed one capital offense today. I've signed my own death warrant. What's one more kiss?

It's petty and childish, but I flip Princeton off before I close the vault door and spin the dial.

"Everything okay?" Millie asks as we get to the top of the stairs.

I nod. "Yeah. No humans go into the basement unless escorted by me. No exceptions."

"Fair enough." Millie nods.

# CHAPTER 46
# MORRIGAN

Intentionally or otherwise, Ansel kept someone in the room with us at all times yesterday. Breakfast, lunch, dinner, and even all the way up until bedtime, one of the members from Corinth Security was with us.

Today, they're gone. The last van packed up, and they're on the way down the driveway.

"Dinah will be here later this afternoon. She landed in Denver about an hour and a half ago," Ansel informs me before walking away.

"Are we planning on talking about what happened between us, in the truck, the day before yesterday?" I ask, following him.

His legs propel him into the house much faster than I can walk. So, I jog to keep up.

"Nope." Ansel pops the *p* and continues into the kitchen.

He digs out the stainless-steel bowl from the dishwasher and starts grabbing meat out of the refrigerator.

I'm standing here dumbstruck again as he makes breakfast

for Princeton. I can't believe he won't even entertain the idea of at least talking about it before she gets here. It's not anger or sadness, and there aren't words. Nothing I can think to say would adequately explain to him why he fucking sucks so much right now, but maybe Dinah can fix it?

With a sigh, I concede to Ansel's refusal to talk about it, us, but not to silence. "He still hasn't shifted back yet?"

Ansel shakes his head. "No. I'll give him another week. If he doesn't at that point, I'll contact his Alpha and see what he wants me to do."

A few more minutes of silence pass before Ansel stills his hands. He sets everything down and looks at me, the tip of his tongue sticking out from where he's biting it. If it weren't for the ticking clock on the wall, I'd think an hour had passed rather than a minute.

"If you don't want to, I'll tell Dinah what's happened between us," Ansel says slowly.

I frown at him. "I don't understand."

"Morrigan, I'm twice your age. According to our laws, you're not even legally an adult." He swallows, looking at me again.

His gaze warms me with fire but not of anger. It's a flush heat that has me wanting more of what he started in the truck.

"Fifteen to seventeen years, Ansel, it's not twice," I correct him. "I'll be twenty in June."

Surely, he's not saying what happened between us is wrong or dirty? *It can't be.*

"I was there when you were born," Ansel argues, again stating our circumstances.

He closes his eyes, but it doesn't stop the tension building between us.

The gravity of what Ansel's saying sinks in. Wolves protect their pups with a strict law of death for misconduct. Not having met sexual maturity, I'm still, under wolf law, a pup. Ansel and I, being together, technically, would fall on the wrong end of that law.

The dead end.

I argue with him. "I remember you kind of being around when I was growing up. But it's not like we ever had a relationship. You were Dad's friend, and then I moved to California. It's hardly inappropriate behavior."

"I've got reason to believe that the issue between us is some sort of twist of fate." He cuts that sentence off. Shaking his head, he draws a big breath and lets it out. Taking his hair out of his bun, he changes the direction of his words. "We're at different places in life. You should have your twenties to date, find someone who matches you well, and go from there."

I shake my head. *I don't have a wolf, so he can't really think we're fated mates?* My heart squeezes at that thought. It fits almost all the feelings I have and how I crave being near him. The notion that we're fated mates has solid logic behind it. I could see it being true. *If Dinah can help me get my wolf back, we'd know for sure.*

I argue against his ridiculous logic. "Ansel, are you telling me to fight fate?"

"Morrigan," Ansel sighs, and our eyes lock again. The green of his murky irises turns darker. "I'm saying that if fate has truly locked you to me, I'm sorry."

*No.* I shake my head, pushing down my screams of frustration because I don't know how to make him listen to me.

When he hangs his head, his hair falls in his face. Running his hand back over the top of his head, he pushes it out of the way and looks at me. "You need to have me killed so you have a chance in life. A chance with someone more suitable."

"No." I can't. I won't. *Death isn't the answer to all things.*

*What did I do wrong? How can I fix this?* My heart sinks as helplessness threatens to swallow me whole.

My feet absentmindedly carry me to the sliding glass door. I open it, and the alarm starts blaring, but I don't care. Closing it behind me, I leave Ansel to figure out how to turn it off on his own and sit my ass down in one of the Adirondack chairs.

*He can't die.* The world is blurry, and I wipe away the moisture from my eyes. Wiping it away doesn't stop the flood of pain. It doesn't keep me from falling apart. Curling up in the chair, I wrap my arms around my legs and let myself cry.

*He thinks we're fated mates.* I shake my head. *How could I be so stupid? Why didn't I see it?*

I've been here for exactly twenty-two days. My wolf might not be anywhere to be found, but what I have found is more. There's no way we're not mates. There's no way he doesn't feel this. It's like I'm burning up on the inside every time we're close enough to touch.

Losing him before we even get a chance to embrace this is too much. Pressure wells in my chest, and I shake my head as I gasp for air. Trying to get air into my lungs, I draw deep breaths, but the more I think about calming down, the less calm I become. He's awful sometimes, and I should hate him. Instead, I'm willing to do anything to keep him alive.

Fracturing is in my bloodline, and I know if someone takes Ansel from me, it'll be the same fate. Dad fractured apart when Mom took me from him.

Twenty-two days is all it took for me to fall in love with him, and I'll never be the same.

*Do I run?* If I'm not here, then I can't talk to Dinah and I can't confirm what Ansel says. It's his word against mine, but mine won't be available. No body, no crime?

Uncurling from the chair, I stand up to get a better look out at the horizon. I don't have to find my way into town. I just can't be here while she's here.

"Please don't." Ben's voice comes from the bottom of the stairs, startling me.

Ben speaks again, catching my eye. "If you run, then I'll have to hunt your ass down. I bet you're thinking that if you're not here, you won't be able to tell Dinah what has happened."

"Nothing's happened," I rebut.

Ben laughs. "You're shockingly good at lying. If it weren't for the fact that Ansel's told me, I would have believed you."

"I can't do what he wants me to do. I won't." I shake my head.

Sitting on the stairs, Ben looks out at the horizon with me.

"I'm here because I strangled a wolf with my bare hands," Ben says nonchalantly.

Somehow, it isn't even all that weird sounding.

His story continues. "The woman I loved was found broken, bleeding, stripped naked, and left for dead. His scent coated her like a skunk. The Alpha told me that he'd be dealt with. But while she was healing slowly, the asshole was walking around with barely a slap on the wrist." Ben sighs and scrubs his hand down his face. "I've been told a few times I should have done the right thing. I should have challenged my Alpha. But I didn't want a pack. I wanted vengeance." Ben's laugh is deep and foreboding.

When he's done laughing, he swipes a hand through his hair and shares his darkness. "His body was found on the Alpha's front porch smelling like piss. I drove myself to Ansel's. By the time the pack caught up with me, Ansel had it all worked out as to how it would go. Your old man laughed his ass off through that entire meeting. Afterward, he said that if anyone did that to his daughter, he would have gutted him. Your dad had a way with words, and honestly, the graphic detail alone should have given us all a hint as to how messed up he was."

"Are you supposed to be helping?" The words come out on a sob, and I fight the urge to cry again.

"All that to say." Ben pauses. "Your old man wouldn't have even blinked that you and Ansel are together. Walt held Ansel in the highest regard. He believed in Ansel when Ansel didn't even believe in himself. Don't stop pestering him." Ben stands up, still looking across the horizon. He leans against the deck rail. "I can promise you not a single Ardelean will blink at the fact you're a minor on a stupid technicality."

I thought all the men here were some sort of monster. I assumed Ben was here to help. But now, knowing Ben's past, I'm not sure if I should be impressed or scared. Ultimately, it doesn't matter because . . . he's an ally in a dark place. Even if I think he probably doesn't like me.

"What do I do?" The whisper turns into a whine midway through.

I sit back down to wait for an answer from Ben, but the chair feels unusual and . . . not right? My skin tingles uncomfortably. It's like my bones and skin don't fit together in this form, and my body doesn't know how to work with this chair. I stand back up to escape it.

Ben pulls in a deep breath and turns to face me. "You tell the truth. You tell the entire truth no matter what."

"Okay." I nod, meeting his eyes.

"It'll be okay, hellcat. I promise." Ben returns my nod, reassuring me.

"Hellcat? I can't even get a cool nickname?" I grumble at him.

He shrugs. "Not my fault it fits."

I groan, "Not cool. But fine."

Slowly, I walk toward him and the door.

"Oh, and Morrigan?" Ben stops me, moving from the railing he had been leaning against before continuing. "Teach the asshole how to turn off the fucking alarm."

Laughing, I slide the door open, and it starts blaring again. "Yeah. On it."

# CHAPTER 47

# ANSEL

DINAH TAKES MY HOUSE BY STORM. SHE LETS HERSELF IN THE BACK door and kicks off her shoes as she calls, "Hello!"

"Hey, Dinah," I call from the kitchen, where I'm pouring flour into the running stand mixer as it beats batter for cookies.

She's her usual self, smiling wide with her braided hair running over her shoulder. Dinah gives me a hug. When we break it, her smile is gone, clearly picking up on my mood.

"Is that the first official food of the coup?" Dinah asks, avoiding diving into my problems. Her nose wiggles as she draws in a deep breath, leaning over to look in the mixing bowl. "Ooo, even better. Oatmeal butter scotchies."

I laugh at the happy memory of the beginning of our lives coming back together when, in my humble kitchen, Cade Alden decided to take back the throne.

Dinah smiles and then hugs me again. "I'm happy to see you. I love you so much."

I don't understand why I get a second hug, and it startles me. I hold still, and it takes a full minute before she shrugs me off and sits on the stool across from me.

She turns, having held back her curiosity longer than I expected. "So, why the long face?"

My eyes dart up to the loft where Morrigan's shower can still be heard running. Dinah's eyes are slow to follow.

"Why don't you put that in the fridge to chill and go get drunk with Ben? I'll keep an eye on Morrigan." Dinah turns back and gives me a soft smile.

"I've a delinquent in the basement," I grumble.

"And?" She shakes her head. "Truly, cousin. I may not be you or Cade, but I think I can handle her and someone in a prison cell through a massive steel door."

Dinah gets off the stool, grabs my shoulder, and turns me around, pushing me down the hallway to my shoes and the door.

"I'll text you when I've fixed all your problems." Dinah laughs. "Or until I can't live without fresh-from-the-oven oatmeal scotchies for another minute."

"Thank you." I nod and slip on my sneakers before heading out the door.

Sitting on the stairs outside, I tie my shoes. But I don't want to go.

Dinah blows into town and takes over my house, and I'm left doing nothing but thumbing around. I turn around to go back inside, but staring at the door, I know what has to happen. They have to have . . . I don't know? Girl time? It's not fair for me to leave it up to Morrigan to tell Dinah what I've done, but I hold on to hope that maybe she'll go through with it.

Slow steps on the driveway drag me down the hill to the pack's cabins.

Ben's already waiting for me at his front door.

"I take it Dinah made it here okay?" he asks, letting me

inside his little house and then closing the door, keeping the cold out.

Looking back at his front door, I question going back.

"Give them some time. She only wants what's best for Morrigan. If she says they need time, then they need time." Ben puts a beer in my hand.

# CHAPTER 48
# MORRIGAN

DINAH IS A FORCE OF NATURE. IF I STILL BELIEVED IN THINGS LIKE 'what I want to be when I grow up' . . . I would want to be as fierce as Dinah. For now, my dreams are small, albeit unobtainable. From upstairs, I heard how she ordered Ansel out of his own house and made herself at home. It's a whole energy I couldn't imitate.

The open stairwell gives me a good view, and I catch the first glimpse of the woman who might be able to fix me. By the way people talk of her, she's a living legend. But in person, she's so . . . ordinary. Not in a plain way. Tall, curvy, and muscular, she's absolutely a wolf and stunning. Maybe it's an Ardelean thing; like Ansel, the more people talk about him, the scarier he seems. Dinah's a person just like the rest of us.

"You must be Morrigan." She greets me with a quick look up and down.

I nod, swallowing hard.

Dinah's eyes leave me to eye fuck the bowl of cookie dough on the stand mixer. Holding her spoon like a weapon, she asks, "So, how much do you think we can eat before Ansel notices?"

"Half?" I guess.

"Excellent." She gives a devious laugh before disconnecting the bowl and grabbing a second spoon.

Flagging me over, Dinah sits on the couch and waits for me to join her.

I'm barely seated when she dives headfirst into why she's here. "So, tell me, what's going on?"

With the bowl between us, Dinah pulls a pillow in her lap, scoops a big spoonful of cookie dough, and waits. Her hazel eyes flicker with the light from the kitchen behind me.

I shake my head, not wanting to say. But from what she said on the phone, I'm pretty sure she knows.

I lay it out in broad terms. "I've never gone into heat. I don't have a wolf."

Those last words are the hardest to push out. *What if she can't fix me?* No one and nothing has yet.

"Well that's some bullshit if I ever heard it." Dinah rolls her eyes. "Who told you that you don't have a wolf?"

The words, independently, make sense. But under what logic does she even think that's remotely okay to say to someone?

Angry, hot tears form in my eyes. For the second time today, I'm fighting tears. But this time, they come with a glare.

With a sigh and a soft smile, Dinah tilts her head and continues. "Morrigan. Wolves don't just disappear. Your parents were wolves. You're a wolf. Somewhere along the line, someone gave you and her permission to stop talking."

I'm literally biting my tongue. She doesn't know me. She doesn't know anything about what's happened. How can Dinah even understand what I'm going through? No one understands. I'm not angry. I'm sick of being alone.

"I don't know what it's like to completely stop talking with your wolf. But I know what it's like to not have the power to control her."

Dinah's admittance disarms my anger.

Pack gossip — 'news' — spreads like wildfire. Everyone knows that Dinah is this badass woman who survived her mate dying. The speculation, of course, is that Ansel killed him. But he told me that isn't true. It doesn't change the fact that wolves are supposed to mate for life. You're not supposed to thrive after losing someone who was meant to be with you forever. By every account, Dinah is doing well. She definitely doesn't seem like someone in the process of dying of a broken heart.

Yet her words, somber and full of an understanding I didn't expect, quench the fire inside me, and I listen.

She draws another breath and lets it out slowly before continuing. "It probably started a long time before your wolf went completely quiet. Bit by bit, word by word, action by action, you and she drifted apart. You were a pup, and the people meant to guide you did a shit job. Was it because they were also lost? Was it because they were blind to the pain they were causing you? Did they see what they were doing as potentially damaging and tried it anyway? We'll never know. Your thoughts and your fears at the center of your insecurity were amplified by those around you. Their beliefs and their words distorted who you are." She hangs her head for a moment before meeting my eyes again. "Who you're meant to be, and the bullshit that's been given to you, has become so internalized that you've forgotten who you are."

"You're saying this is my fault?" I huff, trying to dismiss her suggestion. Disbelief sparks a new fire that anger fuels. Hot, angry, spiteful words keep coming. "I forgot who I am. It's my fault?"

Dinah nods, agreeing with me that I did this to myself.

Each nod of her head cuts me like a dull knife, slowly opening my flesh. "I'm saying your wolf went silent, and you lost yourself in the chasm of her absence. Embrace that fire." She nods toward me. "Get yourself uncomfortable with the silence within and look for what brings her back."

"I don't know how. I'm broken." I realize how dumb that is. *How can I expect her to know what happened?*

Everything about this conversation has been dark and emotional. But with a quick flick of her spoon, Dinah's perky and playful, offering a quick fix. "Well, there's your problem, stop being broken."

"It's that simple?" I roll my eyes. "Just don't be broken?"

"Oh, that's never simple. It's hard work not being what you've convinced yourself you are. When you started believing those things, you lost your way." She puts her spoon down.

Leaning forward, Dinah picks up my hand. She bites her lips together, and her eyes glaze over with what I've learned from Ansel to be a vision.

My heart rate increases. *Do I pull my hand away?*

Before I can make any move, her eyes come back to hazel. "You've got to open yourself up and find which pieces really belong."

"And?" I push.

*What isn't she telling me?*

Shaking her head, she says, "No ands. No buts."

Suspicion grates against me. "So, that's it, then. Be open?"

"Probably." Dinah shrugs, and it's a full-body experience. She nearly lifts up off the couch and then plops back down. "Unless you think there's something medically wrong?"

I hang my head. "I feel fine. But I don't heal as quickly as everyone else. I bruise and bump, and I get blisters that take days to heal. When —" I swallow hard. "When they tried to give me another wolf, it took months."

"They what?" Dinah's voice peaks, and then she growls. It echoes in the open space.

Facing her, I pull my knees up to my chest and brace for her anger.

"Fucking son of a bitch. I should go and kick Gerad's ass six ways from Sunday. Does Ansel know?" Dinah examines me, watching for signs of a lie if I had to guess. Her teeth grind together.

A nod is all I can manage.

"He hasn't killed Gerad yet?" She grips the pillow in her lap like she'll rip it to bits.

"I told him not to," I whisper, tucking my head lower between my shoulders.

That cools Dinah's anger. Completely out of place, like laughter at a funeral, she smiles, then sighs before she speaks. "That man has more strength and gentleness than I could ever wish to possess."

"What do you mean?" I slowly uncurl myself from the ball I had wrapped myself in and pay closer attention.

"Every ending that Ansel has taken part in has made him who he is today. Every fight he's won, every loss he's suffered, and every person who wasn't grateful that he put them back together. Ansel stays strong through it. Even if that means he puts aside every desire, want, and need for himself." Dinah sighs, standing from the couch. "I bet that makes him especially difficult to live with."

She stretches her hands above her head.

My thoughts drift back to Ansel. The feeling of him pressed against me and his taste in my mouth. They're not thoughts I should have. It isn't fair. I want Ansel's hands on me, to hear his growl in my ear, and everything between us that's still undiscussed.

"If I tell you something, are you required to, like, tell

anyone? If I say something, and it's completely insane, do you have to tell Ansel or the pack council or my parents?" I ask quickly before I lose my nerve.

Shaking her head, Dinah remains standing but picks up another spoonful of cookie dough before setting the bowl on the coffee table. Something, probably the dumb expression on my face, causes Dinah to sit back down. She cocks her head, first to the left and then to the right. Her gaze feels heavy against my skin.

"I'm an Ardelean Alpha. The only person I answer to is Cade Alden. And even then, he doesn't get himself involved in things that don't concern him. So, your question isn't do I have to, it's will I?" She clarifies. When I nod, she continues. "If you're at risk of hurting yourself or someone else, then yes, I'll have to, at the very least, tell Ansel. But I'm pretty sure what you're about to say will stay between us."

*Do I trust her? Do I have a choice?*

It's hard to push the words out. "I'm not, technically, a mature wolf." I'm quick to defend myself, words flying from my lips. "But it's not fair. I'm not exactly a pup either. The humans consider me an adult."

Dinah nods, letting me speak freely without any further prompting.

"We've —" Hot tears prick my eyes. He told me to tell her. Everything will change if I do. Wiping the moisture from my eyes, I ask her, "Why is this so hard?"

The rhetorical question hangs between us. It's almost as if Dinah doesn't care. No, not that she doesn't care. That if I decide not to tell her, she won't judge me.

"And it's not supposed to be possible because I haven't gone through heat. I shouldn't know he's my mate. But I feel it. I feel he has to be. Ansel's, of course, not talking about it. He's fighting everything." I barely get the last few words out. I fight back a sob. *What is wrong with me?* "We've kissed, and it's gone a bit further. And I know we shouldn't have because . . ." I gasp for air. "Because . . ."

Dinah's expression is cryptic, with a soft smile and furrowed brows. It's concerned but happy. *Is she some sort of sadist?*

The tears don't stop coming. I wipe them from my face and try a different direction to get past the stuck words. "I know what the penalty is because I'm not . . . but please don't. Please."

She runs her hand back across my head, pushing hair out of my face.

"It's okay." Dinah coaxes while petting my head. "Take a breath."

I draw a gasp. Her touch is so reassuring and relaxing.

"Ansel doesn't believe anyone loves him." Dinah's voice is full of empathy. She grasps my hand. "No matter how many times we've said it, no matter how many times we assure him he's family, Ansel's missed out on so much love. There isn't enough proof. There may never be."

"He's talked about how much older he is than me." I shake my head and wipe more tears. Any part of me worried about trusting Dinah missed its opportunity to stop me. It's too late now. "I don't know, but maybe it's because he was Dad's friend. But I can't believe I feel this way and he doesn't have any feelings about it."

"He has feelings about you, Morrigan," Dinah confirms. Her eyes are glossy, and she blinks hard. "He has a lot of feelings for you."

"Then . . ." How do I say this without painting him like an ass? *He is an ass, so maybe I should say it?* "Then why does he start shit and stop it without warning? It's like one minute we're on fire together and the next he's been doused with water."

"What an asshole." Dinah has no issue saying what I thought. "Give him some time. In two months, if he hasn't come around, have him call me because you're . . . I don't know? *Feeling funny?* He absolutely will call me, and then I'll shake some sense into him." She laughs, demonstrating how she'd shake him. "Ansel can handle himself fine. As far as kissing him goes, I think you'll find yourself walking a fine line with him for a while. At the very least, until he removes his head from his ass."

Her brash assessment of Ansel makes me laugh.

Dinah chooses her words very carefully. "It's very much a possibility that you're right, and he is your mate." Dinah is silent again but bypasses Ansel and directs the talk back to me. "Now that you're safe and healing, there will be changes. I don't know what those will look like. There isn't a guide for 'hey, my wolf wandered off, how do I fix it?' but I would put money on the fact that when your wolf finds her way back to you, you'll go into heat for the first time very quickly after." Dinah cautions me and pauses, probably trying to gauge how well I'm taking this information.

My eyes go wide. The idea of maybe getting my wolf back occurred to me. But heat never even crossed my mind.

Once I nod, indicating I'm ready for whatever else she has to tell me, Dinah forges ahead.

There's a very clinical tone to her voice. "I can prescribe you the meds to stop it from happening. They'll need to be taken very soon after you shift. You'll maybe have one or two weeks at the most. It'll block the hormones and stop you from going into heat. No heat, no sexual maturity. No sexual maturity, no finding your fated mate. It won't stop the draw you're both feeling toward each other from happening. But you won't have that full effect of finding your mate; those 'can't live without you' feelings. If those even exist. Cade, Thalia, Finn, and Lena all gave me different stories and accounts on the subject. So who really fucking knows anymore?"

"Can I have the meds but not take them if I don't want to?" I sigh. It's logical to have them on hand. It's like the dude's cat in the box thing . . . if I don't go into heat, I can't know for sure.

"Absolutely." Dinah nods and gives me a smile. "I'll have Lena overnight them."

Swallowing is hard, and I try to draw deep breaths.

"Birds and the bees?" Dinah sings out slowly.

"I mean, I know what sex is. And that heat makes babies." I get a little too snappy for someone asking for help. "Sorry. I'm nervous."

It's bad enough I had to tell someone I don't have a wolf today. But now we're on to the 'never been fucked' aspect of my life. *Fucking joy.*

"Ohhhhh." Dinah picks up the bowl of cookie dough and hops off the couch. "You need something stronger than cookie dough."

"He doesn't have brownie batter in the fridge or ice cream in the freezer," I call, but she's already in the kitchen.

"It's a good thing I went into medicine with all these young people asking questions about sex and stuff." Dinah cackles, pulling out glasses and a bottle of whiskey. "We're pretending we're in Wisconsin."

"What does Wisconsin have to do with anything?" I follow Dinah to the kitchen.

"Rocks?" She puts ice in one of the glasses. When I shake my head, she continues. "There is? Was?" She waves her hand, dismissing the technicality of the statement. "A law that essentially says if you have your parent, legal guardian, or spouse with you and they consent, you can drink with them in a bar as long as you're like sixteen or some shit."

"So, you're my legal guardian and we're in Wisconsin?" I'm hesitant.

She nods. "Now she's catching up with the program."

"Rocks," I answer her initial question about my drink order, and Dinah adds ice to my cup and pours us both a drink.

"Alright, you know the birds, the bees, and how to get pregnant. Do you want me to ask you questions to see where you're at knowledge-wise, or do you have specific concerns?" Dinah takes a sip of her drink.

I sit on the stool and swirl the ice in my cup, chilling the alcohol.

"How bad does it hurt?" My voice feels small. I've been through so much pain, though, so how bad could it really hurt? *It's a dick, not a knife.*

"Sex? Depends on a number of factors. I guess, fuck, being a wolf is weird." Dinah winces. With both eyes squeezed shut, she answers, "Based on seeing Ansel naked and your physical size, I would say probably not super bad. It's not like you've a Cade and Thalia or Finn and Lena size difference."

It's still so weird to me that I'm sitting with Dinah, and she talks about the Ardeleans like they're normal people.

She pries her eyes open. "But also, what's your pain tolerance?"

"Normal? I guess?" I shrug.

"Yeah. I mean, don't get me wrong, I remember my first heat, and cramps are a fucking bitch. It's like being bitten. From between the legs. By a bear. With a different pair of dentures each bite." Dinah adds each different explanation slowly, trying to pick words. As she does, she absentmindedly crosses her legs before shuddering.

"Fuck. That paints a picture." I draw a sip of my drink.

"Doesn't it?" Dinah snorts. "I understand wanting to go through it in order to know for sure. Especially because Ansel's being difficult."

"But?" I prompt.

Dinah finishes her drink and chews her bottom lip before answering. "I wouldn't blame you if you wanted to give yourself some time to get used to having a wolf again before going through it."

She locks eyes with me. "There is no right answer. We all have to go through it at some point. And because Ansel is your mate —" Dinah squints an eye and catches herself. "Maybe your mate. That doesn't mean you have to have him service you through it. I'm sure Ansel has a couple of ideas on how to keep you alone and safe. Then you would both have confirmation one way or another."

She pours herself another drink.

"Okay." I hesitate and take a sip of my own. "This isn't exactly something he'll talk about with me."

"Oh, I can only imagine." She groans but lets it go. "I can have Lena send a whole care package for you. She loves that sort of stuff. Freaks in bed the both of them."

"And if I decide to do it with Ansel . . ." *How the fuck do you ask someone for condoms?*

Dinah pulls her phone out of her pocket and talks to herself. "Big dumb asshole . . . No, it's 'Fuck In The' . . . No . . . Ah, fuck it, Ireland's area code is 353? Oh, there he is, 'Here Fishy Fishy.'"

She's speaking in gibberish, I'm sure of it.

Ringing comes from her phone, and she turns the volume up.

"Yes, Dinah." An Irish accent comes through the other end of the line.

343

"Is Lena still in time-out?" She physically pouts at her phone.

Finn growls, "Yes, because someone can't learn to keep her hands to herself."

"Kinky. Anyway, can you help her put a care package together, then, if I text you the gist of what I need?" Dinah rolls her eyes.

"For you, anything." Finn laughs. "Send me the supplies and the address, and I'll be sure to get it in the post."

"No, need it overnighted," Dinah snaps.

"Excuse me?" Finn growls.

"You're not the boss of me," Dinah growls back.

There's a giggle on the other end of the line.

"God forbid the two of you spend more time in one place," Finn mutters. "I'll have it overnighted, and when Kathleen figures out how to behave for more than five minutes in public, I'll have her call you."

"Thank you." Dinah draws out the *o* before a quick "Okay, bye!"

She pushes the disconnect button and smiles at me. "Getting Lena in trouble is my new favorite thing."

"Do I even want to know?" After taking the last sip of my drink, I pull an ice cube in and crunch it.

Dinah rolls her eyes. "It's best experienced, not talked about."

Drawing another sip of her drink and finally setting her glass on the counter, she looks toward the back door. "How long do we let him torture himself?"

I snort, waiting for her to text him. She doesn't move for her phone.

"Are you serious?" My mouth hangs open.

Dinah nestles on the couch in response.

# CHAPTER 49
## ANSEL

My beer is warm. I've paced pretty much the entire length of Ben's house more times than I can count.

Ben's been watching me go back and forth, stopping me every time I go to text Dinah.

"Enough's enough," Ben scolds.

He puts his hands on my shoulders and directs me to his couch. I sit and try to stay seated under his scrutiny. Before sitting in his chair, he hands me a glass of whiskey. Once he takes a seat, he mixes whiskey with ginger ale.

Stretching back in his chair, he asks, "Are you more afraid that she is your mate or that she isn't?"

"Is." I take a swig from my cup.

Ben doesn't let up. "The Walt thing?"

This time, I take a drink first, too sober to answer these kinds of questions. "Partly. There are so many reasons. Ben, I can't do this."

"Her as your mate? Or talk about her?" he asks.

*Both.* But the problem is I need help. Ben is my voice of reason. He's never let me live in my land of denial. Laying it out there will only make it more real. Maybe reality is what I need? Maybe hearing how messed up this is will straighten things out. I take another drink, a larger gulp, hoping my nearly empty stomach and the straight whiskey will work.

"I'm fifteen to sixteen years older than her. I was there the day she was born. Walt made me promise to take care of her. Damn well bet he didn't mean it in a mating sense. We're at completely different places in life. Someday she's gonna want kids, and what am I even gonna say to that? No? Because I've got a bunch of fractured wolves down the hill? That our child would be easy prey for an attack? Or worse."

"Or worse?" He kicks off his socks, sliding them off one after another.

"Or worse," I sigh, pulling my hand down my face and through my beard. "Ben, this is a shit situation."

I wait, hoping he deposits wisdom on me. Silence isn't wisdom.

"What if Harry snaps?" That's a truth I don't like knowing.

Ben shakes his head. "No."

That's all he says, and then we sit in silence.

I finish my drink and look at the ceiling. Probably should be painted. When did I last make Ben do improvements on his cabin?

I pull out my phone, but there's no message from Dinah. I set it and my whiskey glass on the small table next to my chair.

I didn't intend to have another glass, but Ben pours me one. "Yes, she's young. Yes, she's Walt's kid. She's got an attitude problem, but is she really any different than Sherman, Zero, or me? Morrigan didn't get a good shake in life and needs time and a gentle hand."

I nod. He doesn't bond with a lot of the fractures sent here. Says it helps him stay objective. So it's kind of a shock that he's comparing her to our long-term residents.

"But, worst-case scenario, if she is your mate" — he pauses to take a sip of his fizzy drink — "then you need to come to terms with it and find a way to forgive yourself like she's forgiven you."

*Why does he make that seem so simple?*

Harry presses wanting to see her. I check my phone again. Nothing.

Shaking my head, I pick up the glass. "There's a letter from Walt to Morrigan in the safe," I confess.

"What does it say?" Ben asks.

I raise my glass with a tilt. "Who knows?"

"You didn't open it?" Ben raises an eyebrow at me.

Shaking my head, I explain. "It wasn't meant for me. But I'm worried 'bout what it'll do to her. I saw her wolf push herself forward."

"And if you give it to her, what's the worst that will happen?" Ben prompts.

"What if it sets back everything she's been goin' through? The progress." I let my shoulders droop as I sit here and really think it through.

The worst-case scenario isn't whatever is in that letter upsetting Morrigan. The worst-case scenario is that Walt's daughter is my mate. If finding your mate is supposed to be a happy occasion, then why am I rooting for Dinah to end it before we know for sure?

Hanging my head, I look at the glass in my hand before throwing back the rest of my drink.

I text Dinah to warn her I'm coming back with the excuse that I waited too long to feed Princeton, but it's a small lie. He had a late lunch, so another hour wouldn't be a big deal, but I've been out of my house long enough.

"Do us a favor and let Dinah tell you how things are before

you make decisions on what your life is and get stubborn about it." Ben sighs.

He picks up my glass from where I set it on the table.

I show myself out while he heads to the back of his cabin toward the kitchen.

## CHAPTER 50

# ANSEL

WHEN I COME IN THE BACK DOOR, DINAH IS WAITING. SHE PROMPTLY holds one finger up in front of her lips, silencing me. Backing away, she points over the top of the couch and turns away from me to walk up the stairs to the guest bedrooms.

If I want her to come back, I have to speak, but I'm guessing she's telling me Morrigan is on the sofa. Avoiding the squeaky boards on the floor, I walk to the couch and find Morrigan asleep. She's curled up under the blanket I keep over the back of the couch. How tightly she's curled up makes it look like she might be cold.

I navigate to my bedroom and pull one of the blankets off my bed. When I bring it back and drape it over her, she wiggles and snuggles in. Her little fingers wrap around the fabric and bring it closer to her face. With a small sigh, she goes right back to her soft, little sleeping noises.

The ache in my chest is back. I rub it, trying to relieve the pressure. *What is this?*

After taking the raw meat I thawed for Princeton out of the fridge, I put it into a bowl while still in the packages and head downstairs. I can prep it on Ben's treatment table to cut down on the noise up here.

Princeton is still in his wolf form. And as usual in this situation, the whole basement reeks of wolf mess.

There is an improvement, though, when he doesn't snarl or fight the cage doors upon seeing me.

"You know, I'm really fucking sick of cleaning up after you. Could you shift back so we can move on with this portion of your life?" I groan, setting the bowl down.

I unwrap the packages and start the usual tasks of creating a pile of various raw proteins in the bowl.

I keep talking to him. "It doesn't have to be this way. You could work on your anger issues. Maybe settle down and get yourself right. Can't imagine there aren't things in your life you want to do. You're smart, and with that argumentative spirit, maybe you become a lawyer or one of those advocates for human kids."

Uninterested, Princeton doesn't even pretend to listen.

"You've four more days to get your shit together before I have to call your Alpha. At that point, he and I gotta make the decision. But most wolves that won't shift meet the same fate. You'll notice there are no permanent residents down here. It's no way to live. I've lived it. I won't let someone else go through that." I look over at Princeton.

His eyes are focused on me, so at least he's decided to listen.

I set the bowl in the adjacent kennel and get ready to unlock his door.

"Move calmly," I command him firmly while sliding the bars open. "Come to the next one."

I keep my eyes on him, and it's less of a fight than it was yesterday. Princeton moves as instructed and starts eating. I lock him in before grabbing the hose and washing up the kennel he was in today.

By the time I make my way back up the stairs, my limbs feel like they weigh a hundred pounds. A shower sounds so good. Lazily, I move from my bedroom to the bathroom and turn on the water.

No one died today. I didn't die today. Tomorrow doesn't look good. But it's a new day, and it's too early to know for sure.

# CHAPTER 51
# ANSEL

MORRIGAN IS STILL SNOOZING ON THE SOFA WHEN I COME OUT OF THE bedroom. The smell of fresh coffee lets me know that my caffeine-addict cousin is awake and lurking somewhere.

It doesn't take me long to find her. Dinah is sitting on the deck and looking at her phone with a very telling grin.

"Tell Soren I say good morning." Yawning, I walk past her to sit in the second chair.

With a laugh, Dinah cocks her head. "Think that probably won't go over so well. But I'll stop messaging him mid-conversation. That'll drive him nuts for a while."

"What does Ezra call that? A red flag?" I shake my head.

Dinah nearly spits out her coffee. "Oh, yeah. I know I'm a red flag. No one expects anything less at this point. But we're not here to talk about my sexual exploits."

She's not wrong. Dinah runs her hand up into her hair and brushes it out of her eyes before resting her hand on her shoulder where her mating mark remains. With a shake of her head, she starts, "What is your problem?"

"My problem is that I suddenly have no impulse control." I

draw a deep breath. It's hard to say. *Time to come clean.* "I've been inappropriate with her."

Unexpectedly, she snorts. "Is that what we're calling it these days?"

"No, you're right. It's probably assault." The hair on the back of my neck rises.

Dinah sighs and wiggles herself down in her chair, getting comfortable. The more she relaxes, the more uncomfortable I become. I pull the hair tie out of my pocket and wrap it around my hair, holding it back out of my face.

"It's not assault. It's not inappropriate." Dinah rolls her eyes and pities me.

"I can't do this," I admit, no longer able to even look in her direction.

My eyes drift through Cade's new windows to look at Morrigan, but that makes my stomach hurt worse.

"Quit torturing yourself!" she whisper yells, looking over her shoulder to make sure her volume didn't wake Morrigan. "For fuck's sake, Ansel. Let it go."

"You know what's happened. I told her to tell you," I hiss back.

"And?" Dinah questions. She draws a sip of her coffee. Shaking her head, she starts and stops whatever she's saying a few times before finally giving me something, anything, to indicate what she's thinking. "You can see it as plain as I can, her wolf is coming back. She'll probably shift before the month's out, and then I would put money on her going into heat before spring Equinox."

*That doesn't make this okay.*

I don't know why I thought Dinah would help.

"Stop," she growls. "Ansel, I'm telling you to stop."

"Stop what? Telling you I've broken our laws?" My words come out sharp.

Dinah sips her coffee slowly. She takes her time to answer my questions. "Please, you break fifteen of our laws every day you keep your pack alive. Let's not pretend either of us are lawful good. We'll leave that job to Judah."

I don't know what lawful good means. I'll have to ask Ben later. Each word she picked seems so important. What is she trying to say? That I'm being selective in my rule following? I guess that's true.

"I love you, Ansel." She smiles at me before standing up with her coffee mug in hand. "It all works out in the end."

The way she says the words, the ones I've said a hundred thousand times, at least makes me smile. I'm not dying for what I've done to Morrigan. I trust Dinah enough to know she means what she says. I wish she'd tell me more. Even with her reassurance, it doesn't mean I'm supposed to continue on this path.

"Give me a hug," Dinah orders with a laugh.

I stand and wrap my arms around her. "You sure you gotta go?"

"Yeah. I do. You don't need me. I'll only be in your way," Dinah whispers.

When I let her go, it seems like she takes some of my sadness with her. It fizzles out like a bottle rocket that didn't get enough fuel.

"Alright, I'll walk you out, then." I slide the new door along its track.

I refuse to acknowledge that it doesn't squeak like the last one, that it moves nice and easy, and that I didn't have to fix it myself. *Stupid security system.*

RATHER THAN WAKE MORRIGAN UP RIGHT AWAY, I GO TO THE cupboard above the dishwasher and open the door. It used to house my snacks, but now the fancy computer systems and charging docks have taken it over. Following the instructions we wrote out together, I push the buttons and navigate the cameras to the basement. The feed stops intuitively on the cell Princeton is in. Where I expected the large gray wolf to be, I get an eyeful of the bits I'd rather not see on Princeton.

*Let's hope he's ready to play nice.*

# CHAPTER 52
## MORRIGAN

FOOTSTEPS ECHO BACK AND FORTH ACROSS THE HOUSE. THEN THE door closes. I could go back to sleep for a little longer. It's not like we're doing anything today, right?

My bladder doesn't get the message. Awake and angry, I escort the stupid little organ up the stairs to the bathroom.

"For fear of sounding stereotypical," Ansel starts as I open the door to the bathroom.

"Uhhh. What?" I look over the balcony at him.

"Princeton decided he was sick of having four feet during the night." Ansel shakes his head. "Can you go through the drawers up there and find something that might fit him?"

"Yeah." I yawn.

When I come downstairs, Ansel's in the kitchen. He has a variety of bowls of ingredients out. A rice cooker sits on the counter behind him, and two baking sheets with white rice are laid out next to it, steam billowing off the top.

"You still don't like oatmeal, right?" Ansel asks without looking up.

"Ew, oatmeal." I lay the clothes for Princeton over the rail to the basement and sit at the counter.

I've barely set my butt on the stool when Ansel starts, "Listen, we need to talk."

"Sure." I eye the coffee pot behind him.

As if reading my mind, Ansel turns around to the cupboard where he put the mugs in his reorganization, pulls out one of the fancy ceramic ones, and pours me a cup of coffee.

The milk sits on the counter a little way down, and I reach over and grab it to pour some into my cup.

"About us." He shakes his head while looking at me.

*Where is this conversation going?* As I sip my coffee, it gives me a reason not to interrupt him and someplace to focus that isn't on worst-case scenarios.

"We have our issues. Just because Dinah says it's not a big deal. Us. You, me." He struggles for words. "Doesn't mean we should do this." Ansel motions his hands between us, indicating.

The silence is uncomfortable. Not forcing any more words, Ansel goes back to cooking.

"I don't want to pretend," I start.

I watch Ansel for any signs, any indication at all, that he's feeling something. Clearly, he is. Because his movements stiffen, but he doesn't stop moving. His knife glides through the onion in front of him.

"I don't want to pretend there's nothing between us. Dinah said connection is important. How we're connecting is probably bringing my wolf back." I weave that lie into the truth so tightly I hope it rings true.

That poor onion didn't stand a chance. Ansel's knife skills in the kitchen are scary. It's off the cutting board in a flash, and he's quickly moving on to the garlic. Quick strokes slice with the precision of a master chef.

"I'm not saying that we jump into bed together." *It would be so good though. What is wrong with me?* I run my hand back through my hair.

Green eyes are locked on me. Carefully, trying to look natural about it, I pull my hair to one side, exposing my neck to him.

His nostrils flaring and the sound of a deep breath are the only indications I need. *Ansel wants me too.* His green eyes darken to black. *Harbinger wants me.*

"I'm saying that spending more time together might be a good thing." The words come out slower, and I raise my tone at the end, delivering my statement as a question.

Ansel's eyes turn deep brown before glossing over white.

*Well, at least he wasn't frying anything.*

I drink my coffee, waiting for him, wherever his gift has taken him. I remember seeing this as a child. It was mystifying and seemed so spectacular. But Ansel wasn't the same after a vision. He was much more somber and sad.

"Fuck," Ansel hisses.

He squeezes his eyes shut and drops the knife. Backing away from the cutting board, he heads over to the sink.

After washing his hands, he turns around and leans his ass against the counter. Crossing his arms in front of his chest, he looks at me before looking down. Free strands of his hair fall forward and rest on his shoulders.

"Princeton won't survive the week." Ansel doesn't look at me.

I swallow. "Oh."

Tension radiates from Ansel. He's clenching his fists and releasing them. The muscles in his forearms ripple. Ansel raises his head, eyes still deep brown. Harbinger is watching me.

"Harry doesn't like him. Princeton's outwardly violent. He's picking fights and failing to find order. I don't want you alone with him. Ever." Ansel's shoulders heave with a very forced deep breath. Brown-black eyes brighten to green.

"Okay," I answer.

"I don't tell people this sort of stuff." Ansel steps up to the cutting board again.

Picking up the knife, he moves on to slicing carrots on the bias. The thin slices will fry in the pan and get crispy.

*He's making Dad's rice recipe.* Happy memories of breakfasts with Dad pull on my heartstrings. But this isn't the time for happy memories.

"Why are you telling me?" I ask quietly, embracing the secret nature of the conversation.

"Because of what you said the other day." Ansel puts the knife down again.

He takes the pans of rice out the side door to the covered porch and returns, picking up where he left off. "Princeton is another predator. You're a very easy target for us."

Frustration leaves my mouth in angry words. "Don't call yourself a predator."

"It's exactly what I am, Morrigan. Even if you don't feel afraid of me. There's little difference between me and the man locked up downstairs." Ansel laughs, but it's dark, ominous. "The only difference is I know how to escape." He points, demonstrating which way for me to go in the basement. "The cell on the far left, when you look at them from the stairs, is the only one I can't get out of." Ansel confides in me. He nods his head. "Ben knows."

This morning had so much promise. But Wednesdays are weird, and this one is no exception. I'm not taking no for an answer.

"I don't want anyone to live in a kennel if they don't have to. Prolonging the inevitable isn't fair to him." Ansel swallows hard and starts tossing onions, garlic, and a squeeze of ginger paste into the wok, where he had oil warming up on the stove. They crackle and hiss.

"So, what you're saying is you're letting Princeton out knowing that you're putting the guys at risk. And you don't want me to leave your side because I can't protect myself." I start piecing together what I'm thinking.

Ansel nods. "The guys can fend for themselves. Princeton's small. They know he doesn't fit. They're good about working together to defend themselves against someone who has snapped." His jaw grinds before he finishes the thought. "If I didn't feel so shitty after I do it, I'd take him out now and end him. Harry doesn't care. Violence is violence. But I get to feeling guilty, knowing I could have given them more time to say goodbye."

"So, you're telling him his time is up?" I pick my words slowly.

He shakes his head and tosses sliced asparagus into the wok next.

Ansel explains further. "That ends in frenzied violence. I drop hints and try to nudge them in that direction. I don't know if it even helps the fami . . ."

Ansel's voice trails off. He stirs the contents of the wok.

"I don't know," I admit. Tears sting my eyes, and I hate them for betraying me. This newfound emotion hurts. I'm not used to it. "I've always wished I could have said goodbye. If I could have made that last hug longer. Or if I could have, I don't know. Told him I loved him. Would it have fixed him?"

His words are firm. "No. Walt was gone. He was gone long before your last visit. Morrigan, nothing you could have done, even being here, would have stopped it."

Somehow, what he says makes it better. It doesn't take away the pit of grief that holds me captive. But the grave feels less deep. Maybe there's hope, even a little, that it won't always hurt this much.

Ansel quickly whisks egg yolks and seasonings in a bowl with a fork. He then beats together egg whites in a different bowl, and I know he'll fry them separately and make golden fried rice. Grief holds that hollow part in my heart as I think of all the times Dad made this for me for breakfast.

"Do . . ." *Can I ask this? There isn't a reason not to?* "Do you remember anything from before Dad?"

Ansel shakes his head. "Nothing good. I learned everything from your dad. Ersilia helped after he met her too. But from that first day in the pack, Walt walked up, kicked me in the shin, and told me we were friends. I'm not sure it's the best way to make friends, but I was so glad to not be alone." He laughs, shaking his head while he starts frying egg whites with the onions. "But to answer your question, there isn't a whole lot of normal people things I know how to do that your dad didn't have a hand in."

I shake my head. "We have a lot in common."

"Yeah." Laughter breaks the tension. Ansel shakes his head and continues. "We do. But he was a lot more gentle with you than me. Then again, he had more practice, and it wasn't like you could even help yourself. The day you were born, he was terrified to even touch you. Walt practically cried every time you did. You were perfect and, he was certain, made of porcelain. Obviously, he eventually got it in his brain that you're a wolf and even as an infant, you'd be resilient, but the first week, I almost moved out."

"Shit, it was that bad?" I find myself laughing with him.

"Worse." Ansel rolls his eyes. He goes out to the covered porch and comes back. A gust of cold air comes with him. "When you were starting to walk, you fell over and hit your head on that coffee table." Ansel indicates with his head toward the living room. "You didn't even get a goose egg. But he wrapped the table in four blankets and wondered if your mom would notice if he got rid of it."

Ansel carefully pours the rice off the pans into a large bowl. He breaks apart the rice clumps and forms a hollow in the center. Then he pours the yolk mixture in with it.

He groans. "Can you stir this while I see if Princeton can play nice for a meal?"

"If he can't, can I have his share of the food?" I bargain.

"Absolutely," Ansel answers, walking around the island toward the stairs and me.

His hand brushes my shoulder, and my skin heats from that touch, running through my body. A chill strikes me as the warmth dissipates.

*Come back.* The little voice whispers, and my mouth almost echoes the call.

## CHAPTER 53
# MORRIGAN

PRINCETON SUCKS, AND I HATE HIM. YOU WOULD THINK AFTER spending four days in the kennels in wolf form, he'd at least have the common sense to act humbled. Alas, the minute he's done scarfing down two bowls of the delicious golden rice and vegetables, he opens his mouth and words come out. They don't stop.

Princeton's voice reverberates through my brain. He spews lies mixed with facts, like having 'gone' to Princeton. How he 'dated' a senator's daughter.

I don't know how long it's been. All I know is that it's been too long.

How does one person talk this much? Is there a daily limit on words that people are allowed to speak?

Princeton crossed it for sure.

I look up at the clock, hoping to gauge how long I've been tortured …

*It's only been ten minutes?*

A knock comes to the back door, and Ansel actually gets up

from the table. Ansel hasn't let anyone in the entire time I've been here. Pretty sure the reason isn't the new security system.

"Hey, Zero. Come on in, bud." Ansel's voice is uncharacteristically loud. "Princeton's leaving, so you and I can get a chat in."

I stand up from the table and take my bowl and fork to the sink. Ansel turns to Princeton, and I watch out of the corner of my eye.

"You should go get cleaned up. Maybe stretch out and unwind a bit. We're back on a jobsite tomorrow," Ansel instructs Princeton.

"Well, if you two are talking . . ." Princeton eye fucks me, and I fight the urge to gag. He continues his sentence. "Maybe . . . Morrigan and I can hang. Get to . . . know each other . . . better."

This time I do gag, and I cover it behind a cough.

"Oh, well." I'm quick to reach for an excuse.

Ansel rudely lets me speak.

If I was human, I would being fake sick, say I'm feeling unwell and want to go lie down. But being a wolf means there's no excuse. We don't get physically ill.

With a shrug, my brain finally finds something that's almost logical. "I'm gonna do an oil treatment for my hair. It's still not in great shape, and with how cold it is today, I'd planned to spend the day in the bathroom, making it my own personal spa. You know, being girly."

Princeton, of course, has an objection. "Shouldn't you do that Saturday, so it has a full day to rest before you pull it up for work?"

"Princeton. Boundaries." Zero rises to my defense. "She said no."

"What? You the boss now?" Princeton snaps at him.

Ansel steps toward him. "No. I am. Go out the sliding glass

door and go to your place. I'm not asking. I'll use the command if I have to."

With a massive, immature sigh, the alleged Princeton graduate turns and walks out the sliding glass door.

"Thanks, Zero." I give him a big smile.

He nods, not answering me.

Without any questions, Ansel lets me raid his kitchen for ingredients. Sugar, salt, honey, olive oil; it's a whole slew of ingredients for a day at the makeshift spa upstairs. The idea of even doing it myself is delightful. Would I love a professional wash and cut? Yes. Absolutely. Am I making the most of this? One hundred percent.

I DON'T KNOW HOW LONG AGO ZERO LEFT, BUT ANSEL'S HALFWAY through a rom-com when I emerge from the bathroom wrapped in a towel. He laughs at a scene that runs across the screen with a bit of slapstick comedy.

*How does he do that so easily? Why does joy come so easily to other people?* Retreating to my bedroom, I comb through the clothes Ansel's gotten me over the past few weeks. My size is still changing. It's frustrating, but it's a good thing. Maybe.

Clean and cozy in sweats, there's only one bit of self-care I haven't done . . . But it'll only be a disappointment. What I want is downstairs on the couch, chuckling at the television, and, as he's made absolutely clear, not on the table.

But, with some coaxing, maybe I can get it on the menu. Fortune favors the bold kinda worked last time, so maybe it works better this time.

Tying the back of my T-shirt up, I expose my mid-section. I'm absolutely not above playing to a man's weakness. Not when I know what I want. *And he wants.*

*Ours.* The soft-spoken voice in my head is much more regular now.

As much as I hate to admit it, Dinah might be right. I've been embracing the empty, and it's helping. But she's also louder when Ansel is near, so I'm embracing anything that brings her back. Even if he is being stubborn about it.

Hearing my footsteps on the stairs, Ansel looks over his shoulder at me. His eyes go wide before he looks away. When I walk past to sit next to him on the sofa, he moves over to the far side.

Am I being too forward? Am I chasing a man? Is this pretty much the most stereotypical thing in the world? Woman chases man she can't have. Well, desperate times call for desperate measures.

Ansel is firm against us being together, but I can see that shield coming down. Wolves are physical. We crave touch. He can't hold out forever.

When I go into heat, we'll know for sure. Dinah said soon. But maybe I can't wait that long, and hopefully, Ansel can be worn down. I follow him across the sofa, and he's trapped between me and the arm.

Ansel makes a terrible pillow. He's rigid and uncomfortable while I lean against him. I rest my hand on his leg, and when he places his on top of mine, I think I'm getting through.

Access denied.

He removes my hand and goes back to focusing on the movie.

# CHAPTER 54
# ANSEL

I'VE REMOVED HER HAND. AFTER GETTING UP AND MAKING US popcorn, I settled in on the other end of the couch, but Morrigan moves with me each and every time.

She's lying down with her head resting on my knee while her feet rest on the arm on the end. It's pure torture. There's no way, with her tied-up T-shirt and low-hung pants, Morrigan isn't trying to push all my buttons.

It's working. The zipper on my jeans hurts. My pants are way too tight when sitting down to deal with the proximity of her head in my lap.

The end credits roll, and I gently pet her shoulder. "I'm heading to bed."

"Yeah. I bet the workday comes early." Morrigan sits up and yawns, stretching her arms over her head.

The T-shirt rises and barely covers the bottom of her breasts.

Morrigan catches me looking at her and smirks. "I don't have to go to bed upstairs."

"You really do." My mouth feels dry, and I flee to the kitchen.

Morrigan meanders about the living room, picking up the popcorn bowl and napkins.

I close my eyes to avoid watching her lithe hips swing back and forth as she walks closer. *Get some fucking self-control, Ansel.*

Indicating to the switch with a nod, I walk over to the glass door and flip the locking mechanism. My feet don't move fast enough as I walk toward the back door and flip that one as well. Then I head to my shoe bench space, where the security station for arming the house is.

"House secure." The panel beeps at me.

"Well, if you're sure." Morrigan lingers at the edge of the kitchen counter for a moment.

With a nod, I answer, "You know I am."

A sad sigh escapes her lips, and Morrigan flips the final light switch and heads up the stairs.

My bedroom is cold. The heating register has been closed since the hired intruders were in here installing my new window. Normally, I don't sleep with the bedroom door open. But even for running hot, my room is too cold to be comfortable. After sliding the vent open, I strip my jeans and pull on pajama bottoms.

Closing my eyes, I beg sleep to find me quickly. Anything to stop the replay of thoughts of us on the couch together.

Sleep doesn't arrive. The sounds coming from my loft chase it off. Morrigan always sleeps with her door open, and tonight, she's using it to her advantage.

Loud and clear, her little moans cut through the quiet of the house. A telltale sound as she begins to pleasure herself. I picture her lithe hips rising off the bed.

My cock pitches a tent against my sweatpants. Gripping the bedsheet, I force myself to stay right where I am.

I'm not doing this. Taking her. The first violation, that kiss, one minute of weakness, was enough of a mistake. Breathing deeply, I try to block her and the raging hard-on out of my mind.

"Ansel." My name leaves her lips.

I slam the pillow down over my head. No. No. We aren't getting out of this bed. Her begging doesn't change the fact that what I've done is disrespectful. It's dirty. Disloyal.

"Ansel. Please," she whimpers.

It's louder. I can hear her pleas through my pillow.

Her begging pushes me out of bed, but I catch myself on the doorframe. It creaks from the pressure of squeezing it with my hand.

No. I'm stronger than this. Extending my arm, I grab the door and slowly push it closed. I know it won't completely cut out what I can hear of her lust.

I press my head against the door. The physical barrier between us helps lessen the disgusting urge to commit a repeat offense and touch her the way I did in the truck.

I'm strong enough not to run up the stairs and give her what we both want but not strong enough to keep my hands out of my pants. My sweats are on the floor, and I've stepped out of them before I get back to bed. I'm pumping myself before I lie back. The memory of how good she felt with her arms wrapped around me hits at the same time a muffled cry comes from the loft.

Guilt again. This is just as bad as fucking her, isn't it? *Fuck.*

She calls my name again.

My hand squeezes along the shaft on its way up to the tip. Precum has beaded there, already coating me. It's been an agonizing couple of days resisting her. I'll work her out of my system. Alone.

"Ansel. Please. Fuck me." It's muffled, but Morrigan's voice still floats down from the loft and through my closed door.

My hips rise, bucking into my hand. Traitorous thoughts continue, like how good she felt pressed against me, my lips locked on hers, the feeling of my fingers wrapped around her neck. In the truck, her hesitation melted away as she trusted me to make her feel good. All I did was push us to this point.

I want to watch her finger her clit while her eyes focus on my cock sinking into her.

I'm coated with sweat. My cock gives an angry throb, wanting to be buried inside her sweet pussy.

Morrigan screams upstairs. The sound of her orgasm echoes through the entire house and seeps into my bones.

I clench my jaw, keeping my own release quiet. My cock throbs. My heels dig down on the bed, and I brace myself with my shoulders.

It's an unsatisfying release.

I'm gasping for air, and my lust isn't sated.

I breathe, trying to bring my heart rate back down.

*Why does she have to be so perfect?* Morrigan is driving me to madness.

*This can't happen again.* It's a quick acceleration. One kiss, an inappropriate touch, and now this. It doesn't feel like there's anything I can do about it either.

No one died today. Soon, but not today.

# CHAPTER 55

# MORRIGAN

Work was brutal. It was cold, and the falling snow just made everything more glum. Ansel said nothing at all about my stunt last night. And now, walking in the door at the end of the workday, Ansel stops in his tracks.

"Ansel?" I ask behind him, pushing on his back.

His body moves to stop itself from falling over, but it doesn't look like he's paying attention. The step he takes forward, though, is enough for me to get in the door and close it behind us.

Not moving any farther is even more spooky.

I step up onto the shoe bench to get in front of him. His eyes are glossed over with his gift.

The security panel on the wall beeps. Ansel didn't change the security code, so I enter the password I helped him set up, and the beeps stop.

Taking off my jacket and shoes, I wait. Nearly five minutes pass, and Ansel hasn't moved from his spot.

*What do I do?* I sit on the bench, looking at him standing perfectly still. *I guess start dinner?*

I pull things out of the fridge and slice an assortment of veggies, but Ansel still hasn't moved.

Nearly twenty minutes pass, and Ansel is still wearing his coat. I can only imagine, with the heat on, that he's over-heating.

"Ansel?" I stand in front of him, calling his name. "Ansel, can you take off your coat?"

He doesn't answer.

"Harry?" I'm talking to a wolf I don't even know. This is ridiculous. "Harry, can you let Ansel come back, please? I need him."

Ansel's eyes flash dark but go back to white.

*Okay, so Harry can hear me.* I try one more time. "Harry. I need Ansel. Give him back."

This time there's no movement.

Putting my shoes back on, I forgo the coat and step over the bench again. I head back out the door to the driveway to go get Ben. I think I saw his truck on the way in. If anyone knows what to do, it'll be him. I think.

"Hey, Morrigan. I was coming to find you." Princeton's slimy voice hits me before I even get the door closed.

It's too late to go back into the house. I look over my shoulder through the window in the door, and Ansel is still frozen, facing the inside of the house.

When I look back, Princeton is significantly closer than I expected. He's in front of me, with his arms outstretched, grip-ping the railings and blocking my path down the stairs.

A knot in my belly tells me there's no way I can turn, open the door, get inside, and lock it before he ascends those four small steps into the house. Would that bust Ansel out of his vision or just get more messy?

*Get an excuse and get moving. To open spaces where . . . what? I can outrun a wolf? No, where someone could see or hear.* There's safety in a pack.

I steel myself with a game plan. It has to work.

Motioning with my hand, I look down the road toward where the cabins are. "I need to go borrow some salt from Ben."

*Really? Salt?* What a dumb lie. I've lied a hundred times before, and that's what I come up with? Pathetic.

Princeton steps aside, opening my path, but his body still blocks me from Ben's. *Well, it's not stupid if it works.*

He stepped out of the way of the path that would lead me toward the garage. It's the opposite way. Someplace more secluded. *No. Nope. Fuck.*

I walk down the stairs and look back over my shoulder at the door one more time. With no movement coming from inside, I redirect toward the pack and Ben's cabin and attempt to go around Princeton.

A hand grips me just above my elbow. I pull back, trying to get away from him, but Princeton wraps his arm around my shoulder.

*I don't want you alone with him. Ever.* Ansel's voice is in my brain.

Ansel doesn't mince words. I need to get away from him right fucking now. I can handle this. *Don't show him any distress. Be calm like Ansel would be.* I may not have a wolf, and the wolf I had may not have been an Alpha . . . but if I keep cool and casual, this doesn't have to go poorly.

"I'd really like to get to know you better," Princeton coos like he's trying to seduce me.

Swallowing hard, I shake my head and try to divert Princeton's advances. "I don't think that's a good idea. There are intentions out against me. My stepfather wouldn't like it."

Ben's house is to the left down the hill. Stepping in that

direction doesn't work. Princeton's bigger and stronger than me. He guides my steps toward the garage.

When I plant my feet, Princeton keeps moving me, nearly dragging me with him.

"Princeton, I'm uncomfortable with how close you are to me. Move away from me," I state firmly, explaining and giving him no room to argue with what I dislike.

I try to find any air of authority. Anything to get his attention without asking for him to release me. I don't want him to think he should have a choice in any of this.

When he doesn't answer, I try again. "Princeton. You need to let me go. I need to go to Ben's and get back."

Fear may be what gets him off. I have to be in control. Well, the best I can. *He's just a guy at a club, getting handsy. You've done this a million times before.*

"Don't lie, Morrigan. You've been thinking about me like I've been thinking about you. The way you've been flirting with me." Princeton leans closer to me.

*I don't want you alone with him. Ever.* Ansel's words hit me again.

*Fuck!*

We've made it all the way over to the garage. I know it's locked from when I looked at the security panel, which is too bad. I would gladly let him steal Ansel's truck to get out of this.

Looking at the pad, I ask, "Do you want me to unlock the door? You could take the truck."

Princeton pins me between his chest and the metal door, placing his hands on either side of my head. The metal is cold against my back. Not grabbing a coat is now torturing me. I shiver.

He moves his weight from his hands one at a time to shuffle down and lean on his elbows in the same place, removing so much more space from between us.

He whispers, "I don't want to go anywhere. We should stay, you can accept me as your mate. Screw the other intentions."

"That's not how this will work. You know that intentions can be really serious." *What do I say to get him to give up?*

I try to keep my breathing level as if holding back my fear might save me.

"You're afraid of how Ansel will react." Princeton scoffs. "You don't think I've realized who you're intended to? He's old enough to be your dad. Don't be disgusting."

"That's not what this is. You're misreading the situation." I shake my head. At least this time it isn't a lie. "I'm not intended to Ansel."

"I've seen the way you look at me. You wouldn't have invited me to play beanbags with you if you didn't feel this way." Princeton shifts his weight.

He runs his hand down the side of my face and rests it on my neck, stroking my cheek with his thumb.

I fight back a shiver.

"You know how beautiful you are, don't you?" he whispers, leaning closer to me.

Our noses are nearly touching.

"Princeton, move. I don't want this." I try to be firm, but without a wolf, it's about as threatening as a house cat to an elephant.

There's no way I don't reek of fear at this point. I'm fighting to control my quivering.

*Do I push him back?* Ugh. Why don't I know self-defense? *Because I'm a fucking wolf and should have claws and teeth.*

Princeton leans forward and draws a breath, running his nose up my neck.

*Please, Ansel, come back.*

"I can smell your fear, Morrigan. You don't have to be afraid. I'll protect you from Ansel," Princeton presses.

I turn my head away from him. Why are men so dense? I don't understand how he doesn't get that I'm not interested.

"You're afraid your parents won't approve? They don't matter. I'll show you they don't matter." Princeton guesses, and of course, it comes down to his perception of my life.

My knee-jerk reaction is to scrunch my face and betray the calm I'd been trying to keep. *Shit. I shouldn't have . . ..*

"That's okay. I know you want to be a good, obedient wife. You need a man to be head of the house." Princeton spews more misogynistic, sexist bullshit. "I bet you'll look so good barefoot and pregnant with my pups. We can breed our own baseball team."

Lunch was hours ago, but my stomach churns, threatening to bring the contents back up. He sounds like Gerad. More sexist, but just like Gerad.

"Princeton, really. Move. This isn't okay. I need to go," I urge while looking for a way out of this situation.

The self-defense videos online say you need to be commanding and forceful, but my voice is shaking.

To the left is the wooden doorframe, and the right is more open as it runs across the aluminum garage door. I don't know if I can get past him, even with the advantage of surprise and being small.

Princeton tips my chin back toward him and kisses me. I freeze. His tongue pushes against my lips, and my fist bangs on the garage behind me, hoping anyone will hear.

I try turning my head, but Princeton holds me harder.

He growls, "Stop doing that. Don't scream. If you scream, I'll have to do things to you. Bad things. Let me make you feel good."

*No. No. How did this happen?* I close my eyes. *Fuck, I'm an idiot.* Ansel said he was dangerous, and I could have just stolen Ansel's phone to call Ben.

Princeton presses his lips against mine again. My stomach revolts, and my fight or flight instinct kicks in.

He breaks the kiss and whispers, "Fuck, I've got to have my dick in your tight cunt right now. You a virgin, baby? I want to be the first one to split you open and get that virgin blood on my cock."

*Ew. Fuck.* Where is Ansel? How has he not come back from his visions yet?

I push my arms up to try and get space between us, but he's too close to me.

*You know what would be helpful right now? Being able to turn into a fucking wolf.* I try finding one inside me but come up blank. I try begging into that void. *Please, if you're there. Please. Please.*

Princeton moves his hands between us. Without him holding my chin, I have the smallest bit of room to move. As hard as I can, I lift my knee, trying to hit Princeton in the groin. But he's too close to me. And the hitch of my leg does nothing.

I try to sidestep him, but he grabs the front of my jeans. His foot catches mine, pulling my feet out from under me, and he lowers me to the dirt driveway.

He clicks his tongue. "You want to make this hard, baby? Just like you made my dick?"

His hand is tight on my jeans, which are tight on my body. Even squirming, there's no way I can get my hips past the buttoned waist to get out of them. I try to use my hands to push myself away from him, but the compacted dirt doesn't give.

Straddling me, Princeton pulls his shirt off over his head. His skin is pristine white and free of scars or tattoos. It's nearly blinding against the remaining daylight.

I try to squirm harder. My fingers, palms, and wrists burn from pushing against him so hard. It doesn't work. No claws, no paws, and he's about a hundred pounds heavier than me. A rock in the driveway presses against my back. *Fuck! This isn't how this should be!* I whimper as the stone twists by my spine from me turning, trying to escape.

"Don't be this way, baby. I'll make you feel good the first time." Princeton smiles.

"Let me up. That's enough. Stop it. No." I say all the words frantically, hoping he'll hear one that tells his brain to stop.

Words don't work. His hand covers my mouth.

My fingers dig at his hand, but it's not working. Surely, he has to smell my fear. He can't think I want this. *I should have screamed. Why didn't I scream?* I push harder. I'm fighting with every ounce of strength I have, but it's not enough. It won't be enough.

The sound of his zipper is followed by the feeling of mine.

Which is where my torment ends.

With his weight suddenly gone, I draw a lungful of air. My heartbeat, which had been filling my head in my over-whelming panic, is silenced or maybe drowned out by Princeton's screams as he's torn off me.

*Ansel?* Not seeing clearly, I scramble in the dirt, away from the direction his voice traveled when he was flung. More center, in the driveway, I find the reason for my escape. It's not Ansel.

Sherman's gray and white-faced wolf holds onto Princeton's thigh. He starts to shake Princeton's body like it's weight-less. His gray fur with russet tips shakes out around him as he does so, and it makes him seem even larger. It's not like Sherman isn't massive in both forms. But now he's so much larger.

With ease, Sherman starts to pull Princeton apart. The act turns Sherman's wolf's face the same color as the tips of his fur.

I'm too mortified to scream anymore or further call for help. I'd like to think Sherman, who just saved me, wouldn't hurt me, but I don't know that for sure.

Princeton goes limp, and the screaming finally stops.

Covered in blood, Sherman's wolf turns toward me. Ears down, he lowers his head, checking in on me.

My body relaxes with his submissive body language. "Than—"

The white wolf of death bounds down the stairs of the house.

Harry charges Sherman, knocking him over.

"No!" I scream as loud as I can.

I push myself up onto my feet.

You're not supposed to get between two wolves fighting. Not as a wolf and especially not in your human form. And especially not without having a wolf form and wolf healing, but I have to try.

Harry won't understand that Sherman killed to protect me.

"Harry, no!" I scream again.

The two titans are at war. I try to get closer, but they're moving too fast. How do I even get in between them?

"Harry! Ansel!" I scream, trying to distract them. Distractions aren't working, so I shout an explanation. "He was saving me. Sherman gets to live. He did the right thing!"

Snarling and snapping jaws continue. Harry grabs hold of Sherman's leg, and I hear the crunch of bone snapping. Sherman yelps, and it feels like I'll never get through to them. My heart is screaming 'Save Sherman! You have to save Sherman,' but I don't know how.

"Stop!" The shriek comes out as loud as I can. I've never made so much noise in my entire life.

Harry lets go of Sherman's leg. The white wolf of death faces me. Blood coating his muzzle, he cocks his head like he's listening rather than setting his eyes on me as his next victim.

"He gets to live. He was saving me." I try to explain again, and it comes out in begging and whines. "Harry, please let Ansel back. Please."

Sherman whines, neck exposed in perfect submission.

It's a miracle, but Harry retreats and Ansel takes back his shape.

I can't stop myself; I move to Sherman's side. He has a large gaping wound on his side. I can't tell through the fur if it's healing.

"Ansel, please," I beg. I don't know what to do.

Ansel's next to me, combing his fingers through the fur. Sherman whines when Ansel pokes and prods.

"Morrigan. Go in the house," Ansel tells me.

"You can't kill him. Please. Don't. He was saving me. Princeton was hurting me, and Sherman came from nowhere and saved me." I keep pleading for Sherman's life.

Killing another wolf is a death sentence unless you're protecting someone else, unless there's proof that the other needed to die.

"He's not dying. But I'm not having you out here anymore. Not until I know it's safe." He nods, locking eyes with me. "I'm getting Ben. Sherman will be okay." Ansel leads me away from the wolf who saved me. "Sherman will be okay. Go in the house."

# CHAPTER 56
## ANSEL

I KNEW WHEN THE FORECAST SHIFTED THAT WE'D BE LOSING Princeton. Now he's dead and locked in a sleeper, waiting for a final resting place.

Sherman is down in his cabin with his leg up and in a brace. Ben set his leg and brought him a smorgasbord of food to help him heal as fast as possible.

I've rinsed the blood off me and dressed in clothes I keep in the basement for this kind of situation. There's only one party left who needs help.

"Morrigan?" I call, opening the door between the basement and the house.

She doesn't answer, but I hear sobbing. Closing my eyes, I try to pinpoint the sound, but it's echoing through the great room. I walk up the stairs from the basement and look around.

Morrigan's sitting on the landing of the stairs. The sight of her tears burns in my soul like acid.

"Hey, sunshine. It's okay. I promise. You're okay. Sherman's okay. Princeton's gone. It's okay." I step closer to the bottom stairs, and she curls in on herself, further wrapping her arms around her legs.

"Ohhh, okay," I coo softly. "You're okay."

It tears me up inside to retreat, but even if she hasn't shifted, she's a scared wolf backed into a corner. *Should I call Mrs. Hoppe? Maybe another woman around? I can't get Dinah or Lena here fast enough.* My heart hurts, and I rub my sternum, trying to get it to stop.

I crouch down, squatting down below her. Giving her the high ground and space, I keep talking softly. "Sherman's okay. I promise. Ben took him back to his cabin. His leg's reset, that gash in his side was superficial. He's not even mad. Just wants the kitchen scraps for his chickens and wants me to make him cupcakes with sprinkles."

I leave out the part where he wanted to bring Princeton back to life and kill him again for hurting his friend. Now's not the time.

Morrigan's sobs subside for a second.

"You did so good. I'm so sorry. I don't know why that vision caught me for so long." I don't know what to say to her.

It's not like I can explain all the things Harry was showing me. Between memories, Harry showed me Vito's, Ripley's, and Sully's deaths. Their timelines are ever changing, but what snapped Harry out of it was seeing Princeton attacking Morrigan.

My knees ache, and I sink onto my butt, kinda mimicking how she's sitting. *How the fuck did she get Harry to stop? Sherman should be dead.* I try to pull back what Harry will let me see. I hear her voice, and then he broke.

Silence between us doesn't feel right. But I'm not moving until she moves, in any direction, or until she invites me closer, whichever happens first.

I've spent a lot of time sitting and talking to wolves in the basement. Hours trying to remind them they're human. Sometimes it works, and other times, I'm just talking. Usually, it starts with something local or the news or whatever book Lena sent me to read. I don't start there with Morrigan.

"I don't have any actual memories before I was nine or ten. I have flashbacks that Harry's shown me, but I don't know if they're real or not. It's bloody, brutal, and I guess . . . I don't know." Talking about me is always hard, but this feels right. "I think he killed people when we were young. But no one's ever said anything about it, so I don't know."

Morrigan's sobbing starts to become more sporadic, kinda quieter the more I speak.

I continue softly. "I was evidently timid and shy. The pack theory on how to fix it was essentially to throw me to the wolves, or, well . . . the pups. And kinda let me sink or swim."

Morrigan's not looking at me, but her shoulders rise and fall with deep, regular breaths.

"No one ever gave me a proper family, but Walt . . . He decided I would live in his room, sleep in his upper bunk, and that was the end of that."

Morrigan doesn't laugh with me, but she's still drawing deep breaths. While she's still ball shaped, she's less tense.

*What do I tell her?* I choose the first thing that comes to mind. "I always played it cool for your dad when it came to you. That man was a nervous Nellie, but I was hanging on to my breaths right with his. He was a wreck. Every fall, every tumble, every second you wandered off and we couldn't find you. And, fuck, did you do that a lot. Guess not much changes with you, huh? We were both scared. But he held my hand through becoming a person, and I held his while keeping you alive. I never felt that fear quite like he did, not when it came to you. Not until today."

There's a little shuffle in her movements.

"I will say, I'm glad someone taught you to drive other than Walt. From everything I can tell, you're better at it. Then again, I don't think there was anyone worse. He was terrifying to ride with. No focus on the road and anything happening around the vehicle." I scrub my hand down my face. "Even with you in the vehicle. No, with you in the vehicle, it was worse. He was fussing over you and trying to drive. He almost put the truck off the embankment, and I said enough was enough. He cussed me out."

Morrigan rolls her head to the side, looking at me.

I offer her a small smile and mock the gruff tone of his voice. "I taught you how to speak and read, and you've the balls to tell me I can't drive."

"That's why you always came with to pick me up at the airport?" she whispers.

Nodding, I confess, "I couldn't trust your dad not to try to turn the truck into an airplane."

Morrigan snorts.

Every fiber of my being wants to ask her if she's okay. But I know she's not. There's a universal equalizer though. "Want some peanut butter cookies?"

"With chocolate chips?" She blinks.

"The first official food of the coup," I inform her. "It's what Cade, Thalia, Ezra, and I ate the day Cade decided to take back the throne."

"That's probably not the most couth food for a revolution," she informs me.

"Couth," I repeat. The word is fun but not something I recognize.

"Refined," she explains.

Shaking my head and squinting at her, I defend myself. "Excuse me, my cookie recipe is very refined. I only use the finest store-bought peanut butter."

She rolls her eyes and slowly unrolls herself out of the ball she turned into.

My heart feels a little bit lighter in my chest.

# CHAPTER 57

# MORRIGAN

*Shouldn't we be working today?* I move my feet as fast as I can down the stairs as I pull my hair into a messy bun.

The house is empty. There's no sound anywhere.

The vault door at the bottom of the stairs is closed. But on the counter is a piece of notebook paper and an envelope.

Good morning sunshine,

I thought you could use some sleep today, so I didn't bother trying to wake you. There's food in the fridge, and the house is armed. The stupid beep thing will let me know if you try to leave. Please don't. We're down in Nameless today doing some work.

The envelope is a letter from Walt to you. It feels like the right time, but maybe it's not. I've never opened it, so I don't know what it says. But he wanted you to have whatever it is. If you're not ready, don't feel like you have to read it now. It's a decision you've gotta make. I can't make it for you. It can go back in the safe if you don't wanna see it around the house.

We'll be home sometime this afternoon.

Love you,

-AA

Studying the note, I see that Ansel erased something before signing his name. Telltale signs of the little pink rubber eraser are still stuck to the paper. I raise it up to the light.

There's proof. Physical proof that Ansel feels something for me. Dinah's right. Now all that's left is to get him to accept it.

But that's not all. That's maybe not even the most important bit.

On the counter in front of me is a letter from my dad. Mom got rid of everything from him in our lives. Even my T-shirt that still fit from the dinosaur museum was scrubbed from my life.

Here, in his own handwriting, is whatever he thought was important enough to leave with Ansel to protect for me.

Picking it up off the counter, I look at the handwriting. He was left-handed, and everything had a strange slant. Grandma and Grandpa had tried to teach him not to be left-handed, but I get my stubbornness from him.

My fingers shake as I stumble to open the seal. The paper slides out without protest. I wander over to the couch. In preparation, I pull the box of tissues toward my end of the sofa.

I've never really sat and thought about how much I miss him and tried to remember his voice.

Pup –

I don't know how much time has passed since we last saw each other, but knowing you are reading this assures me that you are exactly where you're meant to be. Ansel's is where you're meant to be.

Now before you roll your eyes at your dear old dad, take a breath and listen. Really listen to what I have to tell you.

Ansel is not responsible for my death.

I can only imagine the things your mother and her mate told you or didn't tell you, but don't spend another minute being angry at Ansel. He did everything he could. In the end, I wouldn't have asked for anyone else to have done what he did.

Pup, I always knew I was gonna die young. Don't ask me how but I did. I'm sorry I won't be there to see you take your mate or welcome a pup into the world, but I know you will have the right person, the right people beside you when it happens.

I always knew I had a purpose in my life and it wasn't until Ansel landed in it that I understood what that purpose was. I wasn't meant to be a granddad as much as I would have enjoyed spoiling your pups or to find my fated mate. My job was to make sure Ansel helped as many wolves, people as possible in this world. And even though my time was short, I knew it had to end for him to help you.

It's your turn to take the spot beside my best friend and help him help the world. Of this, I am positive. Regardless of how you've made your way back into each other's lives, embrace it. Don't hold off being happy any longer than you have to.

A wise woman once told me that it'll take a pig headed woman full of spirit to make Ansel see he's worthy of love. If I know anything about my daughter, it's that all the worst parts of me are the best parts of you.

Life's too short, pup. Hatred has no place in your heart. With every fiber of my being, I love you more.

Dad

Waterworks are on. Tears, thick and wet, run down my cheeks. My nose becomes congested, but I fight breaking down. The slanted text gets another read through. This time, I hear it in his voice.

Fat tears drop to the paper, and I quickly move to dry them off the page, stopping them before they can get to the ink and ruin it.

The back door clicks open, and the alarm starts beeping. Springing up off the couch, I see Ansel carrying a stack of bakery boxes. I leave the letter on the counter and go to help him in the door.

"Cade and this motherfucking alarm system that no one fucking wanted," he starts mumbling under his breath.

"You'll get used to it. I promise." I take the pies from him.

Ansel tips his head to the side and furrows his eyebrows, all his features putting me under deep scrutiny.

"I'm fine," I assure him, shaking my head before walking away with the pies.

The entry code is punched in, and the alarm stops beeping, and then Ansel's footsteps follow me to the kitchen.

"You're sure?"

"I'm sure." I use the firmest voice I can.

The hum of disapproval draws my eyes to him. But Ansel doesn't press.

"I brought pies. We're doing family-style dinner and a pack run. I hate to say it, but Princeton's — fuck, I have to call." Ansel stops and pulls out his phone. He sets it on the counter and points to the open letter.

Shaking his head, he goes to his bedroom. He leaves the door open, and I stand at the threshold. The room smells strongly like him, not in a bad, dirty way, but it's so thickly *him* it beckons me to break the unspoken rule and step inside.

*Home*, the little voice in the back of my head whispers.

The clank of the safe door closing echoes in the room before he turns to look at me. He's holding a manila file folder and a plastic bag. I step out of the way, and Ansel goes back to the kitchen.

He stands there and grips the countertop with both hands, staring at the folder a minute before finally opening it and picking up his phone.

The phone rings through to voicemail.

Ansel sets it down on the counter and scrubs his hands down his face before letting his hair down.

He eyes the letter. "I want to ask about that, but I don't want you to feel like you have to tell me. It's between you and him."

"It tells me not to hate you and that Dad hoped we'd find a way together." Summarizing is hard, but Ansel deserves some of this letter just as much as I do.

Ansel hangs his head, and his fingers turn white when he pushes them against the countertop. He draws a deep breath.

"Somethings never change with Walt, do they?" He laughs before stepping away from the counter.

He roots around in the refrigerator and digs out a variety of things before finishing his thought from earlier. "Without Princeton, things feel easier, and the pack is back to well, back to less chaos. The pecking order didn't change at least. So, they're going on a run tonight after dinner."

"Okay." I shrug, feeling antsy. *Maybe we could also go outside?*

Ansel's phone rings. "Can you see who it is?"

"Mercutio — Alpha Louisiana."

Ansel sighs and picks up the phone. "Hello?"

Ansel's phone volume is up, and I can hear the thick Southern accent. "Ansel, where ya at?"

"I don't call for the good times, Mercutio," Ansel answers.

"Oh, cher, his momma will be sad to hear it. But I told her it was too late. His daddy got too deep into him." The thick Southern drawl continues. "It was you, then? He didn't hurt nobody?"

I freeze in my chair.

"His momma don't need to know," Ansel answers.

"That bad, then." Mercutio makes a tsking sound with his tongue. "I'll make arrangements for him and send up pack to bring him home. He needs to return to the swamp. I'll get you all the riches. Cher, you did all you could for that boy. I told her before we sent him that he was gone. Nothing comes from someone that sick inside."

"I appreciate it. I'll send his belongings with the body." Ansel draws a deep breath.

"It was good talking to you. You make sure to come down to The Big Easy for something less dark. We'll raise your spirits," Mercutio answers.

"We'll talk soon." Ansel nods and pulls the phone away from his head, letting out the air from his lungs.

Ansel doesn't dwell on the negative call. We laugh and swap stories with the guys all through dinner. No one brings up what happened yesterday, but Sherman still favors his leg and doesn't stay too close to me or Ansel.

As the pack slowly makes their way out the door to their cabins to strip and shift, Sherman hangs back in the backyard with us. Ansel starts making a fire, giving us space.

"I hope you're okay." Sherman doesn't look at me. "I'm sorry."

I try to wrap my arms around him, but he's massive and I

realize how much smaller I am than him. I squeeze. "You did nothing wrong. Thank you for saving me."

He gives me a very gentle hug back. "I want you to stay."

"You're stuck with me for almost a year, for sure." I give him one last hug, trying to squeeze all the reassurance into him.

When we part, he gives a small wave to Ansel before joining the rest of the pack.

I want to go with them and belong. It feels wrong to be left behind, like maybe someday I won't be.

## CHAPTER 58
# ANSEL

I don't deserve someone as good as Sherman in my pack. He didn't blame me for trying to kill him. Sherman is quick to forgive, and when the day comes that we put him in the ground, we'll find his heart is, in fact, made of gold. Sure, he kept his distance, but I could tell it was more so out of fear of Morrigan than me.

"He didn't ask why I didn't shift," Morrigan whispers, sitting down next to me in the swing.

My fingers pick at the wood of the table. "It's because he knows."

"He knows?" Morrigan turns to look at me, but I keep watching the flickering light of the fire.

"He knew when he first met you. Asked me why you couldn't be a wolf," I answer with a shrug. "I told him it was a secret and that when you figured it out, he'd get to be the first one to know. Looking back, maybe I should have questioned him a little more."

*It'll be soon, so he'll be super excited. Maybe we'll bake a cake and celebrate.* I shake my head. *I was so dumb not to question*

*Sherman more. Would have saved a lot of time had I asked a question or two . . .*

Sully's bugle of a howl erupts as the fray starts to run. Ben answers with his deep baritone.

Harry paces inside, his focus darting between Morrigan and the call of the wolves. It's a tough choice. I trust her to stay. Something feels right about her here. But it's . . . not right. As the howls and barks move away from the house, Harry focuses less on them and more on Morrigan. It's not predatory.

"You could run with them," she offers softly.

Shaking my head, I sigh. "Me not going with them isn't about me being worried you'll run off."

"Oh?" Morrigan shifts in her seat, turning her body toward mine.

"It's not fair to lock you away inside." I nod. Turning to look at her, I explain, "You've been restricted for so long, what if it's a little freedom you need?"

"I've started to hear something, someone," Morrigan admits slowly. A smile pulls up the edge of her mouth. "It's weird. But it's there. I think it's her."

My heart beats faster in my chest.

Harry is acutely aware of her. He pushes, wanting to get out. I can't handle sitting still. The movement of the swing isn't enough. I stand and roll my shoulders, stretching them out. Maybe if I can give him more space inside, he'll relax.

Morrigan gets up and quickly steps closer to me. She leans against me lightly, breaking the no-touching rule. When I turn to adjust her off me, I see her golden eyes. Morrigan's wolf is there. She's awake.

As I look into her eyes, I feel the electrifying pull of a wolf ready to shift.

"I think she might be back." I back up a step, locking eyes with the wolf inside Morrigan. "Trust me?"

She hesitates, biting her lips together, but fear mixes with anticipation, and the fluttering of her heart assures me it's time.

When she nods, I pull my T-shirt off and motion for her to do the same, encouraging her.

Hesitantly, Morrigan follows my lead as I back away from the fire pit, stripping off clothing. Wandering eyes check in on me, her tongue darting out occasionally, and her cheeks flush. But she keeps undressing at a distance and matches me step for step and piece for piece. It's nervous energy, but fear isn't in the air.

Her body twitches and shivers as her wolf nearly pushes out on her own. We're a safe distance from the flames, and I offer her my hand. The feeling of her delicate touch awakens something inside me. It's more than the desire to shift. It's heavy and lustful, but I focus past the fire burning between us and instead lock eyes with her wolf again.

If Alphas see an animal on the surface, they can force the shift, but from experience, it's unpleasant. It's not an experience I want for her. I want her rewarded for coming home, not suffering and confused.

With at least a little understanding of what I'm asking from him, Harry slowly takes my body; it's not forced or rushed. We've learned to work in an instant, but this is peaceful and leisurely. My hope is it coaxes her wolf to join us.

And it works.

Morrigan's body folds. Her wolf follows Harry to the ground.

Waiting, we watch as her body adjusts. Her wobbly, unpracticed legs struggle to balance. Gently, we sniff down her neck and side, nudging and helping her shift her weight to steady herself.

Between the light of the crescent moon and the fire behind

her, it's enough for me to see her coat, flecks of black dusting along her shoulders and hindquarters. Walking before her, we arch, stretching out, inviting her to move.

Her steps are not graceful. She takes uncoordinated puppy-like steps, raising a large paw and trying to squarely connect it with the ground. The sight makes it impossible not to feel her joy.

Harry feels worried and uneasy watching her. He forces us near her with small, shuffling steps. It's a constant need to check on her.

When she takes a few steadier steps, we spring and bounce, encouraging her. Our tail wags when we arch to play.

It's light and non-predatory with him. It's something unfamiliar that I don't know or understand, but like hell if I'm ever letting it go.

Footing gained, Morrigan relearns coordination. She walks more easily. Slowly, we make a large circle around the yard. We stay right by her side. Harry wouldn't let me pull away if I wanted to, which I don't.

She's panting after the trip around the yard. Back within feet of the fire pit, Morrigan collapses and shifts back. I follow her to human form, lying on the ground next to her.

"Fuck." She rolls onto her back.

She wipes tears out of her eyes with the back of her hands.

"Did it hurt? You okay?" I ask, rolling closer.

Harry's locked on her still. Panic sets in. *Please don't be hurt.*

"Did we pull her out too fast?"

She shakes her head. Which I'm not sure if that means she's okay or not.

"I'm okay. I just. I didn't believe." Her eyes, reflecting in the firelight, hold so much happiness. It's contagious.

She bites her bottom lip.

We're so close. I can't resist the pull to lean forward into her space.

I've thought about this, and I've fought this behavior.

But I'm weak for her.

For the first time, I see a genuine smile, but it's laced with a devious look. She shuffles closer to me.

It feels so right.

And just like that, I abandon my firm grip on my rules.

I brush the remaining tears from her cheeks, and my lips find hers.

Harry's focus on her changes, demanding she be closer to us. Wrapping my arm around her back, I pull her closer. Her soft skin pressing against mine makes my cock throb. It's all for her.

Morrigan drives us. Her hand finds my shoulder, pushing me back against the dirt.

*Little sunshine thinks she's in charge.* I pull her on top of me before running my hands from her ribs down her sides to her ass.

She grinds against me, and I feel the wet tease of her along my shaft.

Instinct takes over as I guide her hips to grind against me. Morrigan moans, and I need her pleasure more than I need air. To be inside her and feel her come undone.

When she rocks forward, I break our kiss and hold her hips up while my cock teases her entrance. The flickering light of the fire paints across her skin when she raises herself up. With her hands pressing against my pecs, her fingers dig in, clawing me.

"Please, Ansel. I need." Morrigan bites her lip. She tries to slide me in her. She pants, "Need you. Please."

That last needy plea breaks my resolve. I can't deny us anymore.

With my arms wrapped around her, I enter her. She gasps, and I hold her steady, letting her set the pace of descent.

I grit my teeth from how good the warmth of her pussy feels as she takes my cock.

Our pelvises meet, and she tries to grind again, slowly raising her ass, her body begging for more.

I allow it and watch her work herself closer to orgasm, even though there's no way I'll let her come this way.

She moans, whimpering and biting her lip. When her eyes fall closed, I know it's time.

Morrigan's eyes fly open when I easily lift her off my cock. She hisses, "No."

I smile and sit up from the earth with her resting in my lap, my cock pressed against her clit. I nibble her bottom lip, and she grinds, chasing the orgasm I withhold from her.

My hand dances up her back, and her body shivers, pushing against me.

I whisper in her ear, "You come when I say you do, sunshine. Not before."

She whimpers as I hold her against my chest. Her knees and thighs squeeze my legs as I put her beneath me, and her chest rises and falls with her panting.

Biting her lip, she reaches for my cock. I let her wrap her hand around me, wanting her to feel it. The palm of her hand caressing the tip has me forcing myself to stay still and let her explore.

When I can no longer hold myself back from fucking her, I separate her legs and wrap them around my waist. I adjust her hips for a better angle, holding her to me. The delicate touch of her hands slides down from my chest toward my cock again, and I move my hips, pressing against her entrance.

Pausing, I command, "Pet that perfect clit for me. But don't you dare come before I say."

The corner of her lip pulls up into a smile. She taunts, "Or what?"

"Or you get to find out what a ruined orgasm feels like. It's worse than denial," I whisper, sliding myself down onto my elbows and burying my cock back where it belongs.

I feel her hand working her clit between us, and I drag out my thrusts, slowly building, watching her eyes close as she focuses on what she's feeling. I kiss her soft, full lips and pick up some speed.

"Ansel," she mutters. "Close."

"Not yet. A little longer, Morrigan. Wait." I press my forehead to hers.

Allowing myself pleasure, I grind my hips into her faster.

My release builds.

We're both panting, but heady moans and whimpers come from her.

She pleads. Her obedience and self-control cut at me as my body begs for release.

When her moans are constant and I'm positive she'll fail, I whisper in her ear, "Come. Come for me, Morrigan."

Her pussy clenches and her body spasms. Morrigan comes undone quickly and hard. I follow, my cock throbbing and pulsing as I fill her. Her body contracts around me, and Morrigan's mouth is forced open in a silent scream. I grit my teeth.

Through our pleasure, we're both aware of how sound travels in the desert.

Morrigan's hand slows, and I stop my thrusts. When I kiss her, she gives me a contented grumble of approval. Her body is lax beneath me, but when I separate us, she whimpers.

"Shhhh," I comfort her. "Be with me. I've got you."

I roll and pull her onto my chest. She rests her head on my shoulder and nuzzles into my neck. I stroke her back and notice the fire is dying before us. A few moments later, she shivers.

"Let's get you to bed." I coax her.

When Morrigan stands, the glinting moon shows the beautiful mess we made between her thighs. I wet my lips at the idea of licking her clean.

Then I catch the scent of blood. Her blood. It's mixed with the smell of sex and leaves no question as to what I've just done. A chill runs down my spine.

She starts hunting for clothes, and I'm pulled back to the task at hand.

"Go inside. I'll clean up," I urge her.

Counting articles of clothing, I look until I've found them and go into the house. The sound of the upstairs shower running greets me.

Reality sets in when I toss our clothes in the washing machine. I scrub my hand down my face and rake my fingers through my beard.

I fucked Walt's daughter. I deflowered Walt's daughter.

Guilt knots low in my stomach. It's not right what we did.

*No, what I did.* I'm responsible for this. My entire job is to protect her and keep her from trouble. Trouble like being fucked, for the first time, under the stars the night she finds her wolf.

By the time I walk the four feet to the bathroom, the guilt has spread from my stomach into my chest.

I broke every single rule I put in place to prevent exactly this. The kiss may have been Morrigan's action, but I failed to stop it.

I turn on the shower to a lukewarm temperature and quickly wash away the dirt and her blood from my body.

My unsettledness rattles Harry. He bristles, and the hollow feeling in my stomach grows. He's not pushing thoughts of bloodshed but happy and content thoughts of her. The draw to be closer to her doesn't lessen.

When I unlatch the door to the bathroom, I hear the rustling of drawers in the kitchen. I round the corner. But I don't need to see her to know it's her.

Morrigan's wearing one of my flannels, and when she reaches for a glass above the sink, it hikes up, exposing her naked ass.

My guilt battles against Harry's dirty thoughts. Time outside with Morrigan naked is what got us into this mess. It's not the answer out of it.

"Want a sandwich?" Morrigan offers, returning to the cutting board, where she has the necessary items laid out.

She pours a glass of cold water from the fridge.

I can't get words out to answer. I slump against the wall.

Morrigan repeats, "Ansel? Sandwich?"

I shake my head. "No. No thanks."

There's this need to talk, and this need to tell her I fucked up, but I can't do that to her right this second. I fucked up. Telling her what we did was wrong right now doesn't reinforce her wolf. It doesn't build her up. She's innocent in this, and hurting her with my need to establish boundaries again isn't right or fair.

# CHAPTER 59
# MORRIGAN

There's something wrong. Ansel isn't saying it, but I know I fucked up. No, no. He held my hand. He kissed me. But I leaned on his shoulder. There has to be math or something that makes this make sense. What didn't go right?

There's one burning hot factor that I can think of, and it's the tenderness between my legs and the blood I washed away during my shower. *Was he mad that I was a virgin? Should I have told him?*

Steeling myself against whatever he'll say next, I finish making my sandwich and head over to the couch to eat.

"Eat at the table," he instructs.

I stop midway between the two.

*Follow his command. Show him we can be good,* my wolf whispers.

I'm too afraid to lose her again to not agree. I divert my course and sit at the table.

He's not moving. Ansel standing there, watching me from where he's leaned up against the wall, is uncomfortable at best. Trying to eat with the intense feeling of his eyes on my back is as easy as swallowing sand, but I'm not moving to turn and face him.

Despite being focused on him, I don't hear Ansel move across the house to me. His hand runs across my shoulder, and I jump as he sets the water glass I left on the counter in front of me.

He then goes to the kitchen and comes back with a glass of water for himself.

It had been like eating sand before, but when Ansel comes back with a glass of water for himself and sits down, the food is more like eating ash.

"I didn't know," Ansel says quietly, "I wouldn't have. I—"

"I wanted it too." I cut him off and try to find words that maybe will make him less mad. "It's not like I wasn't consenting. I should have told you I hadn't before, but it felt so good. And it's . . ." I'm panicking, gasping for words. "Don't be mad."

He whispers, "It's okay. No one's mad."

Ansel reaches across the table and wraps his hand around mine, squeezing tightly. The touch soothes me. A wave of relief runs through my body from the crown of my head down to the soles of my feet.

Ansel doesn't say anything more while I eat. I don't know if it would make it better if he did or not. But when I finish my sandwich, he stands me up and gently leads me to the stairwell.

My wolf wiggles, and I look back past him to the sliding glass door.

*We can run.*

*No. We can't run. Not tonight.* I disagree. It feels so weird she's here. I do remember this feeling. It's not foreign like I expected it to be.

"Get some sleep, sunshine." Ansel encourages me with a push of his hand to my lower back.

422

Obediently, I nod and go up the stairs, not looking down at him as I do.

The farther away I get from him, the more lonely I feel. My heart remains on the first floor, leaving me more and more empty. I feel his eyes until I crest the landing. But it's clear he doesn't want to be by me.

Going to bed alone after my first experience isn't how I ever pictured this happening. . . I had sex with Ansel Abbot.

I had sex with Ansel Abbot, and it was amazing.

## CHAPTER 60

# ANSEL

Morrigan hadn't taken the letter from Walt up to her room, and it being mostly unfolded on the kitchen counter seemed like an invitation enough to read it. So, I did. Four times.

At first, it was just an attempt to feel closer to him, or so I told myself. I thought maybe reading his words would help me understand what Morrigan took from the message behind his letter, and it would fix how I'm feeling. It didn't. Not really.

The letter from the asshole I called my best friend to his daughter doesn't make me less angry. It just changes the direction I guide my anger. For once, in the last month, I'm not angry at myself.

*He fucking knew.* I racked my brain for hours, *hours*, last night as to when Dinah could have told him. It triggered two episodes with Harry and fucking awful sleep.

My mind had a violent night, which turned into a morning reliving memories I don't fully have or understand. But my lack of memory doesn't make the words in his letter less true. Not remembering when they could have had that conversation doesn't make it less real.

Dinah didn't answer the phone when I called her. I pick up my phone to call her again. There's one of those stupid little text messages.

DINAH:

> She's your mate. Suck it up, buttercup. Got babies to catch. Love you lots. I'll see you later and you can hug me then.

ME:

> You couldn't have told me? I could have found a way to keep us apart.

> Someday I'll grab your head and shake some sense into you. But today, I'm busy. I love you. I love you. I love you. Be good to her.

> Fine.

The little bubbles show that Dinah is typing, but no message comes through. But now knowing what she knows, knowing what Walt knew, and acting on it? Very different things.

*Fuck. I was an asshole last night.*

The third step from the top creaks. I turn on the stool and watch Morrigan make her way down. Her steps come slowly. It's clear from the way her wolf has her pushed against the wall, far away from me, that I fucked up.

Harry presses me toward her, but I let her approach.

"Now you know?" Morrigan's voice still holds the gravelly sound of an angry wolf.

"I am —"

"If you say anything other than sorry, I'm going down to Ben's and getting a tranquilizer dart to stab you with," she growls.

Her wolf floods to the surface, further punctuating her threat. The little wolf is protecting Morrigan from me.

426

"I am sorry." I finish my sentence and start a new one. "I was awful. And I wouldn't blame you if you did march down to Ben's to find something to stab me with."

"Do you get it now? Are you done resisting us?" She moves her hand back and forth between us.

Morrigan places one foot directly in front of the other, getting closer with each step.

I hang my head, and my hair falls in my face. I push it back up and out of the way.

"And I'm the stubborn one," Morrigan snarls.

Harry rises to meet her snarl, but I stuff him down.

"The facts don't change, Morrigan. You're —"

"Call me a child or tell me I'm Walt's kid and I'll find something *here* to stab you with. I know where you keep the sharp knives." She changes course, taking the farthest path from me around the kitchen island.

She caught me that time. I change what I was about to say. "Dinah's gift isn't always accurate. We can't know until we know."

"Until I go into heat." Morrigan spells it out.

"That." I draw a deep breath. "The pills came in. They're on top of the fridge. It's your choice."

"I'm not taking them," she states firmly, holding my gaze.

"That's your choice," I say again. *Does she think I won't respect that?* I squeeze my eyes shut and look away. "Morrigan, nothing has to change. You're maybe my mate."

The fact Harry lets me submit in that way to her says mountains about what's going on.

"May —"

"I know what the letter and Dinah say" — I take my turn to interrupt her — "is convincing, but we can't be sure right now."

"All the more reason to go into heat," Morrigan interjects.

My heart is heavy. Harry keeps pushing me toward her, so I quit resisting him and slide off my stool to lessen some of the distance between us.

We both want her. All the signs point to yes, so why can't I be happy?

I can't keep talking about this. I'm holding on by a thread as it is.

*What can I fix? What can I control?*

"Let's take you into town and get you some clothes today. I'm doing a shit job remembering, and I want to keep you comfortable."

It's safer to take her to town than stay holed up here, where those damn thoughts of all the terrible things I could do to her run through my head.

MORRIGAN'S STOMACH RUMBLES AS WE WALK INTO THE DINER TO GET some lunch. The complaints about buying flannel clothes and jeans were minimal. But she was pleased to find some sort of legging things that fit. And I was pleased seeing her try them on, the skin-tight fabric wrapping up her legs and the curve of her ass. It's hard to believe she was skin and bones a month ago.

Wrong or not, I want Morrigan for myself. It goes against everything, and it's not fair to her, but I want to be selfish. Just for once. I want something, someone, just for me.

Fries, burgers, milkshakes, and soft drinks ordered, Morrigan flips the ends of her hair up, examining them closely.

"You want to get a haircut?" I offer.

"I mean . . ." Morrigan huffs with a little laugh.

She slowly lifts her eyes. They're heavy looking.

I know that look from seeing it on other's faces.

My cock stiffens, and I shake my head. *Not here.*

Morrigan smirks. "Yeah. A haircut would be nice, but not today."

*So, this is it, then? This is all the harder it has to be?* It's one of those 'too good to be true' things, her not making a fuss. Life seems too easy. But the reality is, I have to be prepared for the fact that we're all wrong. *I don't remember switching to wanting her to be all right?*

"How many days are you stuck here for?" I ask, taking a drink of water.

I may cross days off my calendar, but I'm not one for numbers. Morrigan was counting before though.

"I don't think of it as stuck," Morrigan says softly. "But three hundred and thirty-eight."

A smile creeps across my face. Despite counting down the days, Morrigan did turn a new leaf.

"Any thoughts about what you want out of life?" I push.

*Like, when you leave.* I bite back that thought; it's bitter in my mouth.

Harbinger doesn't like something. He presses at my skin, hackles raised.

Morrigan opens up, playing with the straw wrapper. "I didn't have a ton of plans outside of anywhere that's not with Gerad and that'll let me get a dog. I'd love to be able to sew and do mending full time, but on my schedule, not someone else's."

The first real information, that's not circumstance based, is wholesome. It's not lavish dreams, it's not some huge festival or even going back to traveling. My mate wants a simple life.

*No. No. Not my mate.* There's no guarantee she is. Dinah isn't foolproof. Life changes; it's ever fluctuating.

Morrigan will go into heat, and it'll prove she's here temporarily like everyone else. I'll even start calling her Ben's dumb nickname, hellcat, like the rest of the temporaries here.

Then, in a little under a year, she'll move on, find her mate and be happy.

Harry snarls inside me. I ignore him.

"Do you think about getting a degree? Maybe fashion or business to help you?" I press, wanting to set her up for success.

"Maybe. But without money, it'll be hard." She gnaws on her bottom lip.

Our plates arrive before I can respond. But once our server leaves, I do. "The pack fund will pay for it."

"You say that like you make decisions," Morrigan sasses and picks up a french fry off her plate.

My phone vibrates in my pocket. Then it starts chirping. I fish it out and am not surprised he would be ruining our lunch. He has a sixth sense for when I'm getting somewhere with Morrigan.

"Gerad," I tell her before answering.

"Update me on Morrigan," Gerad snaps like I'm some sort of robot on the other end of the line.

"Gerad, I appreciate you calling. But we've nothing to discuss. Morrigan is here. Pack register is in process of being updated. I'll take your payment anytime. But don't call me, I'll call you." I hang up before turning the little volume bar down until it disappears and the angry red slash mark appears through the icon.

I flip the phone over so I don't have to watch the screen light up fifty million times while he calls.

Morrigan stares at her burger and then looks over at her milkshake.

"Don't tell me you're not hungry because he called." I try to encourage her past his inconvenient call. "He doesn't have the authority to ruin our day."

Morrigan pulls her milkshake over and takes a drink.

430

*That's my girl.* I want to praise her, but instead, I smile and do the same.

"Life's too short to not eat dessert first." I wink at her before drawing a sip of chocolaty goodness.

Morrigan is ravenous. Her wolf being back looks good on her.

We're almost done with our meal when Morrigan's eyes dart back and forth between me and my phone. Tension radiates off her.

"Why do they call them french fries if they're made in Idaho?" I try to lighten the mood.

"How can you make a joke about this?" Morrigan groans.

I play with the fry between my fingers, watching as the potato, which is a little soggy, bounces. "Because, much like the fact that Idaho isn't getting the credit for the potatoes, I'm not getting the credit for the muscle behind what I do. See, all fries are made with potatoes. Regardless if they're French or Idaho, an Ardelean is an Ardelean. It's this idea people have in their heads of the French fry getting more respect than an Idaho fry."

Morrigan rolls her eyes. "You're saying you do all the hard work, but Cade gets all the credit?"

"No, I'm saying it sounds cooler when he does it." I shake my head and flip the phone over. There are fifteen missed calls. "Why doesn't he take the hint?"

"Because he's a self-important narcissist who only thinks about what is good for himself and no one else?" Morrigan growls.

Harry whines, pushing me toward her.

"Oh." I nod. "Yeah, that makes sense. I was gonna say because he's stupid and an asshole, but we can pull out the ten-dollar words."

That gets Morrigan to crack. She smiles at me. "It'll be . . .
okay?"

"More than okay. Whatever happens, I've got your back,
and Idaho or French, I'm still a potato." The joke's not that
funny, but I laugh anyway.

Morrigan snorts and shakes her head.

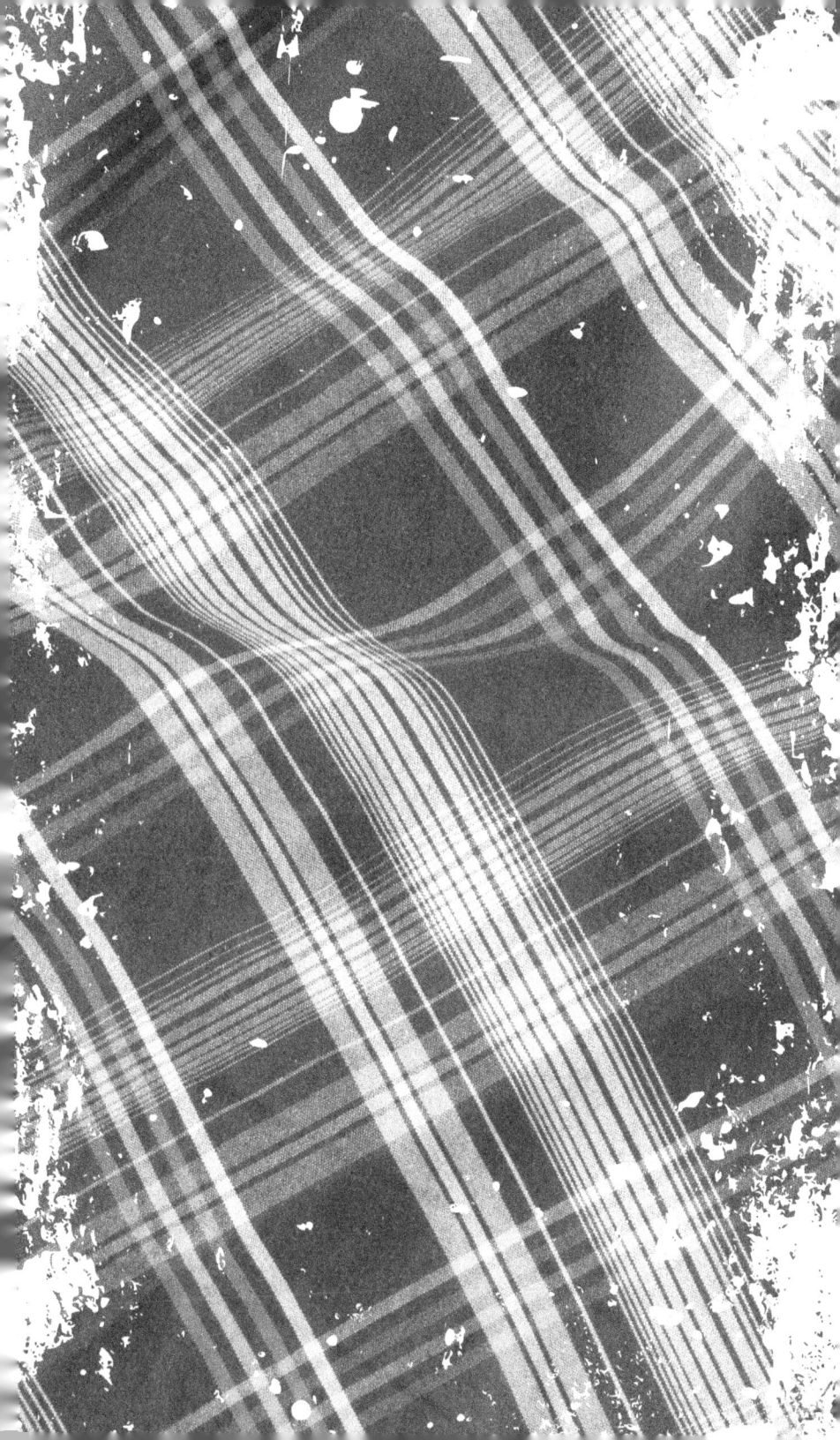

# CHAPTER 61
# MORRIGAN

"Why are you being so difficult?" I huff at Ansel as he loads the last plate in the dishwasher.

Pack dinner was delicious, but I'm exhausted. I don't remember having a wolf. But it's draining being around other wolves while having one. So many different mannerisms and trying to keep her in check, but she's been out of control all day. For whatever reason, though, Ansel's pack has been incredibly patient with me.

Well, almost the whole pack.

I look over at Ansel, waiting for a reply to my question.

He's shaking his head without an answer.

"Between you and Ben, it's like I can't win. I don't have wolf skills. I'm trying to remember them," I snarl, letting my wolf back my words. "I would think you'd know what this is like, but no. Instead, you two keep being such dicks about everything."

She's snappy and sharp.

I try to comfort her. *Fuck him. He's a jerk. We don't need him as our mate.*

Everything feels wrong, like when your sock twists around in your shoe, and there's no possible way for you to fix it, and you sure as fuck can't ignore it. I can't find a way to be settled.

He throws his hands up in the air and walks away toward the hallway to the back door.

It's like he's given up on me.

"Maybe the wolf is wrong. We don't need him and Harry." My thoughts leave my lips at a whisper.

Ansel turns around. Harbinger is darkening his eyes. Ansel stalks back to me, and his steps are fast. In a half of a second, he's nearly on top of me with a hand gripping my throat.

The squeeze of his fingers isn't gentle. With my chin tipped up, I'm forced into eye contact with Harbinger. It's uncomfortable at best. My wolf submits to him, and I divert my eyes.

"Is this what you wanted, Morrigan?" Ansel's voice is all growls and darkness.

I don't answer but swallow hard against his hand.

"You've been fightin' for dominance with every wolf here all day long. You were even challenging poor Zero, who wants to be friends." Ansel increases the pressure on my throat.

The frustration my wolf was bringing, the aggression, melts away at his touch. Everything wrong feels better.

"Maybe I should let Harbinger put you in your place." He hums.

I flick my eyes up to see his. Harry is still there, and so is a very new smirk across Ansel's face.

That fire, constantly threatening to ignite between us, is already hot. When his lips sear against mine, it warms my core. Ansel's kisses are intense.

Hungry for more, his fingers bite into my neck. No longer a squeeze but forming a firm grip, he drags me with him.

With me pinned against the wall, Ansel pushes his body tight against mine. His cock presses against my stomach.

I want it. I want it so bad. The dampness in my panties only proves it. It was only two days ago that I shifted and we were together.

But if it was two days, it was an eternity.

Ansel's tongue claims my mouth, deepening our kiss.

Moans escape from me to him. I'm unable to hold myself back. My tongue fights with his as I'm running out of air. I try to gasp but come up short. I squirm against him but still at his growl. Can you die from a kiss? Well, it's not just a kiss. It's not just a kiss when his hand is cutting off my air supply.

Fuck, I don't want him to stop, but I can't . . .

When I push harder, Ansel breaks the kiss.

He laughs darkly. "Isn't this what you wanted, Morrigan? You wanted me to let loose for you? You wanted to feel what Harbinger really is?"

The edges of my vision are turning dark. *He wouldn't let me die, would he?*

My wolf squirms, pushing forward and trying to save us.

Ansel releases my throat, and I gasp for air as he steps back away from me.

"Go get cleaned up and get to bed. We've an early day tomorrow." His instruction is a sharp, cold contrast to the warmth that was between us.

My heart is still beating hard in my ears. I do as I'm told, but I don't understand him.

*Why is he so hot and cold?* Tears well in my eyes, but I refuse to let them fall as I make my way up the stairs to my domain.

When I get to the top of the stairs, Ansel's lost to a vision. *Asshole.*

Thrashing, my wolf looks down at him. *Go back downstairs and give him a piece of our mind.*

Her sass matches mine, but this view is nice. It feels imposing. Rather than head straight into the bathroom, I stand there watching him.

The vision passes, and Ansel squeezes his eyes shut before opening them to look at me.

"Who's dying?"

Ansel shakes his head. "No one if I can help it."

"So, you're willing to change fate for them, but you're what? Not willing to accept it for us?" Condescension drips off every syllable, and it feels amazing.

"When you go into heat, we'll know for sure one way or another." Ansel dismisses me while walking away, crossing beneath the loft back toward his bedroom.

"You're such a fucking asshole," I shout over the railing.

I know it's childish, but I'm sick of him and his hot and cold nonsense. This isn't fair.

Ansel huffs but doesn't answer.

*Stubborn jerk.* My wolf huffs.

I feel warm all over. It's uncomfortable, and I retreat to my bathroom to take a cold shower. My face is flushed in the mirror as bright pink tones paint my cheeks.

*It's from the blood flow cutting off.*

I shake my head. Dinah said my heat would be soon after I get my wolf back, but it hasn't even been a week. That's way too soon.

# CHAPTER 62
# ANSEL

She's going into heat. I don't think she even realizes it.

Ben and I spent all day putting ourselves between the guys and her. No one seems immune to the draw of her going into heat. Me included.

There's no proof she's not my mate, but that doesn't excuse what I've done.

I keep touching her. I keep *wanting* to touch her.

The knob on my shower is set all the way to cold.

After stripping quickly, I step under the freezing cold spray. I shiver before drenching my hair.

Harry is still looking for her, not wanting to let her out of his sight. He pushes me to leave and find her again.

I've been hard all afternoon. It hurts from throbbing so much.

I let Morrigan make the choice not to take the suppressants because I wanted to know. How this feels, which could all be her heat talking, is intense, but is it a mating bond?

Finn said with Lena, it's a pull toward her. His wolf is equally as obsessed with Lena as he is.

But the problem is Harry gets this focused on people we're about to kill. It would be equally believable that he wants to end her and that she's still at risk of not adapting. She got her wolf back. Who knows if that wolf is even stable?

No, if Harry was so sure she wasn't safe, he wouldn't have been so free with her when we shifted. Harry's not behaving normally when it comes to her. Whatever's different isn't that she's in danger.

The cold water helps pull me out of whatever sex-crazed monster I'm becoming. After getting clean, I towel off and crack open the door to the bathroom.

Morrigan is still in her shower.

The image of her naked, from when she shifted, is broadcasted into my brain, and she was flawless. And her wolf; I didn't think it was possible to be attracted to a wolf. But she is the most beautiful gray wolf.

I push myself across the hall to my bedroom, and in the short distance, my feet only try to change my direction toward the loft twice.

With the door closed and locked behind me, I lie down on the bed and open my phone. Lena gets mad if I don't check the messages every day. Seeing only messages from Gerad, I opt to ignore those and clear the notification thing, and then I hit Lena's contact.

ME:

> Hey, can you order a sewing machine out to the house? And whatever sort of things sewing machines need in order to be usable?

Lena's phone answers back.

LENA:

Hey, it's Finn. Once Kathleen is done
misbehaving, I'll have her order one. Talk to
you soon.

They have the strangest relationship. Not that I've room to
judge. I want a woman who probably isn't mine.

# CHAPTER 63
# MORRIGAN

I'm going into heat, maybe. Yeah. Pretty sure I was right last night, mostly.

It's lunchtime, and I've broken out sweating while working twice. The waves of warmth come and go. They're short and uncomfortable. Intrusive thoughts of Ansel taking me in various ways flood those short moments.

Our pack is taking notice. And it's uncomfortable.

Sully's the worst of them. He's hinted at knowing what is wrong with me and wanting to help. I want to appreciate him being helpful, but it's creepy.

Sherman seems to know I'm not happy and offered me his sandwich and water and to pet one of his chickens when we get home. That thought actually helped a little. I want a pet.

The pack member I want isn't giving me the time of day. Ansel's lack of attention is creating more and more frustration. We're building a retaining wall, and Ansel is constantly working on something that doesn't involve me.

I down another bottle of water and watch entranced as

Ansel carries two retaining wall blocks from the back of one of the trucks to the small area where we're building up the space to make a parking pad.

# CHAPTER 64
# ANSEL

THE AGITATION BETWEEN US GROWS. HER HEAT IS INCHING CLOSER. No conversations Morrigan and I have had in days have gone well.

I'm biding time, hoping that some sort of idea will come to me that doesn't suck. I try to stay away from her, not wanting to force myself onto her. All the guys are affected by her, so I know it's not just me. My attraction to her isn't anything special.

Harry is focused on Morrigan, and he's making it my problem. He takes up constant space in the front of my head. It's hard to listen or focus on anything that isn't her.

"I think I'm going into heat." Morrigan pulls out a stool, and it scrapes across the floor. I feel her eyes on my back while I preheat the oven. "I don't know for sure. I don't know what this is like. It sounds like it from what Dinah said."

I nod. *Oh, sunshine, we know.* My cock twitches. And I forget what buttons I'm pushing. I look at the baking sheet next to me. *Focus. Cookies. Three-fifty or they get too done on the bottom.*

Oven set, I answer her, trying not to embarrass her. "Yeah. The guys and I noticed. They're all gettin' testy."

"Embarrassing," Morrigan groans.

*Well, that didn't work.* I turn back to face her and offer her the last three days' worth of thoughts. "You've got some options. Do you want to talk about them?"

Much to my surprise, she nods.

I go through the least problematic options I've come up with. "I can lock you in the kennels with a couple week's worth of food. There's no shower down there, but we could rig the hose, probably. I've got a container cabin down the hill. It's roughed in enough. I can getcha a couple appliances on short notice and a couple weeks of supplies for out there. Lock you in, you'd be safe. I'd say a furnished one might be nice, but I don't think you'll be comfortable in Princeton's. I cleaned out quite a bit, but it's still not clean by any means. Or even Ezra's 'cause it has so much of his scent and I never know when he's gonna turn up."

Morrigan is listening but doesn't comment on either option.

"You're old enough to consent. You're more than welcome to find someone who can service you through it. I'd ask that you pick the container rather than the kennels for that." I press out those words despite the internal struggle.

Harry fights me, rage-fueled lunges in my brain, hateful that we are even considering letting these options happen. Images of corpses of people who would dare put a hand on Morrigan flood with the insistence she uses someone else.

*Don't be selfish. This isn't about us.* He isn't going to understand.

Morrigan's fingertips are turning white as she grips the edge of the counter. Her eyes are laser focused on me as if I have more options.

"That's all I got." I shrug, holding my empty hands out to her as evidence. "Dinah said once you start having symptoms, it's too late to take the blocker. So, that ship has sailed. I know Dinah said she's been able to find a rotation of humans for her cycles in the past. Seems we're a little short on time there." I like that plan the least.

It's why I didn't want to offer it at all. But she needs the options.

"Why are you saying these things?" Morrigan's voice trembles.

Wincing, she pushes herself off the stool. Once standing, she leans against the counter, rolling her hips out and stretching out her lower back.

My cock throbs with the idea of taking her over the edge like that. My control is wavering. Her heat is closer than we have time for. There's no way the container will be an option.

I choke on the words. "Sayin' what?"

Morrigan whimpers. Her pain is strong. "Like you're not an option."

Harry likes the sound; his ears prick, standing up and focusing on her.

*Fucking predator.*

I don't know how to explain. "I don't want to be your only option. If you're pickin' me, it's not because I'm the Alpha or the person makin' you be here. My job is to make sure you're safe and to not be taken advantage of."

"Ansel." Morrigan half moans and half groans my name. "Fuck me. Quit pretending we aren't mates. It hurts. It fucking hurts."

Harry paces, fully focused on her, the sounds of pain taunting him.

If we do this, will I be able to stop him from claiming her as ours?

Morrigan's pleas butcher me. It's not quite time yet. I may not have spent a season with a female before, but I know it's not time.

I stand behind her, keeping my pelvis as far from her ass as I can. She stays folded over the counter, arching her back. I take a deep breath and rest my hands above her ass. Sliding them upward, I run my thumbs along her spine and push tension out of the muscles there.

Her knees nearly buckle, and she sighs. I work the knots again. She whines, and I watch where her body moves the most. When she winces away from me, I know I've hit the most sensitive, painful areas. I work on them slowly and more gently.

It takes her a minute, but she mumbles against the counter, "I want you, Ansel. You were my first, and I want you to be my forever. My only. Dinah has said I'm yours. Dad even encouraged us."

"I didn't handle being your first fantastic, Morrigan. I'm sorry for that." I've let that guilt hold me captive inside, and apologizing doesn't even seem to release it fully. *I'll make it up to her.* A stupid promise to myself, knowing that this is me accepting what we're about to do. "I'm not claiming you during this heat," I tell her and my heart, hoping at least one of them listens.

*I can't tie her to me forever without feeling the mating bond. It's cruel.* The pain in my chest is there, strong and burning hot. But I don't really know what that is.

She winces again, body tensing when my thumb hits another sore spot in her lower back.

She lifts her head from where it rested on the counter. The wounded tone in her voice further adds to my guilt. "We know we're mates."

"I want to believe that wholeheartedly." I've spent hours

thinking about all the ways I want this to work but keep coming back to the reality of how it won't. I try to tell her in the fewest words possible. "You're not old enough to consider matin'. You shouldn't be tryin' to plan forever. I shouldn't be thinkin' about the what-if and how it could be with you. We're at different points in our life."

Morrigan stands back up, the passing episode leaving her hot. She reaches for her hair and pulls it up, but there isn't a hair tie on her wrist. I pull my hair out of its position on the back of my neck and offer mine to her.

"Thanks." Morrigan's voice is small.

I feel how insecure she is in the tension coming off her. Her body is wound so tight.

I wrap my hand around her ponytail and use it to spin her head toward me. Pulling it down forces her gaze up to meet mine.

"You're welcome." I pull her into a hug. "I don't know how to explain how I feel. I'll try to figure out words. But I can't claim you. Not right now."

Despite panting and the incredible amount of warmth she's giving off, Morrigan nuzzles in against my chest. She nods. "You promise to be with me through heat?"

I nod against her head. "I promise."

I shouldn't be selfish like this. It'll be the biggest mistake of my life.

# CHAPTER 65
# MORRIGAN

I'T'S THE MIDDLE OF THE NIGHT, AND I KICKED ALL MY BLANKETS OFF and threw the pillow across the room an hour ago. I'm dying from being too hot, and my heart is racing. *Fuck.*

I get out of bed and walk down the stairs. Fuck being quiet. I'll be waking him up on purpose in a little bit anyway. I don't have the patience to be courteous.

I walk toward the sliding glass door leading to the deck before remembering the alarm and the stupid panel on the wall in the hallway. Back across the house and down the hall, I get to the alarm panel and start entering the passcode.

"Where you goin', sunshine?" Ansel's voice is thick with sleep.

"I'm hot and it's too hot in here and outside is cold." I huff, finishing the code.

When I turn around, he's leaning against the doorframe. His plaid pants hang low on his hips, giving me a perfect view of the many tattoos painting his chest and shoulders. I'm salivating looking at him. The hair draped around his shoulders only adds to the sex appeal.

*Who knew I was the type who liked the bad-boy vibe?* But beyond that, going outside is no longer a priority.

"Guess it's time to open that box from Lena." Ansel walks toward the kitchen.

I don't contain my wolf's whine. *No, need him.*

"Ansel." His name comes out in another whine.

"I know, sunshine. Just a minute. Get in bed," he calls back.

I hesitate at his bedroom door. The door to the room that smells so strongly of him is no longer closed to me. It's always been off-limits, but this is different, invited. Yet I can't push myself across the threshold.

"What on earth does Lena think is happenin'? No, fuck, I don't want to know. Too much information about her."

His voice is far away, too far away as far as my wolf is concerned.

I should go to him. *What is he getting out of Lena's box? No, fuck whatever is in the kitchen. I want this. No, I want to fuck who is in the kitchen. Kitchen or bed, kitchen or bed.*

Ansel's arm wraps around my waist. "Come to bed. You should get some more sleep. It'll probably start hurting soon."

He guides me with soft touches into his space, and just like that, my hesitation dissipates. The bed looks super soft and plush, and his scent is everywhere. Closing my eyes, I draw a deep breath and start relaxing.

*I needed this. How could this be something I needed?* Being a wolf is fucking weird.

Something is set down on the dresser. I look over my shoulder, and Ansel's right behind me. On top of the dresser is a box?

"No pups, Morrigan. We don't need to be figurin' that out." He pushes his hand against my lower back, and I step toward the bed.

*But we want pups,* my wolf pushes.

I shake my head. *He's right. Not this time. Soon.*

She huffs, conceding, for now.

Ansel kisses the back of my neck, and I'm fairly sure I could melt into a puddle.

His hands find the hem of my shirt and pull it up. "You're soaked. Want one of mine?"

I let him pull it over my head. The removal of the fabric cools me a little bit. "No. Too hot."

"I'll fix it," Ansel tells me. "Take off your pants."

*YES!* my wolf demands. *Yes, he fixes it right now!*

"Ansel," I whine again.

There's a click and a mechanical hum, and the fan blades overhead circle around.

*Not. Helpful.* My wolf huffs.

After sliding off my pants, I climb onto the bed. I have no idea if he's gone through heat with a wolf before, but even if he hasn't, it's not like I have much of a choice. He is my option.

*The only option. No one else*, she growls in protest. *We want Harbinger.*

Ansel's sheets are really nice. Silky smooth and unlike the ones upstairs, which are covered in fabric pulls and stretched out.

I crawl across the bed to where it feels coldest. Stretching out my back, I lower my chest against the bed.

"Fuck." Ansel cusses with a low, drawn-out, needy growl.

"That's an excellent idea," I encourage, realizing he has a perfect view of my ass, so I shake it for him.

He laughs, and the bed dips as he climbs in next to me. "Not yet. Rest first."

Despite being denied, the coolness feels comfortable, and I collapse against the bed to lie flat. Inhaling his scent, it only takes a second before I'm drowsy again.

I WAKE UP SCREAMING AND CURLING UP TO PROTECT MYSELF. I'VE BEEN stabbed or kicked or stepped on.

"Shhh," Ansel whispers. "Okay. You're okay. I'm here, sunshine."

"It hurts so fucking bad," I pant and whine and try to turn into a smaller ball. "Why doesn't anyone tell you how much it hurts? This is not like being bitten by a bear. Dinah lied."

Ansel pets my hair before pulling me to him. We lie nose to nose.

"Probably because they don't want you—"

"Shut up," I snap.

Ansel squeezes me tight before letting go, and quieter, he instructs, "Stretch out. I know it hurts. I'll fix it."

Trying to follow his instructions is too hard. I don't want the pain. Letting my legs go, they only unfold a little bit before the pain has tears welling against the lids of my clenched eyes.

"That's it, sunshine." Ansel praises me despite my lack of following directions. His thumb wipes away my tears.

He rolls me in my armadillo state until I'm facing away from him.

"Shhh, sunshine. I've got you."

Ansel slides his hand down my arm, then across the outside of my hip. As he closes the gap between us, his hard cock presses into my back. His hand roams the front of me toward my pussy. Feeling his fingers there, exploring, is already a relief.

Through deep breaths, I force air down into my lungs, expanding my stomach. I stretch out along his body. When I'm more elongated, I roll on my hip, allowing him better access.

Ansel presses his lips against my neck but holds still, not kissing, not biting. He holds us there, connected, all the while making long strokes across my clit. The stabbing pain subsides as he works me with his fingers.

"Mm-hmm. Yes. This."

Ansel murmurs in agreement to my approval.

He slides his fingers up and down my slit before circling my clit, then he repeats the motions, my wetness allowing him to easily glide through my folds.

I moan, torn between the pleasure he's drawing from my body and the pain that's subsided but is still a dull ache.

Keeping the pressure light, he brings me closer to an orgasm without pushing me over the edge, and I'm contented to let him do so.

Until his hard cock throbs against my backside.

"Want." I grind back against him, and his cock slides between my ass cheeks.

He groans, "Fuck. Beg for it, sunshine."

Pushing back again, I do. "Please."

That unleashes him. Ansel rolls me onto my back before commanding, "Stay."

The heat of his body is gone, and I shiver. The box on the dresser is torn open. The light taps of condoms falling to the floor is followed by a soft 'fuck it,' and then the bed dips.

My wolf loans me her eyesight for the darkness, and I watch Ansel roll the condom down his hard shaft. I move toward him with more urgency than he seems to have, wanting to be on him right now. His gorgeous cock is the only thing that will fully chase away the throbbing pain I'm feeling.

He lies on his side next to me and kisses me. Extending my arm, I go to push him onto his back and pull myself over the top of him, but he wraps his hand around my wrist entirely.

Grabbing my other wrist, Ansel pushes them both above my head. Off balanced by his movements, I'm forced flat on my back, underneath him, right where I belong. Taking advantage of our position, Ansel kisses me deeply. He tastes me slowly, and as much as I enjoy his kisses, they won't sate the growing need.

Rocking forward, Ansel teases my entrance with his tip, and I raise my hips to meet him.

"I love you needy for my cock," he whispers against my lips before sinking inside me. "You need it deep inside you, don't you?"

The pressure is so much as I'm forced open. A scream escapes my lips, but it's silenced by his hand over my mouth. The back of his hand presses against my nose, cutting off my breath, and panic hits as I can't breathe.

"What do you want more: to breathe or to come?" he whispers. He raises his hand just enough for me to draw a breath and answer his words. I steal breaths, fast and ragged, but when I don't try to answer, Ansel presses his hand back down and moves to whisper in my ear. "If you want me to stop, tap on my arm, otherwise I'm playing with your breath like I'm playing with the rest of you."

His words send shivers down my spine. I want everything and anything Ansel's willing to give me.

With long drags of his hips, he pulls his cock in and out of me. I'm lightheaded already, but I'm not sure if it's from the way he's restricting my air or if it's from finally having him rutting into me like I need. A rattle in my throat tries to escape as a moan, but it doesn't make it past his hand.

Panic sets in, and my body involuntarily thrashes against him, the movements halting my growing orgasm. I'm battling the impossible choices of holding still and letting Ansel make me come or the base instinct to breathe.

Ansel pulls his hand from my mouth, and I gasp for air, only to be hit with a wave of an orgasm. Screaming, I come hard while Ansel moves inside me, never letting up his deliberate pace. It's perfectly painful, and I'm not sure if I'm coming again or if the first wave never ended.

He doesn't stop, drawing out the single, massive orgasm

until he snarls. His cock throbs, and finally there's relief from the pressure within.

"Shit," Ansel pants. He releases my wrists but keeps me caged in. I look up to him and see that soft, caring smile. "You okay, sunshine?"

I reach up and wrap my hand around his head and pull him into a kiss. He tenderly returns it, but then the bed dips as he rolls off me. His feet pad softly on the floor as he leaves the bedroom.

I shudder under the breeze of the fan, and the cold drives me from the bed to the closet. I pull open the sliding door and reach for one of his T-shirts, but it's not right. I pull a flannel off the hanger and slide it over my shoulder.

Light from the bathroom floods down the hall. Ansel hisses and mutters, "Okay, humans might be right, this kinda sucks." He keeps talking over the sound of the sink running as he washes his hands. "Pups are worse. Pups are so much worse."

My wolf grumbles, upset with the denial of pups.

While I, on the other hand, cover my mouth to stifle the laugh at his dedication.

He returns to the bedroom, and when he sees me standing, he points back to the bed. "Lie down, I want to clean you up."

"Oh, I have to pee anyway." I point toward the bathroom behind him.

Ansel is unwavering. "Wasn't a suggestion, Morrigan."

With a huff, I climb back onto the bed under the irritating fan.

A warm, wet cloth slides up between my legs from my knee to my apex. I hiss as it dips, wiping down.

The scents of sex and blood are all I need to know about the intensity with which he fucked me. It's blissful.

After the soft touches of the cloth are pulled away, Ansel offers me his hand and helps me off the bed.

"Snack or sleep?" Ansel offers. "No, you should probably snack."

It seems he made up my mind for me.

After a trip to the restroom, I button up the flannel on the way to the kitchen.

Ansel's already frying bacon, and I salivate.

"Breakfast okay? Or do you want more savory?" Ansel offers.

"Pancakes?" I try to remember what Ansel has in the cupboard, but after I say that, I don't think I saw any mix.

"No problem." Ansel smiles, watching me as I sit down.

I'm not tender, and I shrug, encouraging him to keep cooking.

Griddles and mixing bowls are pulled out of cupboards along with large canisters of flour and sugar. Baking powder, baking soda, and vanilla. *From scratch? He's making them from scratch?*

There isn't a recipe book in sight. Ansel weighs and measures ingredients, tossing them in a mixing bowl before heating the griddle. It's magic.

"I don't remember Dad knowing how to make pancakes?" I question Ansel's claim that Dad taught him everything.

Ansel shakes his head. "I don't know what it is. Baking has always been easy. It's soothing. I don't know. Sometimes it's the only time Harry shuts up. Maybe he's the one who knows how to bake, and I'm simply along for the ride."

He smiles at me before giving me a wink and ladling the batter onto the griddle.

"Are pancakes baking?" I squint at him.

"Has the word 'cake,' so it's baking." Ansel's smile makes me giggle.

# CHAPTER 66
# ANSEL

I LET MORRIGAN FUCK WITH THE THERMOSTAT OVERNIGHT AS MUCH AS she wants, but she's struggling to maintain a comfortable temperature. In one of her bouts of trying to get comfortable, she opened the sliding glass door and found that the temperature of the deck was mostly okay.

Currently wrapped up in the bedspread but sitting in a pair of my boxers on the cold deck, she's content to watch me work on rebuilding the drip pan of the grill. Which I'm only doing because I feel helpless when it comes to her. I feel like I have to be doing something, even if it's not helping her.

"Where did you learn how to do all this?" Morrigan asks.

Looking over at her, I shake my head. "Where do you think?"

"I don't know." She squints at me. "I've known you my entire life, but I know nothing about you beyond the little involvement you've had."

"I learned a little bit of a lot from Walt, but most of it also comes from the good old fuck around and find out. Plus, every single one of the guys down the hill has taught me somethin', same as the people there before them."

It feels good to talk about myself with someone. For the first time, it doesn't seem like I'm filling the silence and trying to gain someone's trust or respect. Sharing for sharing's sake?

"Dad said you didn't know a lot about what happened to you . . ." Morrigan pauses, and I look back from the dirty grill pan toward her, and she continues. "From before."

I keep my hands busy and turn back to the grill. Instead of stopping to think about what she's asking, I shut it down. "I don't. It's not something I ever really figured I needed to think through. What's happened is done and gone. Use what you have and move forward."

"But you do remember, those memories, they're just with Harry." Her voice is softer and understanding.

When she says his name, he rises from the sleep he's been living in. He pushes me toward her, making it impossible to hold the wrench, and the fight for control gets harder again. I set it down and wipe my fingers on a rag.

Sitting up, I look at her. Morrigan's eyes are heavy with sleep.

"Can you get to bed while I clean up here?" I know there's no going back now; she'll need to talk more about it.

Morrigan nods, and with the blanket wrapped around her, she goes back into the house.

Putting away my tools in the garage, I try not to hurry in hopes that the tiredness in her eyes leads her to fall asleep before I get back into the house. Morrigan deserves rest and peace through this. She doesn't need to get bent out of shape over what's happened to me.

The memories I have are few and far between, but someone told me I should try talking about it. The few people I did tell, at least what I remember, were different afterward. I don't want her to be different with me. Morrigan deserves someone, something, better.

Tools away, I close the garage door and take a look at my phone in one last-ditch effort to stall before going in.

LENA:

Let me know how it's going. I'll assume no news is good news.

BEN:

Everyone's fine. Quit worrying.

DINAH:

Love youuuuuuuuuuu!!!!

Nothing I can say to any of them will make a difference, so pocketing it, I go back into the house through the usual door.

The laundry machine and dryer are running, meaning she flipped over the load of sheets I started before we went out onto the deck. I look inside the bedroom through the open door, but she's not there. Evidently she shook off her tiredness from outside when she walked back in through the sliding glass door. Farther down the hallway, in the main portion of the house, I find Morrigan, in my boxers and nothing else, looking through the fridge.

"What do you need, sunshine?" I lean against the wall to watch the way she moves about in our home. *Our home.*

Harry is back, eyes on her, wanting her.

"Something sweet and something salty. Or maybe both at once," Morrigan mumbles.

"Peanut butter or chocolate?" I ask, moving to the cracker cupboard.

"Uh. Peanut butter, obviously." She laughs. But not even ten seconds later, she pauses. "You have chocolate?"

"Kind of."

I pull out some round crackers people apparently use with

cheese and a jar of peanut butter. Then I reach toward the back of the cupboard and pull out the emergency reserve of almond bark.

"That looks like it requires assembly." Morrigan groans, and her shoulders fall with a deep sigh of defeat.

"Only a little," I assure her.

"I'M SORRY FOR ASKING YOU ABOUT YOUR PAST," MORRIGAN SAYS, biting into the cracker cookie thing.

I've let her come and sit in my lap. Her head resting against my shoulder and the movement of her jaw as she chews is soothing. I love this moment, all these moments, the tenderness and how easy it is to sit with her.

Harry is calm and settled. It's the easiest it's ever been with him. The closer the connection to her and I feel like maybe Harry knows what peace is after all.

*Is this what life could be like? Just as soon as I feel whatever this mating bond thing is supposed to be, life could be this good?*

I lean my head against hers. "I don't know that while you're in heat is the time to talk about this. It's a lot to tell, and I've been told it's heavy and that people don't like heavy things like this."

Morrigan is quiet as she eats more of her peanut butter cracker sandwich things, and I think the conversation is over.

"You know they say everything is different in heat, right? Like, I might not remember everything. Could be a good time to tell me." Morrigan shuffles to look me in the eyes.

I pull my hand off her lap and run my fingers into her hair. After licking the bit of peanut butter off her lip, I kiss her. She melts at my touch, relaxing into my arms.

She smiles, breaking the kiss. "You can't kiss me stupid."

"Wouldn't dream of it." I nudge her cheek with my nose. "Let's get you to bed. I'll tell you as much as I can before you fall asleep or the next wave hits."

I plan to talk as slowly as possible. Based on how long she's been acting like almost-normal Morrigan, I'm expecting the minx with an attitude problem shortly. Maybe I can get away with only telling her the less ugly bits that I remember. She doesn't deserve to hold my burdens.

Sliding off my lap, Morrigan fans herself before pulling her hair up off her shoulder and piling it on top of her head. It's such a simple act, but it's so fucking sexy. With the skin of her neck exposed, Harry and I are fully focused, mouths watering.

I draw a deep breath, and my suspicion is confirmed. Morrigan's getting slick again. It'll be maybe twenty minutes, max, before she's begging for me to take her again.

Harry's focus moves to the sway of her hips as they dance back and forth.

I pull myself up off the couch and follow dutifully to the bedroom.

Letting her hair down, Morrigan climbs onto the bed rather than walking around it. She looks over her shoulder at me and wiggles her ass back and forth.

*Hot. Fucking. Damn. Sunshine.* It's the beginning of the end for me every time she does that.

With that little wiggle, Morrigan has me wrapped around her slender fingers. I'm helpless to do anything but give her what she wants.

My cock throbs, and I step to her, grabbing hold of the boxers she's wearing and pulling them down her hips. I bend and bite her ass playfully.

She moans, "Please."

After untying the string of my pajama pants, I slide them and my boxers down my legs and step out, then kick them toward the hamper. She's so fucking wet her slick is glistening. I want to slide my dick inside her and take her like this, forgoing the stupid fucking condoms. Fisting my cock, I enjoy watching her waiting for me. The memory of how she felt, at the fire, tight and hot . . . *No. Fuck. No. So not ready for pups.*

Groaning, I release my cock before backtracking the two steps to the dresser and grabbing a condom. "Fucking eighty percent chance."

Morrigan whines, "I hate those. Do we have to?"

"Sunshine, I get your frustration, trust me," I agree, rolling it down my shaft. The texture makes my skin crawl. "But no pups. Not right now. We can talk about it later."

Morrigan drops her chest to the bed and pops her ass out farther. Pushing her knees apart, she shows me her swollen, wet pussy.

With my cock wrapped, I slide in. We moan together, and I steady myself, letting her pussy flutter around my shaft.

She rocks back toward me, pushing herself until her ass is seated against me. I let her use me, forcing myself to stay still as she works herself back and forth on my cock.

Morrigan wants me, and I don't think it's the heat talking.

Running my fingers up her back, I ask, "Do you like being able to use my cock like this?"

She doesn't answer with her voice. But the look over her shoulder, her eyes bright with her wolf and her teeth pressed into her bottom lip, says it all.

I lean forward to get closer to her and slide my hand around her hip. She tenses, pussy clenching tight as her body stills.

"Keep going, sunshine. You can use me," I rumble with approval.

Morrigan draws a ragged breath, and her head falls back. As she thrusts her hips into me, the scent of sex fills the air.

I run my hand from her hip straight to her clit and apply steady pressure. Her head falls forward, and I run my other hand up her spine, making her shiver. Fisting my fingers into the hair at the back of her neck, I pull her head toward me a little bit, opening her neck into a more vulnerable position. The sight of it, clear for me to sink my teeth into, sends a jolt of energy and pleasure to my cock.

"Fuck," Morrigan pants. "Fuck."

"Sunshine," I groan. "You feel so fucking good."

I support her low belly with my palm, letting my ring and middle finger slide along either side of her clit. Her whole body shivers.

As her moans grow louder, I recognize the not-so-subtle shift in sound. My cock throbs with anticipation. Her being in control has me captivated, waiting for her and watching her use me. A few more rapid heartbeats pass before Morrigan's body erupts. She screams through an orgasm. The sound edges me on, but even with the clench of her pussy around my cock, I need more of her before I come.

"Fuck. Ansel," Morrigan pants.

I let go of her hair, and she lowers her head to the bed.

"Mm-hmm." I wrap my arm around her waist while leaning forward and pressing myself against her back. "Ready to be fucked, sunshine?" I kiss her cheek.

She wiggles her ass the best she can with me buried deep inside her and pinning her like this to the bed.

No further invitation required.

Harry snarls, demanding through images that I sink my teeth into her shoulder. He reminds me of the taste of blood, and I struggle to push it away. Forcing myself upright off her back, I further remove the temptation.

Fucking hard, fast, and deep into her, I use both hands to support her hips.

"Oh fuck, right there." Morrigan vocalizes what she likes, and I provide the same thrust again and again and again.

"Ansel," she moans, "Fuck. Ansel, please. More."

The begging gets me. I can't deny her needy little sounds.

I snarl. And fuck her harder. Taking her on full thrusts, I pull my cock all the way out and slam back in again. Morrigan's pleas for more drive me to fuck her rougher and deeper until they subside and she's simply moaning. I take her as hard as I can until her fingers curl into the bedsheets and she starts to scream, coming undone with another orgasm.

I follow her over the edge, coming relentlessly while burying myself inside her. I place a hand between her shoulder blades to stop myself from toppling over from the floaty, light-headed feeling of my release.

It takes a minute for the ringing in my ears to subside.

I draw a deep breath and slowly slide out of her.

Her frustrated whine echoes the disgusted feeling I have looking at the condom. I take it to the bathroom.

After cleaning myself up quickly, I bring a warm cloth back to her. Morrigan didn't stay where I left her. Instead she's lying on her back with her hair flipped up over the top of a pillow.

"I don't like this." She looks at me and then glares at the rag with her lip curled up.

"Hate being cleaned up?" I try to figure out what she doesn't like and offer the rag out to her.

"Hate not smelling like you." She doesn't take the rag and lets me tend to her.

"You're lying in my bed and wearing my clothes. You smell like me," I assure her.

When I'm convinced she's clean, I go to the bathroom and come back.

"No, it's not the same," Morrigan says. She's now curled herself up in the bedding, hugging my pillow.

472

"What's not the same?" I ask, climbing into bed next to her, not bothering to put on pajamas.

"When you came inside me, I smelled like you. I felt you," she explains. "With the condoms, it's chemical and it's not right."

"No pups," I remind her.

"Pups wouldn't be so bad." She yawns, but her mouth slips into a sly smile.

I stifle my laugh. "I've done pups, Morrigan. You weren't a walk in the park. I can only imagine. Not right now. Maybe in the future."

"Maybe means no." She sighs, pushing out her bottom lip with a pout.

"Well, I'll talk to Lena. There's got to be something wolves can do to not have more pups. Surely, not everyone is using condoms during heat or risking pregnancy," I answer. I would think more people would be complaining otherwise.

"Okay." Her little defeated noise makes my heart ache.

I pull the pillow she's curled up to out of the way and drag her to me.

Morrigan is quick to wrap her leg over the top of my stomach, pressing herself as close to me as she possibly can. Her head comes to rest against my chest.

"Tell me something," Morrigan whispers. "Tell me something you keep secret."

*What do I tell her?*

Harry helps. Pulling memories, he offers what it felt like, the fear, when we first installed the kennels.

Cade insisted that I needed to know how to get out in case someone trapped me inside. His logic was sound. I told him it would never happen, and it hasn't happened, but those few hours of practicing were absolute torture.

I swallow hard, pushing the images out of my brain. "I

can't handle being stuck somewhere. Especially being tied or restrained. It makes my heart beat too fast, and it feels like I can't get enough air. It hurts like fear but worse."

Morrigan says nothing. She doesn't move, and not until I draw a deep breath do I realize she wasn't breathing with me.

"Does being hugged do it too?" Morrigan's voice is small.

I don't answer but kiss the top of her head.

When she tries to pull away, I drag her back, holding her in my arms. "I don't ever want to let you go."

# CHAPTER 67
# MORRIGAN

*JUST WAKE HIM UP. HE WANTS YOU TO WAKE HIM UP.* I SHIFT WHERE I'm sitting on the bed again. The cramps are making it hard to focus on the words on the page.

My wolf whines as another one rolls through me.

"You okay, sunshine?" Ansel's groggy. He reaches for me in bed.

I put the book back on the nightstand. *Page ninety-six. Page ninety-six.* I try to remember the number. But I'm sure I'll be looking for it later.

"Yeah, couldn't sleep anymore." I lie back down against him, lying about what I'm feeling.

He yawns and rolls over toward me. "Are you supposed to be this chipper all the time? I thought heat was supposed to make you crabby and bitchy."

"Rude." I flare my nose at him.

It challenges Harry, who rises to the occasion. I don't process the room spinning before I'm flat on my stomach, Ansel's weight over the top of me. His hard cock pressing against my ass, paired with the warmth of his exhale, sends a shiver down my spine, making me submit.

"Why didn't you wake me up, Morrigan?" Ansel's voice comes with a thick growl. "I can smell how bad you need me. You've got to be in pain."

Trying to keep my breath even is impossible. I'm panting and grinding myself up against him. I try to separate my legs to give him better access, but with the way he's caged me in, I'm at his mercy.

"Why didn't you wake me, Morrigan?" he repeats, and it's more forceful this time.

"Ansel, please." The next cramp hits hard.

Ansel doesn't move.

"Ansel," I cry, pushing my ass up against him, but the cramps traveling all the way up my stomach leave me weak and unable to really entice him.

He moves and kisses down my back. Trailing his hands down my side, Ansel straddles my thighs, and with a merciful adjustment, he opens my legs for him, no longer straddling both, just one.

I try to grind back against his thigh between my legs, but Ansel picks up my leg, and with a grip around my shoulder, he spins me to face him.

"Tell me, Morrigan. Why didn't you wake me?"

Harry's eyes have darkened Ansel's gaze. Cocking his head to the side, Ansel releases my arm to move directly for my clit. The touch feels so good, but I want to be filled. I want to be consumed. I want to feel myself under him, and this interrogation is so not what I want or need.

"I want you," I whimper. *I want you raw. I want to be fucked without the stupid condom.*

Trying to look innocent, I drop my jaw a little bit, leaving my lips parted and eyes soft.

Ansel shakes his head. "Trouble. So much trouble." He leans over to the nightstand, and I've been defeated.

He has more self-control than ever. It's not fair.

*Fucked. We need to be fucked.* My wolf, sick of my shit, is running the show as she grinds down toward his knee.

Trying to get anything to take care of our need, I take matters into my own hand. I slide my fingers into my folds and play with my clit. It's not enough, but it's something to keep me sane while I begrudgingly watch Ansel slide on a condom.

Plastic, smelly sheath on, Ansel doesn't deny me any further. He hitches my thigh up over the top of his, opening my legs wide for him. Interlacing my fingers into his, he stops me from touching myself.

"You" — he smiles as he scolds me — "touching yourself like this, making yourself come while screaming and begging for me, is the most unfair part of my life."

Playfully, I bring the other hand down to replace the stimulation, and Ansel shakes his head, grabbing that hand too.

"Fuck me. Please," I moan and whine, feeling my wolf come forward, trying to find that bit of Harry within Ansel that gives me what I want.

Having gone so long without her and now recognizing her within me, the feeling is so raw. It's a call for clawing and biting without fear. I want to bleed and bleed him. She electrifies me from the inside out. A spark to a fire I'd been hollow without.

Ansel groans, sliding forward, his cock teasing my opening. He pins my hands above my head and kisses me. When he kisses me with tongue, he presses his cock into me. The stretch is no less foreign than it's been before.

I want more.

*Need*, my wolf corrects.

Tilting my hips up, I try to indicate to him how needy I am for him, how much I want him.

Steady, consistent thrusts soothe the aches of my cramps. I draw even, regular breaths and enjoy the lack of pain while Ansel kisses down my neck. He nuzzles his nose into my hair, releasing hot and irregular breaths as he keeps going.

I'm on the edge already. A little more and I'll fall over.

"Fuck, Morrigan. So tight," he growls into my ear.

That's all it takes. I come undone for him. Silence broken, needy whimpers escape as I try to pull him closer with my leg around him. I struggle to breathe, trying to force air into my lungs between waves of pleasure.

Ansel snarls above me as he holds himself back. He mercifully slows as I try to pant, unwinding from my orgasm.

Ansel repositions me, bringing my hands together and pinning me by the wrists to the bed with one of his large hands.

Our eyes lock.

"Scream for me, Morrigan."

With his free hand, he plays with my nipple before sliding it down my belly, a devious glint in his eye.

I moan when his fingers slide against my clit, and I quickly discover the reason for his sly smile when he pinches the bundle of nerves. Multiple orgasms always sound excessive when people talk about them, but Ansel makes this luxury in the middle of the desert my own oasis.

I'm coming. Pain and pleasure mix into one.

The way his eyes roll back in his head when he finally roars through his own release causes flutters in my heart. Panting, he stops himself from collapsing on top of me.

He rests his forehead against mine, and we exchange soft kisses while he smiles between each one.

And then Ansel freezes.

He looks above my head, and I try to arch and see what he's looking at.

"Fuck," he whispers, letting go of my hand and narrowing his eyes. "Don't move."

Untangling us, Ansel moves gracefully off the bed, then I see his hand. Blood paints his fingertips.

I don't feel hurt. My heart rate accelerates, and the words 'don't move' become meaningless as I pull my wrists back into view.

Red stains them, slick, wet blood, but I don't feel pain.

Ansel's back at the bed, holding a bowl of water and a rag.

"I'm so sorry. I can't believe I lost control." He apologizes again and again as he wipes away blood.

Tiny crescents with little bruises, looking nearly healed, dot my wrists where his nails had dug in.

"Ansel, look, I'm fine." I try to reassure him.

He shakes his head. "It shouldn't have happened. I let Harry go too far forward."

"Ansel. I'm fine." I take the rag out of his hand. "I loved every minute, and all that happened was we made a little mess."

"I could have hurt you. This" — he holds up my hands for clarity — "isn't normal healing. I've never seen someone bleed that much and not even have scabs."

"I'm weird. I had a wolf, I didn't have a wolf, I have a wolf again. And now I heal fast? It's just how I'm supposed to be. Maybe she's making up for lost time," I tell him, but I have no idea if my words are even true or based on some sort of fact. He doesn't seem satisfied with the answer. When I reach for him, wanting him closer, he obliges, letting me bring our noses together. I lower my voice. "You can't fix what isn't broken, and you can't apologize to someone who hasn't been wronged."

His lips disappear as he bites them together. But a steady resolve comes with a nod. "You're right. I can't."

ANSEL IS SOFT AND SWEET WITH ME, MAKING FOOD, DESPITE IT BEING after a normal supper time.

"Want to pick out a movie?" he asks, plating food for the two of us.

It smells so good, and despite seeing him make me a hundred meals before, I'm fluttering inside as I watch him.

*Our mate is such a good provider,* my wolf explains.

"Sure thing." I pick through the DVDs and find a stack with newer, less worn cases. I pull one off the top and check the back. It's a film from a few years ago.

"Have you seen this one?" I hold the case up for him to see.

"Oh, no." Ansel shakes his head. "That one's new. Lena just sent it."

"Uh." I stifle my laugh only a bit. "It's not new, it's like five years old."

"New." Ansel nods, reaffirming his statement.

"New movies come out every month, you know. At the theaters." I shake my head, putting the disc into the DVD player.

Ansel doesn't answer but brings our plates over to sit at the coffee table, which is apparently okay to eat at only when you're in heat. On another trip back to the kitchen, he brings himself a beer and me a glass of water.

He tries to sit down in his chair, and I give him a firm huff. He pulls himself out of the recliner and comes to sit on the sofa next to me.

I didn't expect him to say anything more; the uncomfortable tension hasn't been shaken yet.

But Ansel starts to speak. "Lena prescreens everything for me and marks which ones are sad or have big emotions tied to them. She knows everything." His words stop, and he clears his throat. "She knows everything." He tries one more time. "That's happened and makes sure they'll be okay before she sends them here." He pauses again before admitting, "I've never seen a movie in a theater."

I put my hand in his and squeeze.

"I'm okay watching the same things over and over. There's something nice about knowing what will happen." He shrugs.

"I can put in something you've seen before," I offer, already starting to move.

Ansel holds me still on the couch. "No. I don't mind new things with you."

# CHAPTER 68
# ANSEL

SOMETHING PULLS HARRY AND ME OUT OF A DEEP SLEEP. I OPEN MY eyes to our dark bedroom, and the house is still quiet. I stand, listening, but don't hear anything out of the ordinary. Morrigan is still making her sleeping sounds next to me.

It's not abnormal for a furry desert critter or something settling in the house to wake us. Even the furnace clicking off is sometimes enough to do it.

Wide awake, I can't lie here anymore. Not when things aren't feeling right. I slide out of bed and start poking about the house. Harry checks high and low with me, listening around but pushing back toward the bedroom and Morrigan. It just doesn't feel right.

Morrigan has been so close to me. It's like she feels some sort of pull or draw to me, but it might just be her heat. The only thing I feel is what I've felt around her a million times before. The burning ache in my chest is as present as always.

*Maybe I can't feel the pull until she's out of heat?* I stand at the bedroom door, staring at her. Wouldn't be that hard to call Dinah, see what she has to say about it.

Morrigan is so peaceful, sleeping with her hair draped out around her, curled up with the blanket entwined between her legs.

I pick up my phone off the charger and take it over to the back door. But Harry stops me, pushing me back toward Morrigan.

*I could call Dinah later.* With his insistence, I go back to the bedroom door. If it hasn't changed when Morrigan gets through heat, I'll call Dinah. *Maybe.*

Harry settles as I climb back into bed alongside her. Nuzzling my nose in her hair, I start to drift off to sleep with the familiar feelings and sounds around me.

"Mmm," Morrigan murmurs.

I hold my breath in hopes that she'll go back to sleep. Heat has been ravaging her system hard, and while I've enjoyed every minute of it, almost every minute of it, she's due for some much-needed sleep.

I'm positive she's sleeping, but her body rocks forward against me. She's pressed tight against my side with one leg hitched up over the top of mine.

She murmurs again and grinds her pelvis against me.

I draw a slow breath, and her growing arousal floods my nose and saturates my lungs, sparking excitement in my body. Strange, though, how it hasn't woken her up yet.

A frustrated little groan comes from her, and I note that her hand is between us. She grinds again. Her movements are clumsy, and the little groaning snore she makes continues.

I should go back to sleep, and when she pulls herself from sleep with her need, she can wake me up. But as much as I want to behave, my cock has other ideas. My erection grows, and with where her knee is placed, draped over the top of me, her little movements are playing right into that particular weakness.

When she presses her body against me this time, I feel her hand making tiny movements.

"Morrigan," I say softly, but it doesn't wake her.

Not that I expected it to because waking her up has always been a bit of a struggle. If she's this far under, I should let her sleep.

Rolling her over will make it so she's not as close and not smelling so much of me. It's probably overwhelming her senses.

"Mmmmm," Morrigan moans, pushing herself a little harder against me, her hips rocking back and forth more than once.

My cock throbs, and behaving doesn't seem like the right thing to do. With great care, I roll her and myself until she's lying more on her back.

She still doesn't wake, but she does moan, her body curling toward mine.

With the new positioning, I've a good view of where her hand is. Her fingers are dipping well below the waistband of her cotton panties, but in her slumber, she's unable to satisfy herself.

Trying not to startle her, I slide my hand down the length of her arm, following it under the fabric, and find her soaking wet.

She moans, and it's a little louder than the last, but her deep, restful breathing is still there. I nudge her fingers out of the way. In her sleep, she probably can't understand much, but she moves her hand from her pants, giving me more space to work.

I'm so fucking hard, and her wetness coating my fingers sends a jolt straight to my cock.

Morrigan's body relaxes, and the hand I moved comes to rest near my chest. She makes a needy little whine, and I debate kissing her, but I wonder how long I can play before Morrigan wakes up. *Can I make her come in her sleep?*

I groan, struggling with that thought and keeping still. With one hand cradled behind her and the other playing with her pussy, I can't exactly handle my own pleasure. The way she moans, though, I'll get her off more than once, and then she'll beg for my cock.

# CHAPTER 69
# MORRIGAN

*ANSEL'S HANDS HOLD ME TIGHTER TO HIM. HE PUSHES DEEP INTO ME, cock ravaging my insides, reaching to the deepest depths again and again. His mouth is kissing mine, then my neck, and down my breasts. I grind against him, pushing, wanting more of the pleasure he's offering. My orgasm is so close, but he won't let me reach it.*

*I beg, but he denies, and when I protest, the excitement building disappears. In a momentary blip I'm lost, not getting what I need.*

*"Ansel."*

*"That's it, Morrigan. Come for me." His voice is both too loud and too soft. It's a whisper and a yell.*

MY EYES OPEN, AND MY MIND SLOWLY PROCESSES THE WORLD AROUND me. The dream merges with reality. Ansel's hands are the ones working me over. His fingers are pressed deep inside me. His thumb running slow circles over the top of my clit.

My heart is beating through my chest, and my breaths are hard to catch. Ansel groans, driving me in the height of desire. I pant, trying to catch my brain up with what he's doing to my body.

Ansel locks eyes with me before nudging my head up and kissing me. He presses his mouth against mine, tongue exploring, and it's nearly enough for me to come undone.

I raise my hips, and Ansel presses a little harder.

I'm screaming into our kiss. He swallows it back.

The first orgasm crashes through me, and I'm shaking with pleasure.

Ansel moves over the top of me, pinning me down. I'm trapped beneath him, blissfully forced to feel every orgasm he wants to give me.

Turning my head to the side, I gasp for air as the first orgasm subsides. This is perfect. But I'm not entirely satisfied.

I want more.

Need more.

I run my hands up his back and try to pull him closer. Anything to make us more together. I want to feel him inside.

I turn my head back to him and moan against the kiss. "More."

There's a dark laugh, and Ansel pulls my bottom lip between his teeth and bites. A low rumble reverberates in his chest as he growls in disagreement.

"Always in such a hurry." His words hold the gravelly tone of the growl, but he doesn't stop his motions.

Whining, I try to play to his softer side, hoping for anything that it'll work.

It doesn't. Ansel doesn't give me more.

Bending my fingers, I dig my nails into his back and scratch, trying to force him for more. Instead of giving me what I want, Ansel stops fucking my pussy with his fingers and circles my clit faster with his thumb.

Harbinger rises to the surface, and Ansel smirks. "You want to play rough, hmmm?"

I curl my lip in a snarl, letting my wolf come forward. *We want more*, my wolf agrees, urging Harbinger through me. The whine we let out is supposed to be disarming.

Ansel snaps his teeth in my face, and I look away in a hurry to expose my neck for him. His breath hits my ear, and his thumb stops moving.

I'm throbbing, chest heaving, waiting for Ansel's next move.

He releases a small laugh and then runs his fangs down my neck.

I hold my breath, waiting for the pain of teeth sinking into me.

He nips at the base, but aside from the playful pinch, it's not enough. It's not the bone-deep mating mark that would tie me to him forever.

*More.* I let out my breath and try again to plead for attention. Softening my eyes, I whine, trying to give him puppy eyes. "Please?"

"Only because you asked nicely." Ansel pulls his hand out of my pants, and instantly, I mourn the loss of him touching me as a throb shoots straight through my core.

I curl into a ball with the cramp.

"Hang on, sunshine, just a second." Ansel unties his pajama pants, and in the low light, I see the wet spot on them.

It's fucking delicious. I dig my fingers into the bedsheet, closing my eyes through another wave of pain.

Stupid foil packet in hand, Ansel returns to bed. He's careful unwrapping me and then undressing me. His skin feels ice cold against mine.

A chill rips through me.

"Roll over," he commands. "It'll trap in the warmth better."

Doing what he asks, I tuck my arms up close to my chest, huddling into the sheet. Being face down, away from him, vulnerable, is becoming my new favorite thing. It's so primal having him behind me. It's animalistic, offering him my backside for fucking.

Ansel backs down my body before I feel a long trail of kisses up my calf. At the knee, he begins peppering little nips with those kisses. When he makes it to the globe of my ass, he sinks his teeth into the flesh, and a yelp of surprise escapes me. He jokingly chews, putting more teeth marks on my skin.

The way he slides his hand up my back draws a shiver from my body. When his fingers get to the nape of my neck, he starts weaving them into the strands of my hair until he's secured his hand at the base of my skull.

"Do you know how sweet you smell worked up like this?" Ansel's voice is gravelly and distracts from his hand sliding up my inner thigh.

I struggle against the bed, trying to push myself to his fingers and, ultimately, his cock.

I whine, "Ansel."

"Morrigan," he whines back at me, mimicking the sounds, and removes his hand from between my legs.

Ansel fists his fingers in my hair. Pulling me into a slight bend, he kisses the side of my neck again before giving the hair one last tug. He lets go, and I turn my head to the side to face him.

I soften my features and hope the puppy eyes work this time. *Please, fuck me.*

"I told you, that doesn't work on me." Ansel rubs his hand down my back, pressing into the stiff muscles. His fingers dig into the bite marks he placed on my ass before dipping down between the cheeks.

Expertly he slides them into my pussy and starts to fuck. Tension that hadn't entirely dissipated from the first orgasm only intensifies with Ansel's new movements.

I'm panting and clenching around his fingers.

"Ansel!" I scream as another orgasm takes me.

The world grows fuzzy, and my whole lower body is tense and alive with the orgasm.

My moans growing fewer and further between doesn't stop the ache and need for more.

"You like that?" Ansel taunts me.

I know that's what he's doing, but I can't make myself answer any other way than truthfully. "Yes. Please more."

"Already beggin' for more. Didn't I just give you two orgasms?"

Two fingers inside me become three, and Ansel shifts above me. The head of his cock slides against the bite marks on my ass.

I know he's teasing me on purpose. He's driving me wild because he can, because he wants to. This isn't servicing me through my heat. Ansel is enjoying every minute of us together.

He withdraws the fingers that had been toying with me and splays my legs farther apart, kneeling between them.

The crinkle of the stupid foil and a nearly inaudible growl are the only sounds before Ansel lowers himself down over the top of me, licking and nipping his way up my back.

Pressure and a pinch of pain accompany Ansel sinking his cock deep into me.

"Fuck." My breathing picks up. My heart rate flutters again.

Pressing my knees against the bed, I rise, trying to take more of him. I need Ansel to fuck me harder. It's a deep desire I can't escape.

"You take me so well," Ansel praises, and I push harder, trying to grind into each thrust.

Cruelly, Ansel stops.

Bliss is short lived because, apparently, he isn't ready to let me fully enjoy this.

I snarl as he pulls out. It's got to be illegal to deny a woman like this.

"Frustrated, sunshine?" Ansel rakes his nails down my back and lies beside me, like he wasn't fucking me a few seconds ago and his dick isn't throbbing against my hip.

"Ansel," I snarl, pushing myself up off the bed and glaring at him.

"Yes, Morrigan?" He quirks an eyebrow at me.

I'm done being denied.

The fever of heat is pitching, and I push, hard. Throwing my full weight against his shoulder, I roll Ansel, forcing him onto his back.

Harbinger flashes in Ansel's eyes, but he doesn't move to stop me. Not that I could be deterred anyway. I position myself over the top of him. Pushing my hands against his chest, I pin him beneath me as I straddle him. Ansel grips my forearms, but he doesn't move me. Instead, he's nearly holding me to him.

The tip of Ansel's cock is pressed against my clit, and I grind against it, not sure who I'm torturing more — me or him. But it sure feels fucking good. My eyes fall closed, and I focus on the warmth and the pressure on my clit.

Ansel growls, and I open my eyes. "Eyes on me, sunshine."

"Awfully demanding given I'm the one on top." I bite my bottom lip, sassing him but grinding against him a little harder.

The chuckle that comes from Ansel is the only warning I get before his hands leave my forearms and land on my hips. His fingers dig into the flesh of my thighs, and in a calculated movement, he seats me on his cock, pulling my hips down hard and forcing me to take him all at once.

"Fuck!" I scream, and my eyes close tight.

My fingers dig harder into his chest, and for half a heartbeat, I wonder if I drew blood. That thought passes as quickly as it comes as Ansel rams his cock into me.

He easily fucks me, despite being underneath me.

The gravel sound is back as he growls, "What did I say, sunshine?"

I open my eyes, and Harbinger is still captivated in Ansel's eyes. My wolf pushes forward to meet him, and I let her.

The pace Ansel sets is working me in the exact right ways. Taking advantage of his grip on my hips, I grind hard on the downstroke, feeling myself completely seated onto him. It's blissful to be an extension of him.

An orgasm builds, and my arms shake. With them unable to hold me up any longer, I fall forward.

Ansel, still holding my hips, thrusts steadily. I moan in his ear. His scent trapped in his hair reminds me of how much I missed him.

"You gonna come for me, sunshine?" Ansel whispers. "I can feel you clenching on me. You want that orgasm, don't you?"

"Please, Ansel. Make me come." Begging seems to work with him sometimes, but I don't think he's going easy on me.

Somewhere between waking up and now, Ansel and I have found a new depth. He fucks me fiercely, and I lean over the top of him, adjusting until he hits the exact right spot.

My eyes fall closed, and Ansel's snarl makes me open them again. The moment I do, I scream, coming hard, my pussy clenching around him. His deep bellow follows as he comes undone a breath after.

I wobble and try to hold myself steady on top of him.

This orgasm sates my heat. I'm turning cold. The sweat on my skin is freezing me.

"Easy, sunshine. I've got you." Time moves all funny, and

Ansel's voice fades in and out and flickers with the exhaustion I'm feeling.

Sometime in the last little bit, he's pulled out, left and returned, cleaned me up, and is now standing in clean sweat-pants and a T-shirt, pulling a flannel out of his closet.

I squint, trying to focus the delirium of my mind on him. "What is it with you and flannels and plaids?"

Ansel smiles and helps me into his shirt, buttoning it down my front. "They don't make durable long-sleeve shirts in polka dots. It's only those fancy dress shirts. The Hawaiian ones are kinda nifty, but they're all short sleeves and that flimsy fabric. Rough lifestyle requires rough clothing, so they're the closest I can get to a colorful wardrobe."

"But all year long?" I yawn, reaching for him.

Ansel pulls me to him, and I wrap my arm around his chest. "The tattoos help me hide the scars, but unlike wolves, humans don't care for visible tattoos. So, I always keep one with me for running into town. Never know when you'll need a backup shirt."

"So much to unpack in that sentence." I shake my head. "Humans don't care about tattoos."

"Maybe not an issue in California, sure. When I travel, I get different responses to them. It's a lot more positive than it is here." Ansel sighs and sounds frustrated. "But there's a big difference here. It's just easier if I keep them covered. No need to stand out any more than I already do."

"I guess Utah is known for being a bit more conservative." I move away from the negative thoughts and judgments of others. "So, you'd prefer polka dots?"

*I wonder if the fabric place online has flannel or cotton in polka dots that would work.*

"I'd love a little more variety," he answers. "But I haven't exactly thought too hard about it, I guess."

"Mmm." I curl into him, nuzzling up against him. "Can we nap again?"

"Sure thing, sunshine."

I'm back asleep before I know if he's in bed with me or not.

# CHAPTER 70
## ANSEL

Morrigan is up and out of bed before me. Her side of the bed is cold, and I have to pry my eyes open. Morning light streams in through the blinds, and the smells of bacon and coffee aren't usual. *When has anyone made me breakfast?*

Harry urges me to find her.

The thermostat, turned down for her hot flashes, is a little more chilly than I'd like. I tug on my sweatpants and head out to the kitchen, pulling on a flannel shirt.

I'd much rather have one more day to play house with her. Maybe I'm right though? I'll see her today, and fireworks will happen, something, anything to let me feel this mating bond everyone talks about.

"Good morning, sunshine." Morrigan quotes me as I close the door to our bedroom.

*My bedroom*, I try to correct myself.

Walking the few feet to the kitchen has my heart beating an irregular rhythm, fast and off balance.

*Something. Anything*, I beg.

Cade said when he saw Thalia, something sparked. Finn said he was pretty sure when he saw Lena, and when her scent hit him, it was a missing piece clicking into place. Lena said she felt overwhelming dread, and fuck, I'd take that if it meant I'd get to keep her.

Morrigan is at the stove. She doesn't look up to see me focused on her, but there's nothing out of the ordinary. The warm ache in my chest feels a little funny but still nothing new, nothing different from before her wolf came back.

"Feeling better?" I ask, watching her crack eggs one handed while stirring the wok with a fork.

She nods. "Yeah. I think we're through it."

That pain in my chest is back. *Maybe I should have Ben check it out?*

I shake off the idea. Wolves don't get physically sick. It's all in my head.

"Want a hand?" I walk over to the coffee pot. If I'm staying awake all day, there needs to be caffeine.

She shrugs. "I've got it. You've been taking care of me for thirty-seven days. The least I can do is make breakfast once for you."

"Alright." I walk around the counter and sit on her stool. I suppose it's a good thing she's still counting days. She's thinking about getting out of here.

Harry slinks in through my body. Something's irritating him. But that might be because it's been a while since we've shifted. *Since I shifted.*

I banish those thoughts from my mind. There's no us. There's no we. She'll be back in the loft tonight, and I'll have to wash my sheets and pillows today. I'll have my den back and move on.

Harry snarls at the thought.

"What do you want to do today?" Morrigan asks.

She's smiling, and it's so good to see her this way. Maybe now that she's more in tune with herself, she'll come around.

"I've got to check in on the guys and give Ben a day off. He's probably behind with clients and all sorts of broody." I laugh. He'll be glad this was a one-time thing.

"Sounds good." Morrigan switches from stirring the wok to mixing the eggs.

Her movements are quick and calculated. After turning down the fire, she goes to find spices from the cupboard. I suppose with thirty-seven days, she's learned where everything is from watching. Doesn't take a quick learner to know I don't ever change anything.

"So." I draw a deep breath. "I've been thinking, it might be better for you to help Ben for a while. Before, you didn't have a wolf, and then you were going into heat, and the guys were enamored with you. But maybe until they adjust a little bit . . ."

"Yeah. That's fine. I think Ben might even warm up to me. I got a nickname." Morrigan keeps smiling.

"I'm doing an inventory of Princeton's unit. It's between Sully and Sherman. Once it's habitable, we can get you down with the p —"

Morrigan drops the fork she had been beating the eggs with, and it falls to the floor with a clang that echoes in the house.

Her mouth hangs open as she looks at me. Eyebrows drawn together, she examines me. "You're joking."

"No, I figured . . ." A creeping feeling crawls up the base of my spine into my shoulders, then into my neck. I pull my hair up, but when I reach for a hair tie, there isn't one in my pocket, so I have to let it fall back down around my shoulders. I look down at the wok. "Breakfast is burning."

She turns off the burner, her body stiff and rigid. She leaves the fork on the floor and walks past the end of the counter to the back hallway. The ridiculous security panel beeps as she presses the buttons. Then her shoes and coat rustle as she puts them on.

Harry's instantly on edge watching her. It's predatory, like he's calculating. I've felt this. I know this feeling. He thinks she'll run.

I draw a breath, walking to her in the hallway. "Where are you going?"

"Un-fucking-believable," Morrigan snaps at me. "I'm going to Ben's, you can call him and check."

She glares at me before turning around and slamming the door on her way out.

*Why couldn't I feel the pull to bond? Why couldn't we be mates?* My body runs cold. Tears fill my eyes, and I slump against the wall. *Her reaction is so much different from mine. Why?* If the mating bond isn't here, then why is she so upset? This wasn't meant to be.

I leave breakfast on the stove and go to my bedroom to strip the sheets. No sense in putting it off.

When I get to the pillows, my hands are trembling. I try shaking them out to get control of my fingers. But it doesn't matter because my eyes are watering.

*It wasn't meant to be.* Fate wouldn't bother giving someone with a wolf like mine a fated mate. There's no point in torturing someone with the fear that I might not come home. No matter how good Harry is at his job.

I let myself slump down the wall.

Harry's unsettled and pushing to get at something. I let him have some space in my brain. *Could you just fucking show me her death? Let me have some closure. There's no way she'll die alone. Maybe I can help her find him.*

He doesn't care. I used up all his care for me by simply surviving. I sit in silence with her pillow in my lap. It'll only hurt trying to move on later, but I'm not ready to give her up.

Dinah and Walt were wrong. It happens. Life changes.

# CHAPTER 71
# MORRIGAN

M<small>Y</small> <small>FIST CONNECTS WITH</small> B<small>EN'S DOOR</small>. T<small>HE PAIN IN MY HAND AND THE</small> rattle tell me only one knock is needed.

"Fuck. I'm coming." Ben hollers from somewhere in his house.

The door flies open. "Who's hurt? Ansel okay?"

Tears flood my eyes. "I think the asshole just rejected me."

My wolf whines, hurting right with me. We're hollow, and I draw a deep breath, trying to fill the void with something. But all it does is give me more air to wail.

"What?" Ben doesn't fight when I hug him. "Shhh."

He barely wraps his arms around me, but he does pet my hair, trying to comfort me, but it makes everything worse.

Ben steps back and pulls me into his house. "Come on. Let's sit down and talk about the idiot."

I try to wipe the tears out of my eyes, but more keep coming. My stomach retches, and Ben directs me to his kitchen sink.

There's nothing there, and I dry heave. It hurts.

"Alright." Ben rubs my back. "Let's put some water in you. That's really bad for your stomach."

It's ridiculous. "Do you even have a heart?"

"Anatomically speaking, yes," he answers, turning on the tap and pouring me a glass.

It's pure torture, but I swallow the liquid without tasting it. He hands me a paper towel, and I wipe my nose.

Drawing a deep breath, I try to explain. "I'm not in heat." I state the obvious. "And I thought…it seemed like we were on the same page. He wasn't different, but then he was. It made sense."

Sobs fight against the words, and I'm crying again. He tries to hold me, and this time it hurts. I can't breathe.

The touch is bad. It's not okay.

I push back, and Ben lets me go.

"Okay, then what?"

"He told me I'm moving to Princeton's cabin, and he wants me to work with you," I get out in a big breath. But the tears running from my eyes mean I can't see what Ben thinks about it all. "It's like he can't wait to get rid of me."

Another paper towel replaces the soggy one in my hand. Trying to wipe the tears away, I catch a glimpse of the look on Ben's face. The pity painted in the lines of his forehead is a knife to the stomach. *He knew. He knew we weren't mates.*

Shaking my head, I walk toward the door.

"Morrigan, where are you going?" Ben says the same stupid words that Ansel said.

"Somewhere away from anyone with a penis!" I scream.

My heart is in a million pieces, and there's nowhere else for me to go. On the stupid hill in his stupid castle, Ansel's moving on from my heat, but I'm brokenhearted like some sort of pathetic child who fell in love with my first fuck. What a fucking cliché. Could I be any more naive?

Every fiber in my being, every single last bit of me, presses to run. Physically run.

With a solid push, my wolf charges to the surface, urging me to go.

I let her take over.

THE SUN, HIGH IN THE MIDDAY SKY, TELLS ME IT'S BEEN A LONG TIME since I fled Ansel's. So it's not surprising when my body falters and eventually fails.

She's gone the moment my body falls from my wolf form. Hollowness I recognize all too well settles within me.

It seems I'm back to being broken. Broken wolf and broken-hearted.

Naked in the dirt, I close my eyes as the brightness of the sun's rays cast down against my body. *You can die from a broken heart, right?*

If I lie here long enough, eventually I'll die of starvation or dehydration. But there's no way I can go back. Nothing on this earth could move me from this spot. I'm not even sure where home — No. Not home. I'm not even sure where civilization is from here. Plus, I'm naked. Can't exactly give the poor people of Nameless a peep show.

There's always the original plan. An apartment, a dog, and a sewing business.

No.

That's flavorless. It's no longer a dream. The mundane life of a human can't be anything for me.

Then again, it's not like my wolf is here anymore. Maybe I used her up again. I only get a few hours every five years . . .

Harbinger is a monster. He's incapable of love, and I was

stupid enough to let myself fall in love with the idea that I could tame him.

Death comes for us all in the end. Sooner or later, Harbinger takes fractured wolves. Like my father before me, Ansel will be the end of me.

SOMETIME BEFORE SUNSET, MY TEARS DRIED UP. NOW, LYING HERE IN the dark, I can't even cry myself to sleep.

I look at the stars. I'm nothing more than a speck of dust in the universe, and my existence is futile.

A chill runs over my body. Hypothermia is the next killer of the desert. How cold does it have to get for you to die of hypothermia? Probably colder than this.

"Morrigan?"

My name's being called in the distance. *Fuck.*

Ansel calls again, "I know you're out here somewhere. I can smell you. Come on."

I don't answer him. If he wants to find me so badly, then he can bloodhound me out here in the wilderness.

"Morrigan." Ansel's a few feet away. "Come on, sunshine. Let's get you home."

"Fuck off, asshole." I try to growl, but the wolf won't come back. "I'm not going anywhere with you."

"I'll command you if I have to," Ansel threatens.

"Ha. It'll take more than an Alpha command to get me out of the dirt," I challenge him.

The void remains. There's no wolf, no command, and I'm done pretending.

Ansel drops to the dirt next to me. The bare skin of his shoulder presses against mine. Apparently, I wasn't the only wolf running today.

"Lyra, Hercules, Pleiades, Ursa Major, Ursa Minor, Cygnus." Ansel points up at the sky.

Traitor eyes follow where he points. I try to see the shapes, but they look like randomized specks to me.

The Milky Way spreads out above us. His silence feels like being abandoned all over again.

We no longer have anything to talk about or say to each other. He's here because I'm his job. I'm back to the obligation that I've always been. I've never been wanted as a person. I'm a space filler and a commodity to be passed around when it's convenient. And now it's convenient. My time has come for Ansel to pass me back around.

"I'm sorry," Ansel whispers.

"Whatever, Ansel." I don't forgive him.

There's no way I can forgive him because I don't forgive myself for being surprised. Surprised that I'm nothing to him. *Pathetic.*

He sighs and doesn't speak again.

A satellite blinks overhead, crossing the sky in a slow orbit.

"It's midnight," Ansel informs me. "You haven't eaten today. I can't let you starve to death."

"I'm not hungry. Go the fuck away," I order in a futile attempt to reject him back.

Which is a bluff. If he told me he felt it, that it just took him a day to maybe, I don't know, just feel the feelings, I would forgive him.

"I can't do that, sunshine," Ansel tells me, using that nickname.

The way he would call me that when he'd care for me is an echo in my mind, and it's reliving the nightmare from this morning.

"Fine, show me the way home, and I'll have a sandwich and go sleep in Princeton's cabin. I don't even care if it's gross."

*Home. Fuck.* I correct myself, pushing up out of the dirt. "Which way is your prison, I mean house?"

Ansel follows me to standing. He laughs, either ignoring or amused by my sass. "You really suck at running away."

He points to the left, and I pick a path through the rough cacti and rocks on the ground. He follows a few steps behind, and in two minutes, we're at the back door to the house.

*I do suck at running away.* Irony.

Ansel opens the sliding door for me.

The house is trashed.

"Uh. I think you've been robbed." I turn to look at Ansel.

He steps around me but doesn't say anything.

"Oh, so we're not concerned with the fact your entire house is destroyed?" I accuse him.

"I wasn't robbed," Ansel growls.

*He wasn't . . .* I look closer at the mess. The couch is shredded. But those aren't knife marks from someone cutting into cushions looking for riches. The chairs aren't smashed, they're torn apart with deep gouges. The railing to the downstairs is chewed, and spindles are broken apart. Deep claw marks gouge the floor.

Dread sinks into me. This wasn't a robbery.

"Harbinger got out. He tore up the guest room you had been sleeping in, and worse," Ansel says quietly. He clears his throat and keeps talking. "I cleaned up the worst of it. It shouldn't smell up there, and the other guest room is okay." His voice tells me there's something he isn't saying. "You can sleep up there tonight."

I pick my way through the disaster of the house. The hardwood floors, the rugs, the banister, the barstools, the countertop, the refrigerator, they've all suffered some sort of heavy damage. Ansel's bedroom door is off its hinges.

There's virtually nothing left of his bed. Springs are

exposed. The headboard is in pieces. The dresser is tipped over, with drawers strewn about. The lamp is nearly unrecognizable. Shoes litter the hallway. The back door is dented and looks like the wolf tried to get out. The metallic smell of pennies hits my nose. At some point, he bled.

Shaking my head, I head back to the kitchen.

Ansel's making a sandwich like it's a normal Wednesday.

"Ansel," I call.

He doesn't look up. "Hmm?"

"What happened?" I press.

"Harry got out. He didn't like my decorating style." Ansel's voice is flat and matches the feeling in my chest.

"So you said," I groan. "How did Harry get out?"

Ansel slams his fist on the counter. "Morrigan, I am barely holding it together. Please let me make you a sandwich. Ben is coming to lock me in a kennel, okay? Just . . . I had to find you first."

I stand there, staring at him. What did I do to get this anger and frustration? I'm the one who got rejected. "What did I do wr —"

My words pull his eyes off the counter. Harry is there again, staring back at me. Ansel blinks, pulling him back. Black fades to green, and in the green, I see swirling torrents of emotions. Emotions that'll end me.

"Morrigan," Ansel says, his voice hoarse. "I can't. Please. Just go."

"Fine." I turn away from him and head up the stairs.

He had his chance. A tiny sliver of empathy was taking root for him, but Ansel's made it crystal clear. Whatever's happening in the mind of the Ardelean Reaper, it's not for me anymore. Harbinger reinforced that decision.

# CHAPTER 72

# ANSEL

I DON'T UNDERSTAND. I'M LOST INSIDE. HARRY IS A WRECK. I'VE stopped shifting in my sleep, finally. When I'm awake, he's, well, I don't know that manageable is the right word. I'm keeping him inside, but it hurts.

He keeps trying to pull me toward the pack's cabins. With every breath, he's pushing me away from the house toward the pack. Toward her.

My house is halfway to livable, and I'm exhausted.

I feel like absolute shit. Morrigan's distant. I know she's around because the guys wouldn't lie to me, and I've caught glimpses of her in and about her unit. I was surprised she didn't move into Ezra's but rather tackled Princeton's head-on. Though, I did spell out that he's bound to turn up eventually.

It's noon, and I've finished getting the base cabinets in for the new kitchen island. Even with the furnace set down to a balmy fifty degrees, I'm still sweating. I pull my T-shirt off and throw on a fresh flannel, leaving it unbuttoned. After picking up my cell phone off my new bed, I walk barefoot through the house. I intended to sit in one of the Adirondack chairs and kick my feet up for a bit, but Harry won't settle.

I move back through the house and open the newly hung back door, and it seems acceptable to him that we sit on the back steps. I pull the door closed behind me and sit down, waiting for him to push harder. But the view of the roofs of the cabins is enough for whatever chaos he wants.

I hover my thumb back and forth over my contacts. *Alden, Cade* or *Alloway, Judah* or *Alden, Lena* . . . Judah however . . . Scrolling back up to the top, I pull his name out of the *A*s.

"Hey, Ansel, hang on a sec," Judah says. I hear shuffling, then a vehicle door closes. "Sorry, getting back to the park office. How's it going? You've been quiet for a bit. Cade said you canceled on him for Equinox. Everything okay?"

"Usual bumps that come with wolves who are a little off. Wasn't a good time for company or to travel." My answer is honest, not necessarily the whole truth, but it's honest. "Weather is okay up there with you? Staying warm?"

"Yeah. Came out of a cold snap, but we got another foot of snow last night. But that's the mountains for you." Judah, when he has the time, is almost always good about taking the time to chat. "It sunny out there in Utah? I swear that's why Ezra loves it so much."

"Overcast today. Still a little chilly. But I've been working so hard didn't even notice." I try to direct the conversation a bit because I know I'll stall if he lets me. "I got a question, and you might not be able to answer it, but you seem to get feelings more than most people do."

Judah laughs. "Yeah, comes with the nonexistent gift, I guess. What's up?"

"What does love feel like?" I start broad.

"Uhh." Judah draws that out into a hum. He stomps off his

boots on the other end, and the bell above the ranger station door jingles as he closes it behind him.

"I get it if it's too hard to explain." I try giving him an out. *Might be asking for too much.*

"No. It's not that," Judah says over the sound of a zipper. "I was looking at the snow cornice over the door and wondering if I could get it to fall on Ezra when he comes by later."

I snort. It's not like Judah to sink to that sort of practical joke unless Ezra really pissed him off.

"You feel love in your chest," Judah says. "When you're feeling loved or giving love, it's across your collarbone and shoulders. It kinda wraps around you."

"So, love feels like hugs?" I scratch a spot on my forehead before letting my hand fall away.

"Oh. I thought you meant you specifically." Judah hums. "With a gift that's non-translatable, I can't share it so easily like Dinah, Ezra, or you. It's . . . I don't know. What are you asking specifically?"

"Well, what's the feeling like when you love someone?" I try to rephrase. "I mean like . . ." I draw a breath. "Alright, like your mom and dad, right? They gotta feel a certain way toward each other? Maybe Cade and Thalia?"

"Right," Judah sighs. "Okay, so, like, when Dad thinks of Mom, he gets a flutter in his stomach. It's not quite like butterflies."

"Butterflies." I nod to myself. *Sure, Walt talked about those when he met Ersilia.*

"But Mom gets a tickle in her lower back that wraps around her like when he holds her." Judah groans. "Okay, moving on. Cade and Thalia are really similar. When Cade talks about Thalia, it's like she's standing right by his side. That left side of his body where he holds her matches the right side of her body where she snuggles him. It's cute."

I play with a knot in the wood of the step my feet rest on. I don't understand what he's saying. "I don't feel feelings like that."

"Yeah, you do." Judah laughs, and his chair slides on the floor, scraping a bit. "I said it before. You feel love in your chest. It's that heavy, tight feeling you called a hug. It's a hug that's not actually happening."

My silence must tell Judah something. "Like think about Lena. Right now. Think about when she does something, and you're happy about it."

I think about Lena and how she looked at Finn in Ireland, then the box of supplies that arrived here, or at her mating ceremony.

"Freeze," Judah says quickly. "Take note of how you're feeling. I'd bet your back's a little tight and you're feeling kinda full pressure by your collarbone."

He's right. "Yeah, like a hug."

"That's how you feel love," Judah explains. "But why did you call about that?"

Those feelings in my upper chest that Judah was talking about disappear quickly. *By now, Judah's probably got an idea about what's going on anyway.*

I draw a deep breath before pushing it out with my words. "There's a woman here, and I don't know . . . things are complicated. Harry's obsessed with her, and even I think about her pretty much all the time, but that's not . . ." I run out of air and take a smaller breath. "Those feelings you're talking about don't, I don't know. Cade and Finn and Lena all said they were obsessed. Scared me into thinking it was more than it is. Harry's got a bug up his ass. That's all."

"What do you feel when you think about her?" Judah asks. "The physical. Think about her right now and focus. Tell me what it feels like."

"For a gift that doesn't exist, you sure know how to use it," I grumble but do what he says.

"Being able to explain feelings doesn't make it a gift," Judah quips.

It's that same ache, square in the chest, that intensifies. Harry gets more insistent with wanting her.

"My chest hurts. Square in the center. It makes everything tight and hard. Nothing like when I think about Lena."

"More, right?" Judah asks.

"Hell of a lot more," I answer, curling my toes, grounding me and Harry to the deck.

I let it go, pushing her out of my mind. Better not to get him worked up. Still want to get the countertop installed tonight.

"I know that when I think about people I've been close with and thought might be my mate, it feels different than when I think about everyone else." Judah's voice sounds sad. I perk up, listening to him more intently. "Different might not be wrong. Who is she? Dinah wasn't very forthcoming."

"That's because Dinah is mad at you," I answer him.

"It's because whoever you have out there, Dinah knows is special and she's protecting," Judah corrects. "Dinah quite literally said, 'When it's your business to know, then you'll know, but it's not, so go back to playing with your Squirrel Cadet friends.'"

"Squirrel Cadet friends?" I tip my head to the side and then straighten it. *He can't see you. Stop that.*

"It's fake. They don't exist. That's not the point." Judah groans. "Point is, I don't know, and if you don't want to tell me, then it's fine. But I think whatever your feeling isn't bad."

"It's complicated. She's Walt's daughter. Deserves better than me." I give him the truth.

"There isn't anyone better than you, Ansel. Don't fool yourself." Judah sighs. "I hate to cut this short because you don't sound okay, but I hear arguing outside and I'm alone today."

"No, I got it. Thanks for your time. I'll talk to you later." I dismiss him quickly.

I sure as shit don't want to sit here and pretend that feelings are doing me any good right now.

Harry pushes me so hard I'm forced up off the steps. I stretch and let the cool air brush my skin until I shiver. The intensity of Harry sends me another step closer to the cabins, to her. I focus, thinking about her, the feeling in my chest. It's sharp, painful. It stings but aches. It's like I can't breathe.

If it were a mating bond, you'd think it'd feel better than this, right?

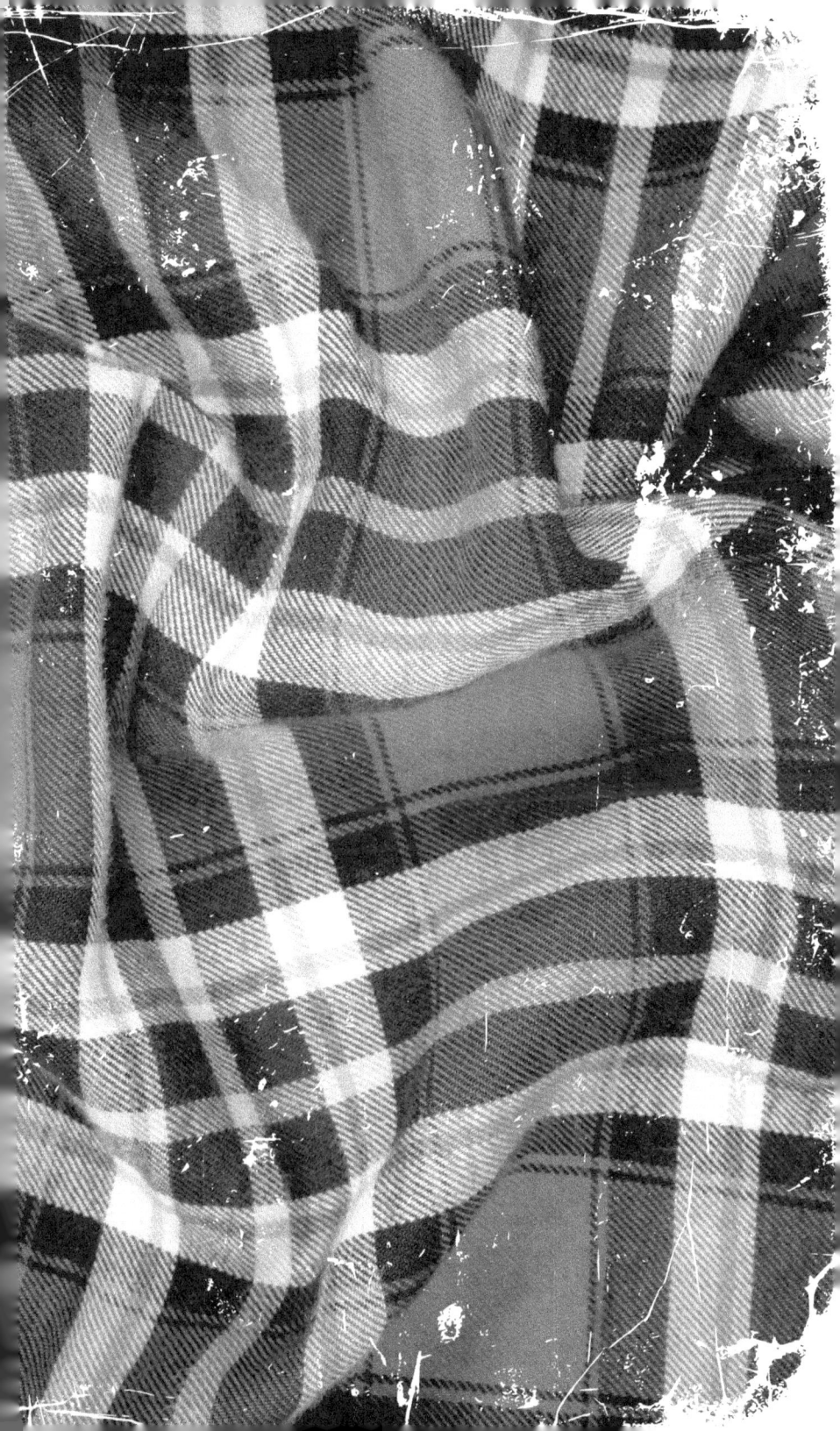

# CHAPTER 73
# MORRIGAN

PRINCETON IS LUCKY TO BE DEAD BECAUSE HE WOULD BE ON DEATH row for the atrocities and war crimes of his previous residence. I have scrubbed every inch of this stupid place, yet it seems every time I turn around, there's another mess or something broken.

Avoiding Ansel has been easy physically. He hasn't come down here. A sewing machine and a mountain of fabric appeared the day after I moved in. And between bursts of cleaning and laundry, I busy myself making a quilt. I don't have a serger or longarm machine, which means I'll be binding it by hand, but fuck it. What else am I doing?

My wolf is gone. She's not coming back. I don't want her, and Dinah said it herself, I'm giving myself permission to not have a wolf and to be broken.

The pain of Ansel's rejection is easier this way.

Knuckles softly rap on my door, and I go to answer it. Zero is standing there with a bag of groceries. I've been living out here in Princeton's trailer for three weeks, and like clockwork,

Zero brings me groceries three days a week. It's all that fits in the tiny dorm-size refrigerator.

When I open the door more, he steps inside and sets the bag down on the counter.

His deep voice fills the small living space. "How's the sewing going?"

"Oh, you know. Straight line here, rotate, straight line there." I shrug and start to put the groceries away. It doesn't really matter what they are.

"Want to come and play beanbags with us?" Zero offers.

"Nope." I shake my head, firm with conviction. Being part of the pack is what Ansel wants, so I will be adamant not to be. "Not feeling social."

He nods, and when I turn my back to face the fridge, I hear him set something on the dining table.

"Well, I'll be going, then." Zero lets himself out before I turn around.

Sliding the grocery bag to me reveals something else on the table. Moving the bag aside, I see what he left me.

A twenty-dollar bill and the keys to his car.

It takes my breath away. *Do I go?*

I close the door to the fridge and cross my arms in front of my chest, staring at my possible tickets to freedom.

Twenty dollars in fuel is about eight gallons of gas. His little import is similar to one of the girls' from high school . . . only a little more beat up. If he gets forty miles a gallon like she did, that's three hundred or so miles. I don't even know what's three hundred miles from me. But I can get a map from a travel brochure stand in Moab.

*Don't be stupid. Of course I go.*

Ansel doesn't want me. Gerad knows I'm here. Staying, with the stupid hope that Ansel admits he's wrong, is a waste of time. Opening the fridge, I look at the groceries Zero gave me. They're all things that don't have to be refrigerated.

*I have to go.*

I WAIT UNTIL AFTER ONE A.M. TO TAKE MY BAG OF GROCERIES OUT TO Zero's car. The headlights were already turned off when I got in. I drive fast past the trailers and Ben's house. Anyone who hears the engine and tires will think they were dreaming it and go back to sleep. I hope.

When I'm down the driveway far enough, I turn the lights on. Coasting as much as possible, I try to conserve fuel. Zero has half a tank in the car.

Past Nameless but before Moab, there's a problem. Smoke billows out of the hood of the car.

"No. No. No. No."

I pull the car off the side of the road. *Of course his beater that's probably older than me would break down.*

Banging my fists on the steering wheel does nothing for the smoke, which tapers off after I turn off the engine.

It's only a matter of time.

I take the box of granola bars out of the grocery bag and bring them with me as I get out of the car. With a small jump, I get my butt up on the trunk of Zero's car and lean back against the rear windshield, looking at the night sky.

THE PURR OF ANSEL'S OLD BEATER TRUCK, THE BROWN TWO-SEATER AND not his usual maroon work truck, comes down the road. When he rounds the bend, the headlights illuminate me and the car.

Hopping off the trunk, I lean against it and rest my elbows on the lid. Pathetic attempt at escape if he found me this quickly. Maybe I should have kept walking. But then all I'd be is another mile down the road.

Ansel slams his truck door without bothering to turn off the engine. The vehicle rocks with the force.

The bright light of the high beams on his faded Chevy obscures my view. I'm envisioning his scowl. The one apparently reserved only for me.

His gait is quick. I expect to be verbally reprimanded with the 'What the fuck do you think you're doing?' and 'You can't leave, are you trying to make me put you down?'

What I get instead is his hands on me. One grabbing my upper arm, fingers digging into me and pulling me close. The other wrapping around my neck to the base of my skull, holding me still, forcing my eyes on him.

I wasn't expecting this Ansel. It's the one from my heat, laced with the commanding force of Harbinger. Yet, it's more than that. There's raw . . . something? Something more, and I feel it growing.

His chest heaves as he breathes deeply. *Is he trying to calm down?*

His lips find mine, pressing against me. The kiss is startling, it's so intense and oh so fucking good.

*No,* I scold myself. *No. We aren't forgiving him because he's good at fucking kissing. This isn't one of those magic 'dick me down and make it all better' moments. I'm stronger than that.*

Ansel's tongue parts my lips, and I kiss back. Our tongues dance back and forth. It's probably only thirty seconds, but it ticks by slowly as my desire builds.

The pain from his fingers digging into my arm fades. His hand on my throat tightens in exchange.

I gasp into our kiss, becoming lightheaded as the blood

flow slows to my brain. My hand moves toward his chest. Flat palmed, I try to push against him while pulling on his forearm with my other hand, attempting to stop him.

He doesn't release his grasp but does break the kiss and goes straight into snarling at me. It laces his words so they sound completely feral. "I'm done chasing. I'm done fighting. I'm done fighting *you*. You're mine, Morrigan."

My eyes have finally adjusted to the shadows cast by the high-beam headlights of his truck.

His thumb presses up into the soft tissue behind my jawbone. And I try to speak, try to tell him off. But his hand has me silenced.

"The house is empty without you. It's too quiet and Harry hates it." At first his green eyes are locked on my own, and then the darkness of Harbinger comes forward. "I'm not the same without you. I don't want to go back to a life without you in it."

An understanding warms me. There isn't a part of my body that doesn't feel his claiming of me, his declaration.

My hollowness dissipates, replaced by warmth. My wolf.

Harbinger, while synonymous with death, brings me so much life. I feel whole again. At last, all the pieces click together, and I realize my wolf wasn't ever missing. She's been tied to Ansel all along. My life, my home, my heart lives here, with him.

As his grip on my throat lessens, I'm able to direct my attention elsewhere. Like to where his other hand has gone, snaked around behind me and tucked into the top of my jeans and panties. One finger teases the top of my ass. With his other hand, he's pulled me closer to him, so my hips are pressed against him.

Slowly, I become more and more aware of what's between us. The heat between my legs grows intensely as I now recognize the shape of his stiff cock pressed against me.

My face flushes.

His breath is heavy and comes with long, drawn-out exhales. Ansel's nostrils flare before he kisses me again. It's not any sweeter. He may have removed his grip from my throat, but the way he's collared my neck with his hand feels like pure possession. His kiss deepens, and he threads his fingers into my hair.

With a momentary pause to breathe, he whispers, "Fuck, what I want to do to you right now."

Ansel kisses me again, his tongue claiming my mouth. This treatment, hot, heavy, and full of lust, burns away the wall I built to protect my heart.

As much as I wanted him to fuck off, he draws out a needy murmur from me. "Please."

His growl turns to a desperate moan. With rough hands, he pulls me from leaning against Zero's car and turns me to face it. Pushed over the trunk, I'm at his mercy. Ansel pulls my arm behind my back, further enforcing my lack of power.

Holding me in place, the growl rumbling through Ansel's voice in my ear threatens me, "There's no going back, Morrigan. There's no leaving. No running."

"Shut up and fuck me, Ansel."

He jerks the fabric from my body, and it gives way, ripping to shreds in his violence.

Fire ignites in my whole body, and my pussy throbs for him.

I hear his belt, followed by his zipper. His strength and weight hold me firmly in place.

I'm exhilarated.

Pushed apart by his knees, my legs feel weak. He slips his hand between my thighs and straight to my already dripping pussy. Every slow slide of his fingers between my folds gently teases my clit, playing with me until I'm moaning, edging, ever closer to an orgasm.

I wait for him to push me over the edge, but an orgasm doesn't come. I moan, pressing back and begging wordlessly for more.

He huffs. "You're not coming now. You'll earn your orgasms from now on."

A frustrated whine is the only response I can give him. *What the fuck does that mean?*

Ansel pulls his hand away. The next sensation is the familiar feeling of his cock along my inner thigh.

I pant, anticipating what's coming. I'm waiting for the delicious feeling of him deep inside.

He's proven Harbinger is always intense. And their exact brand of darkness and dominance calls to me.

The glorious sting of pain pierces my core as he thrusts forward. It's a sharp shooting sting, and it feels like he'll split me in half with his cock. I gasp as he adjusts.

Ansel pauses before rocking forward, cock sliding in much deeper this time. The pain is pushed aside as the satisfying fullness of him inside me wins out.

The way he's taking me is precisely what I need. I push back into him, craving more. He thrusts again, fulfilling that unspoken desire, and his head brushes my deepest part. I move to arch my back, but he leans over me, restricting my movements.

His fingers, covered in my slick, push against my lips and find their way into my mouth. I suck them clean.

"Fuck, sunshine. You take me so well," Ansel whispers in my ear. "I feel you clenching around me. You want to milk my cock? Want to feel me come in you?"

The balls of my feet grind into my shoes, toes curling in

anticipation. Body desperate for more, I whine again, "Fuck me. Ansel, please."

He takes his time; true to his word, he is in control. The pace is so slow and all for him. I want the rough. I want the violence he gave me before.

I try again. "No. Fuck me. Please, I need you to fuck me."

"No, you want me to fuck you. But that isn't how this works. You're not a fuck." He nips my ear. "I'll find a way to make you mine. Harbinger won't settle. The feelings I have don't match what I've been told, but I know what I want. I know what you want."

He punctuates his point, antagonizing me with a long, slow withdrawal. I could nearly cry from feeling him slide entirely out of me and then hearing the sound of him tucking himself back into his pants.

"Fuck you." I squirm as he releases my arm.

I turn around and reach for the fly of his pants.

"No," he commands.

I freeze, forced to stop by his command.

The familiar feeling of his hand around my neck returns once more as our eyes meet. The kiss this time is softer and sweeter.

He slides his hands down my body before gently lifting each foot and removing what's left of my jeans. "Get in the truck."

# CHAPTER 74
## ANSEL

CADE'S STUPID FUCKING ALARM ISN'T THE WORST FUCKING THING IN the entire world. And, maybe at Solstice, I'll tell him that. Probably not, but maybe.

Morrigan had driven around every other driveway sensor but missed the very last one, the one almost to town an hour away. And if it weren't for how insistent the stupid box was that it was a vehicle, I wouldn't have bothered to go look down the guys' driveway.

It didn't make sense that Zero would run. I had trackers installed on all the vehicles I own, but the feisty mechanic turned off his tracker over a year ago. Looking for dumb luck, I opened the app anyway, and the tracker on his car was turned back on.

It made so much more sense when I saw her sitting on the trunk of his car.

Something changed when I saw her sitting there in my headlights.

Then, feeling her pressed against me, the warmth of her skin, hearing the needy moan she made, I couldn't stop myself.

I wasn't gentle with her. But the smell of her arousal next to me tells me it doesn't matter.

"Do you mean it?" Morrigan starts at a whisper but then finds her voice. "You can't call me yours and not mean it."

"What I feel doesn't match what people say this feeling should be. There's no overwhelming connectedness. It's not sweet. Yes, I want to care for you more than anything. I can't put words to this. But everyone makes it sound like it's a gentleness and a calming feeling." I try to explain my frustration, but the words are hard to pick.

Morrigan slides across the bench seat and rests her head against my shoulder. I quit trying to talk about it.

"It's okay. I'll feel it enough for the both of us." She picks my hand up off my lap and interlaces our fingers. "But you don't get to be such a jackass to me about it."

Her frustration is valid. Even if I don't like how she's expressing it, I know I need to hear it, name-calling and all. I have to learn fast how to be a good mate for her.

I leave Walt's truck in the driveway, favoring parking in front of the house rather than in the garage so my sleepy little mate doesn't have so far to walk.

"Come on, sunshine, let's get you to bed." I kiss the top of her head.

With only a little groggy grumble, Morrigan follows me out the driver's side of the cab before leaning against me. "I'm not wearing any pants."

"I think that's your fault." Wrapping my arms around her, I squeeze lightly.

She shakes her head, her forehead pressing on that part of my sternum that hurts when she hurts. With a little adjustment, I pick her up into my arms. Morrigan doesn't object and rests her head on my shoulder. When I get to the door and want to set her down, she unlocks the knob.

"You forgot to turn the alarm on," Morrigan observes.

"Mmm. I thought Zero was having some sort of crisis. Was a little more concerned why my most stable resident decided to bolt than Cade's worry about intruders and that stupid system."

She lets me set her down, and I turn to close the door behind us.

"Ahhh. If you knew it was the delinquent, you would have taken the extra few minutes?" Morrigan rolls her eyes.

"No. If I knew it was *my* delinquent, I wouldn't have bothered closing the door." I toe off my shoes and stalk over to where she's trying to kick hers off. My fingers twitch. I want to feel the way her throat moves when she swallows with my hand around her throat again. But I settle for tipping her chin up to look at me. "Don't you dare run from me again."

"Don't give me reasons to," Morrigan sasses. Her eyes light up and push the sleepy look off her face.

I embrace the desire to feel her throat and press her head back against the wall. My hand catches her high at her jaw, and I turn her head to the side and nip at her neck.

That pain radiating from my sternum, paired with a settling Harry, hums through my body. This is what a mating bond has to feel like. Maybe it's what love feels like because no matter how badly it hurts, I don't want to be without this feeling.

# CHAPTER 75
# MORRIGAN

I FIST HIS SHIRT, AND WITH MY HEAD FORCED AWAY FROM HIM, I CAN'T bite back at him. I want to sink my teeth into him. Maybe I'll claim him first, and then he'll have to accept me. He's already claimed me as his delinquent.

"What am I gonna do with you?" Ansel growls.

"Finish what you started on the side of the road?" I snarl in response.

My wolf, needy and wanting, rushes forward, ready to claim him.

He laughs. It's dark and maniacal, and then he lets go of my throat. "Go to bed. Now."

I fake sadness with a halfhearted pout and try to walk out the door back toward the cabins and test Ansel's resolve. *I mean, if he wants me to go to bed . . .*

Ansel wraps his hand around my wrist, and I'm fairly certain I've broken him. With his eyes wild, Harry forward at the surface, and his nostrils flared, I've cracked that wild interior wide open. "Sunshine, so help me, if you try to go anywhere other than into our bedroom and on the bed with your ass in the air . . . I'll grab you and put you there myself. I'm not askin' again."

He spins me around in almost one of those corny dance steps, and I'm back to facing him. Our eyes lock. "I mean it, sunshine, you're mine."

The little love tap on my bare ass is all the further permission I need to head into his bedroom. *Our* bedroom.

Pulling off the T-shirt over my head, I climb onto the bed, but I'm not into complying with his orders yet. Instead, I stretch out and hang my head off the bed to watch him.

Ansel shakes his head as he strips out of his plaid shirt before undoing his belt and letting his jeans fall to the floor. His cock is already hard, the tip poking at the front of his boxers. A little wet mark lets me know how long he's been horny. I fell asleep in the truck, but it seems Ansel has been thinking about other things.

Our eyes meet, and I curl my legs up and bite my bottom lip.

He pulls his hair up, and the way his muscles flex in his arm, all the way down his chest, has me panting. He means business.

Like the predator he claims to be, Ansel stalks over to the bed and crouches in front of me so our eyes meet. "This was not what I instructed."

"Oops?" I tease.

Upside-down kisses aren't my favorite, but when Ansel separates us, the kiss is inconsequential.

"Open your mouth, sunshine."

Ansel's request is immediately answered. I willingly offer him my mouth. *Fuck. Yes.*

Ansel, despite the tension, frustration, and desire between us, slowly works his cock into my mouth. I force myself to draw air through my nose. It's not what I anticipated. My focus is split as Ansel's hand grazes my breast. He cups it, squeezing gently before the other hand joins the play. He skates it down my body and straight past my clit to push into my cunt.

I gasp, and Ansel pushes his hips forward. He startles me, and I gag. Ever in control, Ansel shifts back and lets me recover before claiming my throat again.

Ansel's thrust into my mouth matches the way his fingers handle my pussy. In and out together, he curls his fingers and presses on the sensitive nerves inside. Finally picking up his pace, he presses his thumb against my clit and works in slow motion.

Gagging on and off Ansel's cock makes breathing hard, and I'm swimming in the different sensations from how he's taking me. My desire to fight against him leaves. I'm here for whatever Ansel wants to do to me. However Ansel wants to claim me is now my only objective tonight.

The pressure growing in my cunt is a new experience. It doesn't feel the same as when I was in heat but equally desirable.

I try to match that pressure with my mouth, pushing my tongue along Ansel's shaft as it moves in and out of my mouth.

"Fuck," Ansel hisses. "You want me to come down your throat? Keep that up and I will, sunshine."

*As a matter of fact, I do.* I want to sass him, but I make my point known by flattening my tongue and pressing against him again.

Ansel snarls and stiffens, stopping his hips.

I growl. *I want it.*

With the little space I have to move, I bob my head on his shaft and then work my tongue around his head.

"Fuck!" he shouts and pushes deep into my mouth.

All the tastes I've had of him are nothing compared to him

SARAH JAEGER

filling my mouth and spilling down my throat. I swallow around him the best I can.

I'm not completely satisfied, but I'm pleased with myself hearing Ansel pant as he pulls his fingers from my pussy.

"Yes. Fuck me," I whine.

I ache for him. I'm dying to have him back inside me, especially without the stupid fucking condoms. I want to feel his wet warmth dripping out of me. It's been too long.

"No," Ansel snaps. He growls, "The next time I fuck you, it'll be when I put a claiming mark on your neck."

Rough hands wrap around my waist, and Ansel pulls me closer to him. My shoulders hang off the bed, and I move my hands to try and catch myself. He claims my wrists in his hands, holding them to the bed against my sides. Pinning me, half slumped off the bed, with his hands and torso, Ansel makes the most of the new position.

His tongue flicks against my clit, and I try to push my focus off how I'm dangling and on to what he's doing to me. I moan with the next long lap up my center.

The pressure building through my whole body throbs.

Ansel worships my clit with long strokes and swirls of his tongue. My pulse is pounding in my ears. I can't catch my breath, and I'm feeling hot all over.

He groans, "You taste so good, sunshine."

That does me in. My body clenches, toes curling, and I try to scream, but it's silent, trapped in the tension of my body, driven further and further by the dedication of Ansel's tongue.

The orgasm hangs onto me. I'm overwhelmed and nearly to the point of passing out when, finally, the languid strokes of Ansel's tongue no longer overstimulate me.

Ansel pulls away, supporting me as he raises me up onto the bed.

540

World spinning and swimming with the change, I cling to him for fear of falling out of bed.

"Easy does it," he murmurs, holding me close to his chest.

There's a happy sound in there, letting me know he's proud of himself for making me a messy semblance of myself.

Ansel's still sleeping next to me when I wake up. His arm makes an excellent pillow.

I can't see over his chest to view the alarm clock or phone screen, but drifting back to sleep doesn't feel right.

Pushing up onto my elbows, I move closer to him and catch a look at the clock. *Oops.*

Kissing him, I rest my hand on the side of his face.

"Good morning," he murmurs against my lips.

"It's noon," I whisper.

"Good afternoon." He kisses me again.

Green eyes open lazily and lock on mine. Untangling our legs, he rolls me over, putting me onto my back.

*Ours.* My wolf whines, looking at him. I feel her emotions so deeply that I follow her lead and push my head aside, exposing my throat to him.

I scold her, *No. We're not letting him off the hook because he fucked us good.*

Ansel pays it plenty of attention, kissing down my neck. He nibbles, and each one gets a little stronger, pinching the skin that much tighter.

With a push against his shoulder, I make him lock eyes with me. I force my wolf forward to see him, to meet him eye for eye. "No more hot and cold."

"No more hot and cold," Ansel agrees. Harry pushes forward for an instant, the darkness stunning.

Ansel runs his hand back along my skin down toward my pussy.

It's still feeling the rough fucking he gave me last night, but then he teases a finger between my folds.

I groan but close my eyes and try to wipe the arousal out of my brain to focus on the guarantee that he'll be serious about us. "When are you planning to make an honest woman out of me and put a mating mark on my neck?"

"Sunday," he answers with a very matter-of-fact tone. "I'm sorry I hurt you and that it took me so long to come up with a way to figure out my feelings. If I'm tying you to me forever, it'll be perfect."

I'M CARRYING ONE OF THE TWO BOXES OF MY THINGS — CLOTHES AND groceries — from the unit I had previously been occupying when Ben stops me by his house, offering to take the box.

"Uhhh, sure?" I hand it to him, and we keep walking toward the main house.

"So, hellcat, I need your help." Ben sighs. "I've got a farm with a bunch of these little goats, and without fail, they get into these tight little places, and I can't get them out, and the people's children are all running around. It's a nightmare."

"You need a kid herder." I bite my lips together.

"Exactly." Ben doesn't catch on to my joke.

"Okay but I want to deal with the two-legged ones." I laugh.

"Goats have four legs." Ben looks down at me. "Oh, human kids. No, those are their parents' responsibility. I mostly need someone fast and small to get into the tight places and get them out." He pauses. "It'll only take half a day."

"It's killing you to ask me for help, isn't it?" I push.

Ben nods. "Yup, but I'm glad the two of you are figuring it out."

Ansel is talking on the phone when we come in the back door of the house. "Yes, please. As soon as you can get it here? Gotta go."

*Suspicious.* My wolf twists around, not liking Ansel hiding something.

Ben places my box on the floor by the railings to the stairs. Ansel finished reframing them in today. It's still weird seeing the house nearly completely changed from Harry's destruction.

"I'm taking Morrigan tomorrow," Ben informs Ansel in a gruff huff.

"What? Why?" Ansel raises his head, squaring up to Ben.

*Is he getting possessive?*

My wolf nods and swoons.

"It's the stupid goat farm with the Dermont heathens, and I'm not spending the whole day trying to fuckin' —" Ben starts ranting.

"Okay." Ansel raises his hands in surrender. "We all know Mrs. Dermont isn't a fan of me, but it's nice they still use you for a vet. Take Morrigan, it's not an issue."

"Thank you," Ben grumbles. He heads out the back door muttering, "Stupid fucking goats and their damn little horns."

When the door clicks behind him, Ansel starts laughing. "Ooft. Someday his head's gonna pop right off his shoulders."

"Why does he go there if he hates it so much?" I ask, climbing onto the new stool in my place at the bar.

Ansel sighs and pulls his hair up into a ponytail. "Oh, it's because he's literally the only vet that will go out to their place. Not even the vets in Moab will go out there anymore."

"And I agreed to go?" I put my head in my hands.

"Meh." Ansel laughs. "I talked to Mr. Dermont at the feed

543

store. They had a light year with the goats, and he promised to send some of his sausages home with Ben."

"Not exactly selling it." I pull my head out of my hands.

"You've never had the sausages." Ansel leans against the wall. He's got his easy smile on and a spark in his eye. "I'll tell you a bit of your surprise for Sunday?"

"Ooo, yes." I nod. *He's serious about claiming me.*

My wolf swishes her tail back and forth. We're both focused on him.

"I've got the dumb projector thing working, so we can do movies on the side of the house with the guys." Ansel raises his eyebrow. "And, apparently, Lena's sent another box of movies, so there's some more new stuff to watch."

"I was hoping for some alone time." I drop heavy hints.

He bites his bottom lip. "There'll be plenty of time left over for that."

# CHAPTER 76
## ANSEL

EVERYTHING HAS BEEN PLANNED. LENA CONFIRMED THAT THE COLLAR and ring have been shipped. The movies and the food have been ordered. Now, all I have to do is survive these overwhelming feelings of anticipation.

My pickup truck sounds like it's throwing a belt, and I don't want to break down when I've got Morrigan out on our date. Though, pretty sure she'd think that's funny. I pop open the hood and get myself elbows deep in parts when I hear a vehicle coming up the driveway.

*Ben finished early? Maybe Morrigan is good help.* I go back to it, finally getting the casing off.

"Ansel." I hear Sheriff Owens's voice in the driveway.

Not who I was expecting. I tip my head around the truck to confirm my ears with my eyes.

Sure enough, Sheriff Owens asks, "Ansel, could you put the tools down and come out here?"

After setting the wrench on the bench behind me, I clean off my hands and step out of the garage. *Did one of the guys go out today?*

Deputy Jayson is with him. That's not usual.

Despite my hesitation, I crack a smile. "Sheriff, didn't expect you. What brings you out here?"

"Well," Sheriff Owens starts, "Ansel, do you know Gerad Gardner?"

"I'm familiar, yes." Something is starting to feel very wrong. *Where's Morrigan?*

Harry paces. We're both on edge, hackles raising.

"Ansel, he called us today, and he's making some wild accusations that, unfortunately, we can't ignore," the sheriff explains.

Ben's truck pulls up the road. The sheriff stops talking, but I've got a feeling I know where this is headed. Morrigan, sitting safely in the passenger seat next to Ben, soothes the uneasiness inside slightly. She's physically okay and still here. *I can live with that.*

Ben parks off to the left, not blocking in the sheriff. I hear him tell Morrigan to stay in the truck. *Please listen to Ben.*

"Hey, Sheriff, Deputy." Ben greets them, eyes darting back and forth between us suspiciously. He's always had good instincts.

Between that and the tension I know I'm giving off in spades, Ben's got an idea of what's coming.

"Doctor Bennett." Sheriff Owens nods to him. I wait for the sheriff to say something more, and he looks at Ben. "You're in charge if Ansel isn't here, right?"

Ben nods.

The pit in my stomach is back. It's one thing to think you know what's happening. Hearing the sheriff ask what happens if I'm not here confirms it. I'm not going to be here. I've been marked dangerous. Humans don't take kindly to dangerous shifters. *Funny how it comes full circle.*

Harry thinks of running, but I won't. He shuffles inside, feet pressing to shift and dart into the scrub brush. He'd rather run than be caged. It's not worth ruining our reputation when the end result will likely be the same.

"Ansel, we've had a formal complaint filed against you and, as such, a warrant for your arrest. They're claiming you're dangerous. You know I'm positive you're not dangerous." Sheriff Owens nods his head.

The deputy huffs with what sounds like disbelief, but he hasn't been around long. I don't blame him for being suspicious.

Sheriff Owens continues. "I've known you the entire time I've been in office. If I thought you were a risk to the public, you and the guys would have been gone," the sheriff admits, running his hand across the top of his bald head. "However, we've got to bring you in and have you evaluated. Get this all sorted out."

Bile rises in my throat, and I swallow hard, covering my mouth with my hand. It's so much harder hearing it than I thought it would be. The pit in my stomach is not hollow, it's a solid rock. I pull my hand away from my mouth. Reaching in my front pocket, I catch Deputy Jayson reaching for his gun.

I move more slowly, using two fingers to pull out my phone. "Ben, you call Judah for me? He'll figure out what to do."

I look at the sheriff for what's next. He steps toward me slowly.

"Ansel Abbot, you're under arrest for the suspicion of endangerment . . ." The sheriff's voice drones on, and I get lost in the words.

I do exactly as I'm instructed, giving neither of them any reason to be afraid of me. I don't know the extent of the law, but being shot in the front driveway because the deputy gets jumpy isn't how I'd like to go out. It also wouldn't bode well for my pack, who'd see it as a personal attack and try to retaliate.

The metal handcuffs are uncomfortable on my wrists. The feeling of them, confining and making us more helpless, sets Harry on edge. He paces in my brain, ready for an attack.

"Ansel!" Morrigan screams.

She tries to run this way, but Ben grabs her arm and pulls her close to him. With his arms around her waist, she fights against him. Her little frame is no match for Ben's, but my scrappy little Morrigan keeps trying to escape him.

Ben whispers to her as she screams for Ben to let her go.

He's not able to subdue her.

"Sheriff, just a minute," I plead.

I toss my head in Morrigan's direction, hoping he understands I can't leave her this way.

He nods, stepping back. "Just a minute."

Ben lets Morrigan go, and she runs to me. Wrapping her arms around my waist, she nearly knocks me over.

"They can't take you. Don't let them take you," Morrigan cries, clutching me tightly. "I'm sorry. I need you. Don't let them take you. Please."

"Shhh. Morrigan, it's okay." I don't believe the words, but I hope she does. I nuzzle my nose against her head, trying to comfort her. I've got to give her more time. "It'll be fine. Please, for my sake, behave for Ben." More words I don't believe come out of my mouth. "Judah and Cade should be able to sort all this."

"You can't go," Morrigan begs. "It's all my fault he's made these claims to get me away from you." Big tears are running down her face as she looks at me.

It pains me to see her take this burden.

Desperately, I want to wipe them away. Handcuffed, it's impossible. There are too many emotions for me to try and sort through, so I lock them all down. I have to choose to stay calm. I can't fall apart, no matter how afraid I am.

I force a smile. "It's not you. He's not doing this because of you. He's doing it because of me. It'll be okay. Whatever happens will happen."

"No," she begs.

"I know." This is what the movies are talking about when they talk about heartbreak.

Ben pulls on Morrigan's arm, and she steps back. He keeps her close as I walk past.

The sheriff puts me into the back of his SUV. When the door closes, I'm trapped.

The air feels thin, I can't breathe. The back seat of the SUV feels so small. I curl my toes in my boots, trying to focus on anything other than the feeling of the cuffs.

"You okay, Ansel?" Sheriff Owens asks.

I can't speak. If I open my mouth, I'm not sure what will come out.

I give a single nod.

Be agreeable. Follow their rules. Do exactly what they ask.

Sheriff Owens seems to sense my distress. "Claustrophobic?"

I nod once more.

The window next to me rolls down. Bars still block the window to keep me in, but this helps, almost.

"I've got a cell you can see outside in. It'll be okay." Sheriff Owens tries to assure me.

*What if Judah can't fix this? I don't want to die. I can't die now.*

# CHAPTER 77
# MORRIGAN

He's afraid of being restrained. He's afraid of being in small spaces. He's afraid to die. The sheriff's truck drives down the road, and I'm helpless.

I turn to Ben, and he's already listening to the phone ring. He puts it on speakerphone and wraps his arm around me, bringing me with him into the house.

"Ansel, cousin, how are you?" Judah, assuming that's who Ben called, sounds kind.

"It's Ben." He pauses.

We're both in shock and acutely aware that Ansel isn't here. Standing in the foyer, I'm at a loss for what to do next.

Ben closes the door behind us. "Ansel was just arrested. The sheriff came out and picked him up, personally, to make sure he went with a friend. Ansel's not okay."

"Okay. I'm on my way. I'll grab the next flight," Judah instructs. His voice is collected and grounded. He's clearly problem-solving. "Ben, you got the pack under control? I can call Milton, the Alpha from Denver, and his son Soren to come out."

553

"I'm okay. The only one who was at the main house when it happened is Morrigan. I'll pawn it off that he's gone to do a pickup. Should keep everyone calm until we can get someone else out. It's not abnormal." Ben looks at me, raising his eyebrows.

I nod. I'll go along with the plan. The guys knowing the truth will raise hell.

Ben goes into Ansel's, our, bedroom, and walks over to the large safe in the closet.

"I'm on my way. Stay cool. I'll get the pack lawyer on the phone. What did they arrest him for?" Judah's breathing is heavy.

Running maybe?

"Endangerment and a bunch of other things I don't know." Ben fiddles with the safe, trying to get it open. "Fuck," he mutters. After drawing a deep breath, he answers Judah first before trying again. "The charges sound huge. I didn't catch it all."

It takes a few tries before he pops it open. "I've only got thirty grand in the safe. I don't think it'll be enough."

"Money's not a problem. For Ansel, it's whatever it takes," Judah answers. He takes a deep breath and exhales it before speaking. "Alright, I've got to call Dinah. Sit back, try to keep things operating as normal. Call Cade. Keep calling. Every two minutes if you have to."

"On it." Ben strides past me out of Ansel's bedroom.

Closing the door behind him, he's scrolling through contacts and dialing again.

# CHAPTER 78

# ANSEL

I'M COLD SITTING IN MY T-SHIRT AND JEANS AGAINST THE CINDER block wall. I wrap my arms around my chest and bring my knees up. There's a small two-foot-by-one-foot window in the upper part of the wall in the hallway access to the cells. Natural light comes in and hits this particular space. I try hard to think about being home. Try to trick Harry and myself that the minimal light I can see from the corner of the cell is the same as when I'm lying in bed, lounging.

Neither of us are fooled. *We're trapped in a cage.*

I'm holding enough control to stop Harry from shifting but not from getting violent flashes, passing in seconds, of every time we've been trapped before.

What I know about the process doesn't help. There's a human somewhere reviewing whatever it is that Gerad's told them about me. They're doing the math as to how dangerous I am and making a decision about me.

*How much am I worth? Is it better for the humans if I'm alive or dead?*

I haven't hurt anyone. That should count for something.

My brain is all fuzzy, and my chest is tight. My skin itches. Time is passing at weird rates. I can't count heartbeats or seconds. There's nothing to focus on and no clock to be seen.

The door to the hallway opens. "Ansel, did you have lunch?"

It's the deputy's voice. I don't think I can eat, but I answer his question. "No, haven't had lunch yet."

"I'll get you something from the café." The deputy doesn't bother coming down to the end of the hall where I am.

Looking at the elements of the cell, I can see why they don't use them anymore. If I got a wild hair up my ass, it wouldn't be hard to dismantle the whole thing. It's less secure than my bedroom, let alone the kennels downstairs. But the good sheriff trusts me not to escape. I won't break that trust between us. Nameless doesn't need the scandal.

Harry is so certain we're dead. All his thoughts circle back to other times we should have died. I've never been able to see my own death. This could be the end.

Escaping and running would only make me seem like I did something wrong. I don't want that. I haven't done anything wrong by human standards. No one's been in any danger. We haven't even had an issue with wolves in town in a long time. Aside from when Morrigan took off in my truck and I had to catch her at the gas station, but even then, no one said anything.

But shit, I don't want to die.

I look at the weak points in the cell bars again. If it keeps me alive, maybe running is the right thing to do.

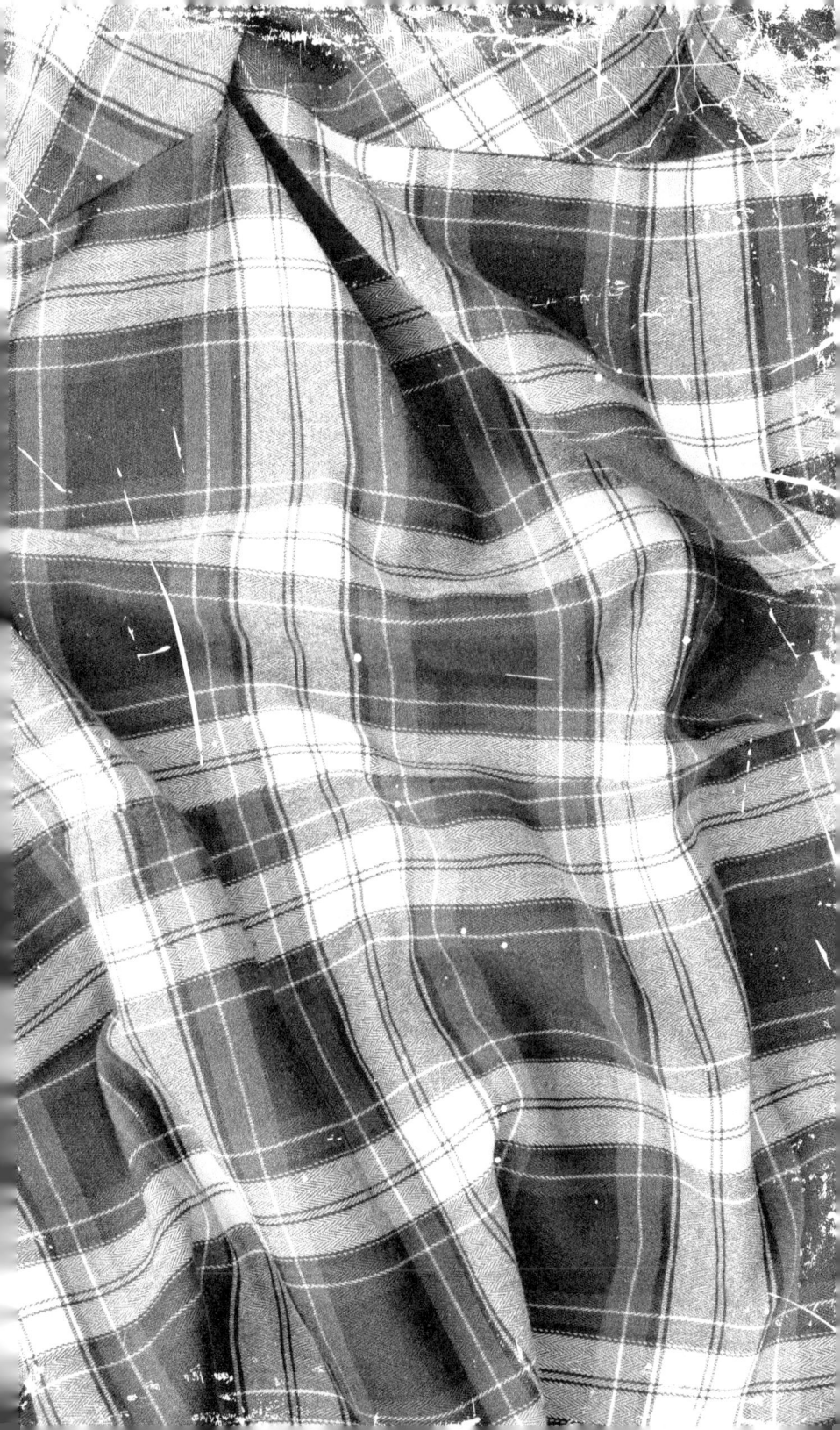

# CHAPTER 79
# MORRIGAN

MY WOLF DISAPPEARED THE MOMENT THE SHERIFF'S VEHICLE LEFT MY line of sight.

Poof, gone.

Ben's been on the phone handling everything, which is good because the only productive thing I've managed to do is make lunch. Instead of being helpful, all I do is wander aimlessly from our bedroom to the back deck, back and forth. I'm numb and empty and unable to settle but with no energy to do anything. I try lying down on the couch and curling up in his blanket, but I know it won't be long until I can't stand lying down lifeless anymore.

The driveway sensors start going off as a vehicle traverses the road.

A knock to the back door comes soon after, and I can't be bothered to get off the couch.

Ben goes and answers it.

"Hey." Ben greets whoever it is.

I curl up into a ball under my blanket.

"Hey, Ben, Judah went straight to the sheriff's office. We came here. How far out are the Aldens?" It's Dinah's voice.

*How long has it been since she got here? How long is the flight?*

"Yeah. I'm surprised you didn't see them at the airport," Ben answers. "Cade and Thalia are flying into Provo with Deacon and Henri. Some hotshot attorneys are driving with them then from Salt Lake. But Finn and Lena are coming in direct to Moab."

"Okay. Where's . . . ?" Dinah's voice pitches with the question, but she doesn't say anything more.

Footsteps sound on the floor, and in a few more steps, Dinah walks around the couch and squats down in front of me, so I have no choice but to look at her. *Oh great.*

"Oh no." She shakes her head. "There won't be any of this. Come on, up, up, up."

I snarl at her, and she pokes me on the nose.

"Boop." Dinah doesn't take my shit. "I know you're sad. I know you're hurting. But there are five wolves down the hill who need you to at least fucking try. They'll know really soon that Ansel's in trouble, and they'll be looking to you and Ben for answers. If they see you falling apart, they will too. If they fall apart, who knows what will happen. Ansel not being here for one of them dying will hurt him. So, time to Luna up."

I don't answer, and she pulls up the blanket, leaving me huddled on the couch.

*I'm not a pack Luna. I'm not ready for that sort of thing.*

"You smell like a barn. Come on. He would absolutely not like you lying here on his couch smelling like this." Dinah taps my butt.

There's only so much you can do to ignore her.

Once I manage to pull myself off the couch, I go to our bedroom and close the door behind me. I sit on the bed and stare at the open closet with rows of flannels and plaids and black and white T-shirts for underneath.

I feel empty.

"Move your butt, Morrigan," Dinah calls from the main portion of the house sometime later.

The window shows the outside world is a little darker as the sun moved to the other side of the house to set.

Frustrated, I move from the bed, grab a change of clothes, and storm across the hall to the bathroom.

*Ansel is going to die because of me.*

# CHAPTER 80

# ANSEL

I FORCED MYSELF TO EAT THE BURGER THE DEPUTY BROUGHT ME FROM the diner. But that was all I could stomach before it felt like it was all coming back up. Lying down on the floor, I stare at the ceiling, trying to do anything other than think about her and home.

Is she doing okay? House full of people with a wolf a little on edge can't be easy for her.

The door to the cells opens.

"Ansel." It's Judah's voice. "You awake?"

"Who can sleep at a time like this?" I answer, sitting up and curling my legs underneath me.

"Fair enough." Judah's footsteps grow closer.

The weird green color of his pants and tan shirt show that he came straight from work, on a plane, and then all the way to Utah. Means it's been at least six hours since I've been here.

"Sorry to bring you trouble. Any idea on what it'll cost to get me out?" I ask, hoping for a number and that we're in the process of cutting a check.

Judah sits down on the floor. "I don't know yet."

There's something he's not saying. But I've no place to go, so I sit in silence. Pull one of Cade's tricks and wait him out.

It takes him a few, but eventually, Judah gets his words together. "Do you know everything you've been charged with?"

Harry stops pacing and finally stands still, his focus matching mine.

"I guess not."

"Gerad's made the claim that you've kidnapped Morrigan, you've been holding her against her will, you've assaulted her, and you cut her off from her family. He claims that he's made many attempts to bring his daughter home, including coming to your house where you threatened him and his pack." Judah stops talking.

I'm shaking my head like an idiot. "We're wolves. What do the humans care about any of that? I thought Cade got the government to agree to stay out of pack politics."

"According to Gerad, you've released wolves back to their packs knowing they were dangerous, and they've reoffended and have hurt people." Judah continues. "He says you're know-ingly keeping wolves alive long past their point of stability and letting them walk among humans despite not being safe."

"That's bullshit," I snap.

Harry charges forward, and I hold him back, focusing on keeping him locked deep inside. Shifting in a human jail cell doesn't look good. It won't look good at all.

"I know it is." Judah nods. "The good part is, he couldn't name anyone in your pack and give examples as to who it is that's dangerous or has reoffended."

I nod in confirmation. The accusation doesn't sit well with me. "If someone wasn't stable, I would have never."

Judah agrees with me. "I know. We know. Cade's buried your pack charter behind mountains of red tape already. His attorneys are working on your case. You'll have a meeting with them tomorrow."

*Tomorrow*. The word sinks from the top of my head all the way down to where my butt is planted on the cold concrete. *I'm not going home today.*

"I promise, Ansel, we're doing everything we can." Judah's words come slower.

I run my tongue across my teeth. It was one thing when it was in my head. The fear was a memory of what I had been through. There was a possibility I was overreacting thinking this would be the end of me.

But Judah gave me the truth. The reality of the situation is I really might not get out of this alive. I might never go home.

My hackles rise and my stomach goes sour.

"You'll be okay?" Judah asks.

I plaster on a brave face. "It's a night in a kennel." I shrug, lying. "It's kinda cozy. They give them mattresses here."

Judah doesn't laugh at my joke. He stands up. "Alright. I'll help get everything in order. Anything you want me to do or handle?"

"Tell Morrigan I'm sorry, but it doesn't look like we'll get to do our date this weekend. Seems we've house guests." A sharp pain hits my chest.

"Nah, it's only Wednesday. Still a chance we can spring ya and get out of your hair before then." Judah stalls. "I'll see you tomorrow. Lena said she wants to come see you," Judah informs me.

"I'll see you. But don't let Lena in here. It's good seeing you. Only you." I can't tell him that if I see anyone else, I'll fall apart. It'd probably hurt his feelings that I can see him fine, but Judah's always seemed to understand me.

He heads for the door with a last backward glance.

# CHAPTER 81
## MORRIGAN

I LOST TRACK OF TIME, AGAIN, STANDING IN THE SOLITUDE OF THE bathroom. I know it took me at least thirty minutes to get into the shower. Tears stopped falling after who knows how long, and when I turn the water off to the shower, the sound of the world outside the bathroom replaces it.

"Should we check on her?" one man's voice pipes up.

"Nah," Dinah answers. "She'll come out when she's ready."

"Maybe some of us should leave? It might be less intimidating if we're not all here at once?" another man asks.

"Dea's a point." An Irish accent is crisp.

A knock comes to the bathroom door. "Hey, Morrigan?"

"I'm coming. I need a minute," I answer, my voice hoarse from crying.

"Let me in? We can have a quick chat?" a woman asks.

"Kathleen, leave the poor girl alone," the man with the Irish accent scolds.

I wrap myself tightly in a towel before twisting the doorknob. Lena Alden, in the flesh, lets herself the rest of the way in and closes the door behind her.

The woman who has been larger than life in the media is barely a few inches taller than me.

"Disappointing, I know. Should have worn heels, makes me seem much more intimidating." Lena rolls her eyes. She grabs a towel off the back of the door and sniffs it before handing it to me. "Hair up. You don't want it to get all gross. He's not dying, so it's not worth letting it go to hell."

"You can't know that." My voice quakes, and I try to button down all the emotions. "No one can know that."

Putting a finger in front of her lips, Lena silences me. She steps closer until we're sharing fractional space without touching and drops her voice. "If we can't win legally, we have a few additional plans to get Ansel to a new life. Cade shouldn't know. And he must pretend not to know. We're minding the discussions about it. But either way, we're not worrying about it."

"So, Dinah?" I push with some hope she can tell me this will be a few rough days. She saw we were mates, after all. That should count for something.

Lena doesn't answer that. "Get dressed, they're all getting antsy. Sherman keeps coming up to the door, and it's making Finn nervous. And, honestly, as much as I would love to see Finn get bloody, I don't want to spend all night with Dinah and Ben patching the boys up."

I nod and pull on the clothes, things that fit me, and one of Ansel's flannels. I hold it to my nose, drawing a deep breath.

Lena waits, scrolling through her phone. The trashy magazines that report the craziest theories claim that Lena is now some sort of member of the Irish mob. I don't know how much I trust it, but given her previous statements and her mate being ex-mafia, there must be some sort of truth to the matter.

"Awwww. You're wearing his favorite one." Lena smiles,

seeing me with the flannel shirt hanging from my frame. "Here, let me help."

Lena rolls the sleeves up and then pulls a hair tie out of the drawer. She cinches the back of the flannel so it hangs loose but doesn't drown me.

"Deep breath," Lena prompts as she puts her hand on the doorknob. Holding up a finger, she cautions me. "Remember, they're all way more afraid of you than you are of them."

"What?" I shake my head as she pulls me with her out into the hallway and then into the kitchen.

*Oh. Fuck.*

The house is full of Alpha wolves, and they're all zoned in on me, your everyday garden variety pack member. Humans like to call us betas, but there's no wolf word for normal. Whatever 'normal' is . . . it's me. Especially in a room of the extraordinary like the Ardeleans.

"Alright, you've got Finn, Irish, asshole, massive can't miss him." Lena points to a man who is, I think, probably a little bigger than Sherman. Then she points to one who looks like he just rolled out of bed. "That's Deacon. He sees ghosts. Ignore him. Unless he's looking you square in the eyes, he's probably not talking to you."

"Rude," Deacon answers. "Not wrong, but rude."

I'm already overwhelmed, and she's only counted off two.

"Then the twins. You probably recognize Ezra, then by default, the other one is Judah." She points to a pair of men who are, in fact, identical twins but with different haircuts and styles. "Judah's the one who seems to know what's going on, and if you try to touch one of them and they move away from you, it's Ezra."

"Dear gods, woman. You've got to come up with a way to explain us better than that." Ezra shakes his head.

I recognize him from when he was here before. It's weird,

but while they're identical, there's a whole vibe difference between them. Black cat versus golden retriever energies that don't mesh.

"You know Dinah." Lena directs my attention past her to Cade Alden and his beautiful red-haired mate, Thalia. "And, of course, His Royal Pain In My Ass, and his better half, Thalia."

"She going to be okay?" Cade draws his words out slowly like Ansel does.

Looking at the two of them is surreal. Meeting celebrities and being introduced like you're a friend and one of them is not something I ever imagined happening to me. You'd think it wouldn't be so weird, having spent my high school years in LA private schools and brushing shoulders with celebrities' children. Cade and Thalia are different. They're royalty. You can't not know who they are.

I swallow and look away out of respect and fear. Breathing is really hard. The room is brimming with Alpha wolf energy.

"Okay then." Dinah sighs. "I call this meeting of the minds to order. What do we know?"

"It's a classic case of a wolf who doesn't want to play by the rules, so he tried to find a way around the higher authority." Finn punctuates his words. "The eejit clearly doesn't look big picture."

I feel his eyes in our direction before Lena leaves my side and goes to stand by him.

Alone, in the realm of giants, I'm a child waiting for direction.

Deacon walks around the island before wrapping his arm around me and pulling me to sit on a stool. He whispers, "Don't worry, we can be alone together."

"Let's get you down to your pack." Cade directs his words to me. "They know we're here, and I suspect they know Ansel isn't. They'll need to hear it from you."

"Me?" I question incredulously.

Thalia nods. "Ben's not an option. He's not handling this well."

That's news to me. He was so calm and collected when getting the Ardeleans here.

I shrug. "I don't know what to say."

"The truth." Finn steps in with an answer. "We're doing everything we can, and you're still here. The hope is he comes home, but we'll make sure they're all taken care of and their lives won't be disrupted any more than they already are."

"Okay." I blow out a hesitant breath and start walking toward the back door.

I had left my shoes untied, so it makes it easier to slip them on and head down to the pack property. I expected to go alone, but Judah and Ezra follow at my heels.

"You don't have to come," I tell them over my shoulder.

Neither of them says anything, and when we get down past Ben's house, the guys are quick to exit their cabins and come out to greet us.

It's a standoff when they gather where we are. I've seen Ansel start a bunch of meetings, but I've no experience.

I shrug and just jump into it. "Ansel's been arrested. It's all my fault. We're trying to fix it."

"She does not beat around the bush, does she?" Judah or Ezra says behind me.

"Did you report him?" Sully asks. He crosses his arms in front of his chest.

"No." I shake my head. "He—"

"Then it wasn't your fault." Ripley cuts me off. "Ansel wouldn't want you to blame yourself. Unless you called the police yourself, then this isn't on you."

"You wouldn't hurt anyone," Sherman adds.

"Agreed," Zero answers.

My eyes are getting all watery, and I wipe at them.

*Luna up*, I remind myself. *Be strong for them.* "We're doing everything we can to get him back. But —"

"No." Vito cuts me off. "Don't talk about the what-if. Get him back."

I nod and look at the group. "I'm so sorry."

"You're sorry?" Sully steps forward and wraps his arms around me. "We're sorry. You don't have to be sorry. You didn't do this."

Sherman comes and hugs me from the other side, and I'm sandwiched between them. Pretty soon the pack is in this giant vertical dog pile of hugs.

"Can't breathe." I fight back against them when my oxygen supply runs low.

Immediately, they all back away, but nowhere as far as when the conversation started.

I shrug. "Is there something I can do? Well, in addition to trying to bring him back home?"

None of the guys say anything. They all shrug.

Zero thinks for a minute and says, "I'll keep an eye on Ben."

I nod. "We all will. The Ardeleans are here to help. I'm betting you know many of them better than I do. But let's all be respectful and get through this together. Check in on each other and with us, okay?"

Murmurs of agreement come from the group, and I get individual hugs as they all go back to their separate cabins.

"Hey," Ezra calls them back.

They stop and turn back to look.

He continues. "Dinner up at the house tonight like civilized folk. Mandatory. I'm cooking, so you'll know it's good."

There's a ripple of laughter and waves as they go back on their courses to their homes.

When I turn back around to Ezra and Judah, they're

wearing the same expression. It's approval in their nods and raised eyebrows.

Judah offers his hand out to me. "You did good, kid. Better than I could have done."

The sun has almost set by the time we get back to the house, and I look back down toward the cabins. *What happens if we're not here for them?* A piece of me, so connected to those men, stings and tears to frayed edges, thinking about what if they're not here anymore.

# CHAPTER 82

# ANSEL

TODAY THE SUN MOVES THROUGH THE WINDOW, AND LIKE ONE OF THE barn cats at Hoppe's place, I move with the ray of light across the floor, staying in it as long as I can.

"Ansel," Judah calls, walking through the door.

He's got two brown bags of food with him. I'm starting to resent takeout.

"Judah," I respond in the same bland tone.

After sitting on the floor opposite the bars, Judah passes a bag through. "There's two slices of pie in there."

His eyes glisten with a smile. I want to smile, I really do. But I'm at a loss. Being fake brave all day is exhausting.

"Morrigan is good. She's amazing with your pack. Rallied them to behave and come visit the main house all by herself."

The mention of Morrigan causes that uncomfortable pressure in my chest.

Judah talks while I pick open the containers. "Sherman and Finn are now friends. Don't know how that happened. There was some growling, and then suddenly, he's trying to learn an Irish accent."

"Sherman will make friends with a rock if you let him." I groan, but it pulls a slight smile at the edge of my lips.

"Zero hasn't come around much. We see him mostly coming and going from Ben's." Judah moves down the row of houses. "Sully is a bit weird. Dinah broke his hand. So, that might account for some of it."

"Why?" I scrub my hand down my face.

"You don't want to know." Judah shakes his head.

*It's not worth knowing. I'm not there. I can't fix it.*

I sigh and nod my head. "How's Vito and Ripley taking it?"

Sherman scares people being so big. But the two who people should be worried about are the most volatile.

"We had some women's studies classes proctored by Dinah last night and this morning. Ripley and Vito are on the course of becoming more civilized and, at the very least, learning to keep lewd sexist comments to themselves. But Ben's been keeping them busy for the most part. I'm not exactly sure what sort of chores he's come up with, but no idle hands." Judah pauses.

And once again, he's holding back.

Rather than ask, I pick up the fork and open the box that contains one of the slices of pie. *World could end any second. Might as well eat dessert first.* The happy memory with Morrigan rots my stomach now that I'm living in a reality where my world could end tomorrow. No one seems to know or wants to tell me a timeline.

Judah lets me eat, and silence hangs between us. It's not long, though, and I have that feeling of wanting more answers.

"What do the lawyers think?" I press.

"They're optimistic." Judah's short answer keeps me on edge.

"Is that lawyer for it's a crapshoot?" I ask.

"To be honest. I'm not sure." Judah bows his head and

wrings his hands. "Cade, however, says they're already getting some of the charges dropped. And that seems like a good thing."

"Hey, Judah?" My heart aches.

"Yeah?"

"I don't have a will." I chew on my bottom lip. "I meant to have the attorney in Nameless write one up one of these years. I didn't really have anyone to leave anything to. I figured . . ." I draw a deep breath and get back to the important stuff. "I didn't claim her formally, but I'm counting on you to get the house in her name. And treat her as you would me. You all keep telling me I'm one of you. Then, whatever you'd give me, give her."

Judah's quiet, looking at me, but he doesn't say anything.

"What?" I pull on the hair in front of my eyes, willing it out of my face. When he doesn't respond, I continue to speak, fighting against the constricting feeling in my chest. "If it's not a thing, could you have Sheriff Owens go to records and get a copy of the deed to the property on the edge of town? I bought it with my own cash working odd jobs, not from The Ardelean Fund. She should get something. It's the least—"

"Ansel," Judah calls, and I stop.

I glare at him and wait.

Motioning me to draw a deep breath, he doesn't start talking until I take one.

"Morrigan is your mate. You have always been and always will be an Ardelean. I will have the property transferred from the fund to her name if it'll make you feel better, but as far as any of us are concerned, she's family. You're family, and that last bit has never been up for debate."

I swallow hard. "A place to live, a dog or a cat, and her sewing machine. It's all she wants, and it's the least I can give her."

LAWYERS ARE EXACTLY HOW THEY'RE DEPICTED IN MOVIES. THE formalities and the way they speak. I've never felt more stupid in a room. They go over information with me again and again and again. Everything from Morrigan to Ersilia to Gerad to anything out of the ordinary that's happened in the last two months. I don't know what they're looking for, but they mutter in big words between themselves after answers.

I guess, what does it matter if I can understand them if they can do their job?

"Is there anything we can get you to make you more comfortable?" the attorney with the blue tie asks me.

I think his name is Hank. But that seems like a dumb name for an attorney.

Shaking my head, I answer, "I suppose it's jail, it's not meant to be fun."

"Pillow, blankets, are you cold at night?" the attorney with the green tie asks.

I have no idea what his name is, and I'm not sure he gave it to me.

"It's okay." I omit the part where it's nicer here than my kennels back home. That's probably not something they want to know about.

"Food, are you eating well, getting enough to eat? Wolves have increased dietary needs; are they being met?" Attorney Hank with the blue tie pushes again.

"It's okay. Food's fine. Deputy Jayson gets me my favorites." I swallow hard. Is it okay to ask them questions? *Won't know unless you try.* "When do we find out if I'm dying this week or next?"

"Mr. Abbot," the green tie scolds me, "we have every reason

to believe we can get this case wrapped up quickly with a favorable outcome."

Belief is kind of like hope. I guess it's time to hang on to it.

"Can I . . ." I don't want to ask for anything or make a fuss, and the words get caught in my throat.

"Can you?" Attorney Hank with the blue tie probes.

"Can I write a letter?" I shake my head. "It's dumb. I'm sure it's against the rules."

"As long as it's not incriminating, there isn't a problem with it." Attorney with the green tie nods and pulls a piece of paper off his legal pad. He slides it over to me before also pushing over the fanciest pen I've ever seen.

It takes a minute to get the words out. I know that no matter what I write, it'll never be enough to explain. But I scribble down my thoughts as best I can and read it once. There's only one last thing. And I debate not putting it there in ink for everyone to see, but I do . . . then I slide the paper and fancy pen over to the lawyers.

They look it over between themselves, nodding.

Attorney Hank with the blue tie nods. "Yeah. This shouldn't be a problem to pass along."

# CHAPTER 83
## MORRIGAN

"What do you mean that they're pushing for —" Cade's shout turns into a snarl, which he stifles before continuing at a lower volume. "A federal investigation to be opened? I thought we had answers from the state of Utah? He was coming home."

*Federal?* I poke my head out of the bedroom. Being out of the way is easier in here. It's not that the Ardeleans aren't nice. This is where it smells like him.

"We did get the charges dropped, all but the endangerment in the state of Utah. But we got blindsided with another set of charges, this time on a federal level." The other end of the phone squawks back.

I round the bedroom door. Cade's sitting at the dining room table with his laptop open. Deacon startles me, walking out of the kitchen.

"So, what exactly does that mean?" Cade is firm talking into the phone.

"It means that we need to bring in some of the upper managing partners who were consulting on the case to handle the case directly." The man's voice on the other end of the phone trembles. "And that they're petitioning to have him moved from the county jail to a max security center."

"Federal or just max?" Cade asks.

"Federal in Colorado." The man on the other end of the phone sounds like he's wincing at being the messenger.

I don't blame him. I wouldn't want to be on the other side of that phone either.

"He won't survive Florence," Cade says firmly. The Leviathan present in his eyes is a calculated, cold look. "We need that transfer blocked. He'd probably be okay in the supermax in Salt Lake City, but if he moves out of the state of Utah . . ." Cade looks at me. "Block it. Whatever it takes."

"We understand, and we're doing what we can," the phone answers.

Deacon wraps his arm around my shoulder and leads me to the couch.

I keep looking at Cade, swiveling my head as Deacon takes me there.

"The thing you need to know is that with the passing of the new emergency stipulations, which we know you're fighting" — there's a pause on the phone line — "there is no middle ground."

My heart sinks. *No . . . middle ground?*

"The Federal Government is pushing hard to make an example out of Mr. Abbot." The attorney is talking slowly like he's afraid of what Cade will do.

Cade starts to growl.

I feel lightheaded.

Deacon's hand runs across my back. He's whispering, but I can't make out the words. Blood is thundering in my head. It throbs. I can't focus on anything because there's something they're not saying, and someone, anyone, has to say it. Because maybe . . . maybe it's not what I think they're saying.

"So, you're saying they're pushing for an execution?" Cade asks.

The room feels so full.

I'm gasping for air.

Deacon keeps petting me. Pulling my hair off my neck.

My heart is beating a thousand beats per minute, and I can't breathe around it.

I try to push him away, but he's stuck to me like glue. But being held together by Deacon is probably better than falling apart.

"Yes. They're pushing for Ansel to be transferred to maximum security pending execution," the attorney answers.

"I should have fuckin—" Cade's rant is cut off by the attorney clearing his throat.

"Sorry." Cade pauses. "Stall it. I don't care what you have to do. He doesn't leave the county jail today."

"We're working on it as we speak," the attorney answers before Cade hangs up.

He gets up from the table, leaving his chair out and exiting out the back door.

The air is only slightly easier to breathe, but I'm too hot and my stomach hurts.

"He's not dying," Deacon assures me.

"How can you all keep saying that?" My voice is hoarse, and I try to clear my throat.

Deacon holds me tighter and whispers, "Because Cade may be king of the wolves, but he's not the only person with leverage. But you may need to learn how to drive on the other side of the road."

I don't have the energy to figure out what Deacon means. But it seems like he knows this because Deacon pulls the blanket off the back of the couch and tucks me in.

THERE'S SOME SORT OF LARGE MACHINE RUNNING SOMEWHERE. THE sound is loud, and there's rattling in the house. *What is Ansel doing?*

When I open my eyes, the sunlight streaming in through the living room windows reminds me that he's not here.

"You awake?" Deacon's voice comes from the kitchen.

"Are you talking to me or someone else?" I poke my head over the back of the couch first to look at him.

Deacon laughs. "Yeah, this time I'm talking to you."

"Well, okay then." I sit up with a sigh.

"They're remodeling the guys' huts, cabins, containers, thingamajigs if you want to go watch and tell Cade it's rude, so you can tell Ansel that you tried to stop him." Deacon smiles at me.

There's a stack of peanut butter and jelly sandwiches on a plate, and he's closing up another one.

"They're what?" I walk to the back door, confused by the sound and what Deacon is saying.

I slip on my shoes and walk outside to find a crane and tractor trailers. The guys are all standing together off to the side of the road. Boxes in neat-ish piles are set off to the side of the main path. Which, based on the contents poking out of the top, contain the pack's personal belongings that had given their container homes a comfy feel.

I start on a brisk jog down to them as quickly as I can and slide to a stop next to Vito. "You guys okay?"

"Oh, fine and dandy. We even got to pick out the colors we wanted," Ripley answers. He offers his fist out for a fist bump. I accept the casual touch as comfort. "How will boss man feel about it when he gets back?"

The words sink hard in my stomach. I want to believe, as

much as they do, that he's coming back, but I don't. Not after hearing Cade's call.

*Luna up*, I remind myself.

It would be so much easier if I was an Alpha wolf. But truthfully, whatever's happening with their homes is really above my head since no one told me. "I mean, what were we supposed to do? Say no?"

"True." Sully laughs.

"They're building me a new chicken coop. One that I can walk into!" Sherman crows loudly, demonstrating how tall he is with a hand at the top of his head. "All the ladies gonna have nice nesting boxes. We'll have all sorts of eggs." He's so excited he pats me on the back a little too hard, and I nearly lose my balance. "It's like Equinox, just a little late!"

"Exactly," Zero adds in his deep voice. He cants his head, watching with the rest of us as people scramble about down below. "Boss will be spittin' mad though."

"Oh, for sure," Sully agrees.

Watching the crew of at least twenty people pull out the old, broken down, mashed-together houses that were here before is entertaining. The bottom of Sherman's house drops out as they lift it up, and Ripley's house collapses like a house of cards.

"Where are the ladies?" I ask Sherman, horrified at the thought of them getting crushed in the move.

"Don't worry. Ben got me a big dog kennel for them. They're safe with food and water up in the garage. All nice and cozy like."

I draw a deep breath. *One crisis averted.*

While we're watching, the guys migrate lawn chairs from the firepit and we set up our own viewing party. Deacon brings out his plate towered high with sandwiches and passes them out to all of us.

The whole pack's housing, less Ben's house, is torn out. The construction crew works in tandem; as each container is removed, a new unit is brought into place. Then I notice more than a few extra ones are added, extending the pack's driveway.

*Interesting they'd add more housing if they're not sure Ansel will be here.* I look down the road to where Cade Alden's talking on the phone. Over the roar of the machinery, I can't hear what he's saying, but the pacing back and forth with a furrowed brow doesn't seem good.

# CHAPTER 84
# ANSEL

THE MORE THE LAWYERS TALK ABOUT WHAT'S HAPPENING, THE HARDER it is to keep Harry locked away. The cage is becoming harder to handle than the promise of death. Today they informed me there's been a change in my case, and I might not be staying here anymore. But they didn't want to tell me where it was I was going.

Judah plops down across from my current spot on the floor. It puts him on my level since I've been tracking the sun again today as it moves across the room. "This isn't fair."

"Nothing in life is. They're not wrong about who I am. If you take away our rules and customs and play by the rules of the humans, it's not wrong." I don't even have the energy left to pretend to be anything other than numb.

Harbinger is thrashing inside me, and I'm using all my extra energy to contain him.

Judah shakes his head. "Don't give up now. You've fought to live for too long."

I hang my head. I know he's right. But for how long do you have to be strong in life? Doesn't anything come easy?

"Do you want to hear the newest plan?" His voice turns up like he believes whatever plan they've hatched will work.

"Does it include a metal file and a horse tied up out back?" I can't help but make the dumb joke.

But at this point, maybe I should be thinking about running. No matter how guilty it'll make me look. Wouldn't be very kind, though, to the people left behind to clean up in my wake. Better to go out without a fuss.

With a half-hearted laugh, Judah shakes his head. "No, we're going to the court of public opinion. Every single pack, wolf, person, and, I'm fairly certain, the entire county is writing letters. Hell, the sheriff is dictating one to the secretary as we speak."

A small flame of hope builds in my chest. It feels lighter. Just a little bit lighter.

I squash it.

I'm back and forth between wanting to be hopeful and knowing the time left on the clock. We only get seven days to bail a wolf out. I'm sitting here at day three. We're getting awfully close to that limit where shifters don't leave human jails alive. It's a garbage feeling, hoping to be rescued but bracing for the fact that I might not be.

"How are the guys holding up?" By now, I'm sure they've been told what's happening and that I might not be coming home.

I push my hair out of my eyes again. It'll only fall forward in like twelve seconds, but for now, it's out of my eyes.

"Truthfully, they're taking it in stride, but there's a little bit of anxiety about what happens if you don't come back. Morrigan and I have assured them they won't be out on their own. That we've plans and they'll be okay. But we are trying our hardest to get you out of here. We're not letting you go down without a fight." Judah tries to spin this nicely.

I draw a deep breath and pull my hair back out of my face again. My voice shakes as I start to walk Judah through what's been plaguing my mind between thoughts of Morrigan. "Zero is stable. He just needs someplace to go. Please take Sherman or get him into Cade's pack. He's not fractured, but it's like his brain never developed all the way. He's just a little slow and particular about how stuff needs to be."

Judah shakes his head. "Ansel. No."

"Shut up and listen," I growl at him. "Sully is almost ready, but if you get him in a pack with a strong Alpha who is good at guiding people, he'll do fine. He's just a little young, and his wolf is taking a bit longer to steady." I feel comfortable with that assessment and move on to the two I don't know what to do with. It's not like I ever had to think out alternative plans for them beyond life and death. "There's something happening that was giving Ripley more time, but he's the least stable. He has about eight months now. If I have to guess, which I kinda have to, his mate is a human in town, and he's running across her path. I just can't figure out who it is."

Judah seems to understand that I need someone to know and care for them. "Vito?"

I shake my head. "A year, unless something changes. It's not set in stone, but it's counting down." I swallow. "If I don't go back home, it might be safest to put him in the ground earlier rather than later. But between you and Ezra, and those handy-dandy gifts of yours, you can probably figure it out."

Harry fights hard as Morrigan comes into my thoughts again. My whole body writhes with the fight to hold him back.

I'm wearing thin. I don't know if I can keep him contained for much longer.

Judah draws a deep breath. "You tell anyone I did this, and I'll kill you."

I look at Judah, and he runs his hand down his face. His wolf's eyes come forward, and then everything fades away.

I feel happy. It hits hard, and I laugh. I can't help it; nothing is funny, but I'm laughing anyway.

It fades a little bit, and Judah breathes deeply.

I shake my head. "So, the gift that doesn't do much of anything?"

"I can't do that a lot. I don't have a ton of control. Reading people is one thing. But whatever you'd like to call that is hard and not always effective." He scratches the back of his head.

"Times up," Deputy calls.

"Alright, I'll be back tomorrow." Judah nods. "We'll get you out."

I nod because saying anything more might cause everything I've bottled up to come out. I'm just not sure what writing letters will do to fix anything. Probably only a couple dozen people even know my name.

# CHAPTER 85
# ANSEL

"Guess Judah probably doesn't have a lot of say over what you do. If you wanna do something, you just do it." I speak loudly.

I don't need to turn to see him in the jail block. The Leviathan is a presence you can't miss.

"Well. I have news. And it came after Judah left last night." Cade's voice gets louder as he gets closer.

Day four, and I'm still on the wrong side of the bars.

"Oh?" I turn my head toward where his shoes have stopped outside my cell.

I can't force myself to look up at his face, so I just look at his shiny black dress shoes.

Despite the fancy dress pants, Cade drops down and sits on the concrete floor next to me on his side of the bars.

"You're getting dirty," I tell him.

"It'll wash," he answers before drawing a deep breath. "I know you know the timeline. So, I know that even if you don't admit it out loud, you're thinking about how much time you should have left. I've been working nonstop, and I was able to get you a stay of execution pending a hearing."

"Shifters don't get trials." It's a dumb thing to say, but it feels like I should say something.

Cade moves his hand through the bars of the cell and rests it on my knee. "Well, trials and hearings are different. No jury, that could get messy. It's just a judge and the law."

*She was a fucking minor. I couldn't keep my dick in my pants and* . . . I try to stop those thoughts. "Our laws or theirs?"

"Theirs. Which should work out in our favor. There are a few things I'm worried about, but Judah already told you about the letters." Cade nods, squeezing my knee.

"I don't know how much a dozen letters will do." I shake my head. "Maybe it would be better—"

"Don't lose hope, Ansel. It's not over. And I don't think it's just a dozen letters." Cade runs his other hand back through his hair.

"So, what's the real reason you're here?" I ask.

He's always had a tell, and Cade's stressed that I won't like something he has to say.

"The hearing is next week on Wednesday." Cade draws a deep breath. "The government doesn't like you here. They don't like that it's, for lack of better terms, a cardboard box with paperclips."

That gets me, and I laugh. "So, what, I'm going someplace else?"

*Is it too much to wish I was going home to my own kennels?*

"They want to take you to a human supermax prison." He tries to find the nice words to soften the blow.

"Federal facility?" The words come out, and I barely make it to the toilet before I heave, despite nothing being in my stomach.

Federal custody is death row. I've never been able to get a wolf out of federal custody.

*I'm going to die.*

"No." Cade shakes his head. "It's a state facility, still in Utah. I called in a few favors, and I owe some people some things. But I made sure you'd stay in Utah."

Cade gives me time to pull myself together.

I pace back and forth, pulling at my hair. I'm not sure why it was so important I stay in Utah, but it doesn't change how it all really is.

"It's more cages, on top of more cages, on top of crowded places." I spell it out. "And I've got to find a way to not cause a blip in the system and not scare anyone. Keep Harbinger locked away."

"Yeah," Cade agrees. "It's only less shitty, but it's still shitty."

"Fantastic." I rub my nose with my palm.

Harry is already pacing at the thought of more cages. The Leviathan's presence helps. How Cade can be so grounded all the damn time isn't fair. But that's life. It's not fair.

My hair feels like it's suffocating me. I pull it up off the back of my neck. What I wouldn't give for a hair tie. *Just fuckin' cut it all off.*

Cade stands up and dusts his butt off. "Do you want me to bring Mo —"

"Absolutely not. I don't want her anywhere near this place. She needs to keep her nose clean." I snap with the force of Harry. Thinking about her drives me to my feet, and I square off with Cade.

"Easy, Ansel." Cade pushes out the Alpha command, and I draw a deep breath, stepping back from the bars.

"Sorry." I hang my head and turn away.

I don't want to watch him go. Maybe in the end, it doesn't matter if someone is there or not, we all die alone.

# CHAPTER 86
# MORRIGAN

"Miss Hart." Cade's attorney, Hank, greets me. "The state and the government haven't talked to you yet. Is that correct?"

I nod. Cade sitting next to me calms my nerves only a little bit.

Being in this conference room, in the county's government building, puts me back to sixty-seven days ago. When Ansel picked me up, he was trying to save me. The irony isn't lost on me.

"The federal government is asking for your presence in court. It's quite possible your testimony is the main difference between Ansel's release or not." He makes eye contact with me, nodding.

"Then it's easy. I'm not pressing charges. Ansel's not hurting me. He's not keeping me against my will. He's not doing anything wrong." I'm firm and try to keep a level tone. It's not working, but I tried. "If this is all it's about, why haven't I been able to just tell someone that, and we could go home?"

The attorney frowns but doesn't say anything.

"I want my mate," I say firmly.

"He knows, Morrigan," Cade acknowledges.

He puts his hand on mine where they've come to rest on the table. I draw a deep breath, letting the connection between us stabilize me. For his wolf being The Leviathan, known for war and conquest, he sure exudes calm.

"It's just not that simple. They'll probably ask you a lot of questions that are . . ." Cade pauses, and with a look, I understand that he's not saying what he would normally. He continues with his edited version. "More invasive in nature."

"Like what?" I squint at Cade for clarity. *What was he about to say?* He looks at the attorneys, so I direct my attention back to Hank and the other attorney. "Like what?"

"They'll want to know the extent of your relationship with Mr. Abbot." The attorney heavily emphasizes the word 'extent.'

*Oh. That invasive.* My heart sinks because the answer to this isn't something that sounds good on paper. "So, they want to know why we've had sex, but he hasn't claimed me?"

The attorney nods. "Exactly."

"Dammit, fucking Ansel. Of all the times he wants to have some traditional bullshit. I have been begging him to. He'd pulled his head out of his ass, and we were planning to make it a big deal over the weekend. He said he had a plan, and he wanted it to be perfect and . . ." The words come out of my mouth with a little bit more anger and a lot more ferocity than I wanted, or that's warranted, given they're just trying to help.

"That's good." Hank nods. "That matches what Lena said about her conversations with Ansel. Let's leave off the expletives when in the courtroom."

Cade snickers. "I don't know, might be funny."

"Really?" I snap at Cade, jerking my hand away from him before I think the actions through.

Quickly, I fall back in my chair and pull my hands over my mouth. *I just snapped at The Leviathan.*

"I'm sorry." Cade nods, touching my shoulder and gently rubbing it. "We're all nervous, and I need to do better."

*The Leviathan just apologized . . . to me?*

I take the physical reassurance and the way there's no tension in the room as a sign of honesty in the action. At the very least, he'll wait until we're back home to chew me a new one.

"The last thing we need to discuss is that, above all, you need to highlight that the human laws declared you an adult at eighteen. That you are not a minor and haven't been a minor for almost two years. Which is longer than your relationship with Mr. Abbot." The other attorney is nodding along with his own words. "It hasn't been stated in the federal case that they're claiming you to be a minor, but it could be brought up and —"

"I understand. If they want to play this out in human court, pretending like I'm human, then the wolf laws don't apply. Gerad can't have it both ways." I cut the second attorney off.

Cade huffs and coughs to cover what I'm fairly sure is a laugh.

"You'll make a hell of an attorney if you want to be one, Miss Hart." The second attorney does laugh.

"There's more to it though." Cade draws my attention from them. "The judge may ask why you hadn't gone into heat, and that's not a question we're going to answer." There's no Alpha command in it because there doesn't need to be. "When or if it's brought up, deflect the question to your physical state that stopped your recovery to being healthy."

Cade's attorneys aren't looking at us. They're pretending not to be here.

"Why don't they care about what Gerad's done? Why is no one questioning him?" I push, trying to help.

"Gerad Gardner isn't the one on trial," Hank answers,

apparently paying more attention than less. "We can build a case against Mr. Gardner, but that would not negate the fact that Ansel is the one of interest to the court."

Before he can say any more, a knock comes to the door before it opens. Another attorney I had been introduced to earlier speaks to Cade. "Mr. Alden, they're getting ready to move him and would like you there."

With a nod, Cade stands up. "I'm trying again to get him to see you. But I can't guarantee he will. Judah said he's been very clear about not wanting to see anyone. He's struggling with Harry."

"Please." My voice is small again.

Left alone in the room with Hank and the other attorney, I wait for more questions.

"Oh." Hank shuffles through the file folder in front of him, flipping through a stack of papers until he pulls out a tri-folded piece. "Mr. Abbot wanted us to give this to you."

*What could Ansel want to give me?*

I take the paper from him, and it shakes like a leaf in my hand.

Once I unfold it, I see his messy handwriting on the page. The mix of letters.

I nearly fold it back up and take it home, but my heart is hurting. It's killing me from the inside out, and I'm dying for a connection to him.

Sunshine

I once made a promise to my best friend that I would always be there to take care of his daughter. When I made that promise, I didnt know exactly how hard it would be to keep it and until now I have never broken a promise to your dad. Seems his and my reunion will look a bit different than I had hoped.

I wont apologize for keeping you away from me these last few days but I am sorry that it took me so long to see what Harry was trying to show me all along. I love you Morrigan. No matter where I am or what happens, I will always love you.

If this is the end for me there are some things I need you to know. I have asked that my share of The Ardelean Fund and the house be passed to you or at least the property at the end of Nameless. Take the house and make it everything youve ever dreamed a house of your own to be. Get that dog work for yourself and do what makes YOU happy. Dont worry what everyone else says. Their opinions dont matter. Its all for you. Always for you.

If you choose to stay in town keep an eye on the guys. Tell them to be good to each other. And for Christs sake be good for Ben. Dont give him too much grief regardless if he deserves it.

You have a full life ahead of you Sunshine. All I ask is that you remember how much I love you. How much we love each other.

- AA


PS. I hope you never need to know this but the trick to escape the kennels is to pull the door toward the kennel, then push the pin up and slide. The one on the end the pin has to pass a horizontal. Its too far to reach from the inside.

SARAH JAEGER

I FOLD THE LETTER UP AND STAND FROM THE CHAIR BEFORE RUSHING TO the door. The attorney's chairs scrape against the floor as they follow.

Through the window on the door, I can see Ansel being led out the back of the building. His long hair is down, covering his face and blocking me from his view. My hand rests on the doorknob, but I can't bring myself to spin it.

Ansel is struggling with Harry. If he can't keep it together, things could get so much worse. But I can hold it together. I'll be strong for Ansel. He needs me to stay out of his sight so he can focus on holding it together. I can contain my worries and what-ifs, even if that means not thinking about him, because thinking about Ansel and what he's going through releases a flood of emotions begging me to go to him.

Instead, I'll stay here and take a last glimpse out the door, watching him go. I'll lock away the fear and helpless thoughts that this may have been my last chance to say goodbye.

It's a lot like Dad. Had I known it was the last hug, I would have made it last longer. Maybe I'd have never let go.

# CHAPTER 87

## ANSEL

I'M PACING WHEN THE DOORS TO THE CELLS OPEN. JUDAH, CADE, AND Sheriff Owens walk in, and my stomach dips.

"I'm guessing you're not here to release me." I look between the three of them.

The sheriff looks to Cade, who hangs his head. "Federal government won't budge, they want you in a more secure facility. I'm still waiting on some things."

"Ansel." Judah's voice grounds me. "You're not going to die. I won't let it happen."

Harbinger moves forward while I laugh. "Judah, if you had much say in the matter, I wouldn't be here."

"We brought Morr—" Cade offers again.

"No!" my voice echoes in the space around me.

If I wasn't going to die, they wouldn't have brought her. They know I'm fucked and are being nice. They don't want me to fight back. It makes wolves look bad if I break down. Least I can do is hold it together. I might die alone, but I'll go with as much dignity as I can.

I know the handcuffs are coming. And I clench my fists as

609

the metallic clank hits my ears at the same time the metal circles my wrists. I keep my eyes on the floor. If I see any more of the people who have called me family, I'll lose it.

The whole office is quiet as I'm led out the back door to an armored car. Inside, they chain my waist and hands to the seat and my feet to the floor. Something has numbed my mind because the physical reaction to being trapped, held in place, doesn't hit.

It's a three-and-a-half-hour drive from the county to Salt Lake City, and nothing matters anymore.

*Apathy? Is that what this is called?*

"HEY. WAKE UP," A MALE SNAPS.

My eyes open to the vehicle stopped, the back doors open. And my chains being unhooked from the armored car.

Prison is exactly how I thought it would look: large gray and white buildings.

"Ansel Abbot?" a man in a uniform asks.

I nod.

His wolf flashes forward.

Harry rises in response. I could have held him back, but my wolf is the reason I'm here. Might as well own it. When Harry flashes through my eyes, the other man drops his head, submitting.

He raises his eyes to look at me again. This time there's a soft smile. "My name is Isaac Kingston."

I recognize the last name. Someone in his bloodline died last year, wasn't savable.

Swallowing hard, I nod. *What do you say to that anyway?*

Isaac nods. "Thank you for what you did. I know you would

have saved him if you could. I'll do everything I can to make sure things go well here."

Isaac is called away but assures me this won't be terrible, so long as I just follow instructions.

I don't know if Isaac was trying to lie to me, but he's not one to be trusted. Prison intake is terrifying. Sheriff Owens had his processing people skip me, said he didn't think I'd be there long, and it wasn't worth the paperwork.

But as I'm stripped down, they photograph each one of my tattoos. My fingerprints are scanned, and then my whole hands.

I'm led into a room with shower heads, and there's an explanation of what'll happen. The guard that was okay gets called out and another steps in to take his place.

Immediately, the new guard gets in my face.

"You wolves think you're so tough. You're not even all that big." His words come out with spittle, and I try to back up.

"Where do you think you're going?" the second guard, who had stayed, taunts.

Harbinger is scary quiet. The quiet I know that comes before violence. I brace myself for what could be a hard forward charge. No matter what happens, I can't shift. I can't give them a reason to hurt me.

It might be my fate to die here. But I have to make it so that the world knows we aren't violent. It's just a little more pain.

"He's awfully small for a shifter. You sure this is the one?" They talk around me.

"Show us your eyes," the one in front of me orders. "Wanna see your tough ass wolf."

When I don't comply, keeping the green of my irises, he raises his hand and smacks me across the face.

Harry snarls at our mistreatment, but I hold him back. There's no way I'll let them win. I keep Harry out of my eyes.

He'll be contained in my body until there's absolutely no choice.

A kick comes to the back of my knees, sending me forward down onto them. The pain of hitting the cement floor radiates up through my legs.

The new position, lower than the other man, leaves me very little choice but to look up at him or at the fly of his pants.

My throat is thick. I keep my eyes on the floor, locking out thoughts and memories I think are my own.

Harry snarls, slamming forward, trying to escape me. *Please, Harry, I know. I know what you feel. I know we're afraid. This time you have to stop. Please.*

He doesn't stop, and I know he won't. I just have to hope I can hold on for longer than whatever they plan to do to me lasts.

"Hey!" Isaac calls through some of the bars to the left with a gruff voice.

The door clicks open.

"What the fuck do you think the two of you are doing?"

"Nothing." The one behind me gives a chirp of appeasement.

"He just fell, and we were helping him up." The man in front of me grabs onto the cuffs. He jerks hard on them, and I'm pulled to my feet.

I'm stiff from days sitting in a cell, and I wince.

"See. All better." The man behind me huffs.

"You two are past duty time. Go." Isaac presses with the power of an Alpha command.

Weird to use it since it won't work on humans, but this is a weird place. Throw the rules out the window, I guess.

Harry snarls a little more, but when the door closes behind them on the way out, he moves silently, stalking through me.

"You alright?" Isaac walks around me when I don't turn to look at him.

I shrug. "As good as I can be."

"Cade Alden won't let you die in here," Isaac says assuredly. "You're all over the news. Humans across the country are enraged about you being locked up."

I nod. Everyone's faith in Cade should give me something to hold on to. Some sort of hope.

But there is none.

"You've a hearing starting in two days. Originally it was supposed to be Wednesday, but Cade moved it up to Monday." Isaac motions me to follow him.

*So today is Friday?* I don't even know what day it is. This is what it's like in the end?

He removes my handcuffs and lets me dress myself, all the while rambling. "The stay of execution is good for two weeks. If the hearing takes longer than that, they'll have to request another one. I don't think it will. No one will want to be on the wrong side of that angry mob."

*Angry mob?* I don't question it aloud. I suppose my family is big enough to look like an angry mob.

The orange pants and scratchy gray T-shirt aren't terrible. But I miss my flannel.

Isaac doesn't handcuff me again but leads me through another door into more of an open area. "We, me and the other shifters who work here, tried to petition to get you into general population, figured you'd do well with the social hierarchies and your wolf would appreciate other people around. But . . . well, the powers that be want you in your own cell."

"Doesn't matter." It's a lie. I don't want to be locked in a cell. I don't know what general population is like, but the idea of further confinement has me on edge.

"Well, I got your one hour outside your cell to consist of

actual time in the yard. Seeing the sky . . . That'll help." Isaac tries to cheer me up.

I'm shown to a cell, and it's marginally bigger than my cell at Salt Lake City, but my kennels in the basement are nicer, except again for a mattress.

I get the dignity of walking freely into the cell.

"Everyone's rooting for you. I know it seems hopeless. But there are five of us here. Plus, two bears. We all got assigned to you, hoping it'll make this easier. The human guards are wary of you. Some don't like shifters at all. But we'll all show you our animals to . . ." Isaac's voice trails off as I open my mouth.

"I'm here because they're planning to kill me. Isaac, I 'preciate you, but there's no splitting hairs to it. I'm on death row, and the attempts at comfortin' me is nice, but I've done my job well for a long time. Humans have every right to be afraid of me." I nod, looking around the cell again. "I promised the Sovereign I'd do everything I could to keep shifters in a positive light through my end. In exchange, he's gonna take care of my mate. Now, all that's left to do is figure out how people manage to live their final days knowin' that's what they are. Irony isn't lost on me."

"Don't get too comfortable with death." Isaac gives me a smile before closing the door to the cell.

*For so many, I am death. It's only fair.*

Harry sits still in my mind. It's like he's calculating every inch of our new space. It's not like at home, where there's a bunch of fun things for him to destroy if he gets out. Maybe it'll be a deterrent.

I lie down on the mattress they've covered the slab with. It's lumpy, but I let Harry have my mind in hopes he'll respect me and leave me our body. I can't let him out, and if that means I have to stay awake and compartmentalize everything, I will. *Come on, Harry. Cooperate, at least for now.*

# CHAPTER 88
# MORRIGAN

Sleep is impossible to come by. I tried really hard to sleep last night, but today could be the last time I see him.

Ansel didn't claim me, and now it might be what kills him while keeping me alive. Sitting on the back step with a cup of coffee that's long since gone cold, I look down the driveway toward the new little houses everyone lives in.

Wednesday? Thursday? I don't know which day is what anymore, but Cade's attorneys had me sign a bunch of documents. I now legally own all the land on End of The Earth Road and the vacant property on Hope Street just inside the Nameless city lines. It's my house, my cabins, and my pack. And apparently, I've a lot of money. It seems completely pointless.

Not having Ansel here? I won't survive. He's the oxygen that feeds my flame, and his absence will only snuff out the fire. All that remains will be a scorch mark marring the earth as proof we were here together. Maybe that's how we're supposed to be remembered, as the remnants of a flame. A flame that burned hot and fast and is gone before you know it, until there's nothing more than another soot mark in the Utah desert.

I walk down the driveway toward the guys' houses. It's lonely up here at the top of the hill, and I know they're all getting up to start the day soon. Sherman first.

As I walk toward his house, he's already outside. Squatting down inside his coop, Sherman has a chicken on his head, another on his shoulder, and he's petting a third while at least three more are running around in the pen.

"Hey, Morrigan. Do you wanna hold a chicken?" Sherman offers me a brown speckled hen. "You can hold this one. Her name is Cinnamon."

"Nah, maybe some other time. I just wanted to come down and see how you're doing. I know we won't be around today, and I don't want you to think I'm not thinking about you," I answer and half listen as Sherman starts talking to his chickens and telling me all about the gossip with 'his girls.'

The way he prattles on is calming.

The door across the road opens and closes. Ripley crows as loud as he possibly can. "Good morning, Miss Morrigan."

"God, would you shut up," Vito shouts, equally as loud, from the unit across from him.

Zero comes out and walks over with a second cup of coffee and exchanges it for the cold one in my hands.

"What, no Sully?" I ask, looking at the four of them.

"He's hungover," Zero answers with his deep voice.

"Tried to keep pace with Ezra and Deacon last night," Vito says, tying his shoes.

"That's dangerous. He should know better by now." Ezra's voice comes from farther down the row where the 'guest' houses were set up.

He doesn't seem hungover at all.

It shouldn't be funny, but it is, and I snort.

With his hands in his pockets, Ezra approaches, but once he's past the wall that the men of my pack made around me, he wraps me up in a hug.

*"Magnus O'Brien is here in the States. He's brought reinforcements, and if today doesn't go well, Ansel is pulling a Houdini. If you want to go with him, just think it really — really — loudly, and I'll make sure you and he escape from Alcatraz."*

Ezra kisses the top of my head and lets me go.

*"I'll go. I don't need to think about it,"* I answer him.

Ezra looks around at the pack and shrugs.

*"I'm not an Alpha Female. I can't anchor them. I've held it together for them this long, but without Ansel, this isn't my home."*

Ripley and Vito start talking about the new solar panels and how the voltage is who knows . . .

"I don't know, guys." Ezra cuts in between them, his eyes locked on me. "Does it really matter what the housing looks like? Makes a difference just knowing it's all contained."

The heavy hint doesn't make sense.

Ezra goes off and gets involved in the great debate with them while Zero and I stand there watching Sherman's chickens.

Zero stoops down and whispers, "Ezra said he'd stay here, permanently, with us. So do not give up a life with Ansel for us." He looks at the rest of the pack. "They'll understand."

The second cup of coffee for the day goes cold before I drink it. I make my way back up the house to get dressed in clothes that, according to Lena and Dinah, will make me look older and more responsible. Dinah curls my hair, and when they're done, I don't think I've ever looked this good.

When we get to the courthouse, there's a crowd of people and reporters.

Cade, sitting in the front seat, addresses me without turning around. "Stay between Michael and me. The reporters will be shouting questions and trying to get close to you. It'll be scary and overwhelming. Keep your head high and look directly ahead of you."

"Okay." I confirm that I'm listening.

"The crowd is separated by the police barricade based on whose side they're on," Michael Tate, who came to install the security system earlier, tells me. "The people on the left are anti-shifter. They're significantly fewer in number, but they're also significantly louder and will be hostile. The people on the right are pro-shifter, and there will be shifters in the crowd. If you feel like you can't stay true to the course, for the love of God, Jesus, Satan, I don't care, run to the right."

Thalia giggles next to me in the seat. "He's adorable. You'll be fine. If Lena can do this, anyone can."

A phone rings over the SUV's intercom.

"Ready." I recognize Millie's voice.

"Ready." I think it's Ezra's voice.

"It's go time." Finn's Irish accent follows suit.

"Roll out," Cade answers, opening his car door.

Michael opens mine for me, and I step out with his hand helping me down. Two security guards from the SUV behind us come forward, and immediately, flanking police officers walk in front of Cade, Michael, and me.

"Morrigan, over here!"

"Abominations!"

"God has no place for you."

"Morrigan, what's it like living with psychopaths?"

I want to put my head down and tilt it away from the left

side. The remarks drag Gerad's words from the depths of my memories.

*Hold it together. Ansel needs you.*

The hallways blend together, but we come to a stop as a collective group outside a courtroom. There must have been another hearing — Trial? Thing? — before us because people are milling around. Their eyes go wide seeing us.

I hadn't realized until we were coming through security how many of us there are. Cade and Thalia, Lena and Finn, Judah and Ezra, Dinah and Deacon, plus me. Then three of the many security agents from Corinth Security entered the building with us; plus the pack publicist, Henri, and her assistant, whose name I don't think I was ever given, met us here; four paralegals and the two attorneys. It's a small army.

The bailiff clears the courtroom of the stragglers before he allows us in. I'm ushered onto a bench, seated next to Thalia and Cade. The rest of the family flocks in around us.

It's cliché, but the clock ticks by as we wait for something to happen. My toes curl and uncurl in my shoes over and over again.

Next to me, Thalia interlaces the fingers of one hand with mine while the other rests on her stomach, like she'll be sick. I squeeze her hand, and she squeezes back.

No one has bothered lying to me and telling me it'll be okay. Even Dinah, who sees the future, hasn't bothered making any statements one way or another. She says there are too many factors.

"All rise," the bailiff barks. "The Emergency Hearing for the State of Utah and Wolf Commission. The honorable Judge MacKenzie presiding."

The bailiff announces the judge, and I follow everyone else's lead, standing when she comes in.

Unexpectedly, the judge is a woman. She's probably in her

fifties and, I'm guessing, is quite stylish. She wears modest glasses, but beyond that, I really have nothing to base it on because her robe covers everything else. Just the vibe, I guess.

The door to the right of her podium opens, and another bailiff enters, followed by Ansel. He looks hollow. When he sees me, he shakes his head. I know he didn't want me here, but I'm the only one who will get him out.

Despite being put in a suit, Ansel doesn't look dashing or handsome. He looks tired and worn down. With his hair pulled back, the courtroom's harsh fluorescent lights only serve to highlight the exhaustion in the bags under his eyes and etched on his fallen face.

I would say he looks how I feel, but no matter how many negative emotions swirl around inside me, he looks worse. He's so much worse. After he sits down, facing away from me, I close my eyes, letting the tears well. I hold my breath and the tears back so he can't hear me cry. Now isn't the time to break down.

"United States Government versus Ansel U. Abbot," Judge MacKenzie states.

"Waive the reading, not the rights, Your Honor," one of Ansel's attorneys says.

"I've reviewed the facts of the case. In the interest of everyone, I would like to speak with Morrigan C. Hart, please?" Judge MacKenzie pulls her head out of the paperwork.

I wasn't expecting to talk so soon. My heart hammers in my chest, and I quickly make my way to where the bailiff shows me to stand. It's off to the side, and I can see Ansel's face. Harbinger is fighting him from underneath the surface, and he radiates tension.

Even knowing it might not help much, I give him a soft smile.

The bailiff swears me in. It's so bizarre, like being on one of those television crime dramas, but you know the man is innocent and the whole thing is a misunderstanding.

"Miss Hart. It seems that your stepfather, Gerad Gardner, thinks you're in danger," Judge MacKenzie asks over the top of her glasses.

"I am not in danger, Your Honor." I shake my head. "He's wrong."

"Is Mr. Gerad Gardner in the courtroom?" She looks out across the room that's packed but only with us.

"No, Your Honor." One of Cade's attorneys stands. "We contacted Mr. Gardner in notification of the proceedings, and we contacted his legal representation, but they denied wanting to attend the hearing."

The lawyer offers out a document to Judge MacKenzie, and the bailiff moves it between them.

The judge raises and lowers her glasses looking at the document. She sets it down and turns her attention back to me.

"Do you know why he would think those things? It's a serious accusation. It must warrant some truth." Judge MacKenzie motions to me and then to Ansel.

"It does not, Your Honor," I try to explain. I've got to be strong for Ansel. Dinah told me not to hold back the facts. "Gerad Gardner, my mother's mate, has arranged a mating, like marriage, for me, and despite my legal obligation to the state of Utah, he is trying to forcefully remove me to fulfill his arrangement."

She nods, and I continue. "Because Ansel is whose care I've been assigned to, Gerad is trying to take me from him and does not like that Ansel is upholding his deal to the state."

"And how old are you, Miss Hart?" she asks.

"Nineteen," I answer.

Ansel's lawyers nod. Which seems dumb because it's a fact, not an opinion. I haven't said anything profound.

Judge MacKenzie furrows her eyebrow. "This isn't something you're consenting to? The mating arrangement?"

"No, Your Honor." I don't want to be rude, but I have more to say. I continue slowly. "Gerad is upset because I'm not consenting and because I've found my mate, and if my mate claims me, then whatever deal he has struck with the other party becomes invalid."

"And who is your mate?" she asks.

I knew this question would come, but that knowledge didn't any more prepare me for what I have to say. It's one thing for everyone to see and know, but it's time I have to own it. "My mate is Ansel Abbot."

My wolf rises at the announcement. The fickle little creature whispers, *Ours.*

It comes as a shock to my system. I hadn't felt her return, but there she is. Claiming him like we need him to claim us back.

"I see." Judge MacKenzie directs her attention to Ansel. "Mr. Abbot, is Miss Hart your mate?"

Ansel stands. "Yes." He swallows and nods. "Your Honor."

"Miss Hart, are you a ward of Ansel Abbot by the federal government and bound to his care?" Judge MacKenzie clarifies.

"Yes, Your Honor." I nod.

I look at Ansel and his attorneys. They're whispering so well that I can't hear. I look to the faces around them for context clues. Cade's mate, Thalia, doesn't have the best poker face, and her eyes go wide.

"Miss Hart." Judge MacKenzie draws my attention back to her. "I would like to see you in my chambers, please."

Everything is happening so fast.

My heart drops. *What does this mean?*

I look at Cade's attorneys for guidance. They nod, encouraging me to follow Judge MacKenzie.

Obediently, I follow her out the door on the opposite side of the courtroom.

Cade's whispering an Alpha command as I walk by. "Ansel. Stay. Stay. Stay. Ansel. Stay."

It hurts more knowing that we're so close. But if what Ezra says is true, it doesn't matter one way or another what happens today; I can go with Ansel. I can be with him. But I'm still not sure entirely what he means by that.

I follow her down a short hallway to an office similar to the one Ansel saved me in. But there are significantly more feminine touches and no rodeo paraphernalia. She sits down at the large, stately desk and motions for me to take a seat in one of the chairs opposite her.

"Miss Hart." She addresses me once I sit down. "Are you being made to say these things to protect Mr. Abbot? It seems that his family is of very high status. Are you saying these things to protect him because they are threatening you?"

"No. Your Honor. Absolutely not." I shake my head. *How could she think that?*

"And if I were to say that Ansel Abbot is not safe for the world, do you think you would be safe given the family's connections? Or would it put you in greater danger?" the judge says, and fear floods through me.

I struggle to speak. "Your Honor." My voice cracks, and I swallow and try again. "If you take Ansel from me, the only people who can protect me are his family."

Losing the fight to hold back my tears, I brush them away and bite my lips together.

She nods. "I want the rest of this conversation on the record."

She hands me a tissue from a box inside a drawer in her desk.

I can't read her emotions.

*I've messed up. I've said something wrong. She'll have him killed. It's all my fault.*

We return to the courtroom, and my eyes lock with his. How many times can I look into his eyes before she takes him from me?

His cousins sense my fear; they're all very much on edge, examining me and the judge, searching for answers.

Judge MacKenzie sits and addresses Ansel. She scrutinizes him. "Mr. Abbot, if it is true that Miss Hart is your mate, then why have you not acted to claim her?"

He looks at me but doesn't say anything. Loyal Ansel would rather stay silent than spill my secret.

"Mr. Abbot," she prompts.

"Uhm." I try to interject as politely as possible. "Your Honor."

She turns back to me, an eyebrow raised.

"Ansel has yet to claim me because of the same reason Gerad is trying to arrange my mate," I say softly.

"And what is this reason?" Judge MacKenzie prompts, okay with me answering and not Ansel.

I can tell she's trying to understand the situation. Maybe not all hope is lost.

"According to our laws, until very recently, I'd been a minor," I answer softly. The lawyers told me to be clear in demonstrating that our laws have holes. So, I know I have to say this. "I only very recently had my first heat and was considered a minor. By our laws, that means if Ansel claimed me as his, it would be punishable by death."

"Even if he's your mate?" She seems concerned, and rightfully so.

"Yes. Your Honor," I answer, omitting the scary detail that we couldn't have been completely sure we were mates until I went through a cycle. But this feels like the lie of omission that's probably allowable.

"Is it normal that wolves are older than the human laws for age of maturity?" the judge asks the room.

One of Ansel's attorneys stands. "Your Honor, from a statistical report entered into evidence, you can see the average age of maturity is between sixteen and seventeen and a half."

She nods, then looks at me. "Is there a reason in which you had not gone into heat until recently?"

Another uncomfortable question, but Gerad isn't here to defend himself.

*It's not a lie*, I remind myself, drawing a steadying breath. *It's not a lie, it's just not answering her question.*

Cade's warning to deflect toward my physical state that stopped my recovery to being healthy echoes in my mind. She's not a shifter and can't hear lies like we can anyway, but if I'm going to save Ansel, I have to be perfect.

*It's not a lie. I'm just not answering her question.* I'll keep telling myself that, and when I speak, the words feel and ring true. "By wolf standards, I'm a victim of neglect by the Pack Alpha."

"And how do your laws handle these things?" she asks me.

"Uh." I don't know how to answer.

To me, Gerad is above reproach. This wasn't something I had been prepared to speak on.

"Your Honor." One of Ansel's other attorneys speaks. "The course of action when neglect is involved among wolves is to remove the wolf being abused from the pack and place them somewhere else to be protected. Miss Hart had been cut off from access to resources due to her position in the pack as the Alpha's stepdaughter. Given Mr. Gerad Gardner's status as Pack Alpha, he is the Pack Alpha who would be guilty of neglect. It was an abuse of power."

Judge MacKenzie looks back to me.

I confirm his words. "I ran away from home and got into legal troubles trying to escape Gerad, Mr. Gardner. Ansel helped me get well, and I went into heat. He didn't claim me then because it felt too soon. He was trying to give me a choice, even if the fates wouldn't."

"You're dismissed, Miss Hart. Thank you for your answers today." Judge MacKenzie's eyes glint as she looks at me, and I don't know what it means. Maybe a trick of the light.

"Thank you, Your Honor." I walk as quickly as I can over to where the Ardeleans are sitting.

Cade stands and pulls me in, protectively making me pass behind him.

Shaking, I sit on the bench between Cade and Thalia. She wraps her hands into mine, and we sit there squeezing our fingers together.

Sitting back down, Cade snakes his arm behind me and then whispers quickly, "You did good."

After a few moments of silence, the judge looks out at us and asks, "Is Mr. Cade Alden present?"

Cade stands slowly, buttoning his jacket. He steps forward and moves with slick confidence over to where I stood before and waits to be addressed.

The judge doesn't make him wait long. "Mr. Alden has made himself available to answer questions of the court. Mr. Alden, could you please enlighten me as to why the court is handling this and not you?"

My eyes go wide at her tone. *Fuck.* She's not afraid of Cade clearly.

Cade doesn't seem to be afraid of her either. He doesn't mince words but keeps himself levelheaded. "I was only made aware of the situation when I was alerted to Mr. Abbot being arrested. The opportunity to handle this was not presented to me as Gerad Gardner disregarded our laws and involved the human authorities."

Judge MacKenzie holds Cade's gaze as if she's evaluating him before nodding. "I see. And you have laws which would handle this sort of dispute?"

"Yes, Your Honor. I would love nothing more than to take this out of the human courts and handle it within our own laws. Our laws were written long before the United States was founded and have been abided by, to the best of my knowledge, until Gerad Gardner contacted human authorities." Cade nods and answers precisely. "In accepted negotiations between wolf shifters and the federal government, issues between Pack Alphas, such as Ansel Abbot and Gerad Gardner, should be handled by our people. This agreement was signed yesterday morning."

"Do we have a copy of that document?" Judge MacKenzie looks to the legal counsel sitting next to Ansel.

An attorney is quick to present it to her.

"Your Honor." One of the attorneys interjects. "We'd like to make a motion to dismiss as there is no jurisdiction."

Judge MacKenzie's nod has my breath stuck in my chest. I can't breathe.

# CHAPTER 89
## ANSEL

MORRIGAN IS, AT THE MOST, FIVE FEET AWAY FROM ME, BUT IT MIGHT as well be a mile.

The courtroom is uncomfortable as we all sit here in silence. I think it's been a long time. But I can't tell anymore. The longer the judge sits, the more anxious I feel. I'm doing everything I can to sit still and look calm. I don't feel calm.

Harry is smashing around inside me. His anger is evident with the gnashing of his teeth and vicious snarls. It's been days of reliving memories of things I'd lost. Torture that he and I have endured has come back, haunting us both. It's aggravated him even more than when we were separated from Morrigan after her heat.

And being so close but so far from her makes it even worse. I don't know what's finer than a hair, but I'm hanging by it. I asked them not to bring her because I'm not sure if I have enough strength to keep him from destroying everything and anyone in his way to get to her.

I'm so focused on keeping myself together that I'm not

entirely sure what's happening when the attorneys are speaking. I don't know what the agreement is and what it being signed means.

But Cade clearly does. "Hang in there. Dinah has a good feeling," Cade says at a low volume behind me. There's a press of the Alpha command, but it doesn't do a whole lot.

More minutes tick by, and I'm focusing on the wood grain of the fancy desk the judge sits behind, trying to pick out shapes among the squiggles like you do in the night sky or in clouds. Anything to not focus on what feels like certain death and to distract myself from panicking. Being calm is the difference between the sliver of hope for life and a very quick death.

"Mr. Abbot." Judge MacKenzie says my name, and I stand.

Cade's attorney friends stand with me.

"Yes, Your Honor," I answer.

"Do you have any idea how much of a public uproar you've caused?" Her words are angry, but she's almost smiling. Or maybe that's the start of a human snarl.

*Dinah has a good feeling.* Is that because she doesn't have plans for Solstice? If they wanted me to leave, I'd do it. But it probably doesn't matter.

I shake my head before remembering I have to speak. "I'm sorry, Your Honor, I don't know."

"Mr. Abbot, our office has received, on my last count, ten thousand three hundred and fifty-six letters speaking on how much of a difference you make in this world. I have read only a quarter of them. The post office is bringing them in in tubs. Seven court clerks are sorting them. Do you know what I've come to understand about you?"

"I can only imagine what people would write about me, Your Honor." I don't know if that answers her question.

*Do I even know that many people?* I swallow hard. I've killed less than a quarter of that many, so if everyone's parents or siblings wrote in telling them what I've done, that number matches? Maybe.

"Mr. Abbot, I'll change my question. Do you know how many people live in the city where you live?" Judge MacKenzie tilts her head, looking at me.

"I think the sign says seven hundred and twenty, but I think the Waltons moved, so probably seven hundred and sixteen?" I answer her.

Judge MacKenzie smiles and corrects me. "Seven seventeen." She shuffles the papers on the desk before her. "I was looking over your documents, and I have to be honest . . . I thought Nameless didn't exist. Then, when I did find out Nameless does, in fact, exist, I learned I was saying it wrong. It's not Name-less. It's *Na-mal-iz*." She shakes her head. "Apparently, it's named after an idea of 'no more lies' or 'no bad things to say,' which I wish I could have a word with your town's founder. But I digress."

I'm thoroughly confused with what Nameless has to do with all this. *Did the Mullhollands have a boy or a girl?*

"We've received a letter from every single resident of Nameless. All seven hundred and seventeen. There was a baby girl born to the Mullhollands last week, who is apparently very excited to meet you. I say this because we checked the census to confirm that statistic. All seven hundred and seventeen residents had something to say about you," the judge informs me.

She picks up a stack of papers and starts to skim. "Mrs. Hoppe, who apparently owns the local malt shop in Nameless —" She pauses, correcting herself to say it right. "*Na-mal-iz*, says that if you were to no longer reside in their city, the entire town would mourn your loss. The sheriff's office speaks of your nonexistent criminal record and how, despite the strict parking regulations, you have never had even so much as a parking ticket."

Judge MacKenzie flips over a paper on her desk and skims the page before continuing. "There is a letter here from the prime minister of Canada saying that you were absolutely critical in a missing person's case they had. You found several hikers unharmed in Saskatchewan. We've received a letter from Her Royal Highness, Queen Revecca Ardelean of Romania, personally vouching for your character and your wolf, stating it would be physically impossible for you to put someone else in harm's way. It also includes a reminder of your place in Romania and of your official title in the Romanian royal court. Which I will not butcher in trying to pronounce your official title. I do believe it is pending to be accepted for diplomatic immunity, which you will need to take up with the federal government."

*Unexpected. Magnus must have meddled.*

But what Judge MacKenzie is saying doesn't sound bad? All . . . of . . . Nameless?

"Mr. Abbot. I've letters here talking about how you've been patient, kind, and empathetic on all levels. Many letters of which say you rival a saint. There are countless testimonies of how you've given people their lives back. Evidently, you've been inspiration for several children's names." She pauses.

*Who would name their kid after me?* I picked most of my name out of a book on photography and the phonebook.

She takes off her glasses and sets them down on the desk thingy in front of her. "All this to say, Mr. Abbot, I cannot find any indication that which you have been accused of is possibly true."

*That sounds like a good thing?*

Harry, for the first time in forever, stands still. I'm not sure he understands what she's saying. But the way I'm paying attention must cause him to focus.

"Work out the issues between yourself and Mr. Gardner under the laws of your people and the supervision of Mr. Alden." Judge MacKenzie motions behind me to where Cade's sitting. "Motion to dismiss granted. Mr. Abbot, I never want to see you in my courtroom ever again, but perhaps I'll visit Nameless."

"Yes, Your Honor." I try to breathe, but it's not going so well.

The bailiff approaches me too quickly. My body jerks when he reaches for me. I want to be released, but it's startling.

Harry snaps, defending me. I hold him back.

*This is a good thing. Stay still.*

"Ansel, steady," Cade commands.

Moving slower this time, the bailiff unlocks the handcuffs.

Everything is really loud, and I'm not sure why. What's the commotion about?

When my hands are released, Cade's attorneys usher me closer to Cade.

I don't want anything to do with Cade right now. I need Morrigan.

I need my mate, and I need her now.

Not fast enough, she's pushed before me, and I wrap my arms around her. Burying my nose into the top of her hair, I draw deep breaths. *Please let this be real.*

"Pick her up if you have to, but you need to move," Cade commands.

I do as I'm told, scooping Morrigan up in my arms. I won't let her go. Not if I don't have to.

She wraps her arms around my neck.

Harry settles for the first time in a week.

"I love you. I love you so much," Morrigan whispers.

I can't answer her. Love doesn't feel like a strong enough word for what I'm feeling for her. I'm positive I've never heard of a strong enough word for it. The pain in my sternum is nothing compared to the pain of living without her. I'll suffer for Morrigan. I always will.

Cade's led us around the courthouse and to a whole fleet of vehicles. It's only then I feel comfortable setting Morrigan down. And that's because my whole body is revolting at the idea of getting into one of the black SUVs.

"Ansel." Ezra says my name. I turn toward the sound of his voice, and he's holding out a set of keys. "Take your own damn truck."

The keys fly toward me, and I catch them out of the air.

"Let's go home." Morrigan threads her fingers into my other hand.

Cade stops me. "You'll be middle of the pack. Have Morrigan call us if you need a minute or a break. We'll stop, but we need to stay together."

"Yeah. Can do." I squeeze the keys in my hand, focusing on the plastic key chain and rubbing my fingers across it.

It isn't until we're an hour outside of Salt Lake City that it really sinks in.

Morrigan is already holding a cell phone to her ear. It's not mine, so someone must have given her one.

Rudely, she doesn't greet whoever it is. "We need to stop."

I follow the black SUV in front of me off the road to the next exit. When we come to a stop, I'm out of the vehicle and drawing deep breaths, walking into the woodsy area.

No one follows me, and I just walk a little ways away.

Harry isn't fighting. He settles slowly, resting inside me.

I close my eyes and just try to listen and experience everything that tells me I'm free.

"Ansel," Morrigan says softly.

I didn't even hear her follow me out here.

I turn to look, and there she is, and then a hundred yards behind her, my family is standing and watching.

"Ten thousand people?"

"Every single person in Nameless." Morrigan nods.

I pull my hair back, snarling in frustration. It's everywhere and nowhere. It's in my face and touching my neck all at once.

Morrigan steps to me and wraps her arms around me.

I didn't realize what was missing was her touch. I'm a shitty mate if I can't figure out that the reason I'm freaking out is that I'm not touching her.

"Ansel," Morrigan whispers.

"Yeah, sunshine?" I kiss the top of her head.

She murmurs, "You have to promise me not to get mad and yell, okay?"

"Why?" I ask.

"It's better if you just promise now and find out later." She nods against my chest, her head rubbing that part of my sternum meant just for her.

"Okay, I promise. I'll either yell or get mad. I won't do both." When I kiss the top of her head again, she pulls back and looks up at me.

She wraps her arm around my neck and kisses me like she means business.

Harry hums with approval.

"Dude. I get it. She's hot. Let's go home," Ezra shouts from across the way.

I flip him off and then break our kiss.

W<small>E'RE NEARLY HOME, AND AS WE COME TO THE TOWN LIMITS OF</small> Nameless, I slow down, ignoring the order to have Morrigan call him if we need to stop. Surely, any threat Cade might have been worried about would have shit or got off the pot by now.

I've driven past the Nameless sign hundreds of times, maybe thousands, and today it's different. The sign's population number now has a new number screwed in on top of the old one. It's changed the population, with a number, but it's not seven hundred and seventeen like the judge says. It's seven hundred and eighteen. And there's an addition underneath.

Well, I mean, an *A* last name is an *A* last name. I guess whatever title Revecca gave me — told the government I have, whatever — probably includes the bloodline's last name. It's still humbling.

"They love you," Morrigan whispers and squeezes my hand.

Coming through downtown, it's like driving in a parade.

We're crawling at tortoise speed. Literally everyone is here, and people are holding signs.

*OUR HERO LIVES HERE!*
*Good wolves live here!*
*We love Ansel!*

OUR CARAVAN HAS COME TO A FULL STOP, AND CADE WALKS BACK TO the truck.

Using the handle, I roll down the window.

"I didn't arrange any of this," he starts, not apologizing but explaining carefully. "But the mayor wants to talk to you. I told him I'd see. But maybe today's not the best day."

"Well, it'd be a shame to have all these people come out and not be polite and say hello." I deflate but then shrug.

I just want to go home. I want to change clothes and shower and bake something. But everyone is here, and apparently, it's all to do with me.

"Alright. I'm here, Morrigan is here, and if you want to go home, just thank them all for coming out and tell them you've a house full of people and it's rude to keep them waiting." Cade offers me an out.

*Oh, there's a house full of people. In addition to them?*

Morrigan leans over and turns the truck off. She whispers in my ear, "It'll be okay. I promise."

She's right. Harry's calm, and it's just me being tired and cranky.

I didn't die today. And the least I can do is thank the people who made sure I didn't.

Cade opens the truck door for me, and I slide out, Morrigan right behind me.

We make our way to the front of the SUVs where everyone's congregated.

The sheriff's brother has been mayor for at least five years. And he's beaming from ear to ear. I've only had a few conversations, but I've always thought he's a good representative for mayor.

"Ansel!" He's shouting and excited. Opening his arms, he pulls me into a hug.

I hug him back because what else are you supposed to do?

"I know you're probably itching to get home to that lovely property of yours, but I wanted to strike while the iron is hot, so to speak." The mayor looks around at the crowd.

They cheer, and the loud noise is kind of jarring, but I hold my ground.

"We'd like to thank you for the work you've done for the community. There isn't a building you haven't helped fix up. And as a thank-you, it seems the best thing to do is give you the official key to the city of Nameless." He's beaming, and Mrs. Hoppe hands him a large wooden box.

*Cities . . . have keys?*

He opens the box, and there's a big golden skeleton key.

*That's never gonna fit in a door.*

"Keys to cities mean that that person is a personal friend to each and every member. That person is always welcome to come and go. But we think there's a deeper meaning. You're our protector," the mayor explains, offering the box out to me.

With both hands, I accept the box, looking down at it. It's pretty.

"Thank you." I nod.

There's more cheering, and I draw a deep breath. "Well, I appreciate you all coming out, and I don't think there's anything I could ever do that will make this up to you. But it seems I've a house full of people back home, and they're hoping I'll make up a batch of cookies. Maybe we can host one of those fancy town picnics later?"

"Now there's an idea." The mayor clasps his hands in front of him and rocks back on his heels.

Closing the lid on the box, I head back to my truck.

"Good job," Morrigan praises.

I set the box on the seat between us and look at it a few times. *What am I supposed to do with it? Problem for another day.*

# CHAPTER 90
## MORRIGAN

Ansel promising not to get angry and yell was not a promise he could keep. Which, really, I knew when I asked him to try, but I felt like maybe it might work.

"You fuckin' what?!" Ansel shouts, looking down the driveway toward the guys' new houses.

"Ansel!" I shout at him.

He's seething. I haven't seen him this angry since I first got here.

Cade keeps his cool, letting Ansel shout at him.

"You can't just fuckin' demolish and erect buildings 'cause you're fuckin' king now!" Ansel shouts.

"Yeah, Cade, get your erections out of here!" Ezra shouts over the top of him.

Dinah cackles.

Thalia walks right between Cade and Ansel without any sort of fear of the rage brewing in Harry's eyes. She grabs Ansel's hand and pulls it out of the air from where he's stuck gesturing down the hill.

Disarmed, Ansel stops and looks at Thalia. I can't see his

643

facial expression, but by the way his shoulders drop, it's something big.

Looking around at us before she turns back to Ansel, Thalia sighs. "Okay, since the big chicken is afraid to tell everyone that he failed, I'll do it. I won."

"No." Ansel breathes the softest little sound of disbelief.

Nodding, Thalia confirms, "I'm pregnant. And while we know you'd gladly make room for everything we might need at the holidays, we knew this would be easier if we could all have our own spaces."

"Pregnant." He shakes his head. "How can I be angry about that?" He pulls at his hair, looking down the hill, and then back at her a few times. His shoulders drop, and Ansel smiles. "It's just some outbuildings. It was just a year ago the two of you were here for the first time." Wrapping his arms around her, he squeezes her a little bit. "I'm so happy for you both."

When Ansel lets her go, a tear escapes from Thalia's eye, and Ansel uses his thumb to wipe it away.

Thalia laughs. "He's just gone a little crazy since he found out."

I can't look at them right now. I'm jealous of how long he's known them and how he's connecting with her. I need him. And I'm stuck having to share him.

A hand on the base of my neck gently squeezes before pushing me forward.

*"It's not good for you to hold that much grumpy inside. Just go and attach yourself to his hip. He won't mind."* Ezra encourages through his gift.

"They're nice. They're not super luxurious, and I made sure they were functional, and everything is completely modular and easy to replace if necessary." Cade wraps his arm around Thalia, pulling her back as I approach.

Ansel jumps, startled when I touch him, but his lips are

644

pulled up into his dumb grin, and his eyes, despite the deep bags under them, are bright and alive. He slings his arm around me and starts walking toward the house, bringing me home with him.

"Daddy Cade." Judah snickers. "We should have known he'd be a mess when it happened."

"Oh fuck. Judah, did you just? No. No. No. I take that back. It's hilarious." Dinah laughs so hard she fans her face. "I love it. Daddy Cade."

Snickering, Ansel and I lead the way to the house.

"The fuck. Really? Guys?" Cade's groan makes it even funnier.

When we get to the top of the hill, Lena says, "Okay, we're coming in and grabbing our things from getting ready today, and then we're leaving. We'll be back up for brunch tomorrow at eleven. Which I know is lunchtime, but I want pancakes and mimosas."

"Well," Cade pauses, stopping everyone before they hustle into the house. "There are two last pieces of 'business.'" Cade uses air quotes around the word business. "Let's just get them out of the way so we can enjoy the rest of our time here?"

"Sure, why not?" Ansel agrees with a little frustration in his voice.

"Well, first is that your and Deacon's blood work came back, and you're half brothers." Cade treads lightly with that fact.

Ansel cocks his head but doesn't say anything. I look around but don't see Deacon, and I can tell by the movement of Ansel's shirt he's doing the same.

But Cade quickly moves on to his next statement. "I would like to suggest that all of us undergo a name change."

"What?" Dinah draws out. "Top Hot Dog, I'm not sure I'm catching what you're saying."

"Well, I've had a few conversations with Revecca." Cade winces. "She's agreed that now that humans already know we're related and since we're not hiding, we could simply take our family's legacy last name, Ardelean. That way, it doesn't matter who our parents were. It's no longer cousins and explaining who we are. It's just family."

"Cool." Ezra agrees. "Let's do it."

"Yeah. Why not?" Lena agrees, and after a second, she says, "Saves the debate where Finn thinks he's going to win and I'm somehow getting an O that doesn't involve—"

"Careful, faolan. Don't think I won't." Finn's threat isn't spelled out super well, but it's enough that Lena goes quiet, zipping her lips with her fingers.

"Okay, so really, the only one we're asking about this is Ansel?" Judah offers.

"Me?" Ansel yawns. "What do I have to do with this? I'll do whatever. Town has already put it Ardelean on the sign anyway."

"Okay, I'm sorry. I've held it in this long, but the tired pregnant lady excuse starts now," Thalia grumbles and then, with a yawn, directs her attention to the two of us. "Cade's second order of business is that: Ansel, we love you, but we're sick of you pretending you're an island and don't need help. It's not fair to you that these idiots don't chip in more. So, Finn, Cade, and Ezra have all agreed that they want to set themselves up to help with fractures and give you some time with your mate. Here, away from here, just having a life."

"And with that, I'm taking crabby down for a nap." Cade offers his hand to Thalia, and she takes it, letting him pull her into his arms. "Think about it, talk it over with your mate. You and I can catch up when the dust settles."

"Sounds like a plan." Ansel agrees.

He looks at the house expectantly, waiting for his cousins

to clear their stuff out. Ansel pulls me off to the side of the stairs leading into the house and holds me while the eight of them traipse in and out.

In two minutes, we're standing by the small staircase alone in the driveway.

Ansel pauses at the door, holding it open and peeking inside. "How much did they change the inside of my house?"

I shake my head. "My house. And all that changed is the alarm. It doesn't make as many annoying beeps when you push the buttons."

"All yours, sunshine." He follows me inside.

## CHAPTER 91
# MORRIGAN

THE ARDELEANS GAVE US OUR SPACE, AND I DON'T KNOW WHAT I should have expected but it wasn't this. It started with a drink of water before bed, and then it turned into just checking the door. Then a snack.

Ansel paces in the house. He can't be still, and it's a constant battle with himself. From standing at the kitchen counter and trying to measure ingredients, to looking at the movie collection trying to find something to watch, to even starting a load of laundry, nothing can keep his focus.

I've seen Harbinger pull back and forth in his eyes a dozen times. It's been two hours that feel like four hundred. He pulls his hair up into a messy bun only to let it down two minutes later. I don't know what to do or how to help him.

He's pulling on his long hair, nearly ripping it out of his head. I can't watch him pace anymore. I don't know what I can do, but I can't watch him hurting like this.

Approaching slowly, I let him see me get close to him. He didn't fight our touch earlier, but there's something less tame about Ansel now than there was earlier.

I try to wrap my arms around his waist.

"I can't." His voice is pained and pinched. "Fuck, Morrigan."

Instead of wrapping them around his waist, I pull on the sleeves of his flannel.

He lets me, barely, while balling his hands into fists. His shoulders twitch, rising to his ears.

Forcing them down, he says, "Fuck, no. Either cut it or shave it off. It's gotta go. I feel trapped."

"Your hair?" I ask, trying to understand.

He nods, heading toward the bathroom. He comes back with a pair of scissors and offers them to me.

Hesitantly, I reach for the scissors and wrap my hands around them. This feels like when girls have life crises and decide to dye their hair and chop it short. As his mate, I definitely should not let him cut it.

"I think you're stressed. Let's try lying down and decompressing?"

Ansel sighs and follows me to the bedroom. We lie together on top of the bed, but his wiggling toes are an indicator of how antsy and uncomfortable he is. It's unsettling seeing him so stressed in his own space.

"I'm sorry," he tells me, looking up at the ceiling before climbing out of bed again.

He walks from the bedroom to the kitchen, to the living room, and to the deck.

I follow him to the kitchen, watching him pace the house. I'm getting tired just watching, and all I'm doing is sitting here at the counter.

I stalled before, but it's getting to the point where I think he's about to rip it from his scalp. I've seen him fuss with it during the day. Up and down more than usual, pulling it tight against his head, every flyaway piece frustrating him.

"Do we need to go for a run?" I offer, trying to distract him.

*We could fuck outside as his prey. He'll claim us in nature where we belong.* My wolf fantasizes.

It's appealing.

Ansel shakes his head, going for his stand mixer in the lower cupboard. He doesn't even pull it out all the way before his hair falls in his eyes, and he snarls in frustration. "Fuck!"

"Do you really want to cut it?" I feel like I can't help but double-triple-check.

With a nod, he speaks softly. "I know I'll likely regret it, but I feel uncomfortable, and it's never right. It's trapping me."

"Okay." I give a decisive nod. "Let's do it."

Scissors, clippers, a towel, and stripped down to my bra, I pull his hair back in a ponytail and then braid it. I hesitate. "I know it grows back, but last chance to stop."

"Do it." Ansel sounds deflated, but it's the acceptance phase instead of the 'I've lost' phase.

The scissors, clearly not used regularly, cut through the hair quite easily. I put it behind me on the counter so he doesn't see it and just keep working. The trimmers glide through the hair at the sides of his head after I'm done scissoring it into place. I won't claim to be great at this, but I've done it a few times before, and the fade is looking pretty even.

Ansel doesn't stop me; he doesn't even move.

"What are you thinking about?" I ask, trying to gauge the silence.

Harbinger isn't active. It's a calm serenity now, and if it weren't for the fact he's still upright, I'd almost think Ansel fell asleep.

"The last time I went for a haircut was with Walt, and I haven't even tried to get it cut since then. This feels right. I guess."

I turn off the clippers and walk around to face him. My eyes meet his. "I love you."

"I love you doesn't cover it, sunshine." He shakes his head. "It isn't contained in a four-letter word."

It takes me another ten minutes, and I'm very proud of my work. Short sides with it longer on top. When his bangs fall forward, they don't quite fall into his eyes.

Ansel looks in the mirror, and he smiles. "This is good."

I reach up and ruffle the top. He smiles, leaning into my touch.

"It all worked out in the end." I kiss him, wrapping my arms around his neck.

Ansel relaxes. Harry has calmed down, and it's back to more like the last time we were home together and at peace. But there's still something not right, and dread grows in my stomach.

"You're still planning on giving me a perfect claiming, even after all of this, aren't you?" I sigh.

"No." Ansel shakes his head. He pulls me tight against his chest, and I can hear the thrum of his beating heart. But over that, I hear his explanation. "I plan on making sure we're completely safe first. I need to know it's over. Part of me still feels like I'm back in that cell, and that this is a dream I'll maybe wake up from tomorrow with some terrible way to die waiting for me."

"I'm real," I tell him firmly. "This is real."

"I fucking hope so. It'll kill me if it isn't." Ansel runs his hands back through my hair before kissing me softly.

# CHAPTER 92
## MORRIGAN

After brunch, I've just finished getting dressed and have barely closed the bedroom door when I'm ambushed.

"I've got Morrigan. We're taking the truck!" Lena wraps her hand around my wrist, dragging me toward the back door. She whispers to me, "Shoes, now. Move."

"No!" Finn scolds from behind us. His footsteps, quick and heavy, follow us out the door.

I barely get my shoes out of the cubby before I'm dragged out the door.

Lena barrels outside, and I watch as she bumps shoulders with Ansel.

"Where you goin'?" Ansel's confusion matches my own as he steps to steady himself from where he was put off kilter.

"We need groceries!" Lena shouts back. "Hurry up, Morrigan!"

Finn places his hands on my biceps before stepping around me on the small back deck and making his way past Ansel.

Dumbfounded, Ansel and I watch them.

Finn wraps his arm around Lena, pulling her back from the

truck. They start having a quiet conversation when Ansel turns back to me.

"We're apparently going for groceries?" I smile at him. He furrows his brow, and Harry rises to the surface. "I'll stay if you want me to."

"Nope. You've gotta come," Lena shouts from across the driveway.

Finn stands silently, holding Lena against his chest.

Ansel looks over his shoulder at them, then rotates completely to me, blocking his face from them. Half whispering, half mouthing, he asks, "Do you want to go?"

Harry flashes into Ansel's eyes.

*No!* My wolf screams. Neither of us wants to leave, but there's also this nagging piece inside me saying I should go.

With a noncommittal shrug, I answer the question. "I want whatever is best for you."

Ansel sighs. "Go. If Lena is demanding it, there's gotta be something. She's not one for senseless joyrides."

The back door opens behind me, and Dinah steps out of the house. "Oh good, you didn't leave without me."

"Or me!" Thalia chirps. She had been wearing looser, baggy clothes, but since yesterday's pregnancy announcement, today she wears a more formfitting shirt, showing off the tiny baby bump she's sporting.

Ansel smiles. "So, what, all the women folk leaving us to our own devices?"

Dinah laughs. "Yeah. Of course, now go, day drink, and be merry."

"Alright, go before I change my mind." Ansel kisses the top of my head and steps backward down the stairs so he's no longer blocking my path.

I take one last glance over my shoulder at Ansel as I walk to the truck.

Finn must have gotten the keys away from Lena during their conversation because he hands them back to her with a tutting reminder. "Precious cargo."

She huffs at him, rolling her eyes. "I'll be fine. It's practice."

"God help me, Kathleen." Finn's smile doesn't match his scolding tone.

Once inside the truck, I see Dinah and Thalia get in one of the SUVs that the rest of the Ardeleans seemed to have materialized.

Cade stands by Ansel watching at the back door.

Finn buckles Lena's seat belt and gives her one last warning. "I mean it, faolan. I don't care that it's the middle of nowhere Utah."

"End of the Earth." She corrects him. "I will drive no faster than the speed limit. My phone is on, with me, and turned to full volume. If Cade is letting Thalia go, that should tell you something about how safe Nameless is."

With a small growl, Finn closes the truck door and steps back.

"Why did I—"

"Not yet," Lena says.

I sit quietly, no longer sure what to expect. She's been very supportive through this, so I trust whatever mission she's on.

We're fifteen minutes down the driveway when she speaks. "You need to know about Ansel's past."

A chill rakes down my body, and I can't help but shudder. "What about it?"

Lena drums her fingers on the steering wheel. "I'm willing to tell you as much or as little detail as you'd like, but you need to know what triggers him and why."

My wolf's hackles rise, and we're both on edge.

"Ansel's a victim of child sex trafficking." Lena says those words, and the pieces of Ansel, the quirks and what he's said, all make so much more sense. "He was born into it, and from what I've been able to track down, his mother was also a trafficking victim. Deacon says she's safe where she is, but knowing him, that could mean she's dead."

"How did . . . why did . . . what—" I don't even know what questions to ask because isn't that how it always is? In the wake of learning about a tragedy, you're left speechless. Questions swirl in my head, and one of them repeats until I speak it. "Is that what happened to Harry?"

"Yeah," Lena answers solemnly. She nods, following the curve of the driveway past the barely there trail that leads to the cabin my parents lived in. "Ansel didn't know he was a wolf. He didn't understand what the voice in his head was. And a reincarnated wolf, if Cade's explanation of The Leviathan is anything to go by, isn't great at explaining things, especially not to children. Whatever Harry had to do, to save himself and, consequently, Ansel, has broken down the communication between them. For all intents and purposes, he's feral. He's probably the least whole wolf living out here."

"That much I figured out." Visions of the house torn to shreds after my heat come back to me. I know that for a few nights following, Ben locked Ansel in the kennels to be sure he had control again. "Does everyone know, or is it just us?"

"Everyone who needs to know does. No one is concerned about it. Don't think we're waiting with bated breath for Ansel to go off the deep end. Especially after this week . . ." Lena sighs. She looks over at me before putting her eyes back on the driveway. "He really loves you." She pauses and draws a deep breath. "Dinah, of course, sees the future, but intuition says that it won't be long if you want the big fancy mating ceremony or wedding, and I'll absolutely make it happen for you."

"No," I immediately spit out. My face heats. "Not to be rude.

I don't . . ." I draw a deep breath. "I've never seen myself as the traditional hunt-mating-ceremony or big-fancy-dress-human-wedding type. And I know Ansel would be more stressed than he'd enjoy it. He's had more than enough stress over me."

"You don't have to protect him," Lena tells me. "I've been screening his movies, helping him with feeling accomplished in 'catching up' with what he didn't get out of his education." She makes air quotes, taking both hands off the steering wheel. "I know my gift doesn't come in handy a whole hell of a lot. But if it has done one thing, well, it's allowed me to give Ansel a space to be safe. I will gladly continue to do so, without fail and without complaint."

"But you're asking if I want to know so I can do it or help?" I follow along.

Lena nods, her fingers back to drumming on the wheel. "You don't have to. And if it weren't for how well you've held it together for him and the pack through this, I wouldn't have even offered. But you're not even aware of how good you are for him."

"It's because you haven't seen the shit between . . ."

Lena's laugh starts small with the shaking of her shoulders. She bites her lips together until the cackle escapes. "The irony of a fight you two had where he said, 'I'm not the one who ended up in a cell with a death sentence' about killed me the other night. First, I laughed because the two of you are so cute, then I cried because I was worried, and then I had to explain it to Finn, and by the time I was done, I was so exhausted. Not even the promise of an orgasm could make it better." She proves exactly how much she knows.

"Yeah," I groan and run my hand back through my hair. *Ugh. I don't have a hair tie.*

Lena pulls the one off her wrist and offers it to me. "There's probably one in the glove box, but Ansel sometimes forgets to restock Walt's truck."

"I'm surprised he keeps a second truck." I shake my head. "But I always assumed Dad was borrowing Ansel's spare."

"Oh, I saw the vision of your dad bringing it home. Ersilia hated it. Said it wasn't suitable for someone with a pup on the way, no back seat and all that. Your dad kept it at Ansel's house because he couldn't sell it back." Lena explains more about my past than even I knew. "Ansel bought a decent car for himself and let your dad borrow the truck. Because it seemed like a bad idea for one driver to have two vehicles, Ansel turned over the keys to your mom."

"It's weird that you remember . . . know? More about my life than I do." I voice that thought. "What I wouldn't do for more memories with Dad."

"I don't know a lot about trauma and what it does to memories, mostly because I have the gift that I do. But maybe being home, with Ansel, will help unlock it a bit for you?" Lena offers with a shrug.

The road to Nameless opens up, and the beginning of the little houses comes into view.

"I want to know what triggers Ansel." I square my shoulders, the decision made somewhere in my subconscious brain. "I'm not sure I want to know everything that happened. Maybe. But I want to know how to help him."

Lena nods. "On the way back, we can talk about it."

We've made it to the grocery store, and Lena turns off the truck.

She turns to face me in the seat. "Thank you."

"For what?" I frown at her.

"For accepting him as he is and not trying to change him." Lena bites her tongue for a minute. "A lot of people would have seen him as broken and as a project they can fix if they work hard enough. But you see him for him and want what he brings to the table."

My wolf hums with the thoughts of how good Ansel is to us, and I nod. "I'm not sure if I'm supposed to say you're welcome."

"Good. You're as awkward as the rest of us." Lena winks, and I jump at Dinah knocking on the hood of the truck.

"Come on bitches, I'm hangry." She groans and presses the back of her hand to her forehead, slumping her shoulders and looking up to the sky like she's withering away.

"So dramatic." Thalia rolls her eyes, and I climb out of the cab and follow them into the grocery store.

LENA TOLD ME EVERYTHING SHE KNEW ABOUT ANSEL. THE TORTURE, the drowning, the rape, the starvation, and the neglect. At every turn, I thought it would get better, that there would be a bright point. But one didn't come.

"He survived, and then what?" I shake my head, angry at the world. *Who would let this happen?*

"Then Harbinger saved him. Harry literally ripped them all to shreds. From what I've been able to dig up, the house he was kept in, the last one anyway, was found with pieces of at least six adult males." Lena's words bring with them a sickening feeling.

It's that morose feeling of relief that wrenches in your gut. At first you feel good for not being the one who suffered, only in turn to be stabbed with guilt. Guilt that someone else suffered in your place.

"And Harbinger . . ."

"Harbinger killed them and now keeps Ansel safe from those memories." Lena sighs and wrinkles her nose. "Though

I'm fairly certain that humans would be more inclined to recommend he see a therapist and talk through it."

"Good thing we're wolves. I can't imagine Ansel talking to a therapist." I shake my head.

"Oh, I can." Lena giggles. "But the therapist would have to start paying Ansel about midway through their second session."

"Touché." I force my shoulders down from around my ears and try to relax on the last bit of road coming home.

# CHAPTER 93
## ANSEL

DINAH'S WISH IS OUR COMMAND, AND IN TRUE 'FUCK IT' FASHION, we're sitting around the firepit with a roaring fire to keep away the cool spring air, day drinking, and melting the glass bottles and aluminum cans as delinquents do.

Zero comes from the guys' new cabins with a fresh six-pack. He tosses it into the cooler, covering it in ice before plopping down in a chair next to Judah.

In the whirlwind of everything, I hadn't gotten a chance to thank him.

I shake my head. "So, you made a run into town. Funny since that car of yours quit working."

"Oh?" Ezra turns in his seat to look at Zero.

"Funniest thing about that car . . . you're either the worst mechanic in the world or had the worst luck in the world." I finally get a moment to call Zero out on Morrigan's escape.

Zero matches my gaze before turning his head away partly in submission, but he'd have to turn around backward to wipe the shit-eating grin off his face. "Guess I'm that bad of a mechanic."

"Bullshit." Ezra fakes a cough before clearing his throat. "But I do love the meddling to get everyone's second favorite cousin and his mate together. Top-tier work."

The laughter coming from the group gets me. And when Zero looks back at me, I give him a nod of approval. I owe him one, that's for sure.

Two dinky little sedans round the bend of my driveway. I don't recognize the individuals inside the first vehicle, but the second has me locking my jaw.

Harry instantly goes on edge seeing Ersilia and Gerad. He's growling, and it rattles in my chest. I'm unable to stop it. Too many days of being in too much control. If we don't rip them apart before telling them to fuck off, it'll be one of those miracle things.

*At least Morrigan isn't here*, I assure him. They can't hurt her if she's not here.

"Oh, for fuck's sake," Cade groans. "He's really that stupid, isn't he?"

"Who is that?" Judah asks.

The cousins all rise with me to our feet. It's weird having my own little gang behind me. Sure, my pack of misfits behind me should make people terrified, but their reputations are as dangerously unhinged wolves, not deadly, calculated killers.

"Gerad Gardner, and I believe the first vehicle is his pack second, but I haven't had the unfortunate opportunity to meet him," Cade answers Judah for me.

As they head up the small hill to the house and the driveway, it's impossible to pull my eyes off the little cars and the trouble held inside.

Gerad's party parks in the middle of the driveway, blocking the entire area. *Inconsiderate asshole.*

Ersilia steps out of the car, and my heart sinks. The woman I blame for Walt's death casually steps foot on the property. It's more of an insult than that of Gerad coming back here. She should know better.

But that dark part of me inside Harry glows warm, ready for revenge.

"I see you were released." Ersilia folds her arms in front of her chest upon approach.

"Yeah. Apparently it's not a crime for your in-laws to hate you." I shrug, repeating the joke Ezra told earlier.

"Don't be gross," Ersilia snaps. "She's my child. You're twice her age and . . ."

I hate the implication that this was something I wanted. That this was something I planned or had worked for. Morrigan is mine, but not because I willed it.

"Ersilia, you could have called. We could have a conversation like civilized folk like we used to. What do you want? What did you really come here for?"

"We've come to take her home." Ersilia pulls one arm out from where it's crossed in front of her but keeps the other wrapped across her chest, protecting herself.

"My mate is not going anywhere with you," I growl.

The time for being nice is over.

Gerad finally gets out of the car and stands by his mate. He lazily motions with one hand to Cade and Judah standing behind me. "What, Ansel, afraid to face me yourself?"

"Fuck, he really doesn't know you, does he?" Cade laughs.

I shake my head. I'm not meeting Gerad on his level. "You could have faxed or emailed or mailed her papers. You didn't have to fly them out on your own. Awfully long journey for a little bit of paper."

"I'm here to bring her home." Gerad is looking over at Cade again.

Two mistakes: first, thinking The Leviathan is the bigger

threat, and second, thinking that he'll be the one to resolve this.

Harry hums in approval. The memories of the taste of blood in my mouth spur on my own excitement. The excitement to be done with this and to be able to claim our mate in peace.

Gerad continues with a huff of irritation. "Honestly, I'm surprised to see you alive. So, it's best you send her with me before anything . . . unfortunate . . . happens."

"She is never going back to California. You signing over her papers is a formality. I'm Ardelean and can override your pack charter if I have to, but I'd rather not," I respond, pulling out my Judah words and using the knowledge I've gained. *What is his definition of unfortunate?*

Harry snaps and snarls, more and more impatient and not impressed that I'm giving Gerad an out, for now.

I hear Cade's footsteps walking away, obviously turning his back on Gerad as a nonthreat, leaving me to fight my own battle. Judah's right behind him.

"Where are you going, Sovereign? This is your problem. Ansel is out of line," Gerad questions. He unintentionally spits a bit when he talks.

*Gross.*

"Oh, this is *so* not my problem," Cade says with a laugh. "But I'm grabbing a whiskey so I can drink and enjoy the show while Ansel puts the fear of Harbinger in you. Or kills you, whatever he's feeling up to today."

"Me too!" Ezra shouts from farther back in the yard.

"Three," Finn echoes.

The back door closes behind Cade as he goes into the house to get the good liquor.

I stand there staring down Gerad with a smile. I offered him to settle this peacefully. It was my intention to come to an understanding, but Gerad has proven that peace isn't an option. It sure as fuck isn't what I wanted, but I'd have accepted it for as long as I could to protect Morrigan. Peace won't satisfy Harry's call for blood.

No sooner does the door close behind Cade than a black SUV, not the same one Dinah took with Lena, comes around the bend to the house. Since Gerad and his second parked in the middle of the driveway, they're forced to drive through my 'lawn' and park by the garage. The doors open, and I'm not the only one watching them rather than focusing on the current conversation.

Gerad snaps his fingers to draw my attention back. "Just bring Morrigan out, and we'll be leaving. I don't want to have to chal—"

With a shake of my head, I hold up a finger, telling him to wait a minute. I can't think over the distraction. Harry listens, trying to hear his way into figuring out the presence of the black SUV. But the familiar hum of Walt's truck has me relaxing.

Lena, driving Walt's truck, and Dinah, driving one of the SUVs, follow the new SUV up to the house and pull around Gerad's shit parking job through my 'lawn' to park in the garage.

Morrigan sits in the passenger seat, her body tense.

Harry and I both assume fear. And it further escalates my feeling on the subject.

"Well, this got interesting," Cade says from a lot closer than I expected. He holds a glass with ice and whiskey.

"Who is that?" Gerad sneers. He snaps his fingers at me, again, trying to draw my attention back from watching for Morrigan. "I'm talking to you, Ansel. I'm challenging you for Morrigan to come home."

He recoils, not liking my gaze when it returns to him.

Harry is pressed completely forward, my eyes probably so

dark you can't find the pupil from the iris. The monster inside me is brushed so close to the surface of my skin I'm as tightly wound as I was in the courtroom, and this time, I don't have to contain him. He'll be coming out for a slaughtering. First Gerad, then his second, and whoever the other prick is, and maybe I even let him tear Ersilia apart.

Seeing red isn't just an expression. I get it now. The edges of my vision tint with it, focusing, hyperaware of it.

"Cade?" I ask for his attention quickly. "If I kill him, will you redistribute his pack for me? Maybe find someone with more sense to keep it."

"Oh, hell yes." Cade laughs.

I laugh. It's a sick, dark sound that comes out. I refuse to hold my anger back anymore. I'm done pretending life is all sunshine and blue skies, at least for today. Maybe tomorrow, when my enemy is dead and my mate is marked, I'll relax into bliss again. But not today.

Today I'm choosing violence.

It's unintentional, but a vision seeps forward.

*He gasps for air. Gerad's wolf, bleeding out between my teeth, sputters and clings to life. Without strength, his legs kick.*

*"Do it, Ansel." I hear her voice. Softly, Morrigan grants permission to end Gerad's life.*

*The sun hasn't even started to set yet.*

*So very soon.*

When the vision lets up, the visitors in the SUV and the women of my life come walking across the lawn toward us.

"Ansel?" Morrigan asks. Her steps slow, but flanked by

Dinah and Magnus O'Brien at her back, she keeps moving forward. "What's going on?"

I wait for her to get closer. The wind blows her scent to me, and I've missed it. I've missed holding her in my arms.

"I've challenged Ansel." Gerad's smile is wicked, curling up his lip.

"It's not a challenge." I shake my head but don't look away from him. "It'll be a slaughter."

# CHAPTER 94
# MORRIGAN

WE PULL AROUND THE FINAL TURN PAST THE GUYS' HOUSES, AND ALL the relaxing in the last fifteen minutes is worthless. Gerad, his Second, his Enforcer, and my mother are standing on Ansel's lawn.

"Who invited her? Ugh, well, at least this is gonna be interesting. I thought those were Corinth Security SUVs." She's leaned forward over the steering wheel to look around me at the black SUVs we had followed out here. She grimaces. "Don't tell Finn I didn't know it was Magnus."

"I won't. Who is she?" I ask, looking at the SUVs. The individuals are still sitting inside them.

"Meh. She's mostly harmless. It's Revecca Ardelean, my mate's brother's wife. Or my brother's biological sister. Queen of the Wolves and Romania." Lena yawns, opening the driver's door like she didn't just say there's more royalty here. "She doesn't bite. Throws a mean insult though. Don't tell her, but I almost like her."

*My mate's brother's wife.* Finn O'Leary is Magnus O'Brien's brother. The head of the Irish Mafia and The Pricolici.

Seat belt unbuckled, I get out of the truck, trying not to panic. Gerad in the yard. Queen of the Wolves and Irish Mafia in the vehicle next to us. Granted, meeting Cade and Thalia Alden was nowhere near as scary as I imagined it would be, but fuck.

"Breathe." Lena wraps her arm around me. She's already come all the way around the truck.

A behemoth steps out of the driver's seat of the black SUV and quickly walks around to the other side without so much as a backward glance. Then he returns, escorting a woman whose face I vaguely recognize as Queen Revecca Ardelean. She's dressed down from what I assume a queen would wear. She wears dark wash denim in wide flares and a fluffy blouse paired with a pointed-toe shoe. It almost looks like she belongs in Utah. Almost but not quite.

I don't remember if I'm supposed to bow or curtsey or offer my hand out to shake. The ridiculous information from the etiquette classes Gerad made me take wasn't a priority to retain in my mind, so it was purged.

"She's stunning." Revecca's eyes are locked on me, and I'm more than a little on edge. "No wonder Harbinger latched on. But it's deeper than that, your wolf has locked to him. So tight it's probably impossible to pull her from your depths without him." As she speaks, she tilts her head to the side. "We should keep an eye on that."

A knot forms in the pit of my stomach. *An eye on that?*

"Vex. You're doing that thing again," the man behind her murmurs softly, a thick Irish accent clinging to each word. "Look how scared she is."

"Oh." Revecca draws a deep breath and then sighs. She physically purposefully slouches. "I'm sorry. I don't mean to scare you. It isn't a bad thing. There's nothing for you to be fearful of."

Lena snorts. "She tries, doesn't she?"

"Little wolf, good to see you." The behemoth steps forward and wraps his arms around Lena in a quick hug.

"Good to see you, Magnus." Lena greets him before letting him go, and then she and Revecca give each other a quick hug.

*Okay. Maybe The Pricolici isn't scary.*

"May be worth coming over here," Dinah says a little loudly from where she is on the other side of the vehicles.

Magnus ushers us out from between the truck and the SUV.

When we step out from between the truck and the SUV, the view past the silver rental cars down the small hill is exactly what I thought I'd see. Anger and hatred are written all over Ansel's face in the wrinkles of his narrowed eyes and the darkness of Harbinger as he stands toe to toe with Gerad.

"Relax, Morrigan," Dinah says beside me. "Ansel can handle himself."

That doesn't make me feel better.

My wolf presses forward, rising at the call of Harbinger.

Ansel still didn't claim me last night, but after everything we've been through, it feels like we're on the same wavelength. Though, from the solemn faces across the Ardeleans and our pack, it's evident no one is currently happy to be here.

When we reach the group of people, down off the side of the driveway, I hear low growls, and a snarl rolls from Gerad.

I can remember so vividly when that snarl used to scare me. It's just a sound now. It means nothing.

The couple of hours that we were gone to the store and back wasn't long, but seeing Ansel isn't enough. I want to be wrapped up in his arms, but as I approach him, it becomes more and more evident I shouldn't. I stand as close to Ansel as he tolerates. I know when to stop because he pulls his eyes from Gerad, and the look acts like quick-drying cement. Within reach but not so close that I could be hurt in a fast shift. I take all the comfort of proximity I can get.

It's interesting how Gerad used to be a threat in my life. Yesterday, his words held so much power over my world. But today, twenty-four hours later, Gerad is merely an inconvenience in. I desperately want to remove that inconvenience.

"Ah, would you look at that." Magnus walks behind Gerad's pack Second.

The way Magnus is built, large and broad like Finn, he towers over Gerad's Second like he's a lanky teenager and not a mature muscled wolf.

"I didn't know you had business with Gardner." Magnus looks between Ansel and Cade.

"We don't," Cade answers with a groan. "It's a complicated discussion. Why? Has Gerad been doing business with you?"

Magnus only answers with a quiet "Hmmm."

Gerad reeks of fear. His head moves back and forth, like on a swivel, looking at all of us but constantly checking that Ansel hasn't advanced on him.

*What was Gerad doing with the Irish Mafia?*

The other Ardeleans and our pack, mine and Ansel's, stand behind us. A small army of individuals against four.

Mom, Gerad, his Second, and his Enforcer are all realizing how big of a mistake they made coming here.

Magnus comes to stand nearly directly across from me in this semicircle we've all seemed to form. His lips don't smile, but his eyes do. "Small world because in all this, that must make you his daughter?"

Ansel snarls and snaps at Magnus.

"He's my mother's mate. My father is dead," I answer, refusing to even acknowledge a status as his 'stepdaughter' in this world.

Told off, or seeming so, Magnus diverts his attention back

to Gerad. "God didn't give you enough brains to be smart, just enough to be dangerous." Magnus shakes his head and crosses his arms in front of his chest. "Well, Morrigan, you'll have to forgive me, but as Pack Alpha, I'll have to deny your intention to one of my Quartermasters."

If sound was a volcano, then Ansel erupts. My bones rattle against it.

I go to move toward him, but during the blast, Revecca has stepped between us.

She rests her hand on Ansel's shoulder. "Ansel, stop."

It's not an Alpha command; I've heard so many of them in my life. This is stronger in a quiet power sense, like the thunder of a lightning strike you never saw. Her words quiet some of the rumbling coming from Ansel.

"He deserves death, but you can't be his executioner," she says in that quiet voice, urging him to listen.

Beyond her, Gerad has taken a step back. I catch him eye fucking the shitty car, like if he can get there, he can save himself.

Magnus growls, and Gerad stops his retreat.

Revecca is whispering, but I make out enough. "Ansel, I know you must hate him for everything he's done and everything he's put you through, but Harbinger isn't steady enough for you to start killing for anything other than necessity."

Ansel's lip is curled in a snarl. "He has to die."

"At someone else's hand," Revecca agrees, her voice louder but still with a confident firmness to it.

I begged Ansel not to kill Gerad when I first got here. I knew if he killed Gerad, a part of my mom would die as well, being his fated mate. That part of her that died would form a black hole and sink all of her until she ceased to exist completely. I didn't want that for her, but now I don't have the empathy to care. She stood by while I was being hurt. She was complicit in them withholding food. *No mother does that to her own child and loves them. Fuck her.*

Ansel shakes his head, ignoring Revecca's statement, and steps past her to get closer to Gerad.

Revecca looks at me and then to Cade. But I don't know what I can say to make this different or better.

She shields herself from Gerad's watchful eyes and is barely audible. Revecca mostly mouths the words "Did he claim you?"

I shake my head.

Revecca's hand flies to her heart, and relief washes over her features. She nods and mouths, "Good. That will help."

*I don't understand.* I purse my lips, trying to gain more information, but I'm pulled away from my conversation with Revecca.

"I'll fight my Alpha's challenge in his place." Gerad's Enforcer sounds so confident in himself as he tries to draw Ansel's focus away from Gerad.

Ansel shakes his head. "You shouldn't have come. You didn't need to die today. But you're here. Is that you volunteering to go first?"

"Ansel," Mom says, her voice panicked and higher pitched. "We don't have to do this. We'll leave her here. We'll just go."

With a cutting glare, Ansel silences Mom.

Revecca turns away from me and walks to Ansel again. "I can't let you, in good faith, end them, not when Harbinger is so out of control. It was bad before, but if you do this, there will be no leaving it. I will have to put you back together, and I'm not sure what that will mean for you."

"He's feral, isn't he?" Gerad accuses, correctly. It further aggravates the situation, especially since Gerad has lost all sense of fear. His air of superiority, along with the stick up his ass, has yet to be dislodged. "The great and terrible Leviathan keeps Harbinger as a pet, knowing he's a rabid dog, no better than his delinquents."

Ansel snaps.

Mom screams.

Fabric tears.

Snarls erupt.

People move in between me and the fight, backing up, changing places, and I lose track of the messy fight for a moment.

Ansel is gone, lost to Harbinger.

Cade stands by my side, his arm in front of me keeping me back. Thalia pokes her head up next to me.

It's three against one. Gerad's wolf, his Enforcer, and his pack Second are all in a tangle, fighting against Harbinger. My mother is crumpled on the ground, watching in horror.

I push to move past Cade, but he holds me back.

He speaks at normal volume, but it sounds quiet against the noise of battling wolves. "Trust me, Morrigan, he's fine. Getting in Ansel's way will only get you hurt."

The snarling only gets more and more intense.

Aside from Harbinger, I can hardly tell who is who.

One of them clamps down on Harbinger's head, pulling at his ear.

I look away, not wanting to close my eyes and seem weak.

The Ardeleans and our pack have come to stand in groups out of the way of the fight but watching with interest, some more worried than others about what will come.

Revecca looks like she's going to be sick. Her skin is ghostly white, but Magnus rests his hands protectively on her shoulders, ready to move her out of harm's way in an instant.

Finn keeps Lena tucked against his side while Cade protects us, me and Thalia, keeping us back and ready to move us away from the violence.

A massive yelp rings out, again and again, broadcasting pain.

My attention snaps back to the fight just as Harbinger violently shakes one of the wolves by the shoulder. He then rips his teeth into the wolf's side, drenching his white fur in the wolf's blood. Gerad's Second loses his leg as Harbinger rips it from its socket and casts it aside. As soon as the appendage leaves his mouth, Harbinger turns back to the wolf now attacking at his flank.

It's Gerad. He gets a mouthful of Harbinger and pulls. Harbinger responds with a massive snarl and roar. He turns, pulling himself out of Gerad's grasp but not without doing damage to himself.

I count the wolves I can see. Gerad, his Second, and Harbinger. There are only three. I look for Gerad's Enforcer but can't find him.

I look around, waiting for a surprise attack, something, anything that can cause trouble for the fight.

My blood is roaring in my ears, and my breaths are coming short. But I'm not afraid for Harbinger. It's like the energy of a club when you're just moving to the music. We're all standing on edge in anticipation of the fight but not needing to be armed.

That's when I notice it. A body, in human form, is underneath the fight of the wolves, limp.

"It's so funny watching Harry play with his kills," Ezra says from somewhere down the row.

"Ezra," Dinah scolds.

"What?" Ezra shrugs. "We all know Harry could have ended this minutes ago. He wants it to hurt. He's enjoying watching them suffer."

It's morbid, but most of all, it's true. I've seen how fast

Harbinger laid out Sherman. It would have been a quick death had I not stepped in.

Gerad is panting. He's cut badly, his stomach torn open, and Harbinger's jaw is latched around his throat.

"Do it," I whisper. It's barely audible, and maybe it's only correlation not causation, but Harbinger finishes Gerad off.

A shrill cry breaks out through the death gurgle. It's followed by another wolf, my mother's wolf, attacking Harbinger.

"You shouldn't see this." Cade tries to turn me away from the fight, but I stop and don't let him usher me farther.

But there's nothing to see. Harbinger doesn't engage in a messy fight. It's one small, sharp movement, and my mother's body lies still on the ground.

I gasp. I don't know what causes the sound, but it pulls Harbinger's attention to me, and he charges. Eyes locked on Cade, he's coming for the kill.

The Leviathan explodes from Cade's body to protect him. But the legends say that Harbinger can kill The Leviathan.

"No!" I scream at the top of my lungs. "Harry. No!"

Teeth and jaws connect with fur and skin as The Leviathan defends himself from Harbinger.

Revecca runs to my side. She grabs my hand in hers. "Say it again. Loud."

I feel ridiculous holding her hand and screaming. We should be doing something more.

"Do it," she demands.

"Harry! No! Stop!" The words come out, but there's a new power to them.

Harbinger and The Leviathan come to a standstill, panting and bloody.

It's a standoff.

"Tell him to shift back," Revecca says quietly.

"Come back," I beg. "Harry, give me Ansel back."

A wet cough and what looks like an excruciating shift bring Harbinger under Ansel's control again. After a few minutes of all of us doing nothing but staring and breathing, Cade shifts back. He walks to Ansel and offers him his hand.

"You good?" Cade asks, pulling Ansel to his feet.

"Sorry." Ansel doesn't answer the question aloud, but he does shake his head.

Revecca lets go of my hand. She and Cade pass each other without any growls.

He gets to Thalia and wraps her in his arms. It's then I hear something other than the sounds directly connected to my brain or to Ansel.

Thalia's hyperventilating, and he talks her through breathing.

Cade takes Thalia toward the firepit, comforting her with a gentle hand on her stomach.

I focus beyond them. Revecca's staring at Ansel as if she's assessing.

She shakes her head and spits, "I told you he couldn't handle that. Now look at what you've done."

Ansel nods but doesn't pull his eyes off a patch of dirt he's locked onto.

"You can feel him snapped, can't you?" Revecca keeps scolding. I'm not breathing. I know I'm not. "You fractured your wolf over revenge. And what if we weren't here? The only thing that saved your life is the fact that Morrigan was here."

She steps closer to Ansel and yells, getting in his face. "I take no pride in having to separate wolves from their humans. I take no pleasure in having to hurt you to heal you."

Ansel's shock reflects my own. He hangs his head, taking her beratement.

"Think about what would have happened to her." Revec-

682

ca's voice quakes with emotion. "Think about what happened to Lena and imagine how much worse it would be for Morrigan. All of you." Revecca turns and looks at the group of us. "So many of you treat your wolves like they will just always be there for you, and you've forgotten the gift that it is. I can't always put you back together." Revecca turns back to Ansel. "I will put you back together. I will put you back together because it's easier to set a fracture than it is to convince a wolf to live without their mate."

She looks up at Ansel with a shake of her head. "Go get cleaned up. We'll deal with the dead," Revecca orders coldly. "Your mate deserves better from you."

Ansel turns to go, and I want to run to him. When I take a step forward, Magnus's hand is on my shoulder. "You can't go with him. It's not safe."

"It's not safe?" I repeat.

"We need to talk." Revecca walks toward me and then starts walking off toward the desert.

Anger follows her, and I'm not sure that going with her is any safer than going with Ansel.

Magnus turns me and, with a palm to the center of my spine, pushes me. "Go with her. God knows she'll get lost if you don't."

"You're on my shit list, Magnus. Don't tempt me," Revecca snarls.

Revecca walks fast. She finds the trail that leads to the guys' cabins and then starts down the running path.

Ten minutes later, she finally starts speaking. "Ansel completely fractured from Harbinger today."

I stop walking. *No. No. No.*

"Come on." Revecca coaxes softly. The anger is still there, but my fear must trigger something inside her. "I can fix him. But you need to know what the next few days and weeks will look like. I can't stay here that long to make sure everything sets appropriately."

"You're sure you can fix him?" I don't keep moving, not until she looks me in the eye.

"I'm the mother of all wolves. Child, if I say I can do something, I can, and I will." The scolding in her voice softens as she puts a hand on my shoulder. "It was a clean break. It's not like they weren't practically in two to begin with, considering how feral he was." She walks her fingers on my shoulder to my back before pulling me closer to her and then making me walk with her. "I can't stand still. I'm too angry. It's how people get killed."

"Okay, keep the queen walking." I whisper a mental reminder to myself.

Revecca snorts before continuing. "Tonight, I'll separate Ansel from Harbinger. He'll need to sleep. Actually sleep, for a few hours. A full night would be best."

"He'll be . . ."

"Human." Revecca nods. "If it were just that he was still feral, it would be nothing. A few moments to calm his wolf, but a fracture, I'll need time. Tomorrow morning, after Ansel sleeps and gets rest, I'll gift him back Harbinger."

"I thought if a wolf lost their wolf, there was no going back? Like you couldn't get a new animal back." I shake my head thinking about it. "When my wolf was gone, Gerad tried to turn me since I didn't have a wolf. It should have stuck?"

"God, it's a good thing that man is dead. I am very concerned about who it is that teaches you all things about being a wolf here because no one seems to know what is going on." Revecca's eyes are wide and express genuine concern. "To answer your question, it's complicated. He's an Ardelean, so I'm not releasing his animal, but I am reclaiming him."

"I don't understand," I admit.

"It's like . . . a library." Revecca shakes her head. "I can call for each of the wolves of the Ardelean Bloodline and for every gift. I have a limited ability to reclaim them to The Pricolici and keep them to heal them. If you had fractured, it would be another story. Your best bet would be for me to try to reset it and give you a few years before it happened again."

"But Ansel is an Ardelean." I'm keeping up with her footsteps, but admittedly, the thought of Ansel, human, echoes in my brain really loudly and distracts me from everything else.

Revecca stops walking. "Morrigan, until I give Ansel his wolf back tomorrow, he may get those memories that Harbinger has been keeping from him. It may be for just one night until Harbinger resettles and protects him again, or it could be permanent."

"No." I shake my head, but there's nothing I can do.

This isn't up to me. Of course, Lena told me, and now I know. I wanted to keep him safe from them.

"It's not for certain. But Harbinger will be whole. They will be back to speaking again, it won't be this fractured state." Revecca gives me a soft smile. She brings the back of her hand to my face and wipes a tear away with the back of her knuckle. "Don't cry about this, Morrigan. It will be for the best. You'll have many more years together, and the future will be so much brighter for it."

"And what about me?" I thread my hands behind my head and look up at the sky. "I'm not trying to be selfish, but you said my wolf is tied to his, and I just got her back."

"Nothing gets past you, does it?" Revecca laughs. "Your wolf's devotion to Harbinger will help get him resettled. It's one of the reasons I'm not worried about reclaiming him for a night. You'll be fine. You may not be able to shift, but it seems your enemies are gone and you're surrounded by more Ardeleans here than there are in Romania. You should be very safe."

Revecca starts walking again. "Then three days after tomorrow, he will have to claim you, and you will have to claim him back at the same time. Three days is the most important part."

"You won't be here?" I get ahead of her and walk backward to watch her.

"I can't stay that long. I shouldn't have come to start with, but The Pricolici wouldn't settle." Revecca smiles at me. "Don't be scared. Tonight he'll be human. Tomorrow he'll be wolf. You wait two days, and on the third day, you claim each other. I heard all about how you two are as mates. There shouldn't be an issue."

"There's no other way to fix this?" I shake my head, ready to beg for another solution.

"None you'll like." Revecca raises an eyebrow. "Either Harbinger gets reclaimed and returned, or we kill them both."

My steps falter. She might as well have poured a glass of cold water over me.

"See. I told you you wouldn't like it." She stops and holds her hands up, looking at the flat, open desert around us. "How is it the landscape is so barren, and yet his house has disappeared?"

"It's around that hill." I point to the only bit of cover in the elevation.

"Ridiculous. A town with no name, a street with no sign, it shouldn't surprise me. The legends of Harbinger say he always seems to find someplace unique to reside." Revecca continues along the trail, bringing me along with her.

*Nameless, End of the Earth Road, Utah.* She's right. There is no place quite like it.

# CHAPTER 95
## ANSEL

WHEN I ASKED CADE WHAT IT WAS LIKE WHEN HE FRACTURED WITH The Leviathan, I thought for sure he was making up how bad it fucking hurt. For every single thing Harry has ever destroyed in my house, none of it feels like the damage he's doing inside my body currently. I manage to get into the house without falling down, but in the shower, I'm braced against the wall, trying to wash the blood off me.

*Fuckin' Cade tracked down Thalia feeling like this?* I draw slow, deep breaths. *Fuck, when did I get to be so old?*

Morrigan's haircut proved to be well worth it. The blood I wash down the drain would have taken so much longer if I had to clean it out of the long strands.

With the water from the shower turned off, I hear voices in the house, and it instantly stirs Harry back up inside me. He's thrashing and looking for anything he can take his violence out on. As much as I don't want to be locked up anymore, I can't sleep like this. I'll need to be locked up downstairs, at least until we know what we're gonna do with me.

Towel wrapped around my waist, I open the bathroom

door, letting the steam escape. The cold air feels good against my skin.

"Put pants on and get back out here. No time to waste," Revecca growls from the kitchen.

I look over my shoulder but can't see her. She must be standing close to the coffee maker and the sink.

I pull a pair of jeans out of the drawer of my dresser but can't bother to put them on. Cuts are still open and bleeding along my body. The shower cleaned off everyone else's blood, but my own doesn't stop leaking out of all my fancy new scars. I grab a pair of pajama pants and pull them on with my boxers, then head back out to my kitchen.

Morrigan sits at the end of the counter, right where it suits her to be. Harry freezes seeing her, but only for a second, and then he adjusts his focus toward Revecca and Magnus. Threats he wants to destroy and tear apart. It's awful trying to keep him together, but I don't have a choice.

Harry, trying to win against my breaking body, snarls and, with force, slams against the barrier I'm barely able to keep up to hold him inside me. He sends me images of the last fight. Killing Ersilia again and again. He thrashes, fighting me, trying to get out.

Hand gripping my side, I nearly double over in pain.

"No, we don't have time." Revecca shakes her head, but I'm not sure if there had been something else she had asked while I was focused on staying in one piece.

"Vex." Magnus says her name kinda nice like, but with that warning Finn uses on Lena.

"I don't know what you're talking about." I try to catch up, but I can't even keep my eyes open. There's too much input to sort as I fight off Harry.

"Revecca can fix Harry, but she needs to . . ." Morrigan stops talking and swallows hard. "So have you ever imagined what it's like to be human?"

"What?" I peel open one eye to look at her.

"Well, you're gonna find out." She smiles at me, but it's a funny one. Like she doesn't mean it, but not like when she was smiling at Princeton and faking nice.

"Human?" I shake my head. At the thought of Princeton, more anger rises inside me. "Fuck," I whisper and close my eyes again.

*Come on, Harry. Chill just a little bit.*

"At least you're already bleeding everywhere." Revecca's voice is closer.

I force open my eyes to see her within stabbing distance of me, given the knife in her hand.

She runs the sharp edge across the bottom of her palm. Once blood blooms on her hand, she presses it against the open wound on my side.

"Ow." I grit my teeth through Harry snarling. *Don't hurt her.*

Then the pain of holding Harbinger back slips away. Everything seems less intense. Well, everything except every single little cut and bruise I've got on all parts of my body. Those are starting to hurt more. And the clarity of my brain lets me start catching up to everything that's going on.

"Human?" I look at Revecca.

She holds one finger up to me. With her eyes closed, she draws deep, slow, steady breaths. She cocks her head to one side and then the other. And when she opens her eyes, they're nearly black. From seeing the abyss of Harry's eyes in the mirror, I know I'm staring back at a piece of myself.

*Human.* I nod. "No wolf."

I don't know what to think or feel. I guess it's like the dino movie. If you can't handle the responsibility of a monster, you shouldn't be letting them out to play. Today, I definitely had my privilege of being a wolf revoked, and I earned that.

"It's temporary," Morrigan says, quickly drawing my attention. "It's just Revecca's helping. You get him back in twelve or so hours."

"It'll be more than twelve." Revecca puts her hand to her mouth and licks the blood clean. "It's impressive how much pain you've been keeping."

*What are you supposed to say to that?* I don't have an answer to that, so I nod along.

MAGNUS CARRIED REVECCA OUT OF MY HOUSE AND DOWN TO ONE OF the guest cottages they claimed as their own. Finn, Lena, and Dinah come and stitch me up. They used little needles of things to numb the spots where they were stitching, and Dinah procured some sort of cocktail of painkillers I took when they were done. Being stitched up like this doesn't feel real.

It might be the drugs, but I don't even feel all that bad about me. But I feel terrible about her.

Morrigan has stayed out of the way. Dancing in and out and getting things for the medical team trio of cousins the entire time they were here.

"Just turn the light off when you guys go to bed." Dinah nods. "I'm going to hang out on the deck until then. I'll sleep here in the house because you're pretty much one fall from a bad day."

I wince, trying to shake my head at her. "I'm without a wolf, hardly makes me fragile."

"There's literally nothing that can't kill you. It's a miracle all humans survive every day." Dinah laughs and walks out through the back sliding door, closing it behind her.

Silence blankets the main floor, where Morrigan and I are standing practically in the middle of the room.

She watches me with tears in her eyes, bringing her hands to her face and then back down.

Morrigan looks away and fights back a sob.

I don't know where to start with apologizing, but I know I have to try.

"I'm sorry," we say at the same time.

"You don't have to be sorry." I shake my head, not offering her to go first. "You did nothing wrong. You saved my life when it would have better served you to let me die."

Morrigan shakes her head. "No. No. We're not doing that anymore. I don't want to hear it. I want to hear you still love me. That you don't blame me for the fact that you're currently human. I need to know that at the end of this, we're going to be okay."

"I love you. None of this is your fault. We're going to be okay." I tell her the honest answers, the ones that make me feel better about this, about us.

And, fuck, I hope they're true because I killed four people in front of her. I killed her mother in front of her.

"Can I hug you?" Morrigan asks, looking lost, standing there awkwardly.

"I don't know. Dinah made it sound like hugs could be lethal. I've never seen a human hug someone else before." I try to shake the mood through humor.

Morrigan steps closer to me like she's truly afraid she'll break me.

When she gets within reach, I wrap my arm behind her shoulder and pull her to me. I can feel the tender tug of stitches and skin, but the painkillers don't let it bother me a whole lot. And it's all worth it to feel her body against mine.

Each breath I pull is thick and full of her scent. It's not as strong as it was before. But I can still smell her. I know that scent.

"I'm sorry about Ersilia. You shouldn't have had to see that."

"She deserved it," Morrigan says quietly. "She attacked you. But worse, she stood by when they attacked me. No mother, no good mother, would do that to her child. You killed them and saved me from a future of what-ifs and wondering if we're really safe. Just like you said last night."

"Last night, a lifetime ago." I draw another deep breath. "Think Revecca's intending on giving Harry back to me? Or are you gonna be okay keeping a human mate?"

"She'll give him back." Morrigan sounds guilty. "Could you talk me through how to bake cookies?"

"I can make you cookies if you want." I'm exhausted, and it feels like I'm kind of drunk, but if she wants cookies, it's what she'll get.

Morrigan shakes her head. "Yeah. No. You'll sit on the stool and tell me all the things I'm doing wrong, and then you'll eat them when they come out of the oven and not complain."

"You've been hanging out with Lena and Dinah too much." I slide my hand down her back to her ass and give it a squeeze. "You'll want the stand mixer."

"Yeah. I'm going to fan girl and freak out over the fact that I'm on a first-name basis with your cousins later." Morrigan nods. "But we need to talk, and standing here staring at each other is awkward. Now I know why you do your come-to-your-senses chats in the kitchen."

"It's close to the alcohol if I need a drink when I'm done?" I tell her my logic.

"No, because you bake when you're stressed and—" Morrigan struggles to get my stand mixer out of the cabinet.

"Nee—"

"No," Morrigan growls. I stay seated on the stool. "—and then when you're done with the stress you get the chocolatey goodness."

I walk Morrigan through the easy peanut butter cookie recipe, the one we now call the 'first official food of the coup,' and she starts one batch. Then, for the second, she adds chocolate chips. Which makes me think that when we're celebrating a victory, chocolate should always be involved.

I tell her it's a little late to do this much baking, but she shows me a text from Dinah that says she'll clean up as long as one batch has chocolate.

"I talked with Revecca," Morrigan says as she confidently uses the stand mixer. "And without Harry, you might start remembering everything from your past. Or, when you get him back, it'll come back then. She wasn't exactly super clear on that. But she said that he's likely going to talk to you again. It'll be different."

My nodding along with what she's saying worries Morrigan, and she stops talking to turn the stand mixer off.

"What's wrong, sunshine?"

"Why are you so calm?" She shakes her head. "You're just not worried about it?"

"Why?" I shake my head and point to the timer. "Chicken."

It starts ringing, and Morrigan silences it before opening the oven and taking out the first pan of cookies.

"Why are you so calm? Why wouldn't you be worried about what getting to talk with Harry would be like?" She isn't asking what she really wants to ask. But I can't figure out what she's trying to say.

"Cookies are good. Put in the new pan," I instruct. "You can place the hot pan on the stove while you get the cooling stand out."

When she's done moving the trays around, she gives an accomplished huff and smiles.

"I'm not worried about talking to Harry because, at this point, I'm just lucky to be alive. I'll figure out what it all means and how it is to live with a wolf who wants to talk to me." I shrug with the assumption. "I would rather do all that with the possibility of being with you forever than watch everyone else live mated, happy, and raisin' a yard of pups without me. Without you."

I brace for her to tell me there's something else. That Revecca taking Harry to fix him means I've lost this for us.

Morrigan spins the chicken timer and sets it down before picking up a hot, melting peanut butter cookie from the cooling rack. "So, that's it. You're fine? It'll be fine?"

"I never said it'll be easy, but there aren't a lot of options that give me what I want, Morrigan." I smile at her, holding my hand out for a cookie. "I want to live the rest of my life as your mate and discuss how that life is going to look. If that means I've got to face my demons and sort out how to live with Harry being more communicative, then fuck it. How hard can it possibly be? The rest of you do it, why can't I?"

"And the memories?" She pushes on the part I keep trying to walk past.

"Revecca knew for sure I'd get them back?" I question.

Morrigan thinks about it but shakes her head.

"Worry about that when we come to it." I dismiss it.

The sliding glass door opens.

"You two done? Can I have cookies?" Dinah asks sheepishly.

I nod. "I'm fucking exhausted. And I feel hot."

"Mmm, it's called healing. Super fun. You should do it more often." Dinah laughs as she picks up the bowl from the stand mixer.

"Those go in next." Morrigan's concern gets a laugh from me and Dinah.

"Yeah. She really just wants to pick the chocolate chips out of the batter," I tell Morrigan. "I'm not saying Dinah doesn't like fully baked cookies, but there's a reason I have four bowls for that mixer."

"Go to bed, old man. Tomorrow you're getting a wolf." Dinah narrows her eyes at me and pulls the bowl closer to her chest, guarding it with her life. Her expression changes when she looks at Morrigan. "Go. I've got this. I swear I'll even bake some of them."

Morrigan nods, walking toward me. I try to hop off the stool like I normally would and stumble.

"Oh shit." Morrigan catches one of my shoulders.

"I'm good." I brace the counter with my other hand. "Forgot I'm beaten up."

"It's the good drugs. Will make you see things if you're not careful," Dinah says between a mouthful of cookie dough.

Morrigan helps me into the bedroom, closing the door and turning the lights off behind us. I can feel the tension in the room shift.

Lying down in bed with her, I whisper, "I love you, Morrigan. That hasn't changed. It feels different, but it hasn't changed."

"I love you." Morrigan nuzzles in against my side. I can only imagine how the antiseptic smells, but she doesn't care. "As long as you still love me, it's gonna be fine."

"People died today. I failed on a lot of levels. But still can't make myself call it a bad day." I yawn, and my body plummets toward sleep.

# CHAPTER 96

## ANSEL

I've been listening to the sounds of home invaders coming and going in my house for at least a couple of hours. It's not as easy to tell who it is.

"How long do we let them sleep?" It's Magnus's voice this time.

"We're not asleep," Morrigan growls.

I laugh because until about ten seconds ago, she was all sleep sounds and snuggles.

"Stupid fucking bladder." Morrigan crawls out of the bed and opens the bedroom door.

Sunlight streams in from the big windows at the back of the house, meaning it's most certainly closer to noon than it is to dawn.

"Excellent. I'm not suitable for Harbinger, so either you're taking him back or I'm releasing him," Revecca growls from the kitchen. "It's impossible for me to fathom living with him. It's no wonder they claimed that Great Uncle Nicolae was such a terrible person to be around."

I climb out of bed and follow their voices to the kitchen. Revecca's sitting on the island with Magnus standing between her legs. I divert my gaze, but Magnus moves quickly.

"Knife?" Revecca asks, holding her hand out. Magnus pulls one out of a holster on his belt and hands it to her. "Come on, outside. In case he explodes."

"Sure, why not." I follow Revecca out onto the back deck.

Her heels click on the stairs as we descend to the lawn.

I'm nervous, not knowing what to expect. I've seen a wolf turned before. It was terrifying on more than one level. Though I'm already sore, not a lot left to rip open to give me one.

Morrigan and Magnus stand on the deck at the top of the stairs. And the rest of my family and pack mill about in the yard, keeping their distance.

Revecca ushers me away from the deck and starts along the path.

*I guess we're going for a walk.* I walk barefoot next to Revecca along the worn path, glad for no prickly cacti out of place.

"I wasn't able to make him whole." Revecca sighs, sounding disappointed in herself. "I stabilized him. So it will be a vast improvement of what it was before."

"I'm glad to be getting him back. But, stabilize?" I question. *The possibilities for the guys could be endless if I'd be able to stop the spiral they go through.* "What sort of stabilizing could there be?"

"Well, it's . . ." Revecca sighs. "It's the same thing I may have done to Sherman yesterday."

I stop in my tracks and look at her. My body leans away from her. Sure, I was thinking about what it would mean, but why did no one tell me? "What did you do to Sherman?"

"Ansel. He's fine. He'll never notice anything different about himself, and you won't either. What I've given him, and am giving Harbinger back to you with, is a . . ." She holds her hands out in front of her, stretching her hands back and forth. "Elastic? Barrier?"

The way she looks for words I can empathize with, so I give her a minute. But my thoughts are firmly locked on Sherman. *If he's not okay . . .*

"It's like a thing that keeps everything together. His wolf can't become more feral and devolve further, but it also makes it so he won't fracture. Sherman will always have, at minimum, the same control he has now. It can only get stronger, if he so chooses," Revecca tries to explain.

"That's . . ." *Nice?* I bobble my head on my shoulders a little. Now it's my turn to look for words. "I'd have liked you to ask first."

Revecca laughs and rolls her eyes. "Magnus said the same thing, and his pestering insistence is the only reason I told you."

"Asking forgiveness is easier than permission." I nod, understanding.

"Let's get Harbinger back to you and then see how you settle." Revecca smiles at me.

Harbinger is in her eyes, and I nod, ready for whatever this is going to feel like.

Revecca grabs hold of my hand and slices open the stitches that Finn put in last night. It stings like a son of a bitch, and I grimace.

Revecca barely even flinches when she slices open her palm again and presses her wound to mine. "Deep breath. Focus on him."

As I lock gazes with her, it takes only a moment before he fades from her eyes and I feel him slam into my brain. *Some things never change.*

With a relieved sigh, Revecca lets go of my hand, and I close my eyes, focusing on him settling back into my brain. *Alright? We good? Need to shift?*

The space in my brain that was vacant without him is still silent, but it's back to the usual predatory kind. The watching and the waiting of a calculated hunter sits with me. He's silently expecting something.

"Really?" Revecca looks at me. She tilts her head and steps back, waiting for something.

I look around and shrug.

"You feel no different at all?" Revecca's fear shows in her eyes as two different wolves flash back and forth, assessing me.

"Less hollow."

*Morrigan.* A gruff voice in my brain hits.

"And apparently he talks." I nod. *Just a second. We'll see her.* The warmth in my chest burns again. "Oh, there it is."

*Morrigan. Now,* he insists.

"Pushy and kind of demanding. Though, I will say, words are nice." I rub my sternum, trying to take down that pain.

Revecca smiles, me having a reaction to Harry calming her nerves. "You deserve to know that this is as hard as it gets. That if you wanted children, this is all the harder it would be. Cade has said you treat yourself like a loaded gun. You're always worried that you'll snap."

"What you're telling me is that I'm safe and that you can make it so I stay safe?"

"Precisely. You're not a loaded gun and you are not on the verge of snapping." Revecca rotates away from the rising sun blinding her. "I couldn't do a full reset. But I've put him back as whole as he would allow. But he is stubborn, and something makes me think that Harbinger is trying to protect you beyond what is usual. But this, how you feel now, is . . ." She reaches a hand out and tries to grab a word. "The bottom of the rock."

"Rock bottom?" I offer.

*I don't feel any differently.* I reflect inwardly on Harry. He's calm, seated in my brain, and waiting, patiently even. My body is starting to heal. I recognize the tingling in my fingers, and I think about the ridiculous number of stitches we're going to need to pull.

Harry isn't worked up or aggressive, but he's adamantly focused with one thought on repeat. *We need our mate. Morrigan. Need Morrigan.*

"Tomato, tomato." She rolls her eyes.

"We say it tomato potato," I tell her.

She just shrugs in response.

I draw in a deep breath and look off to the left, where the house, clear blue sky, and full sun create an almost picture-perfect backdrop. I rotate and see my family watching but pretending not to watch, and beyond that, the daylight bounces off the guys' new houses and their solar panels.

"That's it, then?" My eyes fall on Morrigan, and Harry's insistence for her is instantly calmed.

"I can understand not wanting to trust that it's better," Revecca says quietly. "You're worried that it changes who you are and what you'll learn about yourself."

I turn to look back at her and blow a raspberry. "More than that. What if I fail and let everyone down? You fixed Harry because I broke him. I've already fucked up, and it took you being here to fix it. What happens if I fuck up again?"

Revecca shakes her head. "You won't. I can't imagine any other enemies you hate more than the four you killed yesterday."

She's not wrong. Just the thought of Ersilia and Gerad has me on edge. A snarl inside from Harry pushes up, and I let it loose.

"Let this fear you harbor, of being uncontrollable, go because I spent twelve hours with that demon you call a wolf and have never felt worse, and you're sitting in peace with him. You are in control, and as long as you don't continue on a path of vengeance rather than justice, it won't be a problem." Revecca smiles. She looks at the others watching us. "So nosy."

"They care." I nod.

"Alright, last caveat." Revecca draws my attention back to her. "You need to claim your mate in three nights." She holds up her finger. "Not tonight. Not tomorrow night. Not the next night."

Harry snarls. *We need her now.*

"Got it." I nod. *Patience.* I draw a deep breath. "Is this an hours thing or a daylight thing? Like at midnight or?"

"It's a connectedness thing," Revecca explains. "You'll need to be settled in with yourself wholly. If you bite and try to claim your mate before it's solidified, the mark will fade, and you'll have to do it again. It's . . ." She turns her head away from me, looking at Magnus and then back. "It's excruciating to have to go through the mating bond and have it fail."

"Are you okay?" I ask, turning away from the house and family. "He may be a friend, but if somethin' isn't right."

"No, it's not like that." Revecca comforts me with a hand on my arm. "Always so quick to defend. You'll need to try not to kill anyone until after you've bonded with your mate."

"Try," I huff.

*Everyone is stable,* Harry says nonchalantly.

"Everyone is stable, apparently." I direct her back on the path to the house. "So, Sherman. You fixed him, kinda?"

"I stabilized him. He's not broken or fractured. But he was very volatile, and he didn't need to be. Whichever pack he lived with before mistreated him greatly." Revecca's intuition about what happened to Sherman is spot on. "He deserves happiness.

I hope you keep him here with you always. He'd be a great au pair."

"Au pair?" I repeat the word, but I'm not sure what it means.

"Uhh. Child caregiver?" Revecca tries for the word. "Nanny?"

"I don't know that I'd let Sherman take care of a child on his own, but maybe." I shrug, considering it.

He saved Morrigan, but I never really thought about how Sherman would be if we had pups. He's not the biggest concern. By far, Sherman isn't even on the top of my radar.

Morrigan is standing on the deck right next to Magnus, where we left her. Tears are in her eyes, and she's wringing her hands.

"Why the long face, sunshine?" I cock my head to the side and open the door for Harry to come forward. It's a controlled, steady movement. I laugh at how easy it feels. "Come here?"

She jumps down the steps and runs to me. It doesn't knock the air out of my lungs, but it's hard enough. The warmth and heated pain in my heart grows with her in my arms.

She kisses me fiercely, hands wrapping into my messy bed-head hair. She pulls me closer to her, and her body brushes against the tender skin, but I push it out of my mind. I thrust my tongue into her mouth, claiming her, and slide my hands around her, pulling her to me.

Howls, wolf whistles, and calls of encouragement echo around us across the landscape, but I take my time, not willing to be embarrassed by them.

Morrigan breaks the kiss about the same time Ezra shouts something about taking it inside.

The way she smiles at me makes me feel like everything's gonna be okay.

She cups my face before pulling at the short strands of my hair. "I love you."

"I love you." I tilt my head toward the house. The growing reminder of having a wolf to feed comes with a grumbling in my stomach. "Breakfast?"

"Breakfast."

# CHAPTER 97
# MORRIGAN

IT'S BEEN THREE DAYS, AND ANSEL GROWS INCREASINGLY MORE secretive. We're supposed to complete the mating bond tonight, and I'm not even sure if he's interested. Every time I say it, fifty times a day, Ansel answers with 'I love you too,' but it's not reassuring when he's avoiding me.

Most of his family has stayed in town, and I want to believe that's why it's so weird, but I'm getting frustrated.

Ansel finds me after breakfast while I'm sitting with Cade and Thalia at the fire.

"Morrigan, can I borrow you?" His tone sounds solemn.

On edge, I nod and look to Cade and Thalia. "I'll talk to you later?"

Thalia beams, the pregnancy glow and her hand on her stomach reassuring me. "Of course."

He leads the way up to the house, and the nervous energy is unbearable. The house is uncharacteristically empty. It's been a bustling, busy space where bonding has been happening, cards played at the table, baked goods made, and meals prepared.

"Ansel, just say it," I prompt him. "If it's bad, just say it."

Ansel shakes his head. "What? No. It's nothing bad."

"You're being weird," I tell him. I draw deep breaths and try to stop panicking, but the nervous energy he's giving off and the conflicting reassurance aren't meshing.

"I was thinking, while I've got some help to use the interwebs and get you everything you need, we could go upstairs and measure that bedroom on the right and figure out space for sewing stuff. If you want a countertop or a workstation? Dress form? Not lying, I've not even the faintest idea what you need. But we can maybe finagle your space to make it work."

"You're sure you want to give up the space?" I ask, trying not to let the insecurities build up.

"I'm not giving up the space." He's quick to answer. "This is our home, and you deserve to have things that make you happy. And I figure rather than putting a furnace in the garage to make space for you, it might be nice for your workstation to be upstairs by the second bedroom."

"Why?" I draw my eyebrows together, examining him.

He takes some steps across the house toward the stairs. "I said we could talk about pups later. And I'm not gonna make any promises. I don't feel the same since . . ." *Since I slaughtered your mother and Revecca reset Harry.* "Since this all happened. But if you still want pups in a year, I'd be open to exactly one. And the room on the left is a little bigger for a nursery."

"You mean it?" I ask. The nervous energy makes so much more sense now.

"Yeah, weird floor plan up there. But it's bigger." He shrugs, offering his hand out to me.

"It's up to you, Morrigan. But I'm leaving the possibility open to an extent." He draws a deep breath and lets it out. "Next year, or in a couple. Choice is yours, but you should have someplace to call your own and do your own thing regardless what we do."

"Okay." I nod, taking his hand in mine.

He leads me up the stairs to the bedroom like a school kid ready to show me what he's so proud of.

AFTER MAKING A SHOPPING LIST THAT LENA CONFIRMS WITH ME, Ansel's beaming. I'm pretty sure she's ordering way more than what we specified, but it'll be exciting to get boxes from her.

"Alright. Next up." Ansel laughs. He's almost boyish as he takes me down the stairs. "I've gotta go into town. Mr. Hoppe wants payment for a pig for the freezer, but I thought maybe we'd see Mrs. Hoppe for some malts?"

"Oooo." I follow him down the stairs. "Suppose she'd make mine with double peanut butter?"

"Guess we won't know if we don't ask?" Ansel wraps his arms around my waist in the kitchen. He fists my hair and kisses me deeply. "Love you, sunshine."

"I love you too." I snuggle against him.

RATHER THAN THE USUAL WORK TRUCK, HE BACKS OUT THE VINTAGE truck that Lena told me was Dad's, and I climb in next to him, sliding across the bench seat to sit mostly next to him the entire trip to town.

Everyone in town stopped us and said something: hello, congratulations, and how glad they were to see us. It's so much love and so much gratitude. Ansel seems overwhelmed but handles it incredibly well. He holds my hand and puts his arm around me. I can't ever remember feeling such belonging.

About the same time the sun is headed to the western

skyline, he yawns and lets me get another peanut butter malt for the road.

It's an absolutely perfect day.

The sun is setting by the time we pull back up in front of the house. My second double peanut butter malt was the best thing in the world, but then he drives around the final turn in the driveway.

The side yard's been completely transformed. A large white sheet is hanging off the screened-in porch, and trucks are parked in a row across from it, lawn chairs up in some of the beds facing the house. Other lawn chairs are in front of the tailgates on the ground.

Tears well in my eyes.

Ansel puts the truck in park, and I turn to look at him.

He has his head hung down a little bit with embarrassment pinking across his cheeks. "I know, it's probably not as big and as fancy as it could be. Given everything, though, I thought a movie night with the guys, and now my cousins, would be a good way to make this official."

He leans over and opens the glove box. When he opens it, he pulls out two jewelry boxes. "I don't know if I should get out and get down on one knee or not, but I kinda thought Walt's truck was probably the best place."

With shaky hands, I unbuckle my seat belt and turn to face him.

Ansel opens the flat square box first. The collar inside is simple in a way that's radiant and intentional. A double strand of thick rolled gold chain sits nestled amongst black velvet.

"It's beautiful." My voice gets caught in my throat.

"If it's too simple, Lena said she had some other ideas, but I just didn't see you as someone who wanted the bold." He shrugs.

"It's perfect. It's beautiful. I love it." I smile at him, reaching out to hold his hand.

He closes the lid of the collar box and holds my hand. "But, then, for the day-to-day. 'Cause as Thalia said, just because they're learning that collars are like wedding bands for us, they don't all know."

"You're rambling," I tell him, squeezing his hand.

With one hand, he flicks open the ring box. Inside is a gold band with a solitaire diamond in a cushion cut. It sparkles even in the low light of the setting sun. "It's a little bigger and flashier. But I just wanted it to be—"

I huff out a laugh and give him a big smile. "And now you're supposed to take it out of the box and put it on my finger and tell me how much you love me and beg me to be your mate forever and ever."

Ansel pulls his hand from mine and takes the ring out of the box. The delicate touch of him sliding the band over my finger feels surreal.

"Morrigan Camilla Hart, you're mine. I'm not asking. I'm telling. I will love you for the rest of my life. You are my world, and I will never stop trying to make you happy."

"I love you. All of you." I slide across the bench seat to his side of the truck and wrap my arms around his neck. "So, let's watch a movie with our family and our pack. Then you're going to take me to bed and make me an honest woman."

Ansel pulls back from the hug enough to kiss me tenderly, but it's no less possessive.

He breaks the kiss first. "Damn."

"What?" I turn and look over my shoulder to try and see what he would be looking at.

He pulls my chin back to face him. "Since we've been together, the mating bond has kinda felt like a burning, stinging feeling in my chest." He puts his hand over his heart. "But it doesn't hurt anymore."

"Oh?" I shake my head. "What does it feel like now?"

He smiles. "Kinda like sunshine, I guess."

MOVIE NIGHT IS AMAZING. ON PILLOWS ON THE GROUND, WE SIT cuddled up in a blanket, but the anticipation is killing me. When the credits roll, we accept a dozen congratulations and finally make our way into the house.

*Outside*, my wolf urges. The closer we get to the bedroom, the more she demands we go back outside into the night and under the stars.

I strip down in the bedroom with Ansel, watching him watch me with hungry eyes.

I'm wet, and I want him so badly.

*Run*, my wolf encourages.

When he's blinded by the T-shirt coming off over the top of his head, I make my move. I sprint half naked through the house and throw open the sliding glass door. The alarm blares as I step outside, but I don't care.

After sliding my panties down my legs, I leave them on the deck, and I barely get out of my bra before my wolf takes my body.

"Morrigan!" Ansel shouts, having seen me take off.

But, before long, it isn't Ansel's footfalls I hear.

The eerie howl of a wolf comes a few seconds later.

*Four feet don't fail me now.* I let my wolf drive.

She pushes us forward, jumping and dodging around the desert plants. A snake slithers out of the way, distracting me, but Harbinger's snarls have me snapping my focus back.

*Harry doesn't want to hurt us though.* My wolf nearly laughs as she pushes us forward faster.

We're breathing heavily, and I feel like I'm about to die from a self-inflicted heart attack when the white wolf gets ahead of us.

His large paws slide in the dirt as he spins in a half circle, matching me eye for eye. He's nearly rabid looking with the darkness of his irises.

My wolf recedes easily, leaving me standing in front of him.

Harry continues growling at me, lip curled into a deep snarl.

Something flashes forward, and I'm forced to the ground under a crushing weight, knocking the breath from my body.

I take a full, deep breath, and as my brain rights itself, I can see that it's not the wolf.

Ansel presses his lips to mine, threading his fingers in my hair, and I run my hands up his side.

I need more.

# CHAPTER 98
## ANSEL

HARBINGER RAN WITHOUT INTENT TO KILL. HE RAN WITHOUT INTENT to hurt. We ran without fear of something or someone dying. And he let me out to feel the softness of her body beneath us.

Morrigan's sweet gasps as I kiss her steer me in all the right directions. Her legs opening for me feel soft, warm, and inviting.

"Ansel," she gasps against my lips.

I rumble happily in response, letting her rock her hips up against me. She wraps her legs around my waist, trying to pull me to her.

My thoughts go fuzzy. I'm lost somewhere between feeling wild and lust.

*Ours.* Harry presses forward but not demandingly so.

Taking Morrigan's guidance, I lower myself to her, the tip of my cock pressing into her wetness. She nuzzles her nose against me, and I feel a nip at the base of my neck.

My fingers entwined into her hair sometime on the course to the ground, and I pull her head aside, kissing down her neck to where I plan to place my mark and claim her as mine.

It's torture to wait any longer, but this isn't something I'm ready to rush. I'm enjoying being alive in this moment here with her.

I kiss my way back up her neck while enjoying the warm, slick feeling of her pussy as I sink my cock deep inside her.

"Ansel!" Morrigan gasps. "Fuck yes."

"That's it, hmm?" I nip at her neck before whispering, "This what you want?"

Morrigan answers in senseless moans and mewls. Her body writhes up against me, and she pulls herself closer to me, fingers pressing into my skin.

The way her pussy clenches down on my cock, trying to keep me in, is driving me insane. I don't want to simply be inside her. I want to dominate, possess, and consume her on all levels.

In long, slow thrusts, it is both pleasure and awful pain of denying myself more. I'm going mad with wanting, but I'm taking her with me. The rough fucks will come, but slow and steady, as torturous as it may be, is to savor us.

She raises her hips to me and begs, "More, please more."

"Do you deserve more?" The words cross my lips with a smile.

"Yes," she snarls.

Harry presses forward a snarl of our own. It's a tiny battle of dominance that neither of us mean. It's instinctive, reacting to each other.

Morrigan digs her nails into my side. I hiss and, using my grip against her scalp, pull hard.

The gold eyes of her wolf rise to meet mine, and she snaps her teeth as she challenges. Morrigan pulls one of her hands between us, and between the feeling of her fingers on my chest and the press of her legs and hips against mine, she's attempting to roll me off her.

*Not happening, Morrigan.* I shift my weight to the side and release her hair. Grabbing hold of her wrist, I easily pull it out to the side of her head, holding her immobile beneath me.

"You're cute when you're mine." I smirk.

She drags her other hand across the back of my shoulder before pressing up against my throat.

Letting her believe she has any control over me physically seems silly because all her control over me is in my heart. But for a little bit, I can let her pretend to have this sort of power.

She squeezes and orders me, "Deeper."

Morrigan shifts her hips and rolls them up to match my long strokes as I pull nearly all the way out before sliding in again and again.

She gasps, "Yes. There. Like that."

It's too easy to hit all her sensitive parts with long thrusts. She moans, head rolling and her neck arching out toward me. Morrigan's hand slacks around my neck.

"Please, let me come, please," Morrigan begs, raising her hips to me again.

"Let's not pretend you're anywhere close to needing to come that badly." I kiss her again and change my pace.

It's fast and deep. I take her as hard as I can, as hard as I need, and she keeps rising to meet me, her moans growing louder.

Harry pushes me, and I can't fight it anymore.

I won't fight it anymore.

"Morrigan. Fuck." I'm on the edge. My fangs elongate, and I'm lost to the feral nature of it all. It's an all-consuming fire, and it burns me alive.

Pressing forward, I come hard through a snarl with the taste of her blood in my mouth.

At the same time, Morrigan's fangs sink in a little higher up on my neck as they catch a mouthful of my flesh. Her bite, hard and deep, breaks quickly as she screams through her orgasm. Morrigan's body quakes underneath me, and the pulsing of her pussy around my cock sends stars dancing across my vision.

Chest heaving, Morrigan falls silent with a contented little murmur.

Pulling myself from her is the last thing I want. I want to stay buried in her. It's the closest thing we have, literally in this sense, to being one. On my back, I lie next to her and pull her to me, wrapping my arms around her and giving her my warmth against the cold desert.

Morrigan lays her head on my shoulder, opposite her bite mark, and draws a deep breath before releasing it on a sigh. "I love you."

"I love you too. My feelings don't make sense, and what I feel for you is so unique. I can't explain it."

I press my nose into her hair and take deep breaths of her scent.

Harry settles, relaxing with us.

Maybe it's the fear of never seeing another one, or maybe it's the mating mark on my shoulder, but lying here in the desert, I'm pretty sure I've never seen such a beautiful night sky.

"I suck at running away." Morrigan looks over my shoulder, back toward the house.

"Nah, you don't suck at running away, you're just a great homing pigeon." I laugh. "Seriously, never seen someone find their way back home so easily."

She snuggles in next to me as we watch the night sky. Amidst the peace and quiet, Harry is calm. And that spot in my chest is back to feeling weird. It's warm and fuzzy. *Judah was wrong about what love feels like. It's not like a hug at all. It's definitely like sunshine.*

# Ansel

## June, After Morrigan's Birthday

"Oh! Ansel!" Morrigan drops my hand and shuffles quickly ahead to where Mr. Hoppe is sitting with his box of puppies.

His eyes light up as he sees me, and I worry he's going to blow it.

The puppies weren't old enough for her birthday, but I figured with how happy she's going to be, it won't matter.

"Awww. Look at the babies." Morrigan's voice turns into that cute coo women folk do when they're in the presence of babies.

She squats down at the edge of the box where the puppies are running about. She runs her hands across them all back and forth.

"They're Blue Heelers — or what those continental people call 'em, Aussies?" Mr. Hoppe starts. "Champion bloodlines. Their grandpappy was a show dog. Momma and Papa run our cows."

Morrigan picks one up, petting its head. She holds it up to her face, nosing it before putting it back down. Her voice is all over the place, cooing. "Oh, you're the sweetest little boy, aren't you?" She sets that one down. "Awww. And aren't you precious, little girl? You'll be so pretty when you get big."

The next one she picks up is a little boy with two black eyes and a heavy merle coat.

She turns to look at me, and I know what to expect.

The puppy dog eyes and pouty lip.

I shake my head and sell the line I had to practice. "We don't need a dog. We're wolves, what do we need a dog for?"

With a frustrated huff, Morrigan keeps petting him. Turning her gaze to Mr. Hoppe, she asks, "How much are they?"

"They're fifteen hundred." Mr. Hoppe quotes her.

He looks at me as he says the large price tag, and I nod. Mr. Hoppe keeps a straight face, playing his part in all this just right.

"Come on, Morrigan." I coax her, stepping toward her to nudge her away from the box of trouble.

"Fifteen hundred." Morrigan's voice falls flat, and she looks at the little puppy in the face.

She has access to The Ardelean Fund, but she's equally frugal with it as I am and constantly tries to justify purchases for herself.

He's wagging his tongue everywhere and snuggling into her hands. She brings her face to his, and he gives her nose a big sloppy kiss.

Not for lack of trying, Morrigan looks at me one more time. "You're sure? Look at how cute he is. I think he likes us."

She's offering me the exact puppy I picked out for her three days ago. I knew he was the one, but there was no harm in having her take a look at them.

I shake my head and crinkle my nose. "Nah. I'm good. Besides, we decided we weren't ready for puppies."

Morrigan sucks her lips in between her teeth, face flushing.

Mr. Hoppe looks at me and draws his eyebrows together before the realization hits. He snorts and coughs to try and cover the sound.

"Fine." Morrigan sighs, putting the little boy back in the box.

She gives him a tender wave before stepping away and walking toward the truck.

I shake hands with Mr. Hoppe and follow her.

# MORRIGAN

## TWO DAYS LATER

The driveway sensor Cade had installed beeps, and I check the notification on my phone. Ansel's truck is coming up the driveway.

I go into panic mode and agonize over the shirt I've made. Pulling it off the ironing board, I double-check it for stray threads again. It's been a really long time since I've made something this tailored, using a shirt he had broken in. *Fuck, if these measurements don't work, I'll be so upset.* It's not like he would have ever let me measure him though.

I take a deep breath and shake out my hands before running the buttons through the holes. The little antique buttons line up with the polka dots as I envisioned they would, and the contrasting inner collar shows the *M* I stitched in where my mating mark is.

Folding it carefully, I tuck the sleeves behind the back, letting the embroidered pocket stand out on the very bottom fold.

The low hum of the engine cuts off.

I rush down the stairs with the shirt in my hands, trying not to be weird when he comes through the door. It's been a long day, and I've missed him. And to finally have the shirt ready . . .

"Sunshine?" he calls out as I hit the landing.

"I'm here." I round the stairs to the kennels.

Ansel walks down the hallway carrying a box. The box makes a yipping noise.

"No!" I rush forward and look in the top of the box.

Inside is the perfect little blue heeler puppy from Mr. Hoppe's box. The little boy with the two black eyes.

Tucking Ansel's shirt under my arm, I pick up the beautiful little baby boy. He licks my chin, snuggling in.

I look at Ansel. "I thought you said no."

Ansel smiles, putting the box on the floor before kicking off his tennis shoes. He steps forward and gently wraps his arms around me and the puppy.

Kissing the top of my head, he says, "I wanted to make sure I got the right one. I picked this one out and had paid for him three days before we saw Mr. Hoppe in town, but I didn't trust my instinct and wanted to make sure."

"You set up Mr. Hoppe being there with the puppies so I could pick him out?" I whisper, so excited.

The puppy squirms, and Ansel lets us go.

The little guy licks my face, and I enjoy the smells of puppy breath, getting to truly look him over. He's perfect. I knew when I saw him in the box that this was the one, and now here he is.

I hold him to my chest as he yawns and take him to the open space in the heart of the house. After sitting on the floor, I set him down, and he wobbles on his feet.

"My only request" — Ansel looks me in the eye, tilting my

chin up toward him with his fingers — "is that you don't name him something ridiculous that I'll look dumb having to explain to the pack."

"And probably not one of the nicknames Ben would give the guys?" I ask, watching the little guy trot around the floor, sniffing and exploring.

His ears are alert, and his little butt wiggles in the cutest fashion.

"Yeah. That too." Ansel pulls out a stool and sits down, watching us on the floor.

"How about Spot?" I look at the little mottled splashes of black and gray and the two large black patches around his eyes. "Either that or Bandit."

"Both are good names." Ansel smiles but points at the puppy. "He's got to go outside."

"Come on, Spot, let's go outside." I stand up. Having forgotten about Ansel's shirt, it falls out from between my arm and side. "Oh!"

"What's that?" Ansel scoops up Spot from where he'd been running around the stools at the island.

"It's uhm. For you, and kind of underwhelming after you got me a whole puppy." I look at the shirt in my hands.

Ansel wraps his arm around me and spins me, taking me and Spot out the sliding glass door. I follow him down the stairs, still locked on looking at the shirt.

"Go potty," Ansel orders in his 'I'm warning you' voice.

He brings his hand to my face and slides it back to my nape, pulling on the hair at the back of my head and adjusting my gaze to meet him.

"I love you, Morrigan," Ansel assures me. "Show me what you have."

He pulls his hand back and waits.

I turn the shift to face him, presenting it carefully with two hands. Ansel looks down at it, and I study his face. His jaw drops slightly, and his brow pulls together.

Gently lifting the shoulders, he unfolds the shirt. The polka dots look so vibrant in the afternoon sun.

I turn and watch Spot stretch out his little body to pee before giving him some privacy.

"You made this?" Ansel asks, his voice soft.

"I did. I borrowed one of your flannels to get the measurements, but I don't know if it'll fit because there's a lot that goes into this sort of thing. I don't know your measurements." I draw a deep breath, waiting.

Turning the fabric over in his hands, he looks at the different colored yolk on the back and then goes back to the *M* stitched in the collar and then back to the pocket detail: 'Harbinger.'

Ansel hands it back to me. "Watch the puppy."

I deflate, turning to watch Spot wander around the edge of the clearing Ansel has declared as the 'yard.'

Fabric drapes over my head, and I get a whiff of Ansel's scent. The green flannel he had been wearing is over my head.

He takes back his gift, and I'm free to pull the flannel off from over my head. I turn to him just in time to see him buttoning the shirt.

"Fits perfectly." He laughs. "You made me a polka-dot shirt. And here I thought I had everything I could want." He squeezes me in a strong embrace and kisses me fiercely. Pressing his forehead against mine, he says, "Thank you, sunshine. I love it. And I love you."

"I love you too." I push up onto my toes and kiss him.

Ansel kisses me back and then quickly looks away. "Spot! No!"

I turn to see Spot about to fuck around and find out with one of the cacti at the edge of the yard. Ansel jogs over to him and distracts him, clapping his hands, and Spot follows him back into the yard, where he finds a tuft of grass to chew on instead.

"And you're sure you want a pup?" Ansel scrubs his hand down his face.

"Yup." I smile at him. "I'm willing to wait another year, but I want one."

"Trying to drive me into an early grave?" He laughs, leaning his head against the top of mine.

"No." I roll my eyes even though he can't see it.

He sighs and wraps his arm around me. "I don't think I want to wait a year."

"Really?!" I move out from under his arm and look up at him.

"I'm not getting any younger." Ansel points to the gray hair that started to come in at his temple about a week after we were mated.

I know logically it's from the stress of everything, and it's not something that should be so alluring, but I like the way it looks.

"Sooo, I don't have to keep hunting for that box that had the suppressants in it?" I'm probably more excited about stopping this hunt for the box than the prospect of pups right now.

It was lost at some point, and despite Ansel and I both remembering it being above the fridge, there's nothing there.

"I'd say that we could stop looking for the box." He nods.

Tears are welling up in my eyes, and I look for Spot rather than focus on the fact that it's the first time I've cried in months. He's asleep, mouth hanging open from where he was chewing on the 'lawn.'

Ansel steps behind me and wraps his arms around me again. "I'm back to really enjoying life again."

"Me too." I look out at the horizon, then over toward where our pack's houses are.

# ANSEL
## SALT LAKE CITY - ONE MONTH LATER

"Okay, this is the best blueberry muffin I've ever had." Morrigan dances in her seat next to me in Walt's truck.

She fell asleep on the way here, but it was only because we were both up half the night worried about what today would bring.

"It'll be okay," Morrigan reassures me. "Cade's attorney said this was a formality and nothing to be worried about."

"I know," I answer, driving over to the courthouse.

Harry is a little on edge. He still doesn't say a lot, but sometimes I think it's because he knows he doesn't need to. We've spent most of our time together in silence, and it's just what we're accustomed to. Revecca had warned us that my memories could start coming back, but they haven't been any more frequent than before. It's just now they're not met with a violent reaction.

"What's the plan for this afternoon?" Morrigan asks.

"Three-hour drive back home?" I question.

I know what I had promised her: a night in the city and

dinner at a fancy restaurant as husband and wife, but I'm anxious to be home. I want her safe where she belongs.

She groans, "No dinner?"

"We'll see."

"We'll see means no." Morrigan sighs. "Ezra is at the house with Ben. We can take a night off. Even with the new guy and things adjusting, Ezra said that Vito not being there isn't the worst thing for the pack."

She quotes back to me my cousin, the mind reader, on the mental state I've gone over a hundred times. Losing someone, especially someone who'd been around for so long, hasn't been easy. But it's been two months, and at some point, I have to accept it.

"I know. It's just that the new kid's only been out of the kennels—"

"Three days." Morrigan cuts me off as I back into a parking space at the end of the lot. "But there also hasn't been any fighting or backlash."

"Alright, let's see how we get through this, and then we'll . . . discuss this further." I change from 'see' since that seems to get me more of her sass.

I love the sass, but at some point, a decision has to be made.

"Fine." Morrigan sighs and opens the door on her side of the truck.

After locking the doors behind us, I meet her at the front of the truck, and we walk to the front doors. As expected, Hank and Franklin, Cade's attorneys, are here with us.

"No white dress?" Franklin asks, looking at Morrigan. "You're getting married today."

Morrigan spins in the flannel and lace dress she whipped up on her sewing machine over the last six weeks. "Untraditional dress for an untraditional wedding in an untraditional world."

"Fair enough. Let's go and get this all cleared up." Hank opens the door for us.

THREE HOURS LATER, I'M OFFICIALLY NO LONGER OF INTEREST TO THE federal government, Morrigan is no longer of interest to the state of Utah, and we are both owners of our very own set of arrest records.

More than that, though, we share a last name and a fancy piece of paper saying 'what's mine is hers and what's hers is hers,' or a certificate of marriage as the fancy people call it.

"Ansel, it's been a pleasure working with you, and I would rather not come to Utah anytime soon." Hank laughs, offering his hand out to shake.

"Agreed. You lawyers are far too smart to be slumming it with me." I shake Hank's hand, then Franklin's, and wrap my arm around Morrigan.

The weight of the world off my shoulders feels really good. But out of habit, I fish my phone from my pocket and check the messages.

BEN:

We're fine. It's fine. Stop worrying.

EZRA:

You've a hotel room booked. I've sent the confirmation stuff to Morrigan. If you even think of showing up out here, I'll rearrange all your cupboards.

Now that's a threat I didn't want to read.

Morrigan, reading over my shoulder from where she's

standing next to me, giggles. "Guess I'm getting fancy dinner after all."

"You set this up, didn't you?" I shake my head. "This is what I get for letting delinquents have smartphones rather than dumb phones."

"Worse, you gave me money." She covers her mouth with her hand, but it doesn't hide her smile. "I've got one more surprise too, but we have to hurry."

She wraps her fingers around my shirt sleeve and leads me toward the truck.

I make a good fuss about following, but I'd go anywhere with her.

"I promise, last surprise," Morrigan says, pushing me around to the driver's side. "Get in. Let's go. We'll be late."

"Where are we going?" I ask, climbing in the cab.

She's already scurried around to the other side and climbing in.

"Follow the GPS thing," Morrigan encourages, turning it on. "I already programmed it."

There's only an address, so there's no name to guess what it is, but I do as she says. Her excitement is getting more and more contagious.

Harry wags his tail, making me steal glances and look right an extra, extra time at the stop signs and lights. We're excited, not nervous, for whatever she's planned.

We pull up in front of a movie theater, and I draw a deep breath.

"So." I squeeze the steering wheel. "I don't want to disappoint you, but I don—"

"You do." Morrigan cuts me off. "I rented out a whole theater. It's fine."

"What?"

Her door slams shut, and I sigh. After unbuckling, I follow

her as fast as I can through the parking lot, my brain trying to catch up.

Harry loves the chase behind her.

I fall in line behind her, walking into the movie theater's vestibule. Knowingly, she walks up to the counter, leading the way. I look around at the large space, the smell of popcorn and other quick foods in the air.

"Morrigan Ardelean, I'm here for our reservation." She smiles at the man behind the counter.

"Excellent! A little jealous. If I had a wife renting out a full theater to see a masterpiece like this." He flirts a little with her and smiles at me.

I shrug because what can I do? I don't have a clue what's going on.

"Morrigan." I caution her. "It's one thing for dinner, and we can leave . . ."

"Ansel, come on. Call Ben if you have to, but you saw those texts, and we talked about it. Everyone at home is already a little more than stable. It's a couple of hours. And if, after the movie, you don't want to go to the hotel, then we can drive straight home." She holds the tickets out to me.

It's so tempting. I've always wanted to see a film in theaters. But what if it's not something I can handle? What if something bad happens back home?

"Trust me." Morrigan keeps her hand out, offering the tickets to me.

I take them from her and look at what they say, recognizing the film's name.

"You mean to tell me you can pay them to put a movie on the screen?" I look between her and the tickets.

"There are some limitations, but pretty much." Morrigan nods as she walks backward away from me toward the concession stand. "I'm getting popcorn and peanut butter cups and a slushy and some nachos."

"Sounds like enough food for us," I agree, hesitantly following her deeper into the building.

She shakes her head. "Oh no. That's mine. You can get your own."

The concession stand is a fun experience of gas station food meets rodeo food. And Morrigan buys almost more food than can be carried. Dutifully, I follow her, and we walk down a long hallway until we get to a theater. Overflow sounds from other theaters pump out into the hallway of different movies that sound interesting.

Finally, we get to ours, and Morrigan explains, "If you sit too close to the screen, you're looking up and can't see anything. If you sit too far back, you're not getting the most out of the sound system. So, you want to be in the middle."

I nod along, but my heart is hammering in my chest as I look at how big the screen is. Sure, the guys and I've put the sheet up on the house and made a makeshift movie night, but this is so much larger.

Once I've settled in next to her, Morrigan lifts the arm on her chair and snuggles up next to me. "I love you."

I kiss the top of her head, but it's not enough. Instead, I tilt the bottom of her chin up and kiss her hard until she hums with approval.

When I let her go, I make sure to hold her eyes. "I love you doesn't cover it. Thank you doesn't quite either."

She smiles. "Alright, now let's watch some dinosaurs."

"What is your favorite dinosaur?" I ask, trying to remember her love for any particular one in the past.

"Oh, easy." Morrigan pulls my arm off from around her and unbuttons my sleeve. She points to the cartoon T-Rex I had done to mask the tail end of a scar at the base of my wrist. "It's this one right here."

The lights in the theater dim a second later, and she pulls my arm back around her.

Harry lies down, resting inside. Warmth radiates within me, and I don't question what it is or how long it'll feel this way because it's Morrigan, and I'll get to keep her forever.

River Mts.
South Pass
Swee
Green R.
Big Sandy R.
Snake R.
Soda Sps.
Camas Prai
Malade Cy.
Bear R.
Logan
Corinne
Brigham Cy.
Ogden
Evanston
Bryan
Bridger
Ft. Bridger
Uintah Mts.
Echo
Coalville
Centreville
SALT LAKE CY.
Gr. Salt L.
Toano
Great Desert
Strawberry Valley
Uintah R.
Provo
Utah L.
Spanish Fork
Oquirrh Mts.
Onaqui Mts.
House Rge.
Silver Cy.
Mt. Pleasant
Little Mts.
White R.
Sevier L. & R.
U T A H
Manti
Gunnison
San Rafael
Fillmore
Wahsatch Mts.
Green R.
Dirty Devil R.
Beaver
Sevier R.
Sage Brush V.
Parowan
Pioche
Colorado R.
Virgin City
St. George
Hyko
Meadow Val.
Highland Rge.
Rail Road Val.
White Pine Rge.
Egan Range
D A
Deep Cr.
Muddy Rge.
Vegas Rge.
Spring Mts.
Gr. Cañon
White Mesa
Little Colorado or Flax
Mt. Sitgreaves
Bill Williams Mt.
Picacho Mt.
Cañon
Cerbat
Black R.
Hardyville
Mohave Cy.
Agua
Mogollon

# PLAIN TEXT OF NOTES

**Chapter 6:**
Morrigan,
You didn't get up when I asked if you wanted food. Here's lunch. Be back after
   work. What kinda life do you want?
-AA

**Chapter 10:**
Morrigan,
What do you want to do when you leave here? How can I help you reach that
   goal? I'll be back after work.
-AA

**Chapter 12:**
Morrigan,
Do you have your diploma? Do you want help enrolling in college classes? It
   would be nice if you'd like to try socializing. I'll be back after work.
- AA

**Chapter 14:**
Morrigan,
What do you do for hobbies? Is it something you'd like to turn into a career or a
   lifestyle? I'll be back after work.
-AA

**Chapter 16:**
Morrigan: What makes you happy? I'll see you tonight. - AA

**Chapter 24**
Little Orphan Annie,
I love you VERY much. I know you don't take care of yourself beyond the essentials, so I tried to find some fun stuff for you. If it doesn't fit you but fits the
   guys, share or donate. Let me know what size you do need.
All these movies are safe. I've put notes in the cases of the ones that are a little
   sad. Please don't be mad, but later, people will be coming by to get you
   some security equipment, etc. Cade's worried that your current system (lit-

erally having no road signs) isn't enough preventative measures for stupid people looking to see the wolves.

We just want you safe.

Thank you again for stopping Finn from getting into trouble in Ireland. You always know what I need, and for that, I can't repay you enough.

Love Always, Lena

PS. If you pick his side over mine ever again, I'll cut your balls off.


**Chapter 57, Note 1:**

Good morning sunshine,

I thought you could use some sleep today, so I didn't bother trying to wake you. There's food in the fridge, and the house is armed. The stupid beep thing will let me know if you try to leave. Please don't. We're down in Nameless today doing some work.

The envelope is a letter from Walt to you. It feels like the right time, but maybe it's not. I've never opened it, so I don't know what it says. But he wanted you to have whatever it is. If you're not ready, don't feel like you have to read it now. It's a decision you've gotta make. I can't make it for you. It can go back in the safe if you don't wanna see it around the house.

We'll be home sometime this afternoon.

Love you,

- AA


**Chapter 57, Note 2:**

Pup –

I don't know how much time has passed since we last saw each other, but knowing you are reading this assures me that you are exactly where you're meant to be. Ansel's is where you're meant to be.

Now, before you roll your eyes at your dear old dad, take a breath and listen. Really listen to what I have to tell you.

Ansel is not responsible for my death.

I can only imagine the things your mother and her mate told you, or didn't tell you, but don't spend another minute being angry at Ansel. He did everything he could. In the end, I wouldn't have asked for anyone else to have done what he did.

Pup, I always knew I was gonna die young. Don't ask me how, but I did. I'm sorry I won't be there to see you take your mate or welcome a pup into the world, but I know you will have the right person, the right people, beside you when it happens.

I always knew I had a purpose in my life, and it wasn't until Ansel landed in it that I understood what that purpose was. I wasn't meant to be a granddad (as much as I would have enjoyed spoiling your pups) or to find my fated mate. My job was to make sure Ansel helped as many wolves, people, as possible in this world. And even though my time was short, I knew it had to end for him to help you.

It's your turn to take the spot beside my best friend and help him help the world. Of this, I am positive. Regardless of how you've made your way back into each other's lives, embrace it. Don't hold off being happy any longer than you have to.

A wise woman once told me that it'll take a pig-headed woman full of spirit to make Ansel see he's worthy of love. If I know anything about my daughter, it's that all the worst parts of me are the best parts of you.

Life's too short, pup. Hatred has no place in your heart.

With every fiber of my being, I love you more.

-Dad

## Chapter 86:

Sunshine –

I once made a promise to my best friend that I would always be there to take care of his daughter. When I made that promise, I didn't know exactly how hard it would be to keep it, and until now, I have never broken a promise to your dad. Seems his and my reunion will look a bit different than I had hoped.

I won't apologize for keeping you away from me these last few days, but I am sorry that it took me so long to see what Harry was trying to show me all along. I love you, Morrigan. No matter where I am, or what happens, I will always love you.

If this is the end for me, there are some things I need you to know. I have asked that my share of The Ardelean Fund and the house be passed to you, or at least, the property at the end of Nameless. Take the house and make it everything you've ever dreamed a house of your own to be. Get that dog, work for yourself, and do what makes YOU happy. Don't worry what everyone else says. Their opinions don't matter. It's all for you. Always for you.

If you choose to stay in town, keep an eye on the guys. Tell them to be good to each other. And for Christ's sake, be good for Ben. Don't give him too much grief, regardless if he deserves it.

You have a full life ahead of you, Sunshine. All I ask is that you remember how much I love you. How much we love each other.

- AA

P.S. I hope you never need to know this, but the trick to escape the kennels is to pull the door toward the kennel, then push the pin up and slide. The one on the end, the pin has to pass a horizontal. It's too far to reach from the inside.

**Chapter 89:**
City of
Nameless
Elevation: 4890 Population: 718
Home of:
Ansel Ardelean

# About the Author

Sarah Jaeger is a human being from the Upper Midwest, even though she is certain she was born to be a shifter. A dreamer since birth, the idea for the Ardelean Bloodlines popped into Sarah's teenage brain and refused to leave. Finally, that idea is taking shape in the form of a fully-fledged paranormal romance series. When she's not writing, Sarah likes to recharge with solid TV show binges, playing cards and games with her family, and caring for her fur babies. Stay in touch with Sarah at www.authorsarahjaeger.com.

# Also by Sarah Jaeger

The Ardelean Bloodline:

**Smoke**

**Haze**

**Blaze**

Stay up to date on all things Sarah Jaeger.

Follow me on social media: